Aemilianus rose up, unsteadily. 'Gentlemen,' said he, 'let us to our stations.' Then he looked down, wearily, upon me. 'I understand,' he said, 'that on the wall, you were nearly hung.'

I looked up at him, as I could, but said nothing.

'Perhaps it is just as well that you were not,' he said. 'Hanging is too swift a death for a spy.'

I struggled, futilely.

'Put him with the other spy,' said Aemilianus.

D1785439

# RENEGADES OF GOR

## John Norman

A STAR BOOK
*published by*
the Paperback Division of
W. H. Allen & Co. PLC

A Star Book
Published in 1986
by the Paperback Division of
W. H. Allen & Co. PLC
44 Hill Street, London W1X 8LB

First published in the United States of America by Daw Books, 1986

Copyright © John Norman, 1986

Printed and bound in Great Britain by
Anchor Brendon Limited, Tiptree, Essex

ISBN 0 352 31861 9

This book is sold subject to the condition that it shall
not, by way of trade or otherwise, be lent, resold, hired
out or otherwise circulated without the publisher's
prior consent in any form of binding or cover other than
that in which it is published and without a similar
condition including this condition being imposed upon
the subsequent purchaser

# CONTENTS

# 1
# THE ROAD;
# THE SLAVE

In a sudden flash of lightning, showing the driving rain, the wagons, the crowd on the road, I saw ahead, above me, and to my left, about a half of a pasang forward, on its stony plateau, the inn of the Crooked Tarn.

"There is less than a pasang to go," said a man near me.

"They will have no places left," said another.

"You could not afford them, if they did," said the first man.

"We will camp on the lee side," said another, "and water the beasts in the moat."

"Wagons will already be circled there," said another.

When groups are traveling together the wagons are often arranged in a circle, end to end, tongues inward, narrowing gaps between the "sections" of the improvised rampart, and chained together, the front axle of one wagon chained to the rear axle of the next, the camp, and the draft animals, and any accompanying livestock, within the circle. This forms a wagon fort or laager. The circle contains more interior space than any other geometrical figure, so the camp is thus as large as possible, given the number of wagons. Too, as every point on the circumference is normally visible from, and equidistant from, the center, this facilitates defense, for example, the prompt and pertinent deployment of reserves. This arrangement, incidentally, is not common with the southern wagon peoples, such as Tuchuks, if only because of the vast numbers of wagons. There the wagons congregate almost to form wagon cities. It is fairly typical, however, with some of the less numerous wagon peoples of the north, such as the tribes of the Alars, particularly when separated from one another on the march, though there one might note the circle is often very large and as many as four or five wagons deep.

There was another flash of lightning, and an earsplitting crash of thunder.

Ahead, and on the plateau of the inn, I saw the large wooden sign, on its chains, jerked in the wind, striking about, pelted with rain. It was in the form of a malformed tarn, its neck crooked, almost vulturelike, the right leg, with its talons, much larger than the left, and outstretched, grasping. Such signs are not untypical of Gorean hostelries, as many Goreans, particularly those of the lower castes, cannot read.

Then again it seemed the world was plunged into darkness and there was little except driving rain and the creaking of wagons.

I had put my cloak over my head. The wagon I was walking beside was to my left. It kept to the left side of the road, as it was moving north on what, in this latitude, was usually called the Vosk Road, but farther south was generally known as the Viktel Aria. My cloak hung down from my head about my shoulders, and thence fell to my waist. I had shortened the straps of the sword sheath, hitching it high, the hilt now before my left shoulder, under the cloak. I kept one hand, from beneath my cloak, on the side of the wagon. In this way I was less likely to stumble in the darkness, and the cold, driving rain. The other hand, my right, held my cloak about my neck. My pack was in the wagon.

To my right, in the line of traffic moving south, I suddenly heard cursing and the startled, protesting bellowing of a tharlarion. There were shouts. There was a creaking of wood, and the slick squeak of an engaged, leather-lined brake shoe pressing against the iron rim of a wheel. "Jump!" cried someone. There was then a sound of sliding, and then, after a moment, that of a wagon tipping heavily into mud. The tharlarion, probably thrown from its feet, was squealing in its harness.

I pulled my pack from the wagon I was trekking beside

and, feeling about, locating the side of the next wagon moving south, felt around it, and went to the side of the road. Another tharlarion moved past me. I reached out and felt its wet scales. In another flash of lightning I saw the wagon in the ditch, tipped on its side, its canvas-covered, roped-down load bulging against the restraining cover, the tharlarion also on its side, lying tangled in its harness, its feet flailing, its long neck craning about.

A man thrust past me, holding an unshuttered dark lantern beneath his cloak. Rain was pouring over the brim of his felt hat. Two others were behind him. They slipped down the side of the ditch. "The axle is broken," said one of the men to the driver. The driver had another fellow with him, too. I stood on the road, at its edge. I felt about with my foot. There were missing stones there. That was probably where the wheel had missed the road. These, I supposed, had loosened, given the heavy traffic and the storm. The wagon, it seemed, had slipped down the embankment, dragging the beast after it. I stayed where I was for a moment. It seemed to me odd that three men, one with a dark lantern, should be so quickly upon the scene.

"Beware," cried the driver through the rain to the men below me, beside the wagon. "I carry a Home Stone in this wagon."

The three men looked at one another, and then backed away. They would not choose to do business with one who carried a Home Stone, even though they were three to two. It was as I had speculated. They were road pirates. Possibly the stones had been deliberately loosened.

"Gentlemen," I called down to them. "Lift your lantern."

They looked upward. I let my cloak fall to the sides so that they could see the scarlet of my tunic.

"Hold your places!" I called.

They stood where they were. I might pursue one. None of them cared to risk being that one.

I slipped down the embankment to join them.

I tossed my pack to the side on the slope.

I took the lantern from the fellow in the broad-brimmed felt hat, and handed it to the fellow of the driver. I did not draw my sword. It was not necessary.

"Unharness the tharlarion," I said to the driver. "Get it on its feet."

He went around to the front of the wagon.

I took the leader of the three men in hand. "You have a wagon nearby," I said to them. "You two fetch it."

"It is not on the road," said one of the fellows.

I flung the leader to his belly in the mud and put my foot on his back.

"Get the wagon!" he said.

They hurried away.

"Do you think they will return?" I asked.

He was silent.

I moved my foot to the back of his neck and pressed his face down into the muddy water. He pulled up, sputtering. "Yes!" he said. "Yes!"

He was correct. In a few Ehn the two fellows returned, leading a tharlarion drawing another wagon. As I had anticipated, it had not been far away.

"Empty your wagon out," I told the two. "And place the cargo of this wagon in what was once yours."

They did so. As I had anticipated the contents of their wagon was a miscellany of cheap loot, taken from other wagons, and from refugees moving south on the Viktel Aria from the vicinity of Ar's Station, on the Vosk.

The driver, his tharlarion freed, and on its feet, hitched it before the other beast, in tandem. It knew his voice, and would respond more readily as the lead beast.

"Give your purses to the driver," I said.

They did so.

I myself took the contents of a metal coin box removed from their wagon and emptied it into my wallet. It contained several coins, the loot, probably, of better than several days' work. To be sure, most of the coins there were small, such as would be likely to weight only a threadbare purse. The number, however, more than compensated for the generally unimpressive denominations. There must have been the equivalent there of seventeen or eighteen silver tarsks.

I located the stones which were missing from the edge of the road. They were in the ditch below their place, half sunk in the mud. Apparently they had been removed deliberately from the road, and might be replaced, thence to be removed again, at will, to again jeopardize the integrity of the road, their absence in the darkness in effect constituting a trap. The three fellows, with my encouragement, in the rain, replaced them.

I again took them to the bottom of the ditch, by the overturned wagon.

"Kneel there," I told the three of them, "between the wheels, with your backs to the bottom of the wagon."

They complied, kneeling with the bottom of the overturned wagon behind them. From this position it would be difficult for them to bolt.

"Take everything, but let us go!" begged the leader.

"I am thinking," I told him, "of tying you naked on your back, over the tongue of the wagon, and fastening your two fellows, on their backs, stripped, over the wheels. It might be amusing to spin them about."

They regarded one another, frightened.

"But you are not female slaves," I mused.

"Men would find us with the loot about, and impale us!" said the leader.

That was not improbable. Thieves are often dealt with harshly on Gor.

"Do not condemn us to death!" begged the leader.

"Strip," I ordered them.

I then tied their hands behind their backs. Ropes were found in the wagon and we tied them by the necks to the back of the wagon. Verr, too, and female slaves, and such, are often tethered to the back of wagons.

"In the south," said the driver, from the wagon box, "there are work gangs. We can probably get something for them there."

"Stay the traffic on the road, as you can, for an Ehn," I said to the fellow of the driver. "We will get the wagon back on the road."

"I doubt even two tharlarion can pull this grade from the ditch, with this weight, with the footing," said the driver.

"Hurry to it," I said to the fellow of the driver. "We shall try it."

He scrambled up the embankment, the lantern in one hand, clutching at knots of wet grass with the other, slipping, sliding back, then regaining his feet, then reaching the surface. In the ditch we were ankle deep in water. The rain continued to pour down in torrents. It ran from the pitched surface of the road downward, in tiny rivers; it struck into the swirling ditch water, lashing it into foam, dashing it upwards, its impact registered in thousands of overlapping circles and leaping crowns of water. We saw the lantern, in the fellow's hand, at the surface, swinging. "Hold! Hold!" he cried in the storm. I think he then literally seized the harness of the next tharlarion. "Hold!" he cried.

"We will never make it," said the driver.

"Try," I said. "Besides we have three stout fellows here who can turn about and put their back into it."

"If the wagon slips," said the leader of the brigands, "we could be crushed, mangled beneath the wheels!"

"See that it does not slip," I said.

There were angry shouts now from the delayed line, moving south.

"Hurry," I said to the driver.

He moved about the wagon and climbed to the wagon box. I heard, in a moment, his shouting to the lead beast, and the crack of the tharlarion whip. The whip, incidentally, seldom falls on the beast. Its proximity, and noise, are usually more than sufficient. Too, it often functions as an attention-garnering device, a signal, so to speak, preparing the beast for the sequent issuance of verbal commands, to which it is trained to respond, Too, of course, like a staff of office, a rod, a baton or scepter, it is an authority device. To be sure, the device has its authority largely in virtue of what it genuinely stands for, and what it can do. Much the same, incidentally, can be said for the whip in the master/slave relationship. There, too, normally, it seldom falls on the woman. It is not necessary that it do so. She sees it, and knows what it can do. That is usually more than sufficient. She will have felt it at some time, of course, so that her understanding in the matter will be more than theoretical. She knows, of course, that if she is in the least bit displeasing or recalcitrant, it will be used upon her. Indeed, she knows that she might be, from time to time, placed beneath it, if only that she may be reminded that she is a slave. It is my belief that women have an instinctual understanding of the whip.

The wagon lurched ahead.

It would attempt its rendezvous with the road by an ascendant diagonal. The brigands were jerked forward, by the neck, behind it. One lost his footing and was dragged for a few feet, through the ditch water, part way up the slope.

"Put your backs to it," I told the captives.

"Look out!" cried someone from the road, above, perhaps a fellow come forward, inquiring concerning the delay, dismounted from one of the other wagons.

"Look out!" cried another.

"It is tipping!" cried the leader of the brigands in terror.

I tried to set myself on the slope, but slipped back, and the wagon slid sideways toward me, the wheels tearing lines in the grass, tilting. Then I got solid footing and, my hands pressing against the side of the wagon, righted it.

"Who is down there?" called a fellow from the surface of the road.

I saw lanterns lifted, up on the road.

"There is a gang of five men on the other side of the wagon," said a fellow. "It is all right now. They have righted it."

The first tharlarion now had its heavy, clawed feet on the stones of the road. I heard its claws on the stone. Some other men, too, came to the second tharlarion, hauling on its harness, and others, too, seized the wagon sides and the forward wheels, lending their efforts to getting the wagon on the road. This was done in part in the comraderie of the road, but, too, men were anxious to be on their way. It was not now safe in the north, in this area, particularly for refugees from the vicinity of Ar's Station.

"I see only one fellow down there," said a man from the road. I went to retrieve my pack from where I had cast it on the embankment. It was soaked through. I was sweating, in spite of the cold and the rain. Too, I had been very afraid, for a moment. I had feared the wagon would tip. I saw it now above me, mostly on the road, though, tilting, the left wheels were still over the edge of the stones. The darkness and the traffic on the other side made it hazardous to pull fully across the road. Harnesses might be fouled. Men can be trampled by tharlarion, wagons can be torn apart.

I ascended to the surface of the road. I put my pack at the back of the wagon.

"It is one of the scarlet caste," said a fellow to another.

"Hold the lantern here," I said to the fellow of the driver, who had now, having arrested the progress of the following tharlarion, released his hold on the beast's harness.

"That is Andron, the brigand!" suddenly said a man, pointing to the leader of the brigands.

There were angry shouts.

"Put their necks under the wheels!" said a man.

"Impale them," cried another!

"Tie their feet together and drag them behind the wagons," said another.

"Kneel," I suggested to the brigands. There was a large number of people here and I was not sure I could protect them. I had not counted on them being well known. "Put your heads down," I encouraged them. "Look as harmless as possible."

"Chain them and hang them in iron collars at the inn!" said a fellow. Sometimes a man lasts two or three days in this fashion.

"Chain them on the boards," cried another. That is a similar form of punishment. In it the victim is fastened, by collars and shackles, on structures of parallel, upright boards, vertical platforms, in effect, mounted on posts. These structures are most common in harbor cities, near the wharves. The fellow who had made the suggestion was probably from the river port of Ar's Station. In the country, impalement is often used, the pole usually being set up near a crossroads.

"Let them be trampled by tharlarion," said a fellow.

"No, let them be torn apart by them," said another. In this fashion ropes are tied separately to the victim's wrists and ankles, these ropes then attached to the harnesses of two different tharlarion, which are, of course, then driven in opposite directions.

"Yes, that is better," agreed the first.

If one shares a Home Stone with the victim, of course, the punishment is often more humane. A common punishment where this mitigating feature obtains is to strip the victim, tie him to a post, beat him with rods and then behead him. This, like the hanging in chains, the exposure on boards, and such, is a very ancient modality of execution.

I saw a knife leave a sheath in the driving rain. "There is no time," said a man. "I will cut their throats now."

There were murmurs of assent.

The brigands looked up, bound, from their knees.

"There is no time to waste," said a man. "If the storm ceases, and the cloud cover scatters, the tarnsmen of Artemidorus may strike at the columns." Artemidorus was a Cosian, the captain of a band of flighted mercenaries.

"In a few Ahn it will be morning," said a man.

The fellow with the knife stepped forward, but I blocked his path.

"These prisoners are mine," I said.

"They are known in this area," said the man with the knife.

"Step aside," said another. "Let justice be done."

"Move the wagons!" called a fellow in the back.

"There are many of us here," said the fellow with the knife, not pleasantly.

"The wagon is still off the road," I said, indicating the left wheels. "Let us move the column forward."

"To cut three throats will take but three Ihn," said the fellow.

"Help me return the wagon to the road," I said.

"You are clever," said the fellow in the rain. "You would enlist our support, and thus have us be your fellows, and thus deny us our will."

"You will not help?" I said.

"Get ten men to help," said he. "I will not be deterred."

"Move the wagons!" called a man from behind him. I heard tharlarion snorting and bellowing, even in the rain. There were some five lanterns where we were. I could see others lit, farther back in the arrested line.

"I myself am prepared to cut throats if we do not move in two Ehn," said a fellow. "I have a companion in my wagon, and two children. I would get them to safety."

"You will not help?" I asked the fellow with the knife.

"No," said he.

"Stand back," I said. I then bent over, and backed under the rear of the wagon.

"Do not," said the fellow of the driver, who held one of the lanterns.

"He is mad," said another.

"Look!" cried another.

I straightened up, slowly, lifting the laden wagon. I looked at the man with the knife. The wheel of the wagon, that to my right, spun slowly, free, the rain glistening in the lantern light on its iron rim. The men were quiet in the rain. I moved to my left, inch by inch. I then slowly, observing the man with the knife, lowered the wagon to the road. It settled on the blocks of fitted stone.

I emerged from beneath the end of the wagon. Painfully I straightened up. I looked down at the fellow with the knife.

He stepped back. He resheathed his knife. "They are your prisoners," he said.

"Get to the wagon box," I said to the fellow of the driver. "Lose no time. Get out of here. When you can I would hood the prisoners, coarse sacking, cloth, anything, and tie it down securely about their necks. Do not let them be recognized for a hundred pasangs. If they are slain on you they will fetch little from the master of a work gang."

"Our wagon was that of Septimus Entrates," he said.

"Very well," I said. That meant nothing to me.

"I wish you well!" he said, hurrying around the wagon.

"I wish you well," I said after him, and drew my pack from the back of the wagon. In a moment I heard the snap of the whip, and the cries to the beast. Other men, too, hurried back to their wagons. The heavy wagon trundled away. I stood on the road, watching it leave, my pack in hand. Some men hurried after it, to strike and kick at the prisoners, who were only too willing to hurry after the wagon. They had been brigands, accumulating loot. Now, in a way, they themselves were loot, and would bring something good, at long last, to honest men, their captors. I continued to look after them, for a time. Yes, they were now themselves loot, as much more commonly were women.

"Perhaps you will now permit us to proceed," said a man.

"In a moment," I said. I wanted the wagon to get a bit down the road. With the slow going, and the storm, and its start, it was not likely another wagon would catch up quickly with it.

"Had some of you lost goods to those fellows?" I asked.

"I have," said a man.

"Most of a wagonload of loot," I said, speaking in the rain, "was emptied out down there, by the ditch. Perhaps you fellows would like to see if you can reclaim anything."

"The loot of Andron!" cried a man.

"Perhaps the tracks of the wagon, too, might lead to some cache, or hideaway," I said.

Men lifted lanterns.

"There is something down there," said a man. Almost immediately he began to descend the embankment. Two other men followed him. "Take the wagon ahead," said another man. "I will catch up with you later." He then followed the others. I moved to one side as the wagons, then, began to pass. "The loot of Andron," I heard someone say. "Where?" asked another. "Where those men are," said another. Two more men left the road. The wagons continued to move by. The fellow who had had the knife looked at me. "Is there really anything down there?" he asked. "Yes," I said. "Well," said he, "perhaps I shall get something for the evening, after all." He slipped down the embankment, to join the others. I went then again to the left side of the road and, when a wagon trundled by, unknown to the driver, I put my pack in it, and, again, as I had before, held to its right side with my left hand, to keep from falling in the road.

I thought the storm might have abated a bit but the rain was still heavy. Too, from time to time, lightning shattered across the sky, suddenly bathing the road and countryside in flashes of wild, white light, this coupled almost momentarily, sometimes a little sooner, sometimes a little later, with a grinding and explosion of thunder.

"It seems the Priest-Kings are grinding flour," laughed a man near me.

"It would seem so," I said.

This was a reference to an old form of grinding, for some reason still attributed to Priest-Kings, in which a pestle, striking down, is used with a mortar. Most Sa-Tarna is now ground in mills, between stones, the top stone usually turned by water power, but sometimes by a tharlarion, or slaves. In some villages, however, something approximating the old mortar and pestle is sometimes used, the two blocks, a pound-

ing block strung to a springy, bent pole, and the mortar
block, or anvil block. The pole has one or more ropes attached to it, near its end. When these are drawn downward
the pounding block descends into the mortar block, and the
springiness of the pole, of course, straightening, then raises it
for another blow. More commonly, however, querns are
used, usually, if they are large, operated by two men, if
smaller, by two boys. Hand querns, which may be turned by
a woman, are also not unknown.

The principle of the common quern is as follows: it consists primarily of a mount, two stones, an overhead beam and
a pole. The two stones are circular grinding stones. The
bottom stone has a small hub on its upper surface which fits
into an inverted concave depression in the upper stone. This
helps to keep the stones together. It also has shallow, radiat-
ing surface grooves through which the grindings may escape
between the stones, to be caught in the sturdy boxlike mount
supporting the stones, often then funneled to a waiting recep-
tacle or sack. The upper stone has two holes in it, in the
center a funnel-shaped hole through which grain is poured,
and, near the edge, another hole into which one end of the
turning pole is placed. This pole is normally managed by two
operators. Its upper portion is fitted into an aperture in the
overhead beam, which supplies leverage and, of course, by
affording a steadying rest, makes the pole easier to handle.
The principle of the hand quern is similar, but it is usually
turned with a small wooden handle. The meal or flour emerging from these devices is usually sifted, as it must often be
reground, sometimes several times. The sifter usually is made
of hide stretched over a wooden hoop. The holes are punched
in the hide with a hot wire.

Most Goreans, incidentally, do not attribute lightning and
thunder to the grinding of the flour of Priest-Kings. They
regard such things as charming myths, which they have now
outgrown. Some of the lower castes, however, particularly
that of the peasants, and particularly those in outlying villages, do entertain the possibility that such phenomena may
be the signs of disunion among Priest-Kings and their conflicts, the striking of weapons, the rumbling of their chariots,
the trampling of their tharlarion, and such. Even more sophis-
ticated Goreans, however, if not of the Scribes or Builders,

have been noted to speculate that lightning is the result of clouds clashing together in the sky, showering sparks, and such. Few people, I suppose, see the unity of such phenomena as lightning and the crackling in the stroked fur of a hunting sleen.

In the wagon ahead, briefly illuminated, I saw, swinging from its strap, slung over a hook on the rear axle housing, a narrow, cylindrical, capped "grease bucket," the handle of the brush protruding through a hole in the cap. Such accessories are common on Gorean wagons. The "grease" in such a container is generally not mineral grease but a mixture of tar and tallow. Applied with the brush it is used, as would be mineral grease, were it more commonly available, to lubricate the moving parts of the wagon, in particular the axles, and where the rare wagon has them, metal springs, usually of the leaf variety. Some Gorean "coaches," and fee carts, not many, are slung on layers of leather. This gives a reasonably smooth ride but the swaying, until one accomodates oneself to it, can induce nausea, in effect, seasickness. This seems to be particularly the case with free women, who are notoriously delicate and given to imaginary complaints.

It is interesting to note that this "delicacy," this pretentious fragility, or what not, and such "complaints," usually disappear as soon as they have been enslaved. That is probably because they are then where they belong, in their place in nature. Too, looking up from their knees at their master they may realize he has little patience for such things. Similarly, circumstances can apparently make a great deal of difference. For example, it has been noted that the same woman who makes a disgusting spectacle of herself as a free person traveling one way on a leather-slung fee cart is likely on the return journey, if then a slave, perhaps tied in a sack, or placed hooded, and bound, hand and foot, on the floor of such a cart, between the feet of the passengers on opposite benches, is likely to remain orally continent, even desperately so. If she does not, of course, she, within the sack or hood, bears the consequences of her own actions, after which she is likely to be kicked or struck while still inside the sack, or beaten while still in the hood, after which the sack might be hung over the back of the fee cart or she herself bound vulnerably on her stomach, her upper body over its rear guard rail. Afterwards, too, of course, eventually, she will clean both herself and the sack, or hood, thoroughly, before crawling back into the sack, to again become its prisoner, or having the hood again drawn over her head and having it fastened on her. She seldom has the same accident twice.

To be perfectly fair, however, most Goreans, and not just free women, will prefer the simple, jolting progress of a springless wagon to the often more rapid progress of a leather-slung fee cart. In the flash of lightning in which I had seen the "grease bucket" on its hook I had also seen, under the same wagon, ahead of that to which I clung, two children in a large, suspended hide. They were peeping out, frightened. Their eyes seemed very large. Such hides are not unusual under Gorean wagons. It is unusual, however, to carry children, or any passenger, or even a slave, in them. They normally serve to carry fuel, which is collected here and there along the route. The children were there now, doubtless, to shelter them from the storm.

In the next flash of lightning I did not see the children any longer. They had apparently decided to pull their heads in. I did not much blame them. I recalled the brigands, now in the custody of the driver and his fellow, those who had been of the wagon of "Septimus Entrates." Perhaps that had been the driver's name, or the name of the owner of the original wagon, that which had fallen into the brigands' trap, where the stones had been removed, that which had slid into the ditch and overturned. Its axle had been broken. I had not, as far as I could recall, heard the name before. It was an unusual name. It suggested the sorts of names not uncommon in many of the Vosk towns, however, names reflecting the cultural mixtures of many such places, reflecting influences as diverse as those of the island ubarates, such as Cos and Tyros, on one hand, and those of southern cities, such as Venna and Ar on the other.

The brigands' loot wagon substituted for their own incapacitated vehicle the fellows, their load transferred, had continued on their way. They had seemed like good fellows. I recalled that the brigands, after having descended to prey upon them, had been prepared to withdraw, hearing that the wagon carried a Home Stone. Those with a Home Stone in their keeping are commonly formidable adversaries. Few men

will knowingly interfere with the progress of such a person,
let alone threaten or attack them. Warning them that he
carried a Home Stone indicated that the driver suspected their
intentions. It had been that announcement, too, which had
encouraged me to enter into the matter. I wondered if the
driver had actually been carrying a Home Stone or if his
assertion had been merely a trick to discourage predation. At
any rate the driver and his fellow were now better off than
they had been. They had an extra tharlarion, three extra
purses and three fellows, hurrying behind them, naked and
bound, ropes on their necks, whom they could now sell to the
master of a work chain, perhaps for as much as a silver tarsk
apiece. Hopefully, if the driver and his fellow wanted to get
the brigands to such a master, they would have them hooded
by the time it grew light. If they were recognized they might
be treated to summary justice.

It had been a narrow thing a few Ehn ago, back on the
road. I did not think a little hard labor would hurt the
brigands. There were one or more work chains, I knew, in
the neighborhood of Venna, to the south. She was repairing
her walls. I had heard, as I had come north, that Ionicus of
Cos, the master of several such chains, was currently buying.
Such chains, incidentally, are regarded as politically neutral
instruments. Thus, Venna, an ally of Ar, might employ such
a chain, even though its master was of Cos. I supposed that if
the Cosians did not mind, there was no point in Venna, who
could use cheap labor, becoming exercised about the matter
either.

It is not universal, but it is quite common, incidentally, for
Goreans to strip prisoners. There are various reasons for this.
It humiliates the prisoner, and pleases the captor. It shows the
prisoner that he is now in someone else's power. Too, it
makes it difficult to conceal weapons. Too, there is no generally utilized type of clothing or garb for prisoners on Gor,
few "prison uniforms," or such. Accordingly, the marking
out of prisoners, identifying them as prisoners, the alerting of
others as to their status, etc., which in one culture might be
achieved by such garb are often, on Gor, achieved by the
*absence*, or near absence, of clothing. The nudity, or semi-
nudity, of the prisoner is likely to alert all who observe it to
his status. Too, even if the prisoner should escape his bonds,

he then faces the additional problem of locating clothing, and of a suitable type. It might also be mentioned, of course, that most Goreans do not approve of criminals. Accordingly, they have no objections to depriving them of clothing, and such. It says to them that they have been caught, and may now expect to be treated as they deserve.

These remarks, incidentally, pertain primarily to free criminals, and not to prisoners of war or slaves. The stripping of prisoners of war, if it is done, is generally a temporary matter, having to do with marking them out, as many Gorean soldiers, particularly mercenaries, do not have distinctive uniforms, and preventing the concealment of weapons. Whether the slave is clothed or not is at the discretion of the master. In the houses of slavers and in slave markets, beautiful women, for example, are almost always kept nude.

In another stroke of lightning, I caught sight, again, of the swinging "grease bucket," it filled presumably with tar and tallow, hanging on its strap from the axle housing of the wagon ahead of me. I thought the brigands, all things considered, would be just as happy to go south to a work gang. Perhaps, in time, they would even be released, in two or three years perhaps, when it was thought they had earned out several times their purchase cost, and if it were thought they had been exemplary prisoners, hard-working and suitably docile. Because of the storm, the rain and wind, another method of dealing with such fellows had not been suggested back there on the road, but it is not unknown. It is sometimes done as part of what is known as "wagon justice." I will not go into detail, but the method involves the tar and tallow, and fire. Goreans, as I have suggested, do not much approve of criminals.

I withdrew my pack from the wagon beside which I was walking and let it pass me, and then, following diagonally behind it for a moment, crossed to the left side of the road. Another vehicle passed me, then, behind me. I looked up. In a new flash of lightning I saw the stony plateau, surmounted by the inn of the Crooked Tarn. The wind and rain lashed at the right side of my head and body. I stepped from the road. There was a graveled wide place here, connected with the inn. It was at least fifty yards deep and wide, affording room where even wagons pulled by ten tharlarion might turn. A lantern was hung on a post ahead of me. I made toward it. In other flashes of lightning I saw roads wending about the plateau. There there would be flat places, where wagons might camp.

I could see several wagons crowded together on the side of the plateau to my left, the lee side. Some other wagons were more ahead of me, turned away from the rain. I felt the gravel of the turn yard beneath my sandals. I paused by some of the wagons. Then I made my way again toward the lantern. It surmounted a post which was at the right corner of the wagon bridge, over the moat, ascending toward the inn gate above me. In a flash of lightning, I saw two girls peeping out from under a tarpaulin on one of the wagons. In the same instant, frightened, they had seen me. When the sky was again lit the tarpaulin was down. I had seen little but their eyes, but I did not doubt but what they were kajirae. They had the look of women who had well learned that men were their masters. I trod the wet gravel toward the left side of the wagon bridge. I paused there to look across the moat. It was some forty feet in width. The ground approaching it sloped down, gently, toward its retaining wall, only some inches in height, too low to allow a man cover behind it. In this wall, at its foot, there were openings every twenty feet or so to allow for water from the outside to drain into the moat. This pitch of the land, too, incidentally, makes it difficult to drain the moat. It could be done, of course, by men working under a shed, to protect them from missile fire, arrows, lead sling pellets, and such, or, say, more safely, and less exposed to sorties, by siege miners, through a tunnel. Either project, of course, would require several men, be costly in time and would constitute an engineering feat of no mean proportion.

There are, of course, various other approaches to such problems, for example, attempting to bridge the moat, perhaps using dugout pontoons, having recourse to rafts on which one might mount siege ladders, and even attempting to fill it. Starvation of a garrison is usually ineffective, incidentally, for various reasons. There is usually a large amount of supplies laid in, often enough for one or two years, and water is generally available in siege cisterns within, if not from rain or the moat itself. Similarly, after a time the besiegers tend to exhaust the food supplies available in the countryside and may well themselves suffer from hunger before the besieged. Maintaining a siege indefinitely generally requires an extensive and efficient apparatus of logistics, arranging for the acquisition, transportation and protection of supplies. To be sure, much depends on the numbers of the besiegers and besieged, the nature of the defenses, and such. For example, if the besieged do not have enough men to man the extent of their walls, their lines must be thinned to the point where in a multipoint attack penetration is invited. Still, statistically, sieges are almost always unsuccessful. That is why cities have walls, and such. Usually, too, within a city, there will be a citadel to which defenders may withdraw, which is likely to be next to impregnable. They are likely to be safe there even if the city is burned about them.

If it is of interest, sieges usually do not last very long, seldom more than a few weeks, before the besiegers, not seeing much point in the matter, and generally feeling the pinch of short rations, or possibly even because the captain's war contract has expired, or the men's enlistment agreements are up, will withdraw. Indeed, sometimes the soldiers, particularly if they are levied citizen soldiers, may wish to return home simply to attend to their own business, such as gathering in the harvest. More towns and cities, I think, have fallen to trickery and bribery than frontal assaults. A good besieging captain is usually aware of the political dissensions within a polity and attempts to exploit them, a promised consequence of his success supposedly being to bring one party or another into power. The traitorous party then, and perhaps honestly enough in its own mind, is likely to hail the conqueror as a liberator.

Dietrich of Tarnburg, one of the best known of the mercenary captains on Gor, is legendary for his skill in such matters. He has doubtless taken more towns with gold than iron. The gold expended, of course, may be later expeditiously recouped from the public treasury, and the sale of goods, such as precious plate, rugs, fine cloths, tapestries, inlaid woods, silver and gold wire, art objects, jewels, tharlarion, tarsks, and women. Indeed, such gains may be levied as a "liberation fee," which fee it will be then incumbent on the party in power to welcome with good grace and vigorously justify to the people.

The water in the moat, from the inpourings from the land about, the drainages, dark and roiling, was almost to the foot of the bridge.

The lantern to my right, to the side, on its post, at the right side of the bridge, swung wildly in the rain and wind.

I looked up. There was a blast of lightning. This illuminated starkly, for a moment, the palisade at the height of the plateau.

Lightning burst again across the sky.

The boards of the bridge were slick with water. It was about eight feet wide. Two wagons could not pass on it. It led upward to a covered gate, which, probably, had a covered, walled hall and another gate beyond it. The two gates, the inner and the outer, are seldom open at the same time. In the covered way, like an enclosed hall between the gates, there would doubtless, both above and to the sides, be arrow ports. Two massive ropes, better than eight inches in diameter, sloped down from the gate structure to the bridge, which allowed for the raising and lowering of a portion of it at will. When the section was raised, pulled up against the gate, further protecting it, the inn would be, in effect, sealed off, an island in its small sea.

Such inns can serve as keeps or strongholds, but they seldom do so. For example, one can simply come to them, and buy entrance and lodging. In that sense they are open, though it is not unusual for them to be closed at night. They can, however, as I have suggested, serve as keeps. More than once such inns have served rural areas as a place of refuge from foragers or marauders. They have been seized, too, upon occasion by the remnants of defeated forces, as places in which to make desperate, perhaps last, stands. Too, such places, particularly in remote, restless or barbarous districts, may be used as outposts, strongholds from which a countryside may be pacified. Within the palisade there would be room for several wagons. In this place I did not know how many.

Too, though I did not think it was now lit, there might be a sheltered tarn beacon somewhere, usually under a high shed. This signifies not only the location of the inn, and its amenities, but also a safe approach, one unimpeded by tarn wire, for a tarnsman, or a tarnsman with tarn basket. One brings

the bird in to the left of the light, of course. By custom
Gorean traffic keeps to the left. In this fashion one's sword
arm, at least if one is right-handed, as are most Goreans,
faces the oncoming traffic.

There was a wagon to the left of the bridge. Its canvas
cover was drawn down. The rain poured from it. Under the
wagon there was a small, huddled figure, a tarpaulin clutched
about its head and shoulders. Within the wagon, then, I
supposed, there might be a fellow and his free companion.
Doubtless, unless it had been displeasing in some way, the
location of the small figure beneath the wagon, huddling
there in misery and cold, was a consequence of the presence
of the free companion within it. I did not doubt but what the
small figure was far more beautiful and attractive than the
free companion. That was suggested by what must be its
status. Free women hate such individuals and lose few oppor-
tunities to make them suffer. I wondered if the fellow in the
wagon had acquired the individual under it merely for his
interest and pleasure, or perhaps, too, as a way of encouraging his companion to take her own relationship with him
more seriously. Perhaps, if his plan worked, in such a case,
he might then be kind enough to discard the individual beneath the wagon, ridding himself of it, its work accomplished, in some market or other.

I crouched down. I could then see the heavy chain passed
through the ring under the wagon. One end of it went between the folds of the tarpaulin clutched about the figure's
throat, probably to be padlocked there, about its throat, or
attached to a collar. The other end went behind the figure and
downward, probably to fasten together its crossed ankles.
Seeing my eyes upon it, the small figure knelt under the
wagon, and, its hands coming from the tarpaulin, their palms
now on the gravel, put down its head, rendering obeisance.

"Oh!" she said, softly, as I lifted the tarpaulin back. She
looked up from all fours. The chain which passed through the
ring was wound twice about her neck, where it was padlocked.
From her neck, through the ring, lifting, and thence descending, it served also to secure her ankles, which were, as I had
anticipated, crossed and chained closely together. This makes
it so that the prisoner cannot walk. It is common to chain
female prisoners so that they cannot rise to their feet. In this

there is not only a security but a symbolism, one that bespeaks their rightful place. Beneath the tarpaulin I saw that she was naked, and, as I had thought she might be, beautiful.

She looked up at me, from all fours. Her body now was streaked with the slanted rain. Her hair, apparently from before, was wet and very dark. It fell about her shoulders. Her knees were on the tarpaulin, within which she had huddled, over the gravel. I knelt her back, and then took her hands in mine. They were small, beautifully delicate and feminine. They were also cold. I rubbed them for a time. Then I put them on her thighs. I touched her body, gently, rubbing the rain about it. She shuddered, her shoulders and breasts wet now, and slick, with the rain.

"You are helpless," I said to her, "and will make very little noise."

"My ankles are chained," she whispered.

I put her to her back, a bit more under the shelter of the wagon. The chain moved a little through the loop ring above us. I heard the wagon creak a little, too, above us. Someone had stirred in it, or was moving, it seemed. The fellow who owned the wagon, I supposed, was turning in his sleep, or was addressing himself to his companion. But it then seemed quiet, and there was little noise except for the wind and rain, and the distant rumble of thunder.

My face was close to hers. "You are slave," I whispered.

Suddenly there was a great burst of lightning and crash of thunder.

I saw her eyes, and pressed down upon her, holding her head, pressing her lips with the kiss of the master.

I drew back.

There was another great flash of lightning and I saw her eyes, looking up at me, wild, frightened, needful. "Yes," she whispered intensely, helplessly, "I am a slave! I am a slave!" Then she lifted her body and seized me in her arms and pressed her lips eagerly, needfully, gratefully to mine.

I put her to her back.

Then I caressed her, and she squirmed, writhing on the wet tarpaulin over the gravel, beneath the wagon, in the flashes of lightning, in the explosions of thunder.

She was small, naked and cuddly. Her thigh, as I determined, in turning her about, and caressing her, first, by feel, and then in a flash of lightning, wore the common Kajira brand, the small, delicate "Kef," for "Kajira," sometimes called the staff and fronds, suggesting beauty subject to discipline. On her neck, beneath the coils of the heavy, padlocked chain, wa a common, close-fitting Gorean slave collar.

"Alas," she wept softly, in misery, in frustration, "my ankles are chained!"

I gathered she might not have been a slave long.

"Oh!" she cried, softly.

I thrust up her legs and slipped between them, and then her legs were tight about me, I within their chained circuit. I lifted her up, and lowered her. "Ohh," she said, softly. She clutched me.

The storm was fierce.

Then, after a time, I lifted her up and slipped back, freeing myself.

There are various ways, of course, to use a woman whose ankles are bound. I had utilized one of them.

"If a question comes up," I said to her, "you were warned to silence, and were helpless." To be sure, this was even true. "You were merely utilized by a casual passer-by," I said. Such things, incidentally, are not that unusual with female slaves, particularly if they are put out, without an iron belt, in effect for the taking.

"I cannot believe the feelings I had," she whispered.

"You must endure such feelings, and more," I said, "when men choose to impose them upon you."

"Yes, Master," she whispered, in awe.

The extent and nature of such feelings, I think, are largely a function of the individuals involved. To be sure, they are usually, too, a function of many other factors, as well. For example, in this particular case, I suspected that her chaining might have been a factor. Restraining the female, sometimes symbolically, sometimes in fashions which are literally physically coercive, making her absolutely helpless, for various reasons, psychological and physical, intensifies her orgasm. This sort of thing, I suppose, is largely unknown to free women, though many seem to suspect it, dimly or otherwise. Its reality, of course, can become clear to them, for example, as they might find themselves on their knees, bound, kissing a man's whip. The most significant restraint, of course, is the condition of bondage itself, in which the woman knows that the male is dominant over her and that she must submit to him, that she is owned, and must, in fear of very life, be obedient, and pleasing. Slavery institutionalizes, in an organized, social, civilized context, the natural biological relationship between men and women. It also, of course, as one would expect, by means of various devices, legal and otherwise, clarifies it and renders it more efficient.

"Oh, buy me, Master! Buy me!" she begged.

"Only a slave," said I, "begs to be bought."

"I am a slave," she said. "That was taught to me weeks ago by the slaver who captured me!"

"You are probably not for sale," I said.

"My master does not care for me," she said. "He bought me only to anger his companion, who is terribly cruel to me. During the day, when my legs are open, he even rents me out to strangers for a tarsk bit!"

"Does his companion grow more attentive and concerned?" I asked.

"I think not," she said.

"Perhaps it should be she who is chained beneath the wagon," I said.

"She is a free woman!" protested the girl, in horror.

"Your master charges a tarsk bit for your use?" I asked.

"Yes," she said.

"Open your mouth," I said.

She did so, and I drew forth a tarsk bit from my pouch, this one not a separate coin in the sense of a round or square coin, but a piece of such a coin, a narrow, triangular, chopped eighth of a copper tarn disk, and placed it in her mouth.

"That is for your master," I said. Many Goreans, particularly those of low caste, on errands and such, carry a coin or coins in their mouths. Most Gorean garments, a notable exception being those of artisans, lack pockets.

She looked at me.

I pulled the tarpaulin up about her, as it had been before, to protect her from the storm.

In placing the coin in her mouth, I had not only, having discovered he was interested in such things, and the price was not too much, compensated her master for her use but had precluded further importunities on her part.

I kissed a little at her face. I had thought the streaks there might have been rain, but they had a salty taste.

I moved from beneath the wagon and picked up my pack.

She looked up at me. She understood, the coin in her mouth, that she was now to be silent.

I looked up to the height of the stony plateau, and the palisade. In a flash of lightning, illuminated clearly for a moment, I could see, over the palisade, hanging from its chains, from the crosspiece on the high pole, swinging in the storm, the huge sign with its emblematic representation of a bird, that with the vulturelike neck and the distorted, grasping right leg and talons, the sign of the Crooked Tarn.

I looked back to the girl.

She was still looking at me.

I pointed to the gravel before her, under the wagon.

Immediately, kneeling, she lowered her head to the gravel, in obeisance.

I then turned away, and began to ascend the bridge, leading up to the gate. I put the girl from my mind. She was, after all, a slave, and her use had been paid for.

# 2
# THE COURT; CHAINED WOMEN

"You are not a female," said the voice from behind the door, a small, narrow door cut in the left panel of the gate, the eyes peering out from a small sliding hatch in the door. "Show that you have money!"

I lifted up a copper tarsk. The fellow inside lifted up a small tharlarion-oil lamp to the opening. I held the coin where he could see it but I did not put it through the aperture.

"Not enough!" he said.

I then held up a silver tarsk. The door opened.

I entered.

He locked the door behind me.

I then followed him through a high, shedlike tunnel, walled with wood, about forty feet long, to the interior gate. There he turned about. "Something for the porter," he said.

"You are paid by the keeper of the house," I said.

"Times are hard," he said. "And it is late. I have opened the door late."

"That is true," I said. I put a tarsk bit into his hand.

"Times are hard," he said.

I put down my pack. I took out a knife and pushed it a bit into his gut, pushing him back against the inner gate. He turned white. I lifted up his purse, on its strings, and, with the point of the knife, opened it. There were several coins within it. I could see in light of the small lamp he carried.

"Times are not as hard as you thought," I said. "How much would you like?" I asked.

"A tarsk bit is quite sufficient," he said.

"You have it," I said.

"Yes, Sir," he said. "Thank you, Sir." He put the tarsk bit from his hand into his purse, as I held it, and then took the purse gingerly from me, and, sensing he was permitted, dropped it, on its strings, so that again it hung from his belt, on his left. If one is right-handed, one normally lifts the purse with the left hand and reaches into it with the right. The weight of the purse, on its drawstrings, closed it.

"It is a violent night out," I said.

"It is, Sir," said he. "What have you heard from the north?"

"I have come from the south," I said.

"Few go north now," he said.

"Most here, I gather," I said, "are from the north."

"Yes," said he, "and we are crowded beyond belief."

"With folks from Ar's Station?" I asked.

"Not many now," he said. "Some managed to flee."

"Most were trapped in the city?" I said.

"Apparently," he said.

"What is your latest intelligence?" I asked.

"Little that is new," he said.

"And what is old?" I asked.

"From whence have you come?" he asked.

"From the south," I said. That I had come from Ar herself was no business of this fellow.

"Only what I hear," he said, "—that the Cosians have invested Ar's Station, on three sides by land, and have closed the harbor, that with a wall of chained rafts."

"Have the walls been breached?" I asked.

"Several times," said he, "but each time the defenders have managed to hold the breach, and repair the wall."

I nodded. Some terribly bitter fighting takes place at such times. So, too, it can, in the streets themselves. "Cosians, as far as you know," I said, "hold no part of the city itself."

"Not as far as I know," he said.

"What are the numbers involved, and your speculations as to the outcome?"

"It is you who wear the scarlet," he said. "I am only a poor porter."

"Surely you have heard things," I said. I sheathed my knife. I sensed it might be making the fellow nervous.

"I have heard there are thousands of Cosians, their auxiliaries, and their mercenaries, at Ar's Station," he said. "If that is true, they must outnumber the regulars in Ar's Station by as many as ten to one."

"Equipment, supplies?" I asked.

"They brought with them the devices for siege work from Brundisium," he said. "I suppose that, too, must be the source of their supplies."

That seemed to me to make sense. If it were true, however, why had Ar's tarnsmen not attempted to interdict these supply routes? If they had, I had heard nothing of it.

"The fighting at Ar's Station, by report, has been lengthy and fierce," said the man. "Her walls are defended by common citizens as well as soldiers. The Cosians, I think, did not expect such resistance."

I supposed not.

"You are of the red caste," said the fellow. "Why is Cos interested in Ar's Station?"

"I am not fully sure," I said, "but there could be various reasons, and some of them would seem obvious. As you know much of the friction between Cos and Ar has to do with their economic competitions in the Vosk Basin. Taking Ar's Station would, in a stroke, diminish the major citadel of Ar's power in the area, and, in effect, drive a wedge between the Salerian Confederation and the Vosk League."

To be sure, in virtue of their mutual distrust of Ar, Cos and the Salerian Confederation normally maintained close relations, and the Vosk League, a confederation of towns along the Vosk, originally formed, like the Salerian Confederation on the Olni, to control river piracy, was, at least in theory, independent of both Ar and Cos. I say 'in theory' because one of the charter cities in the Vosk League is Port Cos, which, although it is a sovereign *polis*, was originally founded by, and settled by, Cosians. If Ar were out of the way in the area of the Vosk, of course, I did not doubt but what friction would develop quickly enough between Cos and the Salerian Confederation, and perhaps between Cos and the Vosk League, and for much the same reasons as formerly between Cos and Ar.

Some well-known towns in the Vosk League are Victoria, Tafa and Fina. The farthest west town in the league is Turmus, at the delta. The farthest east is White Water. Some of the towns of the league are actually east of Ar's Station, such as Forest Port, Iskander, Tancred's Landing, and, of course, White Water. Ar's Station, although it was apparently active in the altercations with pirates on the Vosk, never joined the league. This is probably because of the influence of Ar herself, which might regard her extensive territorial claims in the area as being implicitly undermined or compromised by membership in any such alliance.

The headquarters of the Vosk League is located in the city of Victoria. I suppose there are special historical reasons for this, for Victoria is not centrally located on the river, say, between the delta to the west and the entry of the Olni into the Vosk on the east, which point, incidentally, is controlled by the city of Lara, a member of the Salerian Confederation. Victoria lies rather toward the west, in the reaches tradition-ally more subject to Cosian influence. Geographical position, accordingly, at least with respect to approximating the mid-point between the delta and the Olni, was apparently not the paramount consideration in locating the headquarters of the Vosk League. Had it been one might have expected to find its headquarters in, say, Jasmine or Siba, towns much more centrally located.

"I have heard," said the man, "a large relieving force bound for Ar's Station departed from Ar weeks ago."

"I heard that, too," I said. I knew that it was true. I also knew that Ar, inexplicably, to my mind, had literally invested the bulk of its land power in that very expedition, and had done so with the main forces of Cos not in the north but in the vicinity of Torcadino. This seemed to me a military mistake of almost unbelievable dimension. I had been in Torcadino several weeks ago, indeed, at the very moment when the city, housing Cosian siege engines and supplies, serving as a depot and staging area for the eastward advance of Cos, had, in a daring strategem, been seized by Dietrich of Tarnburg with no more than a few thousand mercenaries. These had entered the city through aquaducts, literally over the heads of unsuspecting Cosian armies camped about the city. This act had stalled the invasion. I expected Dietrich to be able to hold Torcadino through the winter, but little longer. I had borne letters from Dietrich to Ar germane to these matters.

In the intrigues of the time, and to divert suspicion, Gnieus Lelius, high councilor, and first minister of Ar, he who was acting as regent in the absence of Marlenus, Ubar of the city, had even had me brought to the Central Cylinder under guard, as though I might have been arrested, and was to be examined on some charge. There, personally and at length, I had spoken to him. I had urged him to march on Torcadino and confront the main body of Cosian forces. But the troops of Ar had not been recalled, nor diverted to Torcadino. They had continued to march northward, as though the major danger lay at Ar's Station. This, in effect, insanely, or at least inexplicably, in my opinion, exposed Ar and her heartland to the Cosians. It also, in effect, seemed to negate the bold stroke of Dietrich, to slow the Cosian advance, and give Ar time to organize, to arm and march. Ar had not moved against the Cosians at Torcadino. She had marched north, presumably to relieve Ar's Station. Gnieus Lelius had listened to me thoughtfully and patiently. But he would, it seemed, trust to the judgment of his officers.

I had then been kept in Ar for weeks, a guest in the Central Cylinder, waiting, and waiting. Then at last I had been given a sealed letter for the commander at Ar's Station, whose name was Aemilianus. That was all. That very night, on tarnback, I had streaked northward from Ar. I had sold the tarn only two days ago, to proceed on foot. The skies had seemed heavily patrolled. I had little doubt they would become more so as I proceeded farther northward. It seemed to me that my chances of successfully delivering my message to Aemilianus, whatever might be its contents, might be improved if it were borne not by a tarnsman but by one afoot, one who might, say, among mercenaries, or civilians, mix inconspicuously. This speculation was further encouraged by the fact that Ar's Station would surely have its tarn wire strung and the skies about it, as nearly as I had determined, were currently controlled by Cos.

"But," said the man, "such a force has not passed this point."

"I do not know its location," I said. I had stayed at certain inns in the south, past which it had taken its march, taking five days to pass given points. Then, moving northward, I had stayed at inns, also on, or near, the Viktel Aria, which had not seen its passage. It had apparently left the Viktel Aria somewhere north of Venna.

"It cannot have just disappeared," he said.

"It is a mystery to us," I said, "but doubtless to those with access to the proper intelligence network, its movements and position are well known." I had encountered refugees from Ar's Station and its environs even south of Venna. Some told me they had seen the army pass. Some had even told me that men and women they knew had followed the army northward, as though confident of its victory and returning to their homes. What puzzled me most was that the Viktel Aria was the most direct route, for hundreds of pasangs, to Ar's Station. Indeed, Ar's Station, in effect, secured the northern terminus of the Viktel Aria, or Vosk Road, at the Vosk.

The Viktel Aria was a military road, one laid out by military engineers as a military route. It sped almost directly from Ar to the Vosk. It made few concessions to towns or communities. Its primary purpose was to provide a reliable, nearly indestructible surface for the rapid movement of armed men. This being the case, however, why had the army of Ar not kept to it, on its presumed journey to raise the siege of Ar's Station? The most likely hypothesis seemed to me to be that it was making its way not to Ar's Station but to Brundisium, where, months ago, the Cosians had landed. This suggested that either Ar's Station was to be sacrificed in these harsh games, or that it was the thinking of Ar's commanders that a move to Brundisium would lift the siege of Ar's Station, the Cosians there perhaps then being withdrawn to protect Brundisium. Such a move, of course, might isolate the Cosian main forces, both depriving them of their support from Cos and Tyros and separating them from their fellows at Ar's Station. I did not doubt, incidentally, that the military might which Ar now had in the north, if it were what it was said to be, would be sufficient to take Brundisium. The objections to this strategy, of course, were obvious. Ar's bastion on the Vosk, Ar's Station, was being treated as expendable, which it was not, if Ar wished to maintain its power in the Vosk Basin. Even if Brundisium should fall, this would not be likely to constitute a disaster of the first rank for Cos. She could presumably find another port by means of which to keep open her lines of communication and supply. Similarly, Ar, lacking a sizable navy, had no way to follow up the capture of Brundisium, either by interdicting the coast or attempting an invasion of Cos.

The major objection, of course, was that this move exposed Ar herself to the main force of Cosians, which was in the vicinity of Torcadino. It was almost as though the officers of Ar were content to exchange Ar for a port, and one which, strictly, was not even a Cosian port. It this were the case, however, that Ar was advancing on Brundisium, I had, interestingly enough, heard nothing of it. By now, in the normal course of events, given Ar's start, and the typical marches of armies, she would have had time to reach not only Ar's Station but even Brundisium, much farther away.

I did not know where the main force of Ar was. In this sense I was confronted with a mystery, at least as far as my own limited information went. Perhaps, for some reason, the forces of Ar were intending to relieve Ar's Station from the west, thus interposing themselves between the siege forces of Cos and their likely routes of escape, either substantially west by southwest to Brundisium or more to the southwest, toward Torcadino. If this were the case, however, it seemed that we should, by now, have heard something to this effect. Indeed, if this were true, it seems that Ar, by now, should have appeared on the western flank of the Cosians.

"I fear for Ar's Station," said the porter.

"How is that?" I asked.

"I do not think she can long hold out," he said. "The attackers are numerous. The defenders are thinned. The walls are weakened. New breaches are made daily. In places they are being mined. Fires have occurred in the city, from saboteurs, from fire javelins, from flame baskets catapulted over the walls. There is starvation in the city. If the forces of Ar do not soon raise the siege, I think she must succumb."

"I see," I said.

"Too," said he, "the fighting, in which civilians have participated, has been lengthy and bitter. The men of Cos expected an easier time of it. Their losses have been heavy. They will not be pleased."

I nodded.

"I would not care to be there when the gate gives way," he said.

"It is late," I said.

He then opened the door in the interior gate. "The keeper's desk, and the paga room," said he, "are in the building to the right."

I looked out through the door, into the court of the inn. I was soaked to the skin. It was still raining heavily. It was dry, at least, in the covered, shedlike entrance way, between the gates. The inn itself, aside from certain ancillary buildings, was built of heavy logs, and in two parts, or structures, with a common, peaked roof, and an open space, covered from above by the roof, between the two parts. Each part, or structure, contained perhaps three or four floors, possibly joined by ladders. It was about a hundred feet between the door in the interior gateway, where I stood, and, to the right, the covered way between the separate parts of the inn. The flooring of the court was formed largely, leveled and carved, from the natural stone of the plateau. Narrow drainage channels had been cut in it. Through these water now flowed, under the palisade, down to the moat. It also flowed, doubtless by design, midway, here and there, between the palisade's anchor posts and abutments. These latter structures were placed in post wells and bracing recesses, cut in the stone, sealed about with tar. Water was running from the long roof of the two-part structure, perhaps two hundred feet in length, falling some thirty or forty feet down to the court.

I pressed another tarsk bit into the fellow's hand. "Thank you, Sir," said he. He had tried to be helpful, though to be sure, I had learned little that I had not known before. I had gathered, however, that the siege at Ar's Station might be approaching a critical point. I then picked up the pack and went out again, pulling my cloak over my head, to cross the court, in the cold rain. I heard the door shut behind me, and the interior bolt thrown. I hurried across the court to the side of the nearest part of the two-part structure. I had seen something there that interested me. I looked at them, exposed as they were, and in the downpour, and then circled about the building. I would consider them in greater detail later. I thought it well to reconnoiter a little. I suppose it is the training of the warrior.

I examined various of the smaller buildings and sheds, their location and what vantages or cover they might provide. There were stables for tharlarion and covered shedlike structures beneath which wagons were drawn up. There was a place for a tarn beacon, on a platform under a high shed, but it was not now lit. There was a tarn gate, too, but it was now closed, wire strung between its posts. Tarn wire, too, I was sure, would be strung about, most of it presumably from the roof of the inn to the height of the palisade. There was a tarncot, too, but now, within it, there was only one tarn. From the condition of the bird, and its nature, its apparent ferocity and alertness, I speculated that it might be a warrior's mount. Aside from the bird itself, however, there was no indication of this, no emblazoned saddlecloths, no insignia, no particular style of harness. As nearly as I could determine there was no barrack here nor garrison. This place, for most practical purposes, lacked guardsmen, though doubtless it kept a burly fellow or two on hand to deal with possible emergencies. I then made my way back to the main building. It had narrow openings in it here and there through which it might be defended. Its two-part structure formed something in the nature of two keeps, one or both of which, I supposed, might be defended. The number of available defenders, I supposed, might dictate the decision in such a case. Both sections, I speculated, would be joined by a narrow, easily blocked underground passage cut in the stone, one presumably taking its way beneath the covered way between them. Contrary to what one might think, incidentally, it is not easy to set fire to such structures. This has to do primarily with the verticality of the surfaces. The situation is very similar with a palisade. The common fire arrow, for example, usually burns itself out in place.

I was now on the left side of the front of the two-part main building, as one would face the building. It was there I had seen something which had seemed worthy of some interest.

"Redeem me!" cried one of the women. "I beg you!"

"No, me!" cried another.

"Me! Me!" wept another.

There were five of them, naked, and lashed by the rain. Their hands were shackled high over their heads, this lifting their bodies nicely. The shackles were attached to short chains, the latter depending from stout rings. The chains were hitched to different heights, depending on the height of the woman.

"Perhaps you are uncomfortable?" I asked the first woman.

"Yes," she said, "yes!"

"That is not surprising, considering how you are secured," I said.

"Please!" she said.

She jerked at the shackles and squirmed against the wall. She was covered with rain, which had blown back under the roof's overhang. Her hair was sopped, and dark and much about her, adhering to her shoulders and body.

"Avert your eyes!" she demanded.

I took her hair and put it back, behind her shoulders. In that way it was out of the way. Shackled as she was she would find it difficult to get it back again before her body. If necessary, of course, it could be bundled and knotted at the back of her neck.

"Please!" she wept.

In a flash of lightning the entire wall and court was illuminated. There were only five positions there for securing women, and they were all occupied.

"Redeem me!" she begged.

" 'Buy me?' " I inquired.

"Never!" wept the woman. "I am a free woman!"

"We are free women!" cried the woman next to her.

"We are all free women!" cried she beyond that one.

I had supposed this, of course, for I had seen that none were collared.

"Oh," said the first woman, as I checked her flanks.

"Do not carry on," I said. "You have probably been out here at least since the afternoon, and have probably been touched by several men."

I detected no brands on her, at least in the two most favored Gorean brand sites. They were probably, as they claimed, free women.

"Redeem me," she begged.

I saw that above and behind the head of each, thrust over nails driven into the logs, were small rectangles of oilcloth.

I turned one over and, in the next flash of lightning, read the numbers on its back.

"What is your name?" I asked the first woman.

"I am the Lady Amina of Venna," she said. "I was visiting in the north, and forced to flee at the approach of Cosians."

"Your redemption fee," I said, "is forty copper tarsks, a considerable amount." I had read this amount on the back of the oilcloth rectangle.

"Pay it!" she begged. "Rescue a noble free woman from jeopardy. I will be forever grateful."

"Few men," I said, "would be content with gratitude."

She shrank back, frightened, against the rough surface.

"My bill is only thirty tarsks," said the second woman, a blonde. "Redeem me!"

"Mine is thirty-five!" said the third woman.

"Mine is only twenty-seven!" cried the fourth woman.

"Mine is fifty," wept the last of the five women, "but I will make it well worth your while!"

"In what way?" I asked.

"In the way of the woman!" she said, brazenly.

There were cries of protest, and anger, from the others.

"Do not sound too righteous," I said to the first four prisoners at the wall.

"We are free women!" said the first woman.

"You are all debtor sluts," I said.

The first woman gasped, startled, so referred to, and the second and third woman cried out in anger. The fourth whimpered, knowing what I had said was true. The fifth was silent.

I recalled that the porter, when I had come to the outer gate, at the height of the bridge over the moat, seeing that I was not a female, had made me show money, and a considerable amount of it, before he had admitted me. This was probably because of the crowding at the inn, and perhaps inflated prices, in these unusual, perilous times. Women, I had gathered, on the other hand, would not be required to show such money. This, of course, was presumably not so much because such a challenge might be thought to be demeaning to a free woman, as, perhaps, that women on Gor, in a sense, are themselves money. They are, or can be, a medium of exchange, like currency. This is particularly true of the slave, of course, who, like other goods, or domestic animals, has an ascertainable, finite value, whatever free persons are willing to pay for her. Women such as these, those at the wall, would be surrendered by the management of the inn for the equivalent of their unpaid bills. They would then be in the power of their "redeemers," any who might make good their debts. Lacking such a "redemption" they might then expect to find themselves, sooner or later, sold as slaves. In this way the inn usually recovers its money and, not unoften, turns a profit. Particularly beautiful specimens of impecunious guests are sometimes kept by the inn itself, as inn slaves.

"Please do not refer to us in such a fashion," said the first woman.

"In what fashion?" I asked.

"As you did," she said.

"Surely the prices at the inn are posted, or are available upon inquiry," I said.

She was silent.

"Did you not know that you had not enough money?" I asked.

They were silent.

I tightened my grip on the first woman, thrusting her back more tightly against the logs.

"Yes! Yes!" she gasped. "I knew!"

"We all knew!" said the second woman.

"We are free women!" said the third woman. "We expected men to be gentlemen, to be understanding, to take care of us!"

"We counted on the kindness of men!" said the fourth woman.

"They will do anything for free women!" said the second woman.

I laughed, and they shuddered in their chains, against the wall. It was still raining, but the force of the storm had muchly subsided. I released my grip under the chin of the first woman.

"Do not laugh!" begged the first woman.

"In short," I said, "you entered the inn, and remained here, in spite of the fact that you had not the wherewithal to meet your obligations, expecting perhaps you might somehow do so with impunity, that your bills would perhaps be simply overlooked, or dismissed by the inn in futile anger, or that eager men could be found to pay them, doubtless vying for the privilege of being of service to lofty free women."

"Would you have had us spend the night on the road, like peasants?" demanded the third woman.

"But these are hard times," I said, "and not all men are fools."

The third woman cried out with anger, shaking her shackles. She was well curved, and diet and exercise could much improve her. I thought she might bring as much as sixty copper tarsks in a market. If that were so, and the inn sold her for that much, they would have made then, as I recalled, some twenty-five copper tarsks on her.

"When you discovered you had not the price of the inn's services," I said, "you might have asked if you might earn your keep for the night."

"We are not inn girls!" cried the second woman.

"It is interesting that you should think immediately in such terms," I said. "I had in mind other sorts of things, such as laundering and cleaning."

"Such tasks are for slaves!" said the fifth woman.

"Many free women do them," I said.

"Those tasks are for low free women," she said, "not for high free women such as we!"

"Yet you are now at the wall, in shackles," I said, "and have upon you not so much as a veil."

"Nonetheless," said the second woman, "we are high free women, and women such as we do not earn our keep."

"Perhaps women such as you," I speculated, "will soon, at last, find yourself doing so."

"What do you mean!" she cried.

"Are there others like you inside?" I asked the first woman, the Lady Amina of Venna.

"Only one," she said, "she who owed the most. She was kept inside. There was not a shackle ring for her here."

"Why should she who owed the most be kept inside, and

we, who owe less, be shamefully chained here, in plain view, and exposed to the elements?'' asked the fifth woman.

"Perhaps she who is inside has already begun to earn her keep," I said.

The fifth woman shrank back against the logs.

"My arms ache," said the second woman.

"Have other free women entered the court, since you have been fastened here?" I asked the first woman, the Lady Amina of Venna.

"Yes," she said, "and have seen us here. Some of them then, after visiting the keeper's desk, doubtless those with insufficient funds, left the inn."

"There seems a point then in having you chained here," I said, "aside, of course, from such things as having you brought to the attention of fellows who might redeem you and making clear the inn's disapproval of attempted fraud, namely, that you might serve as a warning to other free women, women who might otherwise have been tempted to try similar tricks."

"If we are not redeemed, what will be done with us?" wailed the fourth girl.

"Surely you can guess," I said.

"No! No! No!" she cried, in misery.

"Redeem me!" begged the fifth girl. "I will make it worth your while, handsome fellow."

"Slave!" cried the first woman, angrily, to the fifth woman.

"Slave! Slave!" said, too, the second woman to the fifth.

"Come now," I said to the first and second woman, "she is not a slave—*yet*."

" 'Yet'!" cried the fourth woman.

Too, I was amused that the first and second woman seemed to think that slaves might bargain. They had a typical free woman's misconception of what was involved in total female slavery. The slave is owned. She does not bargain. She owes all to the master, and gives all to the master. She strives to be fully pleasing, in all ways, and hopes desperately that she will prove so. Perhaps they would learn that sometime.

"I am not like these other women," said the first woman, suddenly. "Redeem me! Some women, such as these, doubtless have made a way of life of what you refer to as tricks. I have not! This is the first time I have ever had recourse to such fraud!"

The other women cried out angrily in their chains.

"Once is enough," I told the first woman.

"It costs only forty tarsks to redeem me!" she said.

"You would probably bring more than that in a slave market," I said.

"Please!" she wept.

"I would cost only twenty-seven tarsks to redeem!" called the fourth girl.

"Redeem me," said the second woman. "I am of high caste. Consider the glory of redeeming a woman of high caste!"

"The slave," I said, "has no caste, no more than a verr or tarsk."

The woman cried out in misery, helpless in the shackles.

"I am shapely, and blond," said the third woman, suddenly. "Redeem me!"

"Slave!" chided the fifth woman.

"Slave!" retorted the third.

"I do not want to be a slave!" cried the first woman.

"Obviously you are not a slave," I said, "for you have no wish to be pleasing."

"I wish to be pleasing," said the fourth woman, suddenly.

"I have slave needs, I confess it!" said the fifth woman.

"I find that of interest," I said.

"I, too, have slave needs!" cried the fourth woman.

I had not doubted that. There was something about her body which seemed lusciously slavelike.

"I, too!" suddenly wept the third woman. I regarded her. I thought she would indeed move well in a man's hands.

"But I do want to be pleasing!" said the first woman.

I looked at her.

"Do not consider her," said the second woman. "Redeem me! I, too, have slave needs! I confess it! I have slave needs!"

"I, too, have slave needs!" suddenly cried the first woman.

"You?" I asked, as though skeptically.

"Yes!" she wept. "Yes!"

The first time I had laid eyes on her, of course, I had seen that she was born for silk.

"Let me kiss you!" called the fifth woman.

The others gasped in astonishment, in anger, in protest, in indignation, in outrage, at her boldness.

"Taste me," called the fifth woman, enticingly.

"Slut! Slut!" cried the other women.

It had been a slave's invitation. I wondered where the free woman had heard it. Not all free women are as ignorant as many men believe. There had been many indications that the fifth woman's slavery was very close to the surface. To be sure, she may have often fought it. I did not know.

"The eager lips of a free woman await you," called the fifth woman.

I went to stand before the fifth woman and she, pulling at her chains, leaning forward, tried to reach me. I stood there for a moment, she straining toward me, I regarding her, thinking. She looked at me. I now let her wonder, now that she had made her bold overture, if I would choose to accept it. Perhaps, now, to her shame, to her humiliation, before her sisters in custody, her revelatory, astonishing, compromising advance would be rejected. Perhaps, even, she might be cuffed, or mocked. I saw fear in her eyes. So I took her in my arms and put my lips to hers. It began as a free woman's kiss but, as I held her, and pressed her to me, and she then pressed herself to me, it ended as a kiss which, though doubtless still that of a free woman, hinted at unmistakable latencies within her, that she might, under suitable conditions of helplessness and submission, and perhaps proper training, be capable of at least the nearest reaches of the kisses of slaves.

I released her, and she looked at me, shaken. She grasped the chains above the manacles tightly. Then she recovered herself. She released the chains above the manacles and her small hands now appeared as they had before, the clasping iron of the upper part of the shackles close below the fleshy part of her palms, below the thumbs, and at the sides of the hands. She squirmed a little. "Redeem me," she said, slyly.

"Taste me!" said the lovely, slighter girl, who was fourth, who had seemed perhaps the quietest of the five. I thought she might go the gentlest, and the most willingly, and the most gratefully, to her chains.

"Slut!" cried the third woman.

I then kissed her.

I saw that she would make a superb slave.

"Do you not wish to be redeemed?" I asked her.

"Yes!" she said suddenly. "Yes, of course!" But I saw she would never be truly happy, except where she belonged, in a collar.

"Me!" said the third woman, suddenly. "Kiss me, too! Taste me, too!" I gathered that she, too, did not wish to be left out in these competitions. She did not wish to miss her opportunity to see if she might, by the bestowal of her favors, and the promise of such favors, as well, please me, and, by enticement or trickery, inveigle me into purchasing her redemption. I also saw, from her behavior and attitude, that she regarded herself as the most beautiful of the five, and the most likely to succeed in any such contest. Accordingly I gave her little time but merely took her in my arms and unilaterally, forcibly, briefly, crushed her lips beneath mine, and then flung her back against the logs. She looked at me wildly, disbelievingly. Was she not blond? But she would have to learn to please men.

I then stood back, and regarded the three women.

"You have not tasted me," said the second woman. I think she feared I was pondering a choice among the other three.

I kissed her. I would have to admit it, women kiss well in shackles, even free women. She looked at me. Then, she, too, recovered herself. "Though I am of high caste," she said, "I have permitted you to kiss me, and not merely upon a sleeve or gloved hand, but wholly upon my lips, and not even through a veil, no, upon my exposed and naked lips themselves, unveiled, almost as though I might be a slave! Therefore, in return for this inestimable gift, it is I whom you must now in honor redeem."

"You are a female," I said, "and such are made for the kisses of men."

"I am of high caste!" she said.

"Perhaps—*now*," I said. Slaves, of course, are casteless, as are other animals. No longer is one woman divided from another by artificial distinctions. In this sense there is a democracy of slaves. They all begin the same, regardless of previous distinctions, such as position or wealth. They all begin at the same point, as naked women, branded and collared, who must then strive with one another to see who can be most pleasing to masters.

She looked at me in fury.

"Unfortunately," I said, "I do not have a slave whip with me."

"You would beat me?" she asked.

"Of course," I said.

She shrank back against the logs.

I thought she would look well, in her curves, crawling at the feet of men, reduced to the centrality of her womanhood, the female slave.

I then regarded the four women whose lips I had tasted. Each had, in a sense, though free, prostituted herself to me, that she might thereby influence me to rescue her from her clear and obvious plight, that of a debtor slut. Each was willing to bestow her favors in order to obtain her redemption. These were women, I had gathered, who had made a practice of relying upon the generosity and nobility of men, or of some men, to obtain their way in life, in a sense resorting frequently to types of female fraud, regularly exploiting and, in a sense, making dupes of men. Doubtless they had, at least until now, congratulated themselves on their success in such matters. Now, however, they were chained to a log wall in an inn's court. Frightened now, it seemed that they, even though free, were ready to escalate the level of their artifices. Perhaps in more normal times, perhaps even while they were still fully clothed, and veiled, they might have found eager fellows to make good their bills, perhaps at the first sign of distress, even the moistening of an eye. These, however, were not normal times. I considered the four women. They had requested to be tasted, as slaves. One had even begged explicitly, as I had seen to it she would, she who reputed herself to be of high caste. That had amused me. Only the first woman had not so demeaned herself. She, of all of them, was different.

I heard the small sound of her shackle chains on the ring. "I beg to be tasted," she said.

I looked upon her.

I saw that she was beautiful, and not different from the rest. She, too, was only a slave.

"I beg it," she said.

I regarded her.

"Are you disappointed in me?" she asked.

"If you were a free woman, perhaps," I said, "but not if you are a slave."

Even in the apparently freest of women, of course, there is a slave who waits for her master. There is a Gorean saying to the effect that among women there are only slaves who have masters and slaves who do not have masters. Some men fear the slave in a woman; others provide it with the mastering it longs for, and needs.

"Please," she said.

"Who begs to be tasted?" I asked.

"The Lady Amina of Venna begs to be tasted," she said.

Her sisters at the wall gasped at her boldness, that she should use her own name in this fashion, rather as might a slave.

She looked at me.

She could not pull far from the wall because of her shackling. If she were to be kissed, it would be at my discretion.

"Lady Amina begs it," she said.

She was a free woman. Yet I saw that she was well curved, and would nestle well within the arms of a master.

"Please," she said.

I went to her and took her in my arms. I drew her toward me, from the wall. The shackle chain moved in the ring. Because of the chaining she was bent back. I looked upon her. Though she was free she, like the others, was neither clothed nor veiled. Thus, though she was a free woman, her lips were open to me, naked to me, exposed, in the manner of the slave. She looked up at me, those lovely, vulnerable lips parted. She felt slave good in my arms. I kissed her.

"Oh!" she said, softly, as I drew back.

I had made the determination in which I was interested. She belonged in a collar.

I again considered them. They were all beautiful, stripped, and shackled close to the wall. They had all, it seemed, more or less recently, chosen to live dangerously. But perhaps they had chosen to live a little too dangerously. I thought they might all look well on a slave block.

But I proceeded under the overhang to the open space between the two parts of the inn, the covered way there, with its high roof, that which it shared with the two parts of the inn, and then across it, to the right portion of the inn, in which the porter had informed me was the keeper's desk. In this covered way, too, it might be mentioned, passengers, with some protection from the weather, may board and alight from fee carts, and such. It was late. It was not raining much now. The night had turned chilly, however. I was looking forward to a hot bath, a place to dry my clothes, some food, some drink, a warm bed.

"Please!" I heard the first woman calling after me. "Please!" But I left them behind me, at the wall, stripped and shackled, and tasted.

# 3
# THE INN

I struck the keeper's desk twice.

Behind the desk, on the wall, there was posted a list of prices. They were quite high. I did not think that those were normal prices. If they were, I did not see how the inn could manage to be competitive.

I struck the keeper's desk twice more.

There was a tharlarion-oil lamp hanging on three chains from the ceiling, to my right, above the desk.

Sample items from the list were as follows:

| | |
|---|---|
| Bread and paga ............................................ | 2 C.T. |
| Other food .................................................. | 3 - 5 C.T. |
| Lodging ..................................................... | 10 C.T. |
| Blankets (2) ................................................ | 2 C.T. |
| Bath ........................................................ | 1 C.T. |
| Bath girl ................................................... | 2 C.T. |
| Sponge, oil and strigil ................................... | 1 C.T. |
| Girl for the night ......................................... | 5 C.T. |
| T., Greens and Stable ...................................... | 2 C.T. |
| T., Meat and Cot ........................................... | 5 C.T. |

A comment, or two, might be in order on this list of prices. First, it will be noted that they are not typical. In many inns, depending on the season, to be sure, and the readiness of the keeper to negotiate, one can stay for as little as two or three

copper tarsks a day, everything included, within reason, of
course, subject to some restraint with respect to paga, and
such. Also, the bath girl, and the sponge, oil and strigil, in
most establishments, come with the price of the bath itself.
The prices on the list on the wall seemed excessive, perhaps
to a factor of five or more. The prices, of course, were in
terms of copper tarsks.

For purposes of comparison, in many paga taverns, one
may have paga and food, and a girl for the alcove, if one
wants, for a single copper tarsk. Dancers, to be sure, sometimes cost two. I did not know what the "other food" might
be. One always inquires. It would vary seasonally, depend on
the local suppliers, and, in some cases, even on the luck of
local hunters and fishermen. In most inns the fare is simple
and hearty. If one is particular about one's food, one sometimes brings it with one, and instructs the keeper how it is to
be prepared. Some rich men bring their own cooks. After all,
one cannot always count on a keeper's man knowing how to
prepare Turian vulo or Kassau parsit. The references to
"greens" and "meat," and such, were pertinent to draft
tharlarion and tarns, and so, too, the references to stabling
and cots, respectively.

It might be of interest to note that when I had come to Gor,
some years ago, domestic tarns, like wild tarns, almost always made their own kills. They may still do so, of course,
but now many have been trained to accept prepared, even
preserved, meat. Ideally, they are taught to do this from the
time of hatchlings, it being thrust into their mouths, given to
them much as their mother bird would do in the wild. Tongs
are used. With older birds, on the other hand, captured wild
tarns, for example, the training usually takes the form of
tying fresh meat on live animals, and then, when the tarn is
accustomed to eating both, effecting the transition to the
prepared meat. Needless to say, a hunting tarn is extremely
dangerous, and although its favorite prey may be tabuk, or
wild tarsk, they can attack human beings. This training inno-
vation, interestingly enough, and perhaps predictably, was
not primarily the result of an attempt to increase the safety of
human beings, particularly those in rural areas, but was rather
largely the result of attempting to achieve military objectives,
in particular those having to do with the logistical support of

the tarn cavalry. Because of it, for the first time, large tarn cavalries, numbering in the hundreds of men, became practical.

"Tal," said a grizzled fellow, wearily, appearing through a door to the side.

"Tal," said I to him.

"It is quieter outside now," he said.

"It is still raining," I said.

"It is ten tarsks a night," he said. That agreed with the sign.

"That is very expensive," I said.

"True," he said. "I myself would not pay so much."

"Perhaps I will leave now," I said.

"The rain has slacked off," he said.

"Are these prices negotiable?" I inquired.

"No," said he.

"Are you sure?" I asked.

"Yes," he said. "The keeper, believe me, I know, is a resolute and greedy fellow."

"He is probably not as bad as you think," I said.

"Take my word for it, he is," he said.

"I would like a bath, the sponge, and such, and a bath girl," I said.

"That will add two to your bill," he said.

"Should it not add four?" I asked.

"No bath girl," he said. "Because of the crowding, and the demand, we are using them as inn girls."

"I see," I said.

"You will have to sponge, oil and strigil yourself," he said.

"That seems somewhat barbaric," I said. Also it was hard to reach certain spots on the back.

"Times are hard," he said.

"Where are your baths?" I asked.

"Through there," he said, indicating a passage.

"Where is your paga room?" I asked.

"There," said he, indicating another passage.

"Later," I said, "I would like a girl sent to my room."

"You do not have a room," he said.

"What are the ten tarsks for?" I asked.

"Lodging," he said.

"You do not have rooms?" I asked.

"Not separate rooms, for guests," he said. "There are, instead, common areas."

"There are beds there?" I asked, apprehensively.

"Beds?" he asked, raising an eyebrow.

"Yes, beds," I said.

"Certainly not," he said.

"I see," I said.

"Surely you know where you are," he said.

"On the Vosk Road," I said, warily.

"And within a hundred pasangs of the river," he said. "No inns around here have beds. You should know that. You seem uninformed."

"Perhaps," I said.

"Perhaps you would like to try one of the luxury inns between Ar and Venna," he said.

"They are over two thousand pasangs away," I said.

"You are surely not going to hold me responsible for their location," he said.

"I would not think of doing so," I said.

"Do not be dismayed," he said. "Even in these hard times, the keeper, who has his congenial, noble side, has refused to surrender space lines."

"That is good news," I said. "What are space lines?"

"Most inns," he said, "for your lodging, simply assign you to a large common room, to be shared with others. Quite primitive. Here, at the Crooked Tarn, however, we rent out spaces."

"I see," I said.

"Furthermore, they are clearly marked."

"I am glad to hear that," I said.

"You can accomodate fewer people that way, to be sure," he said, "but then there are fewer fights, and free women almost always prefer to have their own space. Too, with spaces, you can charge more."

"This inn then, in its way, I gather, is a luxury inn for this area."

"Precisely," he said.

"Perhaps then you can send a girl to my space for the night," I said.

"Not for the night," said he, "but only for the quarter of an Ahn."

"Your sign," I said.

"I know," he said, "but we are too crowded now for that. On the other hand, we would charge you only three copper tarsks for the time."

"For a quarter of an Ahn?" I said.

"The keeper is a scoundrel," he said.

"I thought you said he had a congenial, noble side."

"He keeps it under control," he said.

"He may not be the scoundrel you think he is," I said.

"No, he is a scoundrel all right."

"Three tarsks seems a good deal for a quarter of an Ahn," I said. I wondered if I might not have greater success with the keeper himself. But I supposed he was not up at this hour.

"We have a debtor slut serving in the paga room," he said. "We could let you have her for an Ahn for a tarsk bit."

"Does she know she is subject to such uses?" I asked.

"No," he said.

"I will take a look at her, and let you know later."

"That would be fourteen copper tarsks," he said.

"I would count twelve," I said. "Ten for lodging, two for the bath and supplies."

"I thought you might want some blankets," he said.

"Of course," I said.

"Fourteen then," he said. I saw this inked on a tab.

From a cabinet to one side, he fetched forth the bath supplies and put them on the counter.

"I will pick up the blankets after I have eaten," I said.

"I will reserve two for you, with your ostrakon," he said.

"I would like a space near the wall, preferably in a corner," I said.

"So would everyone else," he said. "Your space is S-3-07. That is 97, in the south wing, on the third floor."

"Very well," I said.

"Try not to step on any drovers," he said. "They can be ugly fellows when stepped on in the middle of the night."

"I will do my best," I said.

"If you must step on them," he said, "it is well to do it in such a way as to incapacitate them, at least temporarily."

"I understand," I said.

"Do you wish to give your name?" he said.

"No," I said.

He did not seem surprised. Many folks coming through here, I gathered, did not identify themselves, or used false names.

"We shall make the bill out to your space then," he said, "S-3-97." He put that identification on the tab.

"Excellent," I said.

"Payment is due before, or at, departure," he said. "To be sure, if the inn grows suspicious, we reserve the right to require payment, to date, upon demand."

"That is reasonable," I said.

"We think so," he said.

"Your prices," I said, "as I think you have admitted, or as much as admitted, are rather expensive."

"They certainly are," he said. "I, for one, would not want to pay them."

I looked at him.

"They are not negotiable," he said.

"Are you really sure?" I asked.

"Yes," he said.

"It is hard for me to believe that the keeper is as adamant as you portray him," I said.

"He is, I assure you," said the fellow.

"Surely he cannot be the scoundrel you claim," I said.

"He is," said the fellow. "I know."

"I do not suppose he would be up at this hour," I said.

"But he is," said the fellow.

"Do you think I might speak to him?" I asked.

"You have been doing so," he said. "I am he."

"Oh," I said.

# 4
# THE BATHS

I closed my eyes in one of the second tubs, the cleansing tubs. There were five first tubs, and five second tubs. These were all large, shallow, round tubs, of clay, covered with porcelain, mounted on open-bricked platforms, each platform about a yard high. In this particular bath, adequate enough, I suppose, for the area, the fires beneath the bricked platforms were stirred, tended and cleaned with long-handled fire rakes. To be sure, it was late, and I suspected that the fires had not been tended since perhaps the eighteenth Ahn. The water, however, happily, was still comfortably warm. They would probably be built up again around the fifth Ahn. I had hung my wet garments on racks about the brick platform, behind the tub. They would probably be dry by now. Each tub was some seven feet in width and some eighteen inches deep. On a hook, behind me, kept for towels, and such, I had slung my scabbard.

More than one fellow, and even a Ubar or two, as history has it, had been attacked in the bath. The baths here, of course, were very simple, and primitive. For example, they were heated in the same room, and not in virtue of subterranean furnaces, heat from which would normally be conveyed upward through vents and pipes. Here, too, there were no scented pools, no massaging rooms, no steaming rooms. Too, of course, here there were no exercising yards, where one might try a fall or two in wrestling or, say, have a game of catch, either with the large or the small ball. Similarly, there were no recreational gardens, no art galleries, no strolling lanes, no arcades of merchants, no physicians' courts, no reading rooms, no music rooms, or such.

The baths, in many Gorean cities and towns, are convenient and popular gathering places. One can pick up the latest news and gossip there, for example. Many of these establishments are opulently appointed. Many are capacious and even palatial. Sometimes public funds are lavished upon them, as they are objects of civic pride. Even poor men may feel rich in them, sometimes for as little as a tarsk bit. Candidates seeking election sometimes dispense admittance ostraka to the poor. Some of these edifices, as in Turia or Ar, are monumental in size, almost like vaulted, pillared stadiums, with dozens of rooms and pools. One can become lost in them.

Gorean baths are almost always segregated, incidentally, if only by the time of day. This does not mean that bath girls may not be available to tend to a strong male's various wants in the men's baths, or that handsome silk slaves, if they are summoned, may not appear in attendance in the baths of free women. A latticework separated the bathing area from the outer area. It was open now. I heard a fellow stirring in his sleep a few feet away, on the floor, near the bricked platform. Some seven or eight fellows, the latticework open, were sleeping in the bath area. I supposed they preferred the warmth of the baths to their spaces in the unheated levels, or lofts, of the inn. This sort of thing is not unusual in Gorean towns, incidentally, in cold weather, that folks should sleep in the baths. They are often warmer than their houses. They leave in the morning, of course, some of them doubtless to call on their patrons, hoping for a breakfast or an invitation to dinner.

I opened one eye, hearing the outer door, that beyond the latticework, open.

There are many types of baths, and ways to take them, for example, depending on the temperatures of the tubs, or pools, and the order in which one uses them. A common fashion is to use the first tub for a time, soaking, and, if one wishes, sponging, and then, emerging, to apply the oil, or oils. These are rubbed well into the skin and then removed with the strigil. There are various forms of strigil, and some of them are ornately decorated. They are usually of metal and almost always of a narrow, spatulate form. With the strigil one scrapes away the residue of oil, and, with it, dirt and sweat, cleaning the pores. One then generally takes the "second tub," which consists of clean water, sponges away any remaining grime, residues of oil and dirt, and such, and then, luxuriating, soaks again.

If one has a bath girl, of course, she does most of these things for one. Sometimes the services of a bath girl, including massage and love, in whatever modalities the customer may elect, come in the price of the bath, and, at other times, as here, at the Crooked Tarn, I gathered, at least normally, they are extra. Needless to say, bath girls are almost always female slaves. Sometimes, in certain cities, free women, found guilty of crimes, are sentenced to the baths, to serve there as bath girls, subject, too, to the disciplines of such. After a given time there, after it is thought they have learned their lessons, and those of the baths, they are, commonly, routinely enslaved and sold out of the city. It is probably just as well. By that time they will have been, in effect, "spoiled for freedom."

"Ai!" cried a fellow, stepped on by the newcomer.

Another rose up, in the half darkness, and was kicked aside.

I opened my other eye, to consider matters.

It was a swaggering fellow. He was naked, his clothes doubtless being hung on one of the pegs beyond the latticework, in the outer area. Normally, particularly when the baths are in full use, and the air is steamy in their vicinity, that would be done. Mine, which had been wet, I had put behind the bricked platform to dry. He held a sack in one hand, containing, I supposed, his bath supplies, and, in the other, held by their straps, a scabbard and blade, and what appeared to be a flat, rectangular pouch. He had chosen, too, I saw, not to come unarmed to the baths. It is thought to be very bad form, incidentally, to carry weapons in the baths, and, in large public baths, they must often be checked upon entry. On the other hand, I certainly did not blame him for carrying a blade into the baths, particularly in a place such as this. I had done so, myself. I did not know, but I suspected that on the peg outside, by its straps, there might hang a helmet. I recalled the tarn in the inn's tarncot. Though no insignia or harness had been about, it had seemed clearly a war tarn, a warrior's mount. That he had brought the rectangular pouch into the baths with him, as well as the blade, suggested to me that it might be important, too important to be left back at his space, or on the peg outside the latticework. He hung his blade, and the pouch, on one of the tub hooks.

"What are you doing?" asked a fellow. He was the only other in the room who was actually utilizing a tub. He had arrived later even than I, and was still soaking in one of the first tubs, indeed, that which was most convenient to the entrance through the latticework. I myself, in my choice of a first tub had, and, indeed, of the second, as well, in which I now reclined, taken those farthest from the entrance. In that way I would have the longest reaction interval possible between someone's entry and their possible arrival in my vicinity.

"I take the first of the first tubs," said the fellow.

"I do not share tubs," said the fellow soaking in the tub, not too pleasantly. Most Goreans, in the baths, at least in their own towns or cities, do share tubs, of course. That is one reason the tubs are so large. To be sure, even in one's own area, one usually shares a tub only with friends or acquaintances. If the baths are crowded, of course, it would be only polite to share with one's fellow citizens. The same customs, of course, generalized even further, normally govern the use of pools, which, on Gor, are normally located at the baths, and, indeed, are usually considered a part of them.

"Nor do I," said the newcomer, climbing to the platform.

"Aiii!" cried the fellow in the tub, seized, and, in a moment, flung over its edge to the slotted wooden bath floor. He struggled to his feet, to see, in the half darkness, lit by a single lamp, and the reddish embers within the bricked platforms, the unsheathed sword now in the newcomer's hand.

"Stir up the fire," said the newcomer.

Hastily the ejected fellow seized a fire rake and poked about within the platform.

"Bring more wood," said the newcomer. "Then tend the fire. Do not leave until it is suitable."

From one of the large barrels to the side, open near the bottom, the ejected fellow scooped out, and returned with, a

bucket of wood chips, which he flung into the bricked platform. He then arranged these with the fire rake. He then
returned the bucket to its place by the barrel and, from one of
the wood bins, to the right, near the barrels, fetched an
armload of kindling, then some narrow hardwood logs. In a
few moments the chips were burning well. He then added
kindling, and then, a bit later, thrust the narrow logs into the
platform. He then, the reddish glow of the flames from within
the platform reflected on his countenance, looked up, questioningly, frightened, at the newcomer.

"Get out," said the newcomer.

Only too eagerly the ejected fellow hurried through the
latticework, seized his garments, and took his way from the
bath area.

The newcomer then returned his blade to the sheath. He
then climbed into the tub. "Ahhh," he grunted, settling
back.

I did not think he had behaved well, but then it was not my
affair.

Some of the fellows who had been reclining about the
platforms then came closer to the platform where the fire was
built up. They did take care, however, to leave open a
generous passage through which the tub's occupant, when he
chose, might make an unimpeded and convenient exit.

Being hungry then, and having, to my mind, soaked long
enough, I emerged from the tub, dressed, gathered my things,
and the oil and such, and, picking my way among the recum-
bent bodies, left the bath area.

I did take the opportunity, in leaving, once on the other
side of the latticework, to inspect the pegs. In the light of the
small lamp there, near the exit, I determined that the helmet
bore the insignia of the company of Artemidorus of Cos.

# 5
# THE PAGA ROOM;
# I STOP AT
# THE KEEPER'S DESK

"Stand here," I said. "Closer." I indicated a place to my right, near the low table in the paga room, behind which I sat, cross-legged.

With a sound of chain she came closer.

She then stood there.

I checked the shackling on her ankles. The shackles were lock shackles. They fitted nicely, closely, about her ankles. Their staples were separated by about eighteen inches of chain, more than enough. I pulled her wrists down to me. They wore lock manacles. Their fit was snug, efficient, inescapable. The staples on the manacles were separated by some twelve inches of chain.

"Does my shackling meet with Sir's approval?" she asked.

I did not respond to her. I did release her wrists, and she straightened up.

"Is Sir finished with his inspection?" she asked, acidly.

She was naked, except for her chains.

"Turn," I said, "slowly, and then again face me."

"I am a free woman," she said, angrily.

"Must a command be repeated?" I inquired.

She turned, slowly, and then, again, faced me.

"What would you like—I mean," she said, boldly, haughtily, "—to eat, Sir."

"You are bold, for a free woman," I said.

"I may not be used," she said, "as I am free."

"Is there another free woman serving in the paga room?" I asked.

"No," she said.

This must be she, then, of whom the keeper had spoken. I recalled that he had told me that although the use of an inn girl would cost me, in these times, three copper tarsks for only a quarter of an Ahn, I might have the free woman working in the paga room for an Ahn for only a tarsk bit. To be sure, that perhaps overrated her value considerably, as she was only a free woman. Whereas free women, technically, are priceless, they are also, usually, in bed, worthless. They are not worthy of kneeling and humbly holding candles within a thousand pasangs of a slave. To be sure, they commonly hold an inflated opinion of their expertise and desirability. They are no good, however, until they have been imbonded, and have begun, vulnerably and fearfully, to tread, willingly or not, the paths to fulfillment, and ecstasy. The outrageousness of the price, of course, was doubtless to be expected, given the general inflations of the times. I had told him I would let him know later. I would.

"And may you not be whipped," I asked, "as you are free?"

She turned white.

Although she apparently had not been informed that she was subjectable to the inn's clients, for their pleasures, as much as an inn girl, she had, apparently, been informed that her behavior, even though she was free, surprisingly perhaps, was subject to correction, such corrections doubtless including such things as the attentions of the five-stranded Gorean slave whip.

"What is your name?" I asked.

"It is none of your business," she said.

"Have you ever been whipped?" I asked.

"I am Temione, Lady of Telnus," she said. "No, I have not been whipped," she added.

Telnus is the major port on the island of Cos. Too, it is the capital of that island ubarate.

"What are you doing here?" I asked.

She did not answer.

"Doubtless you followed Cosians," I said, "or their suppliers, smelling booty, lured by the possibilities of spoils, by the supposed imminent passage south of men laden with the plate and coin of Ar's Station, men who might succumb to your claims of need and plight, hoping perhaps even to contract an alliance, a companionship, with an enriched officer, or, if necessary, a profiteering merchant.''

She looked at me, in fury.

"You would bargain with your beauty," I said. I smiled to myself. I suspected that her beauty in the future might, indeed, figure in bargains, here and there, from time to time, but they would not be her bargains. They would be the bargains of others.

With a movement of her head she tossed her hair behind her, angrily.

"Are you angry?" I asked.

"Would you care to order?" she asked.

"What color is your hair?" I asked. "It is hard to tell in this light."

"Auburn," she said.

"A natural auburn?" I asked.

"Of course," she said.

"That color, particularly when natural, often brings an excellent price in slave markets," I said.

"I am free," she said.

"There are some others outside," I said, "who may have had similar ideas to yours, in one way or another. They are now in the court, chained naked to rings. Do you know them?"

She looked away, angrily.

"Lady Temione," I said, "you have been asked a question."

"There are five others," she said, "Rimice, Klio, and Liomache, from Cos, Elene, from Tyros, and Amina, a Vennan."

"What do you think will happen to them?" I asked.

"Doubtless they will be redeemed, and freed," she said. "We are all free women. Men, some sorts of men, will save us. Men, some sorts, cannot so much as stand to see a tear in a woman's eye. To such men it is unthinkable that we might bear the consequences of our actions."

"Do you think I am such a man?" I asked.

"No," she said, "else I would have petitioned redemption from you."

"Men such as those of whom you speak," I said, "those who are so solicitous, so kindly, those who are so eager to render you succor, who will strive so desperately to help you, and please you, do they stir you deeply in your belly?"

"I am a free woman," she said. "We do not consider such things."

"But you must fear the iron," I said.

"It will never happen," she said.

"But you must fear it," I said.

"Perhaps," she said.

"Things, then," I said, "would be quite different."

"Yes," she said. "They would then be quite different." This was quite true. The slave girl is in a totally different category from the free woman. It is the difference between being a person and being a property, between being a respected, legally autonomous entity, entitled to dignity and pride, and being a domestic animal. The same fellow who will go to absurd lengths to please a free woman, and even make a fool of himself over her, will, even with the same woman, if she has been enslaved, simply gesture her with his whip, and without a second thought, to the furs.

"When were you, and your fraud sisters, taken into custody?" I asked.

"Payment was demanded this morning," she said. "When our evasions failed to satisfy the attendants ropes were put on our necks, over our robes and veils, and we were brought to the keeper's desk. We gave him what little money we had, of course, but it was not enough to satisfy our bills. We then spent the morning in a wheeled cage, sitting on hard benches, while men checked out. None would redeem us. Then, at noon, as soon as the tenth Ahn had struck, the cage was wheeled back, into a storage area. It was plain, and cold. There, one by one, taken from the cage, while men waited outside the area, we were stripped and searched by two powerful free women. When they finished with one of us they did not then permit her to return to the cage but rather forced her to stand apart, facing a wall. In this way, one who had already been searched was prevented, and quite simply, from receiving anything from one not yet searched. Our garments were examined carefully, and even our bodies. This yielded them some few extra coins. The women, I assure you, were thorough. Doubtless thay had done this sort of thing before.

"When we were returned to the cage we were both coinless and naked. All that was left then was ourselves. The cage was then wheeled back, by the keeper's desk. As you might well imagine our importunities to the guests now became more earnest. Yet none were gentlemen. We even found ourselves looked upon, in the cage, as though we might be slaves! At the fifteenth Ahn we were removed from the cage and knelt down, to the side, to the left of the keeper's desk. Our ankles were then crossed and tied. This was done with a single length of rope. It served also, thusly, with a minimum of knots to which we might have access, to fasten us together."

"Your hands were left free, of course," I said, "so that you might extend them piteously to passers-by, guests, and such."

"Of course," she said, angrily.

"Continue," I said.

"At the seventeenth Ahn," she said, "the keeper, it seems, grew weary of our pleas and protestations. Also, I think he was not too pleased with women such as we, who had attempted to do fraud and dupery within his inn."

"That is understandable," I said.

"No," she said. "We are not slaves! We are free women. We may do anything."

"I see," I said.

"The keeper," she said, "is not a gentleman."

"I am prepared to believe that," I said.

"It is true!" she said. "Look at me, naked and chained!"

"I have been," I assured her.

She shook the chain on her wrists, angrily.

"But he did, it seems, give you an opportunity to practice your fraud and dupery," I said. "Your primary problem would seem to be simply that you were unsuccessful."

"Perhaps," she said, irritably.

From what I had seen of the keeper, I supposed that his main interest in these matters would be to obtain his fees, if not in one way, then in another.

"Continue," I said.

"There is little more to tell," she said, angrily. "At the seventeenth Ahn, perhaps wearying of our presence there, he had us cleared away from the vicinity of his desk. Five of us were taken outside somewhere, and from what you say, I take it, chained in the court. I myself was shackled, and put here, in the paga room, to serve at tables.''

"Why were you not taken outside?" I asked.

"I do not know," she said.

"There are only five exposition places at the wall," I said. She shrugged.

"Still that would not explain why it should be you who are here, and not another."

"I suppose it had to be someone," she said.

"Two women might have been chained to one ring," I said, "or you might have been chained on your knees, nearby, to a sleen ring."

"Men are lustful beasts," she said. "They seem to enjoy looking upon women. Doubtless I am here because I am the most beautiful."

"But you are not," I said.

"Oh?" she said, angrily.

"No," I said. "She who was at the first ring and she who was at the fourth ring were both more beautiful than you."

"Who were they?" she asked, angrily.

"She at the first ring was the Lady Amina," I said. "I do not know who was at the fourth ring."

"Was she small, and dark-haired?"

"Yes," I said.

"That is Rimice," she said. "She is a small, curvy slut."

I recalled the girl at the fourth ring. She was sweetly thighed with a marvelous love cradle, made for a man's loving.

"I am more beautiful than both," she said.

"You seem vain, for a free woman," I said.

"Not really," she said. "I have no interest in such matters."

"To be sure, all of the women out there," I said, "including the Lady Amina and the Lady Rimice, are not yet truly beautiful. They are still too rigid, too tense, too tight, too inhibited to be truly beautiful."

"You see!" she said, triumphantly.

"But none of them so much as you," I said.

"Sleen!" she said.

"It is interesting to speculate what you women might be like, if you became beautiful," I said.

"Sleen, sleen!" she said.

"How did the keeper seem when he ordered you shackled and put in the paga room?" I asked.

"Amused," she said, angrily.

"Perhaps you had spoken up to him," I speculated, "though you were only a debtor slut."

"Such is my right!" she said. "I am a free woman!"

"You dared to protest the treatment you received?" I asked.

"Of course!" she cried. "How is it that I, a free woman, should be stripped, and searched, and put in a cage, and such!"

"Perhaps you made demands, threatened him, insulted him, that sort of thing?" I asked.

"Perhaps," she said.

"I can see then," I said, "why it might have amused him to put you here, to serve as a waitress."

"Perhaps," she said, angrily.

"How much do you owe him?" I asked.

"A silver tarsk, five," she said.

"That might be another reason," I said. "That is more than is owed by any of the other women." The amount stated was a silver tarsk, five copper tarsks.

"Perhaps," she said, thoughtfully. "He may want to keep me where he or his men can keep an eye on me."

Did she really think they feared her escape, she, within the palisade, shackled and naked?

"They might, too," I said, "consider that your display here, if you will pardon the expression, might enhance your chances of obtaining a redemption."

"Yes," she said, "that, too."

In the morning, of course, the girls outside, at the wall, might have a better chance. They would, by that time, I speculated, be bedraggled, and piteous, indeed. Still I did not think any of them, the Lady Temione here, or the others, outside, in these times, were likely, really, to get some fellow to redeem them.

"Would you care to order, Sir?" she asked, irritatedly.

I looked at her. Yes, I thought to myself, that was probably the main reason she had been put here, that is it, not because it was an accident, the luck in a lot of six, or even really, mainly, because she owed more than the others, but because she had not been found pleasing by the keeper. In its way, it was a punishment for her. Too, he had doubtless seen that she required informing, as to her nature and status.

"I am waiting, *Sir*," she said.

"Do you regard yourself as desirable?" I asked.

She tossed her head, haughtily. "You spoke of beauty earlier, and insultingly of my putative intent to bargain with it," she said. "Perhaps you can see."

"That was not my question," I said.

"Yes," she said, "I regard myself as desirable." She regarded me, angrily. "Don't you?" she said.

I said, "Proper diet and exercise, imposed under suitable disciplines, would doubtless work wonders with you."

"Would you care to order," she asked.

"Have you served others?" I asked.

"Yes," she said.

"And you have not been disciplined?" I asked.

"No," she said. "I am a free woman." She looked at me, angrily. "Are you ready to order?"

"Yes," I said.

"Well?" she asked.

"Kneel," I said.

" 'Kneel'?" she asked.

"That is my first order," I said.

She regarded me.

"Do you not know how a woman serves at table?" I asked.

"I am a free woman," she said.

"Shall I send you to fetch a slave whip?" I asked.

She then trembled, and knelt. But, in a moment, she had recovered herself. She looked at me, angrily.

"You may keep your knees together," I said, "as you are a free woman."

Swiftly she closed them, furious. "I hate you!" she said.

"You may now lower your head, before a male," I said.

"Never!" she said.

"Now," I said.

She lowered her head, angrily. "I have never done that before," she said, lifting her head.

"You may now put it to the floor, the palms of your hands, too, to the floor," I said.

Trembling with rage she obeyed. Then she straightened up, and knelt back.

"What do you have?" I asked.

"Paga and bread are two tarsks," she said. "Other food may be purchased from three to five tarsks."

"Is the paga cut?" I asked.

"One to five," she said.

This is not that unusual at an inn. The proportions, then, would be one part paga to five parts water. Commonly, at a paga tavern, the paga would be cut less, or not cut at all. When wine is drunk with Gorean meals, at home, incidentally, it is almost always diluted, mixed with water in a *krater*. At a party or convivial supper the host, or elected feast master, usually determines the proportions of water to wine. Unmixed wine, of course, may be drunk, for example, at the parties of young men, at which might appear dancers, flute slaves and such. Many Gorean wines, it might be mentioned, if only by way of explanation, are very strong, often having an alcoholic content by volume of forty to fifty percent.

"How much bread?" I asked.

"Two of four," she said. That would be half a loaf. The bread would be in the form of wedges. Gorean bread is almost always baked in round, flat loaves. The average loaf is cut into either four or eight wedges.

"What is the other food?" I asked.

"The Ahn is late," she said. "We have nothing but porridge left."

"It is three?" I asked.

"Yes," she said.

"I do not suppose," I said, "that if one orders the porridge, the bread and paga comes with it?"

"No," she said.

I had not, of course, expected any such luck, particularly after my conversation with the keeper. To be sure, even if perhaps a bit greedy, he was not a bad fellow. He had, for example, put the Lady Temione naked at the tables.

"Bread, paga, porridge," I said to her.

"Very well," she said.

"Very well, what?" I asked.

"Very well, *Sir*," she said.

"Head to the floor before you get up," I said.

She put her head angrily down to the floor, the palms of her hands on the floor, and then straightened up.

"From each of your fraud sisters outside, chained to their rings," I said, "I had a kiss."

"You will get no kiss from me," she said.

I then gestured her up with a casual motion of my finger and away, that she should hurry to the kitchen.

"Lady Temione," I called.

She stopped.

"You may move more swiftly," I said, "if you rise up on your toes and take short steps."

She cried out with rage, and stumbled, and fell. Then, rising, she hurried, as she could, angrily toward the door of the kitchen and, in a moment, disappeared through it. I watched it swing behind her, until it hung motionless on its hinges. Such doors, single and double, are common in inns and taverns, as they may be negotiated by someone whose hands are occupied, as in bearing a tray. Most often, however, on Gor, curtains, often beaded, are used to separate open from restricted areas in taverns, restaurants and such. Lady Temione, I had noted, needed discipline. The sooner she received it the better it would probably be for her, and her life.

In a few moments she returned through the door bearing a tray. She knelt near the table, put the tray on the floor, unbidden performed obeisance and then, as though submissively, put the tray on the table, and put the paga, in a small *kantharos*, and the bread on its trencher, before me. Then she put the bowl of porridge, with a spoon, before me. She then withdrew, taking the tray, put it to the side, on the floor, again performed obeisance, unbidden, and then knelt back, as though in attendance. There had been something false in her subservience.

I looked at her, narrowly. She did not meet my eyes.

I took a sip of paga, and then sopped some bread in it, and then ate it.

As I reached for the spoon I thought she leaned forward a little.

I took a very tiny bit of the porridge. As I had suspected it might be, it was offensively seasoned, salted, almost to the point of inedibility.

"Is anything wrong, Sir?" she asked.

"I will count an Ehn," I said, "that is, eighty Ihn. You have that long to make good what you have done."

"I?" she asked, innocently.

"1—2—3—," I said.

"But what?" she said, alarmed.

"4—5—6—," I said.

"My ankles are chained!" she cried.

"7—8—9," I said.

Swiftly, crying out with misery, stumbling, falling, she tried to scramble to her feet. Then, as swiftly as she could, falling twice more, partly crawling, weeping, she strove to reach the door of the kitchen.

"24—25—26," I counted. "27—28—29—30—31—32—33—34."

She appeared through the swinging door, carrying a bowl in her chained hands, desperately moving toward me in short, careful, frightened steps. She could not risk falling.

I let her approach closely. "Hold," I said.

She stopped, wildly.

"Perhaps in your haste you have forgotten to season that," I said. "I prefer anyway to season my own porridge. See that you do not dare to present the porridge without the seasonings."

She cried out with misery.

"Bring condiments as well," I advised her. "50—51—52."

In a moment or two she had regained the kitchen, and, an instant or two later, clutching a small, partitioned hand-rack of small vials and pots, each in its place, she again emerged into the public area.

"67," I said. "68."

"Please!" she cried. "Have mercy!"

"69—70," I said.

She hastened toward me, terrified, with quick, small steps.

"75—76," I said. "Obeisance."

She cried out with misery, performing obeisance.

"77," I said. "78—79."

Then the porridge, with the seasonings and condiments, was on the table.

"80," I said.

She leaned back. I feared she might faint. Then she again performed obeisance, and shrank back.

"Do not leave," I told her. "You do not have permission to withdraw. Back on your heels."

She knelt back on her heels, frightened.

I tasted the porridge. It had not yet been seasoned. Trying it, with one spoonful or another, from one vial or pot, or another, I seasoned it to my taste. I would later, now and then, here or there, in one place or another, mix in condiments. By such devices one obtains variety, or its deceptive surrogate, even in a substance seemingly so initially unpromising as inn porridge.

She looked at me, anxiously.

"I think this will prove satisfactory, free woman," I said.

She breathed more easily.

I put down the spoon.

"I shall take this other bowl away," she said.

"Not yet," I said.

"Sir?" she asked.

I rose to my feet and pressed her back to the tiles, and pulled her wrist chain down, lifting up her feet. I then slipped the wrist chain behind her feet and ankles, and pulled it up, behind her back. This held her hands rather behind her, at her sides. I then put her again to her knees.

"Sir?" she asked.

"You do have auburn hair, don't you?" I said.

Then I picked up the original bowl of porridge and held it in the palm of my left hand and took her firmly at the back of her head, by the hair, with my right.

"No!" she cried.

I plunged her face downward, fully into the porridge.

I held the bowl firmly, pressed upwards. I held her head firmly, pressing her face down into the bowl. She struggled, unavailingly. Then I let her lift her head, sputtering, choking, coughing, gasping for air, her face a mass of porridge. "I can't breathe!" she wept. "I'm choking!"

Then I thrust her face again into the bowl.

"Eat," I said. "Eat."

Wildly she began to try and take the material into her
mouth. Then she twisted her head to the side. "It's inedi-
ble!" she wept. I turned her head again, and pushed it down.
"Eat!" I said. I supposed it was possible someone could
drown in a bowl of porridge. I pulled her head up then, so
she could breathe, and she gasped for breath. "Please!" she
wept, through the glutinous mask on her face. Again I pushed
her head down, and again, she strove to get the stuff in her
mouth. Then I put the bowl on the floor before her and put
her to her belly before it, and put my foot on her back, so that
she could not rise. Her face was at the bowl. "Eat," I said.
She put her head down over the bowl and, lapping, and biting
at the substance, fed. When I removed my foot from her back
she looked up at me. "Please!" she begged. "Eat," I said. I
then kicked her with the side of my foot, and, as she addressed herself again to the contents of the bowl I settled
myself before the low table, cross-legged, and returned to my
own repast. Once again she looked up at me, frightened,
through the paste of porridge, it thick about her face and on
her eyelashes. "I'm on fire!" she wept. "Water! I beg it!"

"Eat," I said.

Frightened, she again lowered her face to the bowl.

After a time I had finished my own porridge.

When I glanced again at her she had rather finished her
porridge, and was lying on her belly, her head turned toward
me, looking at me.

"You are a monster," she said.

"Lick your bowl," I said.

Miserably she did so.

"Some porridge has been spilled," I said, "It doubtless
overflowed the sides of the bowl when you pressed your face
into it. That can happen when one feeds too greedily, too
enthusiastically. One expects a woman to feed more delicately, more daintly. To be sure, you are a free woman, and
may eat much as you wish. Still, such feeding habits would
disgust a tarsk. If a slave fed anything like that, she would be
under the whip within an Ehn."

She looked at me, frightened.

"You can see porridge about, here and there," I said. "Do
not let it go to waste."

She moaned, and, on her belly, lowered her face to the

floor. Her tongue was small, and lovely. Trained, it might do well on a man's body.

"Are you finished?" I asked her, after a time.

"Yes," she whispered, in her chains, on her belly, looking up at me.

"Rejoice that you are a free woman, and not a slave," I said. "Had you been a slave, you might have been killed for what you did earlier."

She was silent.

"Do you understand?" I asked.

"Yes," she said.

"Approach me, on your belly," I said.

She squirmed to the table, her hands still behind her.

I then reached behind her and drew the wrist chain down and, forcing her legs tightly back against her body, put it back in front of her legs. It was then as it had been before. I let her straighten her legs.

"When you bring the check," I said, "do so in your teeth."

She looked at me, angrily.

"Do you understand?" I asked.

"Yes," she said.

"The check is to be paid, or put on the bill, I gather, at the keeper's desk," I said. One had to pass the keeper's desk after leaving the paga room. That arrangement, I supposed, was no accident. For example, it would save the posting of one employee, which was perhaps a calculated economy on the part of the proprietor. I would not have put it past him, at any rate. Too, in virtue of this arrangement, one need not entrust coins to debtor sluts, slaves, and such. In this house I suspected that they would not be permitted to so much as touch a coin. They would be kept coinless, absolutely.

"Yes," she said.

"Do you wish to say anything?" I asked.

"I hate you! I hate you!" she said.

"You may, after performing obeisance, withdraw," I said.

Swiftly she performed obeisance, and then then rose to her feet, and, moving carefully, with small steps, as she could, hurried to the kitchen.

I would finish my bread, and nurse the paga for a time, and then retire to my space. It was in the south wing, on the third level, space 97. I would pick up the ostrakon, with the blankets, at the keeper's desk. I wondered how I might approach Ar's Station and deliver the message of Gnieus Lelius, the regent of Ar, to the commander at Ar's Station, Aemilianus. If I appeared to be of Ar, I might fall afoul of Cosians. If I appeared to be with Cos I might have considerable difficulty in approaching the defenders of Ar's Station. Still I must do something soon. The siege at Ar's Station, I had gathered, might be approaching a critical juncture.

As I pondered these matters the door to the paga room burst open and the fellow, fierce and bearded, who had been in the baths now appeared, in the uniform of the company of Artemidorus of Cos, which, indeed, I had supposed must be his. He wore his sword, on its strap over the left shoulder. This is common among Gorean warriors, though not on the march nor in tarnflight. In this arrangement the sword may be unsheathed and the scabbard and strap discarded in one movement. He carried his helmet and the intriguing pouch which had caught my attention earlier, that which he had carried with him even in the room of the baths.

I did not meet the fellow's eyes, not wanting to explore the consequences of a confrontation. I supposed I should permit myself, if the occasion arose, to be bullied and humiliated, that I might not risk complications or delay in my mission. Still, I am not always as rational as I might be, and if he threatened or challenged me, I was not at all certain that I could summon the concealments and coolness necessary to endure abuse. I am upon occasion too hot-headed, too quick to act, too ready to respond to any insult or slight, real or imagined. It is doubtless one of many faults. Perhaps I should be more like a Dietrich of Tarnburg, who might dissemble plausibly, and then, later, when it suited his convenience, and if it fitted into his plans, make his kills.

I did not raise my eyes but appeared to be concerned with the paga. I heard him make a sound of contempt. I wondered if he noted that my hand closed more tightly upon the base of the *kantharos*. I should try to control that. I think I myself might have noticed it, in the movement of the upper arm. He stood there, a few feet away. I began to feel insulted. Heat rose in my body. I controlled myself. Surely that is what Dietrich of Tarnburg would have done. I did not look up.

Warriors, of course, are trained to rely upon peripheral vision. If he approached me too closely, coming within a predetermined critical distance, I could dash the paga upward into his eyes and wrench the table up and about, plunging one of the legs into his diaphragm. Then in a moment I could have him under my foot or upon my sword. Some authorities recommend breaking the *kantharos* into shards on the face, taking the target above the bridge of the nose with the rim. This can be even more dangerous with a metal goblet. Many civilians, I believe, do not know why certain warriors, by habit, request their paga in metal goblets when dining in public houses. They regard it, I suppose, as an eccentricity. I heard him make another sound of contempt, and then he strode away, toward another table. He was still alive. I wondered what was in the pouch.

I took another sip of paga.

The fellow, I noted, had taken one of the larger tables, a double table, for himself. To be sure, the paga room was not crowded. He and I were the only customers at this hour. I had taken a small table near the wall. The small table does not encourage the approach of strangers. Its location, too, was not an accident. It permits one to survey the entire room, including the entrance, and, too, to have the wall at one's back.

He smote twice on the surface of his table. It leapt under his blows! "Waitress!" he called. "Waitress!"

I heard the swinging of the kitchen door and a sound of chain. The Lady Temione came forth. I would have to admit that she was pretty, in the half light, in her chains. She had apparently cleaned herself, or had been cleaned, perhaps having her head and upper body thrust into a washing tub. There was no sign now, at any rate, of the porridge in her hair, or about her face, neck, shoulders and breasts. She cast an angry look at me. I was still nursing the paga. I even had some bread left.

She hurried to the newcomer.

It seemed for a moment she was going to request his order on her feet, almost as though in defiance, but then, looking back at me, she suddenly knelt and performed obeisance and then knelt back on her heels, in a waitress's proper deference, to receive the orders of the keeper's customer.

I took another sip of paga. She would, of course, have to return to my table, eventually, to bring the check. Perhaps that was why she chose to observe the waitress's proper forms. To be sure, the waitresses in Gorean paga rooms, and such, are usually slaves. Still, it did not seem inappropriate that she, too, should perform suitable service at table. She was, after all, a debtor slut. Perhaps she thought that I might beat her, or have her beaten, if she omitted these courtesies, particularly after I had taken the time to explain them to her. In this, of course, she was correct.

The fellow was looking at her, narrowly, in the half light. She shrank back under that gaze. Then he rose to his feet and went to crouch near her. He touched her about the neck. Then, literally moving her about, his hands on her knees, he examined her thighs. Then, standing, he pulled her half to her feet, by the upper arms.

"Where is your collar?" he demanded. "Where is your brand?"

"I'm free!" she wept.

He then shook her, angrily, like a doll. Her head jerked back and forth. I was afraid, for a moment, that her neck might break.

"Where is your collar, your brand?" he cried.

"I'm free!" she wept. "I'm free!"

"Bring me a woman!" he cried toward the kitchen, still holding her helplessly before him. "Bring me a *woman*!"

"What is wrong?" asked a fellow, looking out from the kitchen, probably the night cook.

"Where is the keeper!" cried the fellow.

"He has retired," said the fellow.

"This thing is free!" cried the fellow, giving the Lady Temione another shake. "How dare you send it to my table! I do not want it! Send me a *female*! Send me a *woman*!" He then hurled the Lady Temione from him and, with a rattle of chains, she struck the floor. There, terrified, feet from him, she lay on her belly. I was amused to see her lift herself slightly, surely not even aware of what she was doing, a natural female appeasement behavior in the face of male anger. I thought she would do well in a collar. Then, as though she might suddenly have understood what she was doing, she lowered herself as flat to the tiles as she could, trembling with fear and shame. She looked at me, wildly, hoping I had not noticed her behavior. I smiled, and she sobbed. Her womanhood had been observed. The newcomer, as nearly as I could tell, had taken no note of these things.

"Immediately, Sir!" called the fellow from the kitchen door. "In but a moment, Sir!" Then he called to the Lady Temione. "Quick," he cried, "back to the kitchen, slut! No! Do not rise! Crawl!" He then disappeared back through the kitchen door. The Lady Temione paused near my table, on all fours. She looked at me. She had been rejected by a man, thrown from him, in disgust. I saw that she was stunned, that she was confused, that she was bewildered. Many free women regard themselves, without justification, as marvelous prizes. It can come as a great shock to them to suddenly realize they are, for most practical purposes, worthless. This rejection had shaken her profoundly. Like many free women she probably regarded herself as inordinately attractive. She looked at me, piteously, beggingly. She wanted some reassurance from me that she might be at least a little bit desirable or attractive.

"Check," I told her, "and as you are." I then indicated, with a gesture of my finger, that she should proceed on her way. Sobbing, slowly, as she could, in her chaining, she took her way from the room. She had scarcely attained the kitchen door before another woman emerged, swiftly, yet gracefully, drawing a diaphanous silken wrap about her. How she moved! There was a close-fitting collar on her neck. How beautiful she was! What bondage does for a woman! She hurried to the fellow and bellied to him. Immediately he seemed mollified. I felt my fingernails scratch on the lacquer on the table. That must be one of the keeper's best girls, I thought. Indeed, perhaps she was the keeper's preferred slave, sent by him to the customer from his own furs.

I then sopped the last of the bread in the bottom of the *kantharos*.

Now, emerging from the kitchen, came the Lady Temione, on all fours, as I had commanded. From her mouth, on its looped string, dangled the small, closed, hinged, wooden, waxed tablet which would contain the bill. These tablets, and tablets of these sorts, which sometimes have several divisions, and fold up, are often used on Gor for drafts, note taking, temporary tallyings, children's lessons, and such.

They contain one or more waxed surfaces which are written on by a stylus. The smaller ones open like flat books, not roll books, and may be closed with tiny latches, or tied shut.

There was a small sound as the small wooden tablet, on its string, touched the floor near the table, as the Lady Temione put down her head, doing obeisance. Then, lifting her head, crawling, she approached the table, and placed the tablet on the table.

I looked over to the table where the newcomer was. He had now pulled the slave to him and thrown her on her belly over the table.

"Disgusting," said the Lady Temione.

"An attractive slave," I commented. The girl was now gasping and clinging to the table. He was not being gentle with her. But then, of course, she was only a slave.

"Disgusting," said the Lady Temione.

"He may be something of a boor, but he seems to caress well," I said.

The girl was now gasping with love noises.

"I would not know anything about that," she said, acidly.

Yet I noted she did not take her eyes from the abused slave.

"Would you like to be subject to such uses?" I asked.

"No!" she said. "No! No!"

The sudden, tense, almost hysterical ardor of her denial spoke of truths, and needs, and depths within her of the existence of which she must be only too keenly aware, and yet truths, depths and needs which, for some reason or another, she seemed almost tragically desperate to conceal and deny, perhaps mostly from herself. I thought she might serve well herself, on such a table. I recalled that she had chosen to live dangerously, relying much on duping men to make her way through the world. Surely she must have realized that there were dangers in practicing such a livelihood. Not all men are fools. Was she, perhaps unbeknownst to herself, in these peregrinations, truly, searching for a man, or men, who were not, men who would simply take her in hand and give her what she deserved, desired, and needed, her total subjugation?

I picked up the small, closed tablet on the table, unlatched it and examined the amount. It was correct, bread and paga, two copper tarsks, the other food, an additional three.

I then glanced again at the Lady Temione. She had a beautiful face. The auburn hair was certainly attractive. She had good flanks, not a bad belly, and lovely breasts. To be sure, she needed diet, exercise and discipline. Those things, too, besides improving her appearance, would considerably increase her sexual needs. Yes, she was beautiful. Many of the women of Cos are beautiful. We enjoy them in Port Kar. She was aroused, to the extent she could be, as a free woman, in watching the taking of the slave. To be sure, she had been given little choice in this. For example, she had been stripped and chained, and put to the tables. I had seen to it that she had performed obeisance before men. Too, she had been made to crawl in the presence of men, and had been made to bring the bill in her teeth. Such things work their effects on women, even free women.

I closed the tablet and latched it.

The slave on the table gasped, used, serving, clinging to its edges.

The bearded fellow, holding her, was then still for a moment.

"She is moving!" said the Lady Temione, scandalized.

"Yes," I said, "she is cooperating in what is being done."

"Terrible!" whispered the Lady Temione.

"Perhaps she is responding to instructions," I said.

"Instructions!" she said.

"Of course," I said. I wondered if the free woman really thought that the subjection of slaves to orders ended with such matters as cooking and cleaning, the polishing of leather, and such, and that they would not be similarly subject to orders, and also absolutely, where the intimate, marvelous, precious, private, delicious realms of the furs were concerned. Indeed, some think it is most pleasant to command the slave in such places, a couching chamber, a room of submission, a cubicle, and so on.

The bearded fellow drew back for a moment.

The girl clutched the table. She was still for a moment or two. Then she moaned. Then she moved.

"Did you see that!" she said. "She actually lifted herself to him!"

"Surely only a slave would so lift herself to a male," I said.

The Lady Temione blushed, hotly.

"Look at that slut wriggle!" she said.

"She is afraid she may not have been fully pleasing," I said. "She is trying now to interest him, to be pleasing, to entice him. But I think he is not angry with her. I think he is only playing with her, only teasing her." I wondered how the Lady Temione would wriggle.

"Look!" said the Lady Temione.

"He is now again with her," I said.

"Yes!" she said.

"Yes," I agreed. The slave was indeed beautiful. To ground my emotion, so to speak, I gripped the table. It seemed thusly, interestingly, as though my tension might pass through it then, down to the floor, to be dissipated, like a flood. I kept myself from breaking wood from the table.

"Am I attractive?" asked the Lady Temione.

"Yes," I said.

"Ah!" she said.

"—as free women go," I added.

"Sleen!" she sobbed. "Sleen!"

The slave now moaned and whimpered, and then cried out, suddenly, as though momentarily frightened, or alarmed, but then, again, in a moment, understanding what was going to be done to her, that to which she was relentlessly being brought, began to cry out softly, gladly, gratefully, eagerly, anticipatingly.

"Why does that girl reveal her emotions like that?" asked Lady Temione.

"Perhaps she is forbidden to conceal them," I said.

"Oh!" she said. "How naked that would make a woman."

"Yes," I said, "but it also, in its way, makes her free."

"I suppose so," she said, enviously.

Suddenly the girl on the table screamed aloud, again and again, half reared up, began to buck, but could not escape, so tightly and helplessly held she was, uttering the word "Master!" over and over.

"Slave orgasm has been forced upon her," I commented.

Lady Temione quivered in her chains.

"I suspect he will not even have to pay for that use of

her," I said. "It will probably be given to him, as a token of good will, in compensation for his earlier disappointment."

The fellow had resumed his place now behind the table, sitting there, cross-legged, but he had permitted the slave to half lie, half sit, by him, holding to him, her arms about his waist, her head and hair at his side.

"How pleased I am," she said, "that I am not a woman such as that!"

"I see," I said.

The slave now knelt beside him, holding him by the arm, She was looking at him with something akin to awe, for what he had done to her, for what he had made her feel. She kissed him softly, deferentially, gratefully, about the shoulder.

"I am not a servile, wriggling slave," she said, angrily.

"She is not wriggling now," I said.

"Look at her," she said, in disgust. "She is content!"

"But she must fear," I said, "for she may be ordered from him by so little as a word or gesture, and she must obey in all things."

"She is a slave," she said. "She should not be happy. She should be miserable and unhappy!"

"Doubtless, if you owned her," I said, "you could make her so."

"I suppose she is beautiful," she said, "and owned. I suppose some low men might find them attractive."

"Yes," I said, "and Ubars, and such."

"I am not a slave," she said.

"I understand," I said. Certainly she was not a *legal* slave, or at least not yet. She was not, technically, at least at present, a slave in the eyes of the law, as an animal is an animal in the eyes of the law, a tarsk a tarsk, a vulo, so soft and pretty, a vulo.

"Men are not my masters," she said.

"I see," I said.

"How pleased I am that I am not one of those women who must crawl about the feet of men, licking and kissing, and groveling, and begging to be found pleasing!"

"I understand," I said.

She suddenly jerked at the manacles which confined her wrists. They were well on her.

"Why are you angry?" I asked.

"I am not angry," she said.

She looked down at her wrists, in the steel, joined by the chain.

"You look well in shackles," I said.

She put her hands on her thighs, the chain bunched then between them.

"He did not want me," she said.

"True," I said.

"I was rejected!"

"Not every woman is attractive to every man," I said, "and, too, you are a free woman."

"I don't care!" she said. "I am free!"

"I understand," I said.

"How pleased I am that I am not subject to use," she said. "Thus, even though I must shamefully serve, I can still, ultimately, retain my pride and dignity."

"I doubt that that fellow would have been overly concerned with such niceties," I said.

"No," she said, shuddering, "I suspect not."

I glanced at the fellow at the other table. He was now giving his orders to the beautiful slave. She was kneeling back. She must now relate to him as a mere waitress. I suspected he would manage to get more than porridge, even this late.

"Do you want anything else?" asked Lady Temione, irritatedly. I saw that she was terribly jealous of the attention which men might bestow upon the slave, but how could that be, for she was, by her own account, infinitely superior to the slave, and she was free? Too, she was, according to her own account, not interested in such things.

"Anything else, what?" I inquired.

"Anything else, *Sir*," she said, acidly.

She was at table service. Surely the keeper would wish her to observe proper amenities.

"Are you being suitably deferential?" I asked.

"Of course, *Sir*," she said, unpleasantly.

Her attitude amused me. Although she had, doubtless, some theoretical understanding that she was subject to discipline, she was not yet fully aware, as is a female slave, of how such realities might affect her situation. Too, she had not even been informed that she was, in truth, subject to guest use.

"Perhaps you would like to fetch a slave whip?" I asked.

"No, Sir," she said, quickly. "Please, no, Sir." I gathered then she had at least seen slave girls whipped, or after they had been whipped. She would have some idea of what the whip could do to a woman. It is an excellent correctional device for female behavior.

"No," I said.

" 'No'?" she said.

"No," I said, "I do not want anything else, just now, here."

"Would you truly have whipped me?" she asked.

"Yes," I said.

"Sir's waitress requests permission to withdraw," she said.

"It is granted," I said.

She then performed obeisance.

"No," I said, "do not rise. Withdraw on all fours."

"I hate you, I hate you, I hate you!" she said.

"You may leave," I informed her.

She then turned about and began to make her way toward the kitchen. For an instant I saw her lift herself, as though inadvertently, and then, with a sob, she hurried on.

I rose to my feet, the small, hinged tablet in my hand. The bill was inscribed on the waxed surface within. It totaled five copper tarsks. When I added that to my current bill, it would come to nineteen copper tarsks. I must remember to pick up the blankets with the ostrakon at the keeper's desk.

I looked over at the bearded fellow, the fellow of the company of Artemidorus of Cos. The slave had now left his table, to fetch his meal. I wondered what might be in the rectangular pouch he carried, that which he seemed concerned to keep with him at all times. He had taken it with him even into the baths. He had a tarn, I recalled.

I then made my way to the keeper's desk. The keeper was not up now, but an attendant was there. He checked the tablet and added the five tarsks to my bill. He retained the tablet. It would be smoothed, thus erasing it, and would probably then be hung with others, on nails, in the kitchen, ready to be used again. I picked up my ostrakon, on which was inscribed the number of my space, and the two blankets. I had paid the blanket rental earlier. Before I left the keeper's desk, I also had the attendant add a tarsk bit to my bill.

# 6
# SOME THINGS WHICH OCCURRED ONE NIGHT AT THE CROOKED TARN

There were one hundred sleeping spaces, or positions, on the third level in the south wing, although no space was numbered "100." What counted for the hundredth space, so to speak, was a "zero" space in the front, left-hand corner, as one entered the level. In the light of a few dim tharlarion-oil lamps one could see the large numbers posted high on the wall, to the left and the back. The rows, from the front, moving back, were numbered zero through 9; the columns, from left to right, were similarly numbered. One determines the spaces then, rather as on a cipher chart, by the intersection of numbers. The farthest space to the left and front, as one entered, then, was space "zero" and the farthest space to the back and the right was "99." As the first line in Gorean writing moves from the left to the right, according to convention the numbers to the left would be first numbers designating the space. For example, the intersection of row 7 with column 3 would be space 73, not space 37. Similarly the space farthest to the back on the left, as one enters, would be space 90, the intersection of row 9 with column 0, and the space farthest to the right, in the front, as one enters, was 9, the intersection of row 0 with column 9. This arrangement makes it possible, at a glance, to see exactly where one's space lies. My space, as I discovered, was not as bad as the keeper had suggested. It was not in a corner, but it was, at least, at a wall. Had there been been walkways bordering the sleeping area it would not have been bad at all. Unfortunately there were no walkways.

One fellow cried out, suddenly, with pain. "Sorry, Sir," I said. I inadvertently struck another with my pack. The light was not good.

I decided I had better stay rather where I was for a moment or so, to let my eyes better adjust to the darkness. I did, however, take the precaution of moving out of the reach of the fellow I had struck with my pack. He could not reach me now without risking stumbling across a couple of other fellows, big ones, too. I did not think walkways would be a bad idea. To be sure, I suppose, then, one could get fewer spaces of the same size into the area. The keeper was probably balancing out the advantages of reasonably sized sleeping spaces, a yard or so wide, in keeping with his concept of the first-class inn, for the area, with the largest number of them he could put in a given area. Keepers, merchants, and such, have problems of that sort. The second and third levels, incidentally, were reached by narrow stairs, rather than ladders, as in some inns. Doubtless that convenience could considerably strengthen the keeper's case that he was maintaining a first-class establishment, at least for the area. I did not know. Perhaps he was. Certainly he charged enough. Too, my friend, the bearded fellow of the company of Artemidorus, whom I had not had to kill, had elected to stay here, and he looked like the sort who would certainly avail himself of the finest accommodations in an area.

There was some squirming to my left, and, as my eyes grew more accustomed to the light, I saw a couple entwined. At first I supposed they might be companions, sharing a space. The female seemed to be making small angry noises, then frightened noises. A large piece of cloth, probably her veil, had been thrust into her mouth and tied there. As she moved it seemed her hands must be bound behind her back. Her slippers were off, near her feet. Her robes had been thrust up about her waist. She looked wildly at me, the cloth stuffed in her mouth, tied there. She had probably been surprised in her sleep, and rendered helpless. When he finished with her he would probably carry her from the floor, either to his wagon and, if interested in her, leave with her, or leave her tied below somewhere, perhaps to the railing at the stairs, or perhaps in the stable, where she would attract little attention until morning, after his presumed departure.

I thought that perhaps the inn should provide separate spaces for women, not just separate marked-out spaces, but, say, a separate room, or area. She half reared up, making tiny noises. He had gagged her well. Then he pressed her back to the boards. I blamed the keeper as much as anything, three copper tarsks for a girl, for a quarter of an Ahn, was outrageous. It was no wonder that some fellow, under the circumstances, might be forced to make do as he could, even having recourse eventually, if he was desperate enough, to a free woman. I trod a bit further ahead. It was less dangerous now, as I could see better. Too, the tiny tharlarion-oil lamps, here and there, at the walls, were helpful.

"Do not approach me, sleen!" hissed a woman. Her arm was back. She crouched in the center of one of the spaces. Her hand, held back, held a small dagger, of the sort which some women think affords them protection.

"Forgive me, Lady," I whispered, "I am trying to reach my space."

She brandished the weapon.

"I mean you no harm," I said. I do not think it is a good idea for women to carry such weapons, incidentally. Their pretentiousness annoys some men. Indeed, some men will kill a woman with such a weapon rather than take the moment or so necessary to disarm her and make her helpless.

"Do not approach me!" she hissed. "Oh!" she said. "Stop! You're hurting me!"

The dagger fell to the floor. My hand was still on her wrist.

"I shall scream," she whispered, tensely. "Oh!"

"It will be difficult to scream, held as you are," I said. My left hand was behind the back of her neck, pressed tightly against it, and my right hand, moved from her wrist, now covered her veiled mouth, tightly, pressing back.

She looked at me, angrily, over the veil. She squirmed. She made tiny noises. Her small hands were futile, trying to pull my hand from her mouth.

"I mean you no harm," I said. "I am only trying to get to my place."

She nodded, a tiny, difficult movement.

"Will you scream, if I release you?" I asked.

She looked at me, and then shook her head, as she could, quickly, earnestly, negatively. She was lying, of course. But this would give me the opportunity to get her veil into her mouth.

I released her mouth and she pulled back and opened her mouth widely, to scream. I bunched and thrust veil into her mouth. She looked at me, wildly, half gagging, my fingers and cloth in her mouth. Little by little, then, with my fingers, patiently, my thumb holding my present accomplishments in place, and pushing them further back, to make room for more folds, I worked more of the veil into her mouth. Finally I pulled out the pins at the side, and completed the work. Some veils are held not with pins but with hooks or cords, passing about the back of the head. Others are a part of the hood itself. With the hood cords, which can fasten the hood more or less closely about the neck, like a cloak, I fastened the veil in place. She then looked at me, well silenced.

No longer had she the dignity of the veil.

She did not try to dislodge the silencing device I had placed in her mouth but she lifted her hands, shamed, before her face, to conceal her countenance from me.

I noted how her hands were held before her face.

I pulled her hands down, away from her face. I held them, she helpless to resist, and then, for a time, not hurrying, considered her lips and mouth. They were indeed excellent. She turned her head to the side.

I turned her about and put her on her stomach. I then removed her stockings. Her slippers, removed for the night, were to one side. With one stocking I bound her hands together, behind her back, leaving two ends loose. I then crossed and bound her ankles with the other stocking, and, as she winced, pulled her legs up behind her. I looped one of the two loose ends from the stocking securing her wrists twice about her ankle tie and then tied it to the other loose end. This fastened her in a slave bow. I pulled her hood down about her face. In this way her facial modesty was protected. Her lips and mouth, then, were not exposed to the gaze of men, as though they might be those of a slave. I then found her dagger and, carefully, with regard for her modesty, cut and divided her garments, removing fastenings and hooks

from them. This left her fully and modestly concealed, albeit
with only strips and pieces of clothing, the devices for arranging and closing which had been removed. I did not think she
would find that her dignity would be compromised unless, of
course, foolishly, she chose to move. I then picked up her
small dagger, and my pack, and the blankets, and again made
my way toward my space. When I reached it, I put down the
pack and blankets. I also put the small dagger under my foot,
and pulling up on the handle, broke the blade away. The two
parts I cast away, back by the wall. No longer would it
endanger her life.

I looked about. There were some empty spaces on the
floor, for example, space 98, to my left, as I would face the
front of the room, but, on the whole, the level was very
crowded. I would have liked the comparative privacy of
space 99, in the corner, but it was occupied. I suspected that
the empty spaces, or most of them, had been vacated by
fellows who had left early. Some folks leave almost in the
middle of the night, and then stop at another inn, in the early
afternoon. That way they can usually count on obtaining
excellent accommodations. Most inns want you out by noon,
the tenth Ahn.

I glanced back to the space occupied by the free woman
whom I had not found pleasing, she on whose mouth I had
seen fit to impose closure, she whom I had left in precarious
concealments and slave trussing. She was motionless. I doubted,
however, that she was asleep. She would not wish to attract
attention in her present straits. In the morning, with folks
bustling about, she would probably be all right. Now, however, she might be plucked as easily as a larma, one over-
hanging a public path. I had scarcely arranged my blankets
and put the pack down for a pillow when I saw an attendant
enter the room, carrying a stripped female, her hands tied
behind her, over his shoulder, her head to the rear, in slave
position. I gestured to him, and, exciting my envy somewhat,
he picked his way expertly among the sprawled, slumbering
bodies to my space. "I shall return in an Ahn," he said. He
then sat his burden beside me.

"You!" said the Lady Temione.

"Shhh," I cautioned her. "People are trying to sleep."

She tried to struggle to her feet, but I gently placed her on the blanket beside me, on her side.

"This is a terrible mistake," she whispered. "You know I am a free woman."

"Yes," I said.

She had been relieved of her shackles, but her wrists were thonged behind her back. About her neck, however, there was now wound, in three close, unslippable loops, a heavy length of chain. Two links of this chain, not the end links, were fastened together in front with a heavy padlock. The two ends of the chain then, below the connected links, hung down in front, in an attractive tielike, cravatlike, arrangement. There was a practical aspect to this as well, of course. The same chain, in virtue of the links selected, may be worn by any woman. Too, attached to this chaining, near the padlock, was a metal tag of some sort. I could not see it well in the darkness.

"Then release me!" she whispered.

"I do not understand," I said.

"You agreed this was a terrible mistake," she whispered.

"No," I said. "I said 'Yes,' that you were a free woman."

"I do not understand what I am doing here," she said, "naked and tied beside you."

"Really?" I asked.

"It can not be *that*!" she said.

"Why not?" I asked.

"I am *free*!" she said.

"But your bills are not paid," I said.

She made an angry noise.

"It seems that this time you did not manage to inveigle some fellow into paying them for you."

"What are you going to do to me?" she asked.

"What do you think?" I asked.

"Not *that*," she said.

"Precisely," I said.

"I am not an inn girl," she said. "I am a free woman! I am not subject to guest use!"

"Were you told you were not subject to guest use?" I asked.

"No," she said, hesitantly.

"So?" I said.

"But I assumed, of course, as I was free—"

"Are you a virgin?" I asked.

"That is surely a personal matter," she said. "Surely that is my own business."

"It would take only a moment for me to make the determination," I said.

"No," she said, pulling back. "I am not a virgin."

"It would seem then," I said, "that at least once or twice you must have had to pay off fellows for their assistance."

"They were not gentlemen," she said.

"I think you will discover," I said, "that from now on you no longer possess bargaining power in such matters."

"I do not understand," she said.

"In the future," I said, "I think you will find that you will no longer have control over the gratifications which might be attendant upon your uses, nor over the numbers, times or natures of them."

"I do not understand," she said, frightened.

"I am pleased you are not a virgin," I said. "Thus our relationship can be much simpler."

"Am I truly available to you?" she asked.

"Yes," I said. "I paid for you, for the Ahn."

" *'Paid'*?" she asked.

"Yes," I said.

"It must have been terribly expensive," she said.

"The price for an inn girl here," I said, "is three copper tarsks for the quarter of an Ahn."

"That is extremely expensive, is it not?" she asked.

"Terribly so," I agreed. I was not too pleased with the keeper. Surely he was a heinously gouging scoundrel. Other than that, however, he seemed a rather good fellow. Space 97, for example, did have one edge, the top edge, on the wall.

"If a common inn girl costs so much," she breathed, "how could you even begin to afford someone like me? You must have been devastatingly smitten with my beauty!!"

"You are actually a bit fat," I said, "but I think that could be worked off you, with a sparing, judicious diet, complex exercises, suitable disciplines, and such."

"Perhaps I should try to be pleasing to you," she said, impressed.

"Why?" I asked. She was, after all, a free woman.

"You must have paid at least a golden tarn disk," she said, "to have rights over me, for a whole Ahn."

"No," I said.

"Nine silver tarsks?" she asked.

"No," I said.

"Five?" she asked.

"No," I said. "I paid only a tarsk bit."

"What!" she said.

"Shhh," I cautioned her. "Do not awaken the guests."

"That is absurd!" she said. "I am a free woman."

"It is doubtless a great deal more than you are worth," I said.

"I will see to it," she said, "that I do not give you any pleasure."

"I think," I said, "you will find it difficult to do anything about that." I pulled her to me.

"Beast!" she said.

"Your squirming," I said, "is delightful."

She cried out in frustration, and then held herself as still as possible.

I smiled to myself. How fortunate for this woman that she was a free female, and not a slave.

"This is some sort of identifying tag on you, I gather," I said.

"Yes," she said, angrily, trying to hold herself still, her hands behind her, tied.

I felt the tag, attached on the chain, near the padlock. "It seems to have the shape of a malformed tarn," I said, "a crooked neck, an enlarged right leg and talons."

"It does," she said, angrily.

"It resembles the sign within the palisade then," I said, "that which is visible for a pasang or so, down the road, the sign of the 'Crooked Tarn.' "

"Of course," she said.

I jerked the tag, playfully. "And where is this little tag?" I asked.

"It is on me," she said, seething, trying to hold herself still.

"Does it have writing on it?" I asked.

"Yes," she said.

Surely it would.

"They must have shown it to you before they put it on you."

"Yes," she said.

"What does it say?" I asked.

" 'Debtor,' " she said. "Oh!" she said.

"What else?" I asked.

"Please stop it!" she said.

"What else?" I asked.

"My wrists have been thonged!" she said. "My hands have been tied behind my back! I cannot free them! Do you not know what that means? Do you not understand? I am helpless!"

"You should have paid your bills," I said. "I thought you were not supposed to move."

"Oh!" she said, angrily. Then, again, she said, "Oh!" but softly, startled.

I desisted in my attentions.

She controlled herself, and did not press against me.

"The word 'debtor' is in large letters," she said. "Beneath it, in smaller letters, it says 'Inquire at the Crooked Tarn pertinent to Redemption Fees.' "

"Would you like your hands untied?" I asked.

"Yes!" she said.

"Turn about," I said.

Swiftly she did so.

"Ah," I said.

"Are you not going to untie my hands?" she said, anxiously.

"No!" I said.

"Beast! Beast!" she said.

I held her where she was.

"I am a free woman!" she said.

I desisted, again, in my attentions, but I kept her where she was.

"I have never been near a man before," she said, "like this."

"How does it make you feel?" I asked.

"It makes me feel vulnerable," she said.

"You are vulnerable," I said.

The palms of her hands, as she was, faced me. The palms of a woman's hands are extremely sensitive. I traced a little pattern in the palm of her right hand.

"I am not a Kajira!" she said.

The pattern I had traced in her palm was that of a small, cursive 'Kef', the first letter in the expression 'Kajira'. The cursive 'Kef', in one variation or another, is commonly used as a slave brand for females.

"I suppose you had better get done with it," she said.

"With what?" I asked.

"With my humiliation," she said.

"I see," I said.

She pushed back a bit, but, because I held her, she could not reach me.

"You may use me," she said. "I give you my permission."

"Your permission is not required," I said.

"I suppose not," she said.

"You are not in shackles," I said.

"They were removed," she said.

"Why do you suppose that was?" I asked.

"To make me more convenient to guests, it would seem," she said.

"Yes," I said.

"What are you doing?" she asked.

"I am untying your hands," I said.

"Why?" she asked.

"You sound disappointed," I said.

"Certainly not!" she said.

I did wrap the thong about her left wrist, tucking in the ends. In this way it would remain upon her body, and be immediately available, if I wished to make use of it later. The symbolism of this, and the convenience of it, would not elude the Lady Temione. She was Gorean.

"May I turn about?" she asked.

"No," I said.

"Do you think the keeper's man anticipated that the thong might be removed?" she asked.

"He would certainly suppose it might be." I said. "He would recognize, of course, that it might be removed from your body, or, indeed, be used to tie you in any one of a hundred other ways."

She shuddered.

"But now that I am not shackled, or bound," she said, "might I not escape?"

"You are within the palisade," I said.

"That is true," she said, thoughtfully.

"Too, even if you were outside the palisade, I do not think you would get too far, naked, with a chain on your neck, the identifying tag, and so on."

"May I turn about?" she asked.

"Very well," I said.

"Am I attractive?" she asked.

"Yes," I said.

"For a free woman?" she asked.

"Yes," I said.

"I wish," she whispered, "that I was attractive, even for a slave."

"I would not trouble myself, if I were you," I said, "about my lack of slave attractiveness."

"The warrior in the paga room," she said. "did not want me. He rejected me!"

"You are only a free woman." I reminded her.

"You received kisses from the women outside, those chained to the rings," she said, "Amina, Rimice, and the others, if I may believe you."

"Yes," I said.

"And I told you," she said, "that you would never receive one from me."

"Yes," I said, "I recall that."

"I relent," she said.

"Oh?" I said.

"Yes," she said. "You may kiss me."

I did not kiss her.

"May I kiss you?" she asked.

"Yes," I said.

Softly her lips met mine. It was a brief, delicate kiss, frightened. Then she drew back.

"What is wrong?" I asked.

"I am afraid of my feelings," she said.

"They are a part of you," I said. "Do not be afraid of them."

"Let us get on with it," she said, suddenly, angrily.

"With what?" I asked.

"Your use of me," she said.

"I see," I said.

"I owe a silver tarsk, five," she said, miserably. "If you have paid only a tarsk bit for my use, it will take me, at that rate, months to earn my redemption from the keeper."

I was silent.

"So take me in your cruel arms like iron," she said. "Force me to pant and sweat, and kiss. Hurry!"

"There is something I think you must understand, first," I said.

"What is that?" she asked.

"You owe a silver tarsk, five," I said, "and I have paid a tarsk bit for your use, for an Ahn, but that does not mean that you are then reducing your debt by a tarsk bit."

"What?" she said.

"The usual arrangement in such matters," I said, "which doubtless obtains, unless you have been informed differently, is that the money you are earning, you are earning not for yourself, but for the keeper. It does not in any way diminish your debt."

"No!" she said.

"Yes," I said. "In this way the keeper gets some good out of you. Too, in this way he is less likely to lose money on, say, your feed."

"Then," she said, "he could keep me here as long as he wants! I could be kept here at his mercy, in this terrible place, as long as it is his will!"

"You might, of course, be redeemed," I pointed out.

"Yes!" she said, eagerly. "I must find a splendid gentleman, and piteously beg that!"

I did not, personally, think she would now be as successful in that sort of thing as she might have been earlier, when fully clothed. It is one thing for a free woman, tearfully, while in the dignity of robes and veil, to attempt to impose on a fellow's gullibility or good nature, and quite another for her to do so when she is unclothed. When a woman is naked it is sometimes hard for a man not to see her as a female. Clearly, too, the Lady Temione's body suggested the exquisite latency of slave curves.

"Perhaps you will find some fellow willing to do so," I said, "who will then expect that you will fling yourself into his arms, agreeing to be his companion."

"Yes," she said, thoughtfully.

"I gather that that sort of thing has worked for you before," I said.

"Yes," she said.

"And his reward then," I speculated, "would be a grateful peck through your veil?"

"I am a free woman," she said. "I trust not."

"Perhaps, then, a grateful glance, a squeezing of a hand, a heartfelt utterance of thanks?"

"The important thing," she said, "is to make certain that your bills have been paid, and that you are in the clear. After that, you may simply leave. I often merely turn my back upon them, for they are fools. They stand there then, knowing they have been tricked."

"I would suppose that that sort of thing might not work with all men," I said, "perhaps not with even all gentlemen."

"True," she said, "it is wise to reward some with at least the squeezing of the hand, an expression of gratitude, or such, before hurrying away."

"You must leave a few frustrated fellows in your wake," I speculated.

"I enjoy frustrating men," she said, angrily. I gathered from her vehemence that she was disappointed in men, that she had decided to despise them, that she wished to hold them in contempt. I gathered, too, however, that she was fascinated with them, and that something in her feared them, or what they might be.

"Perhaps some of these fellows followed you afterwards," I said.

"Fortunately I managed to elude them," she said.

"I wonder what they had on their mind," I said.

"I have no idea," she said.

On Earth, as I understand it, there are certain romantic notions about, for example, that heroes may expect to "win" damsels in distress, so to speak, by the performance of certain heroic behaviors, behaviors which, for example, might bode little good to dragons, evil wizards, wicked knights, and such. These damsels in distress, once rescued, are then expected to elatedly bestow their fervent affections on the blushing, bashful heroes, and so on. Needless to say, in real life, to the disappointment, and sometimes chagrin, of the blushing, bashful heroes, this denouement often fails to materialize.

Although such notions are not unknown on Gor, the average Gorean tends to be somewhat more practical and businesslike than the average hero of such stories, if we may believe the stories. For example, the damsel of Earth, if she found herself rescued on Gor, might not have to spend a great deal of time gravely considering whether or not to bestow herself on the rescuer. She might rather find her wrists, to her surprise, being chained behind her, her clothing being removed and a rope being put on her neck. She might then find herself hurrying along on foot, beside his mount, roped by the neck to his stirrup. If he finds her pleasing, he might keep her, at least for a time. If he does not, she will be soon sold.

"I must find a gentleman to redeem me," she said, "a true gentleman, one who will take pity on me and nobly buy me out of my difficulties."

"Another fool?" I asked.

"Yes!" she laughed.

I was silent.

"But do you think I will find one?" she asked, anxiously. "Never before have I been stripped and put in a chain collar."

"Perhaps," I said.

"I must!" she said, firmly.

There are many mythologies having to do with human beings. Many function like ideological garments, designed to conceal or misrepresent reality. The misrepresentations and concealments, of course, are then called "truth." Truth, crushed to earth, is supposed to rise again, but if it didn't, we wouldn't know it. Indeed, if it did have the temerity to show up, it could probably count on being suppressed again as rapidly as possible, in the name, of course, of "truth." The name of truth all prize; the face of truth most fear. Yet I think the nature of truth is not that terrible. It is just that it is different, and more beautiful than the lies. The demythologization of a man has yet to take place. His reality exceeds the myths; it is a reality which is darker and more dangerous than the myths; but it is also more glorious and more real.

"But what am I to do until I can find such a fool?" she asked.

"Is it true," I asked, "that sometimes, when a fellow

bought you out of your difficulties, you merely turned your back upon him?"

"Yes, " she said.

"Turn your back upon me, now," I said.

"Please!" she said.

"Do so, now," I said.

She did so. "Oh!" she said, gripped.

"Bend forward," I said.

She obeyed.

"I think I can give you some idea," I said, "as to what you will be doing until you find such a fool."

"Please," she said. "Mercy!"

"Look at it this way," I said. "You lived off men, with very little recompense to them. You will now, in a sense, for the time being at least, merely continue doing that, that is, continue to receive your living from men, only now, as opposed to before, you will be doing something for it, indeed, a great deal. You are, at last, going to be good for something. Men, at long last, are going to get some good out of you."

"I am not a slave!" she said. "Oh!" she said.

"Before," I said, "men, in a sense, were subject to you. Now you are subject to them."

She moaned.

"You may move or not, as it pleases you," I informed her.

She writhed briefly, trying to reach back, but could not escape. She cried out in frustration, and then fear. She then lay extremely quietly.

"I am not a slave," she said.

"At least not a legal slave," I said.

She trembled, her entire body, interestingly, responding to these words.

"—yet," I added.

Again her entire body, helplessly, wholistically, organically, spasmodically, responded.

"Please!" she begged. "Do not speak so."

The wholisticality of the female's response is an interesting one. Their response is a whole, physical, emotional and intellectual. Men have sex; women are sex.

"Why did you pay a tarsk bit for me?" she asked. "Why

did you not pay for an inn girl? Were they too expensive? Could you have afforded one?''

"I think so," I granted her. Thanks, of course, to the coins from the brigands' coin box, taken from them by the road, if nothing else, my finances were currently in excellent order.

"Then it was I, truly I, whom you wished delivered to your space," she whispered.

"Yes," I said.

"Why?" she asked.

"I thought you could use a little humbling," I said, "and a little informing as to the nature of your womanhood."

"I hate you!" she said. "I hate you!"

Her body seethed with hatred. It was pleasant.

"I am giving you pleasure, aren't I?" she asked, angrily.

"Yes," I said.

She then tried to hold herself absolutely still.

"Too," I said, "of course, I find you of sexual interest."

"Really?" she asked.

"Yes," I said.

"Do you think anyone else would?" she asked.

"Certainly," I said.

"Oh!" she said suddenly, softly. "Ohh!"

"You moved," I said.

"I am a free woman," she said, angrily. "Yet I am at the mercy of the keeper! I am a free woman! Yet I was made to serve at the tables! Now I have been delivered to a guest, as though I might be a slave!"

I was silent. I did not tell her that the most common thing that is done with debtor sluts is to sell them into slavery.

"Do you think that I will find another fool?" she asked.

"I do not know," I said.

"I must," she said. "I must! Else something terrible might happen."

"What?" I asked.

"I might be sold to the collar," she said. "Then I would be a slave!"

"If I were the keeper," I said, "such would certainly be my decision."

"What?" she said.

"I would sell you into slavery," I said.

"Never!" she said. "Never!"

"You should be a slave," I told her.

"No! No!" she said.

"You are moving," I cautioned her.

She cried out in frustration.

Then she said, "Oh!"

Then she asked, "Are you going to make me yield?"

"Of course not," I said. "You are a free woman."

"Be done with it!" she said.

But I chose, somewhat perversely perhaps, to take my time with her.

Afterwards she clung tightly to me. "Oh," she sobbed, softly. "Oh, oh." She seemed confused, frightened, bewildered, at what had been done to her, at what she had felt. I thought the keeper's man must be due soon.

"I yielded, did I not?" she asked, frightened. "Did I not yield?" The chain, its loose ends, the padlock, the small metal tarn tag, indicating she was in debt to the Crooked Tarn, clinked on her neck.

"In a manner of speaking," I said. She had actually done very well for a free woman, new to the handling of men who could do what they wished with her. The Lady Temione, though the thought might have horrified her, as she was a free woman, had unusually powerful female latencies. Subject to men and the whip I had little doubt she would become extremely passionate, and eventually, even helplessly so.

"You owe a silver tarsk, five," I mused.

"Are you thinking of redeeming me?" she asked.

"I was thinking about it," I said. I must try to gain admittance to Ar's Station. It was invested by Cosians, and mercenaries. I might have use for such as she.

"I would be afraid to be redeemed by you," she said.

"Why?" I asked.

"If you redeemed me," she said, "I would be in your total power. You would, in effect, own me."

"You are aware, of course," I said, "that you have, ultimately, no control over who redeems you, no more than a slave has, ultimately, any choice over who buys her."

"I know," she said.

I lay there, quietly, thinking. Yes, I thought, I might have use for a woman, or women, such as she.

"You took me like a she-tarsk," she said, poutingly.

"You responded well to the taking," I said. "Perhaps it is fitting for you."

"You do not respect me," she said.

"You do not want to be respected," I said. "You want to be cherished, treasured, handled, abused, mastered, owned, subdued, forced to serve and love."

She was silent.

"Someone is coming," I said. "Do you hear him, on the stairs?"

"No," she said.

"He is on the first landing now," I said. I sat up. "It is a male," I said.

"I hear him now," she said, after a moment or two. "Oh!"

I had turned her to her belly, on the blanket, spread over the boards.

"My wrists!" she protested.

They were then thonged. I had drawn them behind her, and held them together there, crossed, with my left hand. With my right I had removed the restraint from her left wrist. A moment later she was bound. Originally I had assumed it was the keeper's man, but the tread, now, seemed heavier. Lady Temione rose to her right elbow, her hands tied behind her. I thought I must know who it was. I glanced at the space next to me. He had arrived at the inn later than I, I supposed, as he had eaten later. If that was the case it was not at all unlikely that he might have been rented the space after mine. If so, that might make things a great deal easier. I would not even have to search him out, in the darkness. There was a fellow slumbering in space 99, in the corner. He must have come to the inn rather early, I supposed, to obtain one of the four coveted corner spaces. If the fellow coming up the steps was indeed who I expected it was, and had rented the space near me, and if things proceeded as I expected, I thought I might be able to enlist the support of the fellow in the corner. The second portion of my plan required a confederate.

"Ai!" I heard someone cry, a few yards away, near the entrance. The newcomer, it seemed, had had some paga, perhaps a second or third *kantharos*. I wondered if he had paid for them. I heard another cry of rage. There was then a blow. The newcomer continued on, somewhat unsteadily.

Another guest cried out, angrily, and rose up. He backed away a step, however, when he saw that he did not come up to the newcomer's shoulder. Then the newcomer beckoned he should come forward. Frightened, he did so. Then the newcomer suddenly, without warning, doubled him with a blow to the gut, and he sank, groaning, to his place. Another fellow half rose up, and another blow was struck, and the fellow fell back, to the side. Another fellow said something to the newcomer and the newcomer's sword half emerged from its sheath, and the other fellow rolled back, away, quickly, feigning sleep. The sword slammed back into the sheath. Two men moved at the noise. I saw the free woman, whom I had gagged and trussed, to whose clothing I had addressed the attentions of her own knife, which I had taken from her, and later destroyed and thrown away, lying very still. She was absolutely helpless, and her clothing, so cut and divided, could be lifted aside at anyone's convenience. It was no wonder she did not dare to move. I wondered what her thoughts might be, so helpless and vulnerable in her femaleness. Doubtless, disarmed and helpless, her beauty at anyone's convenience, her weakness manifested, she now knew herself much better than she had before. Sometimes such experiences help women understand that they are women. In a moment or two the newcomer was at the space, 98, next to mine. He looked down, angrily. I was pleased to see that he still carried the pouch.

He put it down, by the wall, with his helmet.

"Oh!" cried the Lady Temione, pulled half to her feet.

I noted the pouch had a lock. It would not, thus, be easy to open it and examine, or remove, the contents. To be sure, I was less interested in its contents than in something else. It would, of course, as he seemed to be some sort of courier, be a useful adjunct to a disguise.

He held the Lady Temione before him, her head back, his beard but inches from her throat.

"That is a free woman," I said, drily.

With a noise of disgust he turned and cast her from him, to her side, to the foot of my space, on my blanket.

I did not know if he recognized her from before, from the paga room, or not. He was drunk. It was dark.

He looked about. As I thought, he would prefer the corner

space. I did not think it would matter much to him that it was occupied.

"Ai!" cried the fellow from that space, lifted up, and suddenly thrown against the wall.

The newcomer thrust his face against the fellow's face, holding him back to the wall. "Why are you in the wrong space?" he asked him.

"I am not in the wrong space!" gasped the fellow.

He was then flung again against the wall.

"Why!" demanded the newcomer.

"There must be some mistake!" said the fellow. He was the same fellow, incidentally, happily, as I now noted, whom the newcomer had earlier ejected from his bath, and then drafted into service as a bath attendant. He was probably the sort of fellow who was very well organized and rational, had come early to the inn, generally conducted his life in a sensible manner, and so on. To be sure, fellows such as the newcomer can be the bane of such fellows. Again he was flung against the wall. This was a bit noisy, but then I was not asleep.

"I have the ostrakon for this space!" said the fellow.

"What has that to do with it?" asked the newcomer, again slamming him against the wall.

"Nothing, of course!" said the fellow, trying to get his breath. "I am sorry I am in the wrong space! I apologize! Forgive me! It was stupid of me!"

The newcomer let him slip to the floor and the fellow hastily, crawling, fetched his belongings from space 99.

"You would not be thinking of leaving, perhaps to complain to the keeper, would you?" asked the newcomer.

"No, no, of course not," said the put-upon fellow.

He then placed his belongings in space 98, next to mine.

I frankly doubted that the keeper would be keen to mix into such an altercation, particularly one involving an armed mercenary, a fellow of the company of Artemidorus.

"You are a big fellow, too," said the put-upon fellow, looking at me. "I trust you do not want this place."

"No," I told him.

"If you do," he said, "I could always fling myself into the wall now. I have had experience."

"Do not be bitter," I said.

"Get that thing out of my sight," said the bearded fellow, looking at the Lady Temione. She still lay much where she had been thrown, away from him, on her side, much afraid to move, her hands tied behind her, her head toward my feet, the chain, and the tag, on her neck. She put her head down, not daring to look upon him.

"I rented her for an Ahn," I said. "I think the time must be nearly up, and the keeper's man should be along presently."

"What did she cost you?" he asked.

"A tarsk bit," I said.

"That is far more than she is worth," he said.

"Perhaps," I said.

"In many cities," he said, "one could have a coin girl for that."

"True," I said. Coin girls were a form of street slave, usually sent into the streets around dusk by their masters, who commonly own several of them, with a chain on their neck, to which would be attached, normally, a bell, to call attention to their whereabouts, and a small, locked coin box. And woe to the girl who returns without coins jangling in the box! To be sure, in some places, one might even have a paga slave, or a brothel slave, for as little as a tarsk bit.

"It is too much for a free woman," he said.

"Perhaps," I said.

"Particularly one such as that," he said, contemptuously.

"Perhaps," I said.

"Perhaps it is appropriate," he said, "a tarsk bit for a fat she-tarsk."

"She is not really so fat," I said. To be sure, her figure could be considerably improved, and, if she became a slave, undoubtedly it soon would be.

"I have seen tharlarion," he said, "who were better looking."

Lady Temione, lying on her side, her hands tied behind her, stiffened in anger. I did not understand her response. Certainly she did not think that she was slave attractive— certainly not yet.

"They could not easily have charged less than a tarsk bit," I said, somewhat irritatedly. I must try to control myself. The tarsk bit, of course, in most cities, is the smallest-denomination coin in common circulation.

"For so much," he said, "they should have rented her to you for a month."

"Perhaps," I said.

"Such she-tarsks are worthless," he said. "She probably doesn't even know what to do with her toes."

"Probably not," I admitted.

Lady Temione looked up, startled.

"She should have been put in a slave harness and sent to a training school," he said.

"I doubt that there are any nearby," I said.

"She should have been apprenticed to a slave," he said.

"Perhaps she will be," I said. "As I understand it, it was only tonight that she was put in the chain collar." Such training schools are normally found only in the cities. Usually, but not always, they are attached to the houses of slavers. Needless to say, their students are seldom free women, but almost always slaves. The harness he referred to was undoubtedly not a security harness but a training harness, a complex affair, consisting of numerous straps and rings. It is useful, for example, in helping a woman learn how to serve a master while being denied the use of certain of her limbs, for example, her hands. It is commonly worn naked. Similarly, it helps the woman to adjust to her helplessness and her condition, as, in it, she may be fastened in an incredible variety of attitudes and positions. Its utility is limited by little more than the imagination of the master.

"You must be a strange one," he said to me, "to make do with a free female."

"She does not have to remain free," I said.

Lady Temione shuddered with fear. The tag, and padlock, shook on her collar.

"But she is free now," he said.

"That is true."

He looked at the Lady Temione. She did not dare to meet that fierce gaze. Perhaps it was just as well. She might have been cuffed or kicked. I would not have approved had he done this, but under the circumstances, considering my purposes, I would not have interfered. As she was within my rental, and a free person, of course, the administration of any such discipline was really mine to do, and not his. If he wished to beat her, he should have requested my permission.

Alternatively, he might have waited a bit, and paid her next rent fee himself. Any free person, incidentally, may discipline a slave. If this were not the case, then a slave, outside the knowledge of her master, might dare to be insolent to a free person.

"It would not be worth harnessing her," he said. "She would be too stupid to learn."

"Any woman can be taught," I said.

"I am a free woman!" suddenly wept the Lady Temione.

He went and crouched beside her. She put her head down, frightened, on the blanket.

"You are not a woman," he sneered. "You are a she-tarsk." She sobbed.

"You are not worth sleen feed," he said.

"Do not interfere," cautioned the fellow in space 98, who had been ejected from the corner space. "He is dangerous."

"I do not expect to do so," I said. I did not object, of course, to his abuse of the Lady Temione. Indeed, the insults, in their way, while certainly overdrawn, were not altogether unjustified. The danger, of course, with one of my temper, was that I might suddenly feel a point of honor touched. Then, if I should flare up and, say, pin the fellow to the floor with my blade, my plans would be seriously disrupted. I would be as placid as a larl feigning sleep, as placid as a Dietrich of Tarnburg.

"What are you saying?" asked the fellow, wheeling about.

"Nothing," I said.

He returned his attention to the Lady Temione.

"You are worthless," he told her.

"She does have auburn hair," I informed him. "It may be hard to see in this light."

"Then shave it off, and sell it," he laughed.

"The keeper might do that," I said.

Lady Temione moaned, helplessly.

This was, of course, a genuine possibility, particularly in this area at this time. Women's hair, long and silky, plaited into heavy ropes, is ideal for the cording of catapults. It is far superior, for example, to vegetable fibers. It is also superior, in length and texture, to the hair of sleen and kaiila. By now, the hair of slaves in Ar's Station, and doubtless the hair of most of her free women as well, donated in the case of the latter as a contribution to the defense effort, would have been shaved off, or, perhaps, cropped short. If the keeper did decide to shave off, or crop, the hair of the Lady Temione, and, for that matter, the others, the Lady Amina, the Lady Rimice, and so on, he would presumably sell it to suppliers to the Cosians. Under the current conditions, of course, it would be difficult to get such materiel into Ar's Station. Indeed, in a sense, that was the same problem I faced, finding a way into Ar's Station.

"Worthless," snarled the burly, bearded fellow to the Lady Temione.

The burly fellow stood up. I saw where he had placed the pouch.

He looked down upon the Lady Temione with contempt. "Get that thing out of my sight," he said. "I do not want my digestion spoiled for breakfast."

I myself did not think I would have time for breakfast. I was planning on leaving rather early in the morning.

"Did you hear me?" he asked.

"The keeper's man will be along presently," I said.

"Do you cross me in this?" he asked.

"I would not think of doing so," I said. I located the hilt of my sword. I supposed that it might be less than noble to drive a blade through the body of a drunken fellow in the dark, but it was probably preferable, all things considered, to having one driven through oneself.

"I will take her away," said the fellow next to me, hastily.

"It is not your responsibility," I said, somewhat ungraciously, I fear, considering the generosity of his offer.

"Look," said he. "I am now well practiced in smiting walls with my back, but I have had very little experience in dodging swords, leaping about unarmed, you understand, in the darkness, in the middle of a sword fight."

"Fight?" asked the burly fellow, interested.

"So I shall be pleased to return her to the keeper's desk," he said.

I think the burly fellow reached for the hilt of his sword, but missed it.

My own blade left the sheath. I stood up.

The fellow between us moaned, and prepared to crawl rapidly to safety.

"Oh!" said Lady Temione, lifted now, backwards, to the shoulder of the keeper's man who, unnoticed, had approached. "Slut rent period is up," he said.

"Take her away," said the burly fellow, with a wave of his hand.

"That is my intention," said the keeper's man. He turned his back on us, and I saw, again, the face of the Lady Temione, facing backwards, held upon his shoulder in slave position.

"Put her in a tarsk cage," laughed the fellow. "That is where she belongs."

Lady Temione briefly struggled in frustration on the shoulder of the keeper's man, squirming there doubtlessly more deliciously than she knew, and pulling helplessly at her bound wrists. She would be carried about and done with, of course, precisely as men wished. She looked back now in anger, but also in fear, at the burly fellow. Doubtless she thought she was attractive now. She did not understand, of course, how attractive, truly, she might be, subject to certain alterations in her condition. Our eyes met.

"Who wants a fight?" asked the burly fellow, unsteadily. He now had his hand on the hilt of his sword.

"No one," said the fellow between us, hastily, earnestly.

I did not think the burly fellow could well attack with the other fellow between us, not, at least, without cutting him out of the way. That would indeed be a poor way for that fellow to end his day, which had not been a very good one anyway. I sheathed my sword. I was not even sure that the burly fellow, in the darkness, realized I had drawn it. He himself had not proceeded further than to get his hand on his sword. I do not think he realized he was in any danger.

"Are you the one who wants to fight?" he asked.

"Not me," I said.

"Then it is you!" cried the burly fellow, turning on the fellow between us.

"No!" cried the fellow.

His response was surely prompt, I thought. It was assured and definite. It left little doubt about the matter.

"I am tired," announced the burly fellow.

"It is time then to go to sleep," said the other man.

The burly fellow stood there for a moment considering this possibility. "Perhaps," he said.

I was sure, now, that it would not prove necessary to run the fellow through, at least at this time. In such a thrust, of course, he in his present condition, there would have been little of honor. Too, it is difficult to use a sword in a professional manner in the darkness, and I tend to be vain about such things. The sword is less akin to darkness than stealth and the dagger. A recruit, under the circumstances, could have felled him.

"It is time to go to sleep," announced the burly fellow.

"Yes, you are right," agreed the other man.

This was the second time the burly fellow, this night, had been in considerable danger. He would probably not realize this, even in the morning.

"Sit down," said the burly fellow to me.

"Very well," I said, sitting down. The other man sat down, too, in his space.

The burly fellow then stood there and looked about him. He was the only one standing in the room.

He had taken the first tub in the baths. He had created a disturbance in the paga room. He had had an excellent slave sent to him, perhaps even gratis. I suspected he had had a greater variety of food to choose from than I had been offered. He had traversed the sleeping room like a hurricane. I doubted he would be too popular with the other guests. Indeed, more than one fellow he had struck about, making his way to his space. He had even come directly to his space, in a diagonal, rather than making use, like other folks, of more neighborly, if lengthier, orthogonals. Too, it seemed he had shown me insufficient respect, not to mention the fellow next to me, whose paid-for space he had appropriated, nor those he had trampled upon, and struck about, in his passage to our area. I also did not appreciate his criticizing me, mostly implicitly, for my choice of rent sluts. I frankly thought I might have seen more in the Lady Temione than he had. If nothing else, considering the prices in the inn, she came cheap. He then sat down in the corner space, 99, the safest, most private space on the floor.

"Do you snore?" he asked the fellow next to me.

"Never," the fellow assured him.

"If you do," said the burly fellow, "sit up tonight."

"I was planning on that, anyway," the fellow assured him.

I had little doubt the fellow between us planned on taking his leave as soon as the burly fellow slept. Could one really count, one wondered, on the burly fellow being in a pleasant mood when he awakened? Too, what if he should have some savage dream, and start thrashing about, knife in hand, in the middle of the night?

The fellow between us sat back against the wall. The burly fellow looked across at me, contemptuously. "User of she-tarsks," he laughed.

I noted he wrapped the strap of the pouch he carried about his left arm, three or four times. I supposed, like many such pouches, diplomatic pouches, so to speak, the strap would be cored with wire, and, inside, within the pouch itself, between the leather and a presumed lining, there would be a pattern of interlinked rings. These precautions make the pouch immune to the customary approaches of the cutpurse.

In a few moments the burly fellow was breathing heavily.

I put out my hand and detained the fellow in space 98 who, it seemed, was preparing to depart.

He moaned. "Why is it," he asked, "that I am never abused by small men?"

"What is your trade?" I asked.

"I am a sutler," he said.

"Excellent," I said.

"I used to think so," he said.

That had seemed not improbable to me. There were mostly wagoners, of one sort or another, here, or refugees. He did not seem to be a refugee. For example, he did not have a companion, or children, with him. Similarly, most refugees could not have afforded an inn. Too, he did not seem to have the refinement of a high merchant nor the roughness of the drover. Drovers, flush with coins, would be here, of course, returning from Ar's Station. On the journey there they would be with their animals, probably verr or tarsk. "You are on your way to the Cosians' siege camp at Ar's Station," I hazarded.

"Yes," he said.

I had thought that, too, was probable, as he was at the inn. He would want its protection, probably, for his goods. Coins, or letters of credit, might be concealed about a wagon, but it is not easy to conceal quantities of flour, salt, jerky, paga and such, not to mention the miscellany of diverse items for the field supply of which one can usually count on the sutlers, such things as combs, brushes, candles, lamp oil, small knives, common tools, pans, eating utensils, sharpening stones, flints, steel, thumb cuffs, shackles, nose rings, binding fiber, slave collars and whips.

"I have a commission for you," I said.

"You want me to kill our friend in 99?" he asked.

"No," I said.

"It is perhaps just as well," he said. "If I failed to do the job neatly, and he awakened, and I was kneeling there with a bloody knife in my hand, one could not at all count on his seeing the matter from our point of view."

"You are right," I said.

"He has a terrible temper," he said, "and, under such circumstances, it would be hard to blame anyone for being cranky."

"I thoroughly agree," I said.

"What then?" he asked.

"Listen carefully," I said.

# 7
# THE ATTENDANT

"Attendant!" cried the burly fellow, from one of the second tubs, that immediately behind one of the first tubs, that most convenient to the entrance to the baths. "Stir up the fire!" It was early, but most of the fellows who had been sleeping on the floor of the baths during the night had now taken their leave.

The fellow then attending on the baths, rather large for such a fellow, it might seem, hooded, too, perhaps to disguise scarring of such a nature as might turn the stomachs of bathers, enveloped in a cloak, hobbling, perhaps the result of a fall from tarnback, hurried, seemingly alarmed, to the bricked platform beneath his tub and stirred the fire with the fire rake.

"Build up the fire! Hurry, fellow!" said the bather.

"Yes, Sir, yes, Sir," rasped the hooded, cloaked fellow.

I had been confident, of course, from what I had seen last night, that if the fellow were to bathe he would pick that first tub, and then, behind it, that second tub. Some, and he was apparently among them, regard such as the most prestigious tubs. It was natural, then, that he, such a fellow, should select them. Somehow, it seemed that the fire in the platform under the tub in which he now reclined had not been built up this morning. He who was now in attendance on the baths hurried now, of course, to do so. The fellow, thus, who seemingly was fond of his luxuries, would have to wait for a time, and then, when the water was comfortably warm, could presumably be counted upon, if only in compensation for his discomfort and inconvenience, to dally for a while.

He in attendance on the baths, shuffling about, occasionally muttering to himself, tended the fire.

I had anticipated that the fellow would wish to use the baths in the morning. For example, he had drunk heavily the night before and presumably could be counted upon to awaken in a few hours, thirsty and drenched with sweat. A horrifying hangover, too, considering the entire situation, was not too much to expect. In case he was less fastidious than we had anticipated, we had also taken the liberty of annointing the floor about his place with some representative elements extracted from the level's wastes' bucket. The presence of these in his area, particularly given the nature of his preceding evening, we naturally hoped he would explain to himself in the most natural way possible.

He in attendance on the baths puttered about, scraping the brick platforms, picking up shavings, odd pieces of wood, and such.

"Ahhh," said the bather, leaning back.

"Is the temperature of the water satisfactory?" inquired he in attendance, hobbling over to the tub.

"Yes," growled the bather.

He in attendance put an armload of wood and shavings near the bather's tub, on the platform. In such a way, on a busy day at the baths, might some trips to the bins be saved. It is an old bath attendant's trick. He in attendance, however, was somewhat clumsy in doing this. The striking of a piece of kindling on the tub, for example, rather on the left of the tub, seemed to cause distress to the bather.

"Get out," ordered the bather.

"May I be of further service?" inquired he in attendance.

"Get out!" said the bather. "Get out!"

"Yes, Sir! Yes, Sir!" rasped the bent fellow, hobbling away quickly, as though frightened. Then, in a moment, he was on the other side of the latticework.

On the other side of the latticework I looked back into the room of the baths, not yet straightening up. Beneath my cloak, of course, were the belt, scabbard and sword, his wallet, and the rectangular pouch, taken from the tub hook, under the diversion of the sound and blow of kindling to the left, on the tub. The bather, I noted, now lay back in the tub, his eyes closed. The real attendant was probably upstairs in the paga room, enjoying cakes and Bazi tea, a breakfast popular with Goreans on holidays. Certainly he had the means to do so. I had given him five copper tarsks.

I removed the burly fellow's helmet and clothing from the peg in the outer room.

I then left the outer room of the baths.

# 8
# I TAKE MY LEAVE OF THE CROOKED TARN

I strode to the tarncot.

I did not think I would have much time to waste. I now wore the blue of Cos, the uniform of one of the company of Artemidorus, and carried the blue helmet, these things having been removed from the peg in the outer room of the baths.

I smote on the gate of the tarncot.

My pack was on my back.

There was only one tarn in the cot, obviously a warrior's mount.

An attendant emerged from a shed to the side.

A wagon moved by, to the left. The tharlarion stables were in that direction. Folks were up, and stirring. I glanced up, to my right, at the high shedlike structure which would shelter the tarn beacon. It was not lit now, of course. The inn's tarn gate, as I stood, within the inn's grounds, was to its right. In this way, as one would approach the inn on tarnback, from outside the grounds, the gate would be on its left.

"Ready the bird," I ordered.

It seemed he might hesitate a moment, but he took in my appearance, the blue of Cos, the insignia of the mercenaries of Artemidorus, the helmet, my weapons, indeed, two swords.

"Now," I said.

He scurried back into the shed, where, doubtless, the burly fellow's gear was stored, the saddle, tarn harness, and such. I think he did not wish to delay one of the company of Artemidorus. Perhaps he had done so before, to his sorrow.

I looked back, toward the main building. I could see only normal signs of activity.

The great sign, on its chains, hanging from the supported, horizontal beam on the huge pole was quiet now. Some wagons were leaving. The world about smelled fresh and clean from the rain. There were puddles here and there on the stone flooring of the inn yard, itself leveled from the living rock of the plateau.

The attendant now came forth from the shed. He had the saddle, the cloth and other gear over his shoulder.

"I trust the tarn gate is open," I said.

"Yes," he said.

"Good," I said.

Obviously I was in a hurry. He was doubtless accustomed to impatient guests. On the other hand, he would presumably not suspect in how great a hurry I actually was.

He then entered the cot, to ready the bird.

I went about the shed and cot, and crossed the yard, moving between buildings. I wanted to make certain that the gate was indeed open. It was. It had not been opened to facilitate my departure, of course, but, as a matter of course, during the day, for the convenience of new arrivals. The two parts, or leaves, of the gate, within their supporting framework, of course, opened inward. They were now fastened back. In opening, they swung back across the landing platform, which was a foot or two above the level of the height of the palisade. An extension of this platform, retractable when the gate was closed, and probably braced with hinged, diagonal drop supports, would extend beyond the palisade. There was a ramp leading up to the platform on the inside, on the right. The leaves of the gate were very large, each being some thirty feet in height and some twenty-five feet in width. They are light, however, for their size, as they consist mostly of frames supporting wire. Whereas these dimensions permit ordinary saddle tarns, war tarns, and such, an entry in flight, the landing platform is generally used. It is always used, of course, by draft tarns carrying tarn baskets. The draft tarn makes a hovering landing. As soon as it senses the basket touch the ground it alights to one side. The sloping ramp, of course, makes it easy to take the tarn basket, on its leather runners, no longer harnessed to the tarn, down to the yard. It is also convenient for discharging passengers, handling baggage, and such.

Not all tarn gates have this particular construction. In another common construction the two parts, or leaves, of the gate, within their supporting framework, lean back, at an angle of some twenty degrees. They are then slid back, in a frame, on rollers, each to its own side. This gives the effect of a door, opening to the sky. The structure supporting the gate, in such a case, with its beams, platforms, catwalks and mastlike timbers, is very sturdy. Narrow ladders, too, ascend it here and there, leading to its catwalks and platforms. Such a construction, of course, requires the more time-consuming, hovering landing of all birds, not simply draft tarns, carrying tarn baskets. It does, however, make the landing platform unnecessary. The construction at the Crooked Tarn, incidentally, was more typical of a military installation, in that it permitted the more rapid deployment and return of tarnsmen, coupled with the capacity to open and close the tarn gate in a matter of Ihn. The tarn gate's construction here suggested that the Crooked Tarn might not always have served as an inn. Probably at one time or another, before the founding of Ar's Station, it had served to garrison troops, perhaps concerned to monitor the more northern reaches of the Vosk Road. This was suggested, too, by its distance from the Vosk, which was approximately one hundred pasangs. The ordinary one-day march of the Gorean infantryman on a military road is thirty-five pasangs. The Crooked Tarn, then, was almost exactly three days march from the river.

I loosened my blade in my scabbard and returned to the vicinity of the tarncot.

The tarn was ready.

It was within the cot, tearing at a piece of meat, a haunch of tarsk, hung from a rope. The rope was some two inches thick. The suspension of the meat reminded me of the way peasant women sometimes cook roasts, tying them on a cord and dangling them before the fire, then spinning the meat from time to time. In this way, given the twisting and untwisting of the cord, the meat will cook rather evenly, for the most part untended, and without spit turning. The rope then, drawn tightly as it was, so tautly, so fiercely, toward the tarn, suddenly, a foot or so above the meat, snapped. The tarn then had the meat and the lower portion of the rope on the ground, the meat grasped in his talons, tearing it away from the bone.

I spun suddenly about, the sword half drawn.

The girl stopped, extremely frightened.

She put her hand before her mouth, the back of her hand toward her face.

She stepped back, faltering, frightened.

She was slim, and extremely dark-haired, and very white-skinned. Her hair was drawn back behind her head and tied there with a yellow cord. Her breasts were bared. A black cord was knotted about her waist. Tucked over this cord in front was a long strip, some seven inches wide, of heavy, opaque, yellow cloth. It then passed under her body and was pulled up, snugly, and thrust over the cord in the back. The front and back ends of this cloth hung evenly, and fell about midway between her knees and ankles. The effect was much like that of the curla and chatka, a portion of the garmenture, or livery, in which the wagon peoples of the south place most of their slave females, save that the curla, the cord, was black and not red, and the chatka, the strip, was of cloth and yellow, not of black leather. She had nothing corresponding, of course, to the kalmak, or southern slave's brief, open vest of black leather, and the cord binding her hair was quite different from the koora, the red band of cloth commonly used to confine the hair of the southern slave. In all then, since she wore cloth and not leather, and less than the southern slave, her appearance, if anything, was even more slavelike than hers.

"Why are you not kneeling," I asked her, "and with your knees spread?" She was, after all, in the presence of a free man. Too, clad as she was, I assumed she must be a pleasure slave. Such kneel before men in the open-kneed position.

She sank to her knees on the stone, and hastily spread them. The cloth looked well, fallen between her thighs, on the damp stone.

I looked upon her.

She was now in a position of subservience and respect, suitable for a woman before a man.

I replaced the blade in the sheath.

She looked up at me, frightened.

I regarded her.

She had a beautiful face, exquisitely and sensitively feminine.

She lowered her eyes before my gaze.

She was slimly beautiful.

I regarded her garbing. It did afford her a nether closure, but it was, at least, a precarious one. In compensation it well bared her thighs.

"Are you frightened?" I asked.

"Yes," she whispered.

It seemed to me, interestingly enough, if I did not misread the matter, that she was extremely sensitive to, and timid concerning, the revealing nature of her garbing. I had the feeling, based on certain expressions and tiny movements, that she more than once resisted the impulse to huddle before me, her head down, covering herself with her hands. But she remained much as she was. Indeed, she even straightened herself, and lifted her body before me, timidly, as if for my consideration.

"What is wrong?" I asked.

It seemed she wanted to speak, but lacked the courage to do so.

"What is that in your hand?" I asked. She had something clutched in her right hand.

She opened her hand, holding it out a little, that I might see what she held. There, in the palm of her right hand, was a small sack, bulging, seemingly weighty for its size, from the look of it, a sack of coins. It was leather. It had strings.

"Move your hand," I said.

She did so.

"I see now why you were so frightened," I said. "You have stolen a sack of coins."

"No, no!" she said.

"Many masters," I said, "do not permit a slave to so much as touch money. To be sure, they might let her carry coins in an errand capsule, or an errand sack, tied about her neck, instructions to a vendor perhaps also contained within it, her hands braceleted behind her."

She looked up, frightened.

"And few masters, indeed, I assure you," I said, "even if

so lenient as to let her venture to a market with a coin or two in her mouth, on a specific errand, would permit her to scamper about with a trove such as that which now seems to be in your keeping.''

"You do not understand," she said.

"Kneel more straightly," I said.

She complied. I viewed her. I wondered what her master had paid for her. Probably a goodly price. She was worth such.

"How did you expect to escape the palisade?" I asked.

She looked at me, agonized.

"Were you approaching me, intentionally?" I asked.

"Yes," she said.

"It was your intention, I gather," I said, "to attempt to bribe me, that I might abet your escape."

Tears sprarg into her eyes.

"But do you think I would do other then than to carry you into my own chains?"

She trembled. She clutched the tiny sack.

"You have been caught," I said. "You are a caught slave. I will now turn you over to an attendant, for binding and holding, pending what punishments your master might see fit to visit upon you."

"You do not understand," she whispered.

"What do you mean?" I asked.

"The coins are mine," she said.

"Surely you are an inn girl," I said, "though your collar is now off."

"I do not have a collar," she said.

"That is surely an incredible oversight on the part of your master," I said.

"I do not have a master," she whispered.

I looked at her, puzzled, such a woman.

"Am I truly pretty enough to be an inn girl?" she asked.

"Of course," I said, "and a superb one."

She looked up at me, elatedly, gratefully.

"Who is your master?" I asked.

"I do not have a master," she repeated.

"Do not seek to compound your crime with deceit," I said.

"I am not a slave," she whispered. "I am a free woman. Oh!"

I had seized her, half lifted her, and turned her from side to side, examining her slim, attractive thighs for the tiny brand which would confirm the matter. The most common brand sites, that on the left thigh, the favorite, and that on the right thigh, lacked slave marks. This determination, given the nature of her garmenture, could be instantly made. I then put her on her feet. "Oh!" she said. She was not branded on the lower left abdomen. That is perhaps the third most favored brand site. I then checked several other brand sites, such as the insides of the forearms, the left side of the neck, behind and below the left ear, the backs of her legs, and her buttocks. I even examined the insteps of her left and right feet. Her body was not branded.

"I am a free woman," she said, so rudely handled.

"It seems you have not yet been branded," I said.

"I am not a slave," she said. "I am a free woman."

This did not seem to me possible, of course, clad as she was, in this place.

"Do you not recognize me?" she asked.

"On your knees," I said.

Swiftly she knelt.

"Don't you recognize me?" she asked.

I looked at her, puzzled. To be sure, something about her seemed familiar.

"Crouch before me," she said.

I did so.

She put her hands before her face, the strings of the sack looped twice now about her left wrist. As she held her hands before her, rather to the bridge of the nose, they concealed the lower portions of her face, much as would a veil.

"Ah!" I said. It was not so much at first, however, that I recalled her upper facial features, as they would have appeared over the veil, if only because it had been very dark in the upper level when I had sought my space last night, as I recalled immediately, vividly, the appearance and positioning of her small hands. The small palms of them, with their delicate, extremely sensitive, exposed openness, faced outwards. It was in this way that I first realized who she was. During the night she had perhaps realized what she had done.

Perhaps, then, she had sobbed with shame. Yet now, in the morning, presumably by now fully aware of what she was doing, she dared to again so hold her hands before a man. Even last night, once she must have realized how her hands were positioned, I recalled she had not quickly, shamed, turned them about, presenting their backs to me. One expects a Gorean woman, attempting to conceal her features from a man, to place her hands, cuplike, over her nose and mouth. As I have indicated, the lips and mouth of a female are commonly regarded as extremely sensuous features to a Gorean, hence the concern of many free women, particularly of high caste, in the high cities, to conceal them. A simple way to uncup the woman's hands is to take the small finger of her left hand in your right hand and pull that hand to the side, and then take the small finger of the right hand in your left hand, and pull that, too, to the side. This opens the barrier and reveals the mouth and lips of the woman to you. In this case, however, as she held her hands, with the palms facing me, I simply took her wrists and, gently, drew them apart. This exposed her lips and mouth to me. Her lips were slightly parted. She was breathing quickly.

"I remember," I said. Last night I had face-stripped her, before gagging her with her own veil. It had been very dark on the level last night, with only the tiny lamps far to the side and back, but I could see now, upon close examination, that it was indeed the same woman.

"You gagged me," she said. "You made it so that your will was imposed upon mine. I could not cry out or speak. You did not choose to permit it."

I nodded.

"And you tied me!" she said.

"Of course," I said. I had done so with her stockings, hand and foot.

She looked at me, with awe in her eyes. Perhaps she had never been tied before. I considered her beauty. It seemed made for rope, and steel and leather.

"Did you manage to free yourself?" I asked. I was curious to hear what she would respond.

"No," she said. "I was absolutely helpless. I could not begin to free myself. I was freed by an itinerant metal worker."

"I see," I said.

"You knew I could not free myself!" she said, suddenly, reproachfully.

"Yes," I said.

She shuddered. "Are slaves sometimes bound like that?" she asked.

"Sometimes," I said.

"You cut apart my clothing, and removed the hooks and fastenings from it," she said. "Yet you did not strip me. You left it lying upon me in such a way that my modesty might be protected. You even covered my head and face with my hood, that I might not lie there face-stripped. Thank you."

I nodded.

"To be sure," she said, "the hood in such a placement functioned almost like a slave hood."

"True," I said.

"If I did not move I could not see," she said, "and if I did move I might well face-strip myself."

"The choice was yours," I said.

"And if I had as much as squirmed," she said, "I would have stripped myself."

"Again," I said, "the choice was yours."

"As I am a free woman?" she asked.

"Of course," I said.

"Had I been a slave girl," she said, "I gather I would not have had such choices."

"Probably not," I said. "The slave girl, normally, stays simply as men put her, for example, in such a case, presumably naked and bound."

"After you disarmed me, and made me helpless, what did you do with my dagger?" she asked.

"I destroyed it," I said, "and threw it out."

She nodded.

"Do you object?" I asked.

"No," she said.

"It could have gotten you killed," I said.

"I realize that now," she said. "It was terribly foolish to carry it."

"True," I said.

"Beyond such matters," she said, "I should not have had such a thing. It was pretentious and wrong of me to have had it."

"Perhaps you will avoid such mistakes in the future," I said.

"I will," she said.

A woman's defenses are not steel, but such things as her helplessness and vulnerability, and her capacity to give astounding pleasure.

I stood up.

I glanced into the tarncot. The bird was finishing the meat, that which had earlier been suspended on the rope.

The attendant was near it, his hand on the harness.

I glanced back at the woman.

"I left you an amplitude of garments," I said, "though they would have to be redone, or resewn. They could, at least, have been clutched about you. How is it then, that you are dressed as you are?"

"It is appropriate for me," she said, "that I should have this to wear, or such things, or less, or perhaps nothing."

I did not respond.

She lowered her eyes. She seemed terribly embarrassed. Doubtless she was extremely sensitive about her degree of exposure. Yet she had herself arranged it so. She was extremely white-skinned. Doubtless this was in major part because she was very lightly complexioned genetically, but it was, too, in part, doubtless, because she would have commonly worn the ornate, heavy, stiff, cumbersome robes of concealment affected by most well-to-do Gorean women. The contrast between the robes of concealment and her present revelatory vestiture, more suitable for a property girl, must be particularly, and shockingly, dramatic to her, who knew her own antecedents and station. She must now be experiencing a wealth of new sensations, for example, kneeling on damp stone, and feeling the air upon her body.

I looked into the tarncot. The tarn was finished feeding now, and was being watered. The bone which had been within the meat lay to one side, with a tatter of rope, amidst straw. It was deeply scratched and furrowed. The bird thrust its beak into a tall, narrow vessel. It would draw water into that dreadful recess. It would then put its head back. Then, shaking its head, it would hasten the water down its throat.

"Ah," I said, suddenly bethinking myself of proprieties, "though you are a free woman I have you on your knees before me, as though you might be a slave. How rude! How boorish of me! I am sorry. Forgive me, Lady." I hastened to lift her to her feet.

"No," she said, quickly, again, frightened, kneeling.

I stepped back, puzzled.

"It is here that I belong," she said, "on my knees, before a man such as you."

"I do not understand," I said.

"You disarmed me," she said. "You gagged me. You made me helpless, putting me in a trussing suitable for a slave. You pulled my hood down about my face. You made it so I could not see without risking my own face-stripping. You made my garments such that they were mere covers, strips and pieces, such that I dared not move, lest I be lying naked in a public place, such, too, that they might be lifted from me at a man's pleasure."

"I had not found you pleasing," I explained to her.

"It is my hope that in the future," she said, "I may be found more pleasing."

"The tarn is ready," said the attendant. He led it from the cot, it stalking beside him, its head moving about, its eyes round, bright and sharp.

The woman, at the sight of the bird, shrank back, frightened.

"Farewell, free woman," I said.

"No," she said. "Please!"

"Take it to the tarn gate," I said. It was there that I should mount.

"Please!" said the free woman.

The attendant led the bird about the cot and shed, toward the tarn gate. I followed him. There he led the bird up the ramp to the landing platform. Again I followed him. From this height I could see the countryside for pasangs about. The air was exhilarating. The tarn was excited. It opened its wings. The beams of the platform were very sturdy. The attendant untied the mounting ladder at the saddle.

I think it must have taken the girl great courage to follow me up the ramp, onto the landing platform, in the vicinity of that winged monster.

When I turned about, to regard her, she knelt swiftly, spreading her knees. It was in this fashion that I had had her kneel earlier, in the inn yard, before me, when I had assumed she was slave.

"Farewell," I said.

"No," she said. "Take me with you!"

"What?" I said.

"I have sold my things," she said. "I have now no more than what you see upon me, two slender black cords, and a strip of yellow cloth, and these coins!" She held them out.

"The purse is heavy," I said. "Buy what you need with it."

"I will give you them all," she said. "Take me with you!"

"I do not understand," I said.

"You have conquered me," she said. "You have taught me that I am a female!"

I regarded her. She did look well on her knees.

"Oh, this did not just happen," she said. "I have known this about myself for years. I fought it for years. And now I surrender!"

"Completely, and without reservation?" I inquired.

"Yes!" she said. "Yes!"

"I see," I said.

"I am tired of living a lie," she said. "I am feminine, *truly*."

"I see," I said.

"I belong to men such as you," she said.

That did not seem to me unlikely.

"Who are you?" I asked.

"I am Phoebe, Lady of Telnus," she said.

I smiled inwardly. Cosian beauties make excellent slaves. They are not unusual in Port Kar.

"That is a pretty name," I said.

"Take me with you!" she said. "I will pay!"

"In the direction I ride," I said, "there lies danger."

"I accept the risks," she said.

"Even as you are?" I asked.

"Yes," she said, "yes!"

To be sure, the risks were doubtless less for women than for men, for the dangers would threaten primarily from men, and men would know what to do with women. Perhaps the worst that might happen to her would be that she would find herself in the chains of a slave, and laboring, under whips, as a female beast of burden. To be sure, she did face danger, as she was free. Free women, being persons, are far more likely to be killed than slaves, who are animals. Sackers, for example, particularly when the blood lust has passed from them, would not be likely to slay slaves, assuming they are docile and desperately concerned to be totally pleasing, any more than kaiila. They would simply appropriate them for their own.

"I do not need a slave at present," I said. Such did not accord with the first portion of my plan for entering Ar's Station.

"Take me as your servant," she begged.

"My servant?" I asked, looking upon the slim, kneeling, half-naked beauty.

"Yes!" she said.

"The tarn is ready," said the attendant.

"I beg female fulfillment!" she said.

"You will not receive full female fulfillment as a mere servant," I said. Such is not totally owned.

"Take me then as a slave!" she said.

"I do not need a slave at present," I said.

"Take me then as a servant," she said. She held out the coins. "I will pay you to do so."

I considered her, her needs, her beauty, her desperation.

"And if I serve well," she said, "perhaps later I will prove worthy of the collar."

She lifted the coins higher, pleadingly.

"What sort of servant is it which you wish to be?" I asked.

"Whatever sort of servant you desire," she said.

"A servant without restriction, or reservation?" I asked.

"Yes," she said, "such a servant!"

"A *full* servant?" I asked.

"Yes," she said, "a full servant!"

"It is only as such a servant that I would consider taking you," I said.

"Take me as a full servant," she said.

"In whose name do you ask this?" I asked.

"In the name of all women such as I, and all men such as you," she said.

"You are but a hair's breadth from slavery," I said.

"It is my hope that you will eventually permit me to traverse that hair's breadth," she said.

The tarn opened and closed its wings, and she lowered her head, turning it to the side, and shrank down, frightened, cringing, so low that her head was but inches from the ground. She was terrified of the bird.

I considered the mounting ladder.

"Take me with you," she begged, lifting her head.

I saw the desperation in her.

"I want to be myself," she said, "what I really am!"

"Do you know what you are asking?" I asked.

She shuddered.

"Where I am going," I said, "men do not compromise with females."

She looked up at me, trembling.

"And clad as you are," I said, "I assure you men will see you as a female."

"It is what I am," she said.

"Do you understand the nature of such men?" I asked.

"I do not desire a relationship with any other sort of man," she said.

"Such men prefer slaves," I said.

"I will serve them as such!" she said.

The tarn moved again, shifting about, and she cried out, frightened, again shrinking small.

How terrified she was of the tarn!

She was very beautiful, so slim and piteous, kneeling on the heavy beams of the platform.

"No slave need I now," I said.

"Take me then now only as your servant," she said.

"My *full* servant?" I smiled.

"Yes," she said. "Then afterwards do with me what you will."

"You tempt me," I said. "You are a beautiful female, one worthy to be sold from a slave block."

"Let me buy my servitude," she said.

"I hesitate to carry a free woman into danger," I said.

"You would surely hesitate less," she said, "if I were a captive, or servant."

"True," I said.

"Then," said she, lifting the coins, "let me buy my captivity, and servitude."

I took the coins from her, and put them in my pouch. "Stand," I said. "Put your head back. Open your mouth, widely."

I determined in a moment or two that she was not concealing any small coins or tiny jewels in her nostrils, her ears, her hair or mouth. I then conducted her by the arm to the side of the threshold of the tarn gate and stood her there, her feet well back, her arms extended, the palms of her hands leaning against the wood. There was nothing concealed beneath her arms, as was easy to determine, she in this position. I lifted her feet one at a time, checking the insteps and between the toes for any taped materials. I then examined the rest of her body. "Oh!" she said. "Oh!" I then pulled the cloth up again, snugly, as it had been. I then pulled her back from the side of the gate, standing her again on her feet

She looked up at me, reproachfully.

"It would appear that you are coinless," I said.

"I am," she said.

"Put out your hands," I said.

She did so, and cried out, suddenly, startled, as slave bracelets danced upon her wrists.

She lifted her wrists before her, as if not understanding how they could be so suddenly clasped in steel.

"You are now my captive," I told her, "and I am going to keep you, for a time, though for perhaps no more than a few Ehn, as merely my servant, though a *full* servant. At the end of that time, however long I choose for it to be, I will do with you as I wish, perhaps making you a slave, perhaps giving you to another, perhaps selling you into slavery, whatever I please."

She looked at me, frightened.

"Do you understand?" I asked.

"Yes," she said.

I then thrust her, not gently, toward the tarn, until she stood near the foot of the mounting ladder, it dangling from the saddle.

There, in the proximity of the winged giant, she trembled.

"Hold still," I said. I then, with a piece of scarflike cloth taken from my pouch, a wind veil, sometimes bound across the mouth and nostrils of a tarnsman, usually at high altitudes, blindfolded her. A great many women, particularly the most sensitive and intelligent among them, fear tarns greatly. It is not unusual for them to become hysterical in their vicinity. It is not uncommon then for the tarnsman to hood or blindfold them. This aids in their control and management. Too, of course, if the woman is a captive, or slave, one may not wish her to understand where she is, or be able to retrace her route, or know where she is being taken. It is enough for her to know, when the blindfold or hood is removed, that she is in perfect custody. Sometimes a woman does not learn for weeks, sometimes until, say, the very night of her sale, where she is, in what city she finds herself.

"I can't see!" she said.

"That is the purpose of a blindfold," I said.

"You could punish me, couldn't you?" she said.

"Yes," I said.

"And you would, wouldn't you?" she said.

"Yes," I said.

I then put her to my shoulder, her head to the rear, as a slave is carried, and mounted the ladder. I put her before me on the saddle. She grasped the pommel desperately. At the sides of the saddle there are various rings, and straps, which may be used in fastening things to it, or across it. Needless to say, such may be used to fasten females in place. Lady Phoebe of Telnus was, of course, a free woman, and though she was a capture, in a sense, she had a special status with me. I did not, thus, throw her across the saddle, on her belly, or back, fastening her there in utter helplessness as I might have a common capture. I did, however, loop a left strap about her left wrist, and tie it back to its ring, and loop a right strap about her right wrist, tying it back to its ring. In this way, as she wore slave bracelets, although she might slip, she could not fall, and her hands would be kept in the vicinity of the pommel. I then put the safety strap about myself, and buckled it shut.

Once before, long ago, in the vicinity of the city of Ar, I had been lax in doing that. It had been fortunate that I had survived. It was a precaution which, if time permitted, I had seldom neglected thereafter. I thought of lithe, sinuous, olive-skinned Talena, the daughter of Marlenus of Ar until disowned, she having given evidence that she was a slave. After she had been returned to Ar by Samos, of Port Kar, into whose chains she had fallen, Marlenus, shamed, had had her sequestered, freed, but statusless, in the Central Cylinder. Now, in his absence, he having vanished in the Voltai Mountains, on a punitive raid against the tarnsmen of Treve, it seemed that her fortunes were recovering. She had appeared at public functions. Her palanquin was now again seen abroad in the streets. Doubtless she was once again becoming proud and haughty. I had not seen the slave in her. On the other hand, Rask of Treve, and others, had. I, too, now, I suspected, might be more perceptive. Though she had been the daughter of a Ubar, and now, again, it seemed, stood high in Ar, she was, after all, only a female. I wondered what she might look like, naked and in chains, or writhing at my feet, trying to interest me.

"Oh!" said Lady Phoebe, softly.

"You are slim," I said, "but you are well curved."

"Thank you," she said.

"It is pleasant to caress you," I said.

She was silent.

"Do you object?" I asked.

"No," she said.

"Why not?" I asked.

"I am a full servant," she said.

Her body was unusually sensitive for that of a free woman. It was not slave hot, of course, but then she was not a slave. Such transformations in her, of course, might easily come with the collar, and discipline.

I again, briefly, considered the proud, haughty Talena, who had been the daughter of a Ubar, and who now, again, it seemed, stood high in Ar. Yes, she would, I thought, considering the matter carefully, look well in chains, or writhing at my feet, trying to interest me. Too, I recalled she had been contemptuous of me, and haughty and cruel to me, in Port Kar, scorning even the memory of my love, when I had been paralyzed, helpless to move from a chair, the victim of the poison of Sullius Maximus, once one of the five Ubars of Port Kar, before the Sovereignty of the Council of Captains. I wondered if she thought that I was still in Port Kar, perhaps huddled before a fire in that same chair, an invalid, its

prisoner. But I had recovered, fully, receiving even the anti-
dote for the poison in Torvaldsland. I suspected, however,
she might have seen me from her palanquin in Ar. The
following night an attempt had been made on my life in the
Tunnels, one of the slave brothels of Ludmilla, from which
the street called the Alley of the Slave Brothels of Ludmilla is
named. Too, I had seen evidence near Brundisium that she
was guilty of treason against Ar.

"Oh!" said Lady Phoebe.

Ah, yes, Talena, I thought, Yes, I thought, now, upon
reflection, that there had been a slave in her. Perhaps I had
been a fool to let it get away. Yes, she might make an
interesting slave, perhaps a low slave. Then I dismissed
thoughts of her from my mind.

"Ohh!" gasped Lady Phoebe, crying out in the blindfold,
squirming on the saddle before me. I heard the tiny sounds of
the linkage of the slave bracelets. Her white thighs contrasted
nicely with the smooth, dark, glossy leather. Sometimes they
were flattened against the leather, as though gripping it for
dear life, and, at other times, they rubbed, and squirmed, and
moved helplessly, piteously, against it. I considered the glossi-
ness of the saddle leather. I did not think she was the first
woman who had been carried on it, or so handled. Her knees
suddenly bent and she almost climbed up, about the pommel.
I wondered if I should have fastened her ankles to rings,
holding her thighs down and apart, on the saddle, forcing her
to endure her sensations, for the most part relieflessly, within
physical-restraint limits of my choosing.

"Oh, ohh," said Lady Phoebe.

"Be silent," I said to her.

"You have stopped!" she whispered.

"Be silent," I said. Had she been a slave, and not a free
woman, this causing of the repetition of a command might
have earned her a beating.

The attendant looked about. There was the sound of some
commotion coming from the vicinity of the court.

"Here, my good fellow," I said to him.

"My thanks, tarnsman!" he cried, not having expected a
gratuity of such size.

I was reasonably confident as to what the commotion might

well be about, and so I thought I might as well take my leave of the Crooked Tarn.

"You are generous, indeed, tarnsman," said the attendant, backing away now. It would scarcely do to be struck or swept from the platform to the moat some seventy or eighty feet below, particularly as one had just made an entire silver tarsk. Giving such a coin, of course, was, in its way, I suppose, a bit of braggadocio on my part, something of a gesture or flourish. On the other hand, I would not really miss it that much as I had extracted it from among the coins I had taken from the wallet of the fellow I had left in the tub, in the baths, the burly fellow who was of the company of Artemidorus.

I drew up the mounting ladder and secured it at the side of the saddle.

The shouting, angry shouts, a tumult almost, was clearer now. Four or five fellows must have been involved. There were, too, if I am not mistaken, the sounds of blows, or, at least, sudden grunts and cries of pain.

I moved the harness, drawing the straps evenly, and the bird, anticipatory, alerted, stalked to the front edge of the landing platform, outside the portal of the tarn gate. From such a platform the bird, with a single snap of its wings, addressing itself to flight, is immediately airborne.

"Hold tightly," I told my servant.

She moaned. She clutched the pommel with all her strength.

"There is a fellow back there," said the attendant. "He is naked! He is fighting!"

"Oh?" I said.

"Yes!" he said.

"Interesting," I said.

"He has probably not paid his bills, and is trying to escape," speculated the attendant. To be sure, he did not seem eager to rush down and join the fray.

"Disgusting," I said.

I myself had paid my bills properly before leaving the Crooked Tarn. It is the thing to do. Inns, after all, if no one paid their bills, would have a difficult time making a go of it. It is not really practical to hold every fellow for ransom, or every lady for redemption. This is not to deny that some outlying Gorean inns, particularly where female travelers are concerned, function as little more than slave traps, an arrangement usually being in effect with a local slaver.

"He seems to be trying to come in this direction," said the attendant.

"Interesting," I said.

If the fellow was really trying to escape without paying his bills, and this was a peculiar direction for him to be coming if that was the case, then I could hardly blame him. The prices at the Crooked Tarn were indeed outrageous. My own bill, for example, all told, had come to nineteen copper tarsks, and a tarsk bit, the latter for the use of the Lady Temione last night. The itemization of that bill, frightful to contemplate, had been ten for lodging, two for the bath and supplies, two for blankets, five for bread, paga and porridge, and the tarsk bit for the use of the Lady Temione, the only particular on the bill which might have been argued as within reason. I had done without breakfast this morning primarily to save time, but it could also have been done, and I think legitimately, in protest over the prices of the Crooked Tarn. Fortunately I had some dried tarsk strips in my pack. I did not know if the Lady Phoebe would find these appealing or not but she would learn to eat them. Too, she would learn to take them in her mouth from my hand. This would help her to learn that she was now dependent on men for her food.

"How is our friend doing now?" I asked.

"He is down! They have him. No! He is up!" reported the attendant. "Hah! Now they have a chain on him!"

"I wish you well," I said to the attendant. I had thought I might wait on the platform in case the fellow managed to reach it, and then take flight, but it did not seem now that he would get this far, at least this morning.

"I wish you well!" called the attendant, clinging then to a stanchion of the tarn gate.

I drew back, decisively, on the one-strap, and the tarn screamed and smote the air with its wings, and, my servant crying out in terror and clutching the pommel, was aflight!

Those who are horsemen know the exhilaration of riding, the marvelous animal, its strength, its pacings, its speed, its responsiveness, how one seems augmented by its power, how one can feel it, and its breathing, the movements of its body, sensing even the blows of its hoofs in the turf. It is little wonder that peoples knowing not the horse fled in terror when they first encountered riders, taking the rider and his mount for one thing, something half animal, half human, an awesome, unbelievably swift, gigantic, armed chimera, something that could not be outrun, that seemed to fly upon the earth, that seemed tireless, something irresistible, merciless and relentless to which it seemed the world must rightfully belong.

To such initial glimpses, fraught with fear, might harken the stories of the centaur, half man, half horse. And the legendary nature of the centaur, its appetites, its rapacity and power, harken back, too, perhaps, in the canny ways in which half-forgotten historical fact colors the fancies of tamer times, to the first perceptions of the horseman, and his ways, among those afoot. And even later, when the separation of man and mount became clearly understood, the fear of the horseman, and his ways, would abide. Fortunate that they lingered largely on the fringes of civilization. And yet, how often, as with the Hyksos, in Egypt, did they ride in from the desert like a storm, their horses among the barley. The mystique of the rider lingered unquestioned for centuries. Alexander would turn cavalry into a decisive arm. Centuries later the stirrup and barbarian lancers would crush the world's most successful civilization. The very word for "Knight" in German is "Ritter", which, literally, means "Rider."

The ascendancy of the cavalry would remain unchallenged until the achievement of revolutions in infantry tactics and missile power, such things as the coming of the massed pikes, and the flighted clothyard shafts of a dozen fields. Something of the same joy of the rider, and mystique of the rider, exists on Gor in connection with the tarn as existed on Earth in connection with the horse. For example, if you have thrilled to the movements and power of a fine steed, you have some conception of what it is to be aflight on tarnback. There is the wind, the sense of the beast, the speed, the movements, now in all dimensions, the climb, the dive, soaring, turning, all in the freedom of the sky! There is here, too, a oneness of man and beast. There is even the legend of the *tarntauros*, or creature half man, and half tarn, which in Gorean myth, plays a similar, one might even say, equivalent, role to that of the centaur in the myths of Earth. Too, the tarnsman retains something of the glamour which on Earth attached to the horseman, particularly so as the technology laws of the Priest-Kings, remote, mysterious masters of Gor, preclude the mechanization of transportation. The togetherness of organic life, as in the relationship of man and mount, a symbiotic harmony, remains in effect on Gor.

I was aflight!

For a time I muchly gave the bird its head, and then, some pasangs out, drew it about, to sweep the sky in a vast circle, this centering about the inn, far below.

"You will caress me again, will you not?" asked my servant.

"Perhaps," I said, "if you beg it."

"I beg it!" she said.

"Hold to the pommel, tightly," I said.

She did so.

I would have time for her later. This was not the moment.

When one first ascends a new mount, or, indeed, masters a new woman, it is well to put them through their paces, to see what they can do, to see what they are like. In the case of the tarn one's very life can depend on such things as understanding its speed, its rate of climb, the sharpness of its turns, and so on.

My lovely, half-naked, blindfolded servant cried out, flung back, her arms almost straight, her small hands, the wrists braceleted closely together, gripping the pommel.

The bird hovered well, arrested in flight.

The girl gasped and cried out again, in fear, her back almost horizontal as the tarn climbed. The ascent was steep and swift. The air grew cold. Such a maneuver is often useful. More than once it had carried me above adversaries, their attack speed prohibiting so swift an adjustment in their trajectory. The girl clung desperately to the pommel. She seemed very frightened, for some reason. Too, now, clad as she was, in what was, in effect, no more than a curla and chatka, fit garments for a slave, not a free woman, she must be very cold. Doubtless she was in extreme discomfort. In a few Ehn I had established the approximate ceiling of the bird. The earth seemed far below. I could see the surface of a lake, like a shimmering puddle, to my right. I had not even hitherto known it was there. On the left, far below, I could see the

Vosk Road, like a bright thread in the sun. "Please, let us go down. Let us stop!" she wept.

"You are braceleted," I told her. "Such matters are no longer within your control."

"Let us go down!" she wept.

"Are you cold?" I asked.

"Yes!" she wept. "But I am frightened, too! We are high, are we not?"

"Yes," I said.

"Please, let us go down!" she begged.

"It was my mistake to let you ride in such honor," I told her. "It is more appropriate for a woman on tarnback to ride differently, to be tied across the saddle on her back or belly, or, say, if she is one of a brace, perhaps wrist-tied to one end of a shared rope thrown over the saddle or, say, tied to a ring at the side, this, too, providing a balance with the other captive."

"I am a free woman," she said. "Surely you would not dare to tie me so."

"I would think little of it," I informed her.

She shuddered, though whether with the thought of this restraint which I might, if I wished, impose upon her, or of cold, I do not know.

"Please, let us go down," she said.

"What does your will mean?" I asked.

"Apparently it means nothing," she said.

"Hold tightly, woman," I said.

" 'Woman'?" she said. Then she screamed, a long, wild wailing scream, as the tarn, responding to the four-strap, began a sudden, precipitous descent. With one hand I kept her on the saddle. Her hair flew above us, trailing like a flag. The tarn dove well. The swiftness of that descent is incredible. Its force, even arrested at the last moment, can break the back of a full-grown tabuk. I let the bird come within fifty yards of the earth before I reined back, and it swooped, low, leveling, over the grass.

"Stop! Stop! Stop!" she begged. "What are we doing! Where are we?"

"We are within a man's height of the ground," I said. In such flight one can use the screening of a forest or of low hills, even buildings, to make an approach to an objective.

Too, of course, lower flight, in general, reduces the possibilities of sightings.

"We are going too swiftly!" she said. "Please, stop!"

"It is better that you are blindfolded," I said.

"What are you going to do?" she cried.

"One must try out a tarn," I said.

"Monster!" she wept.

"Hold tightly," I said.

She moaned. She hunched over the pommel, clinging to it, sobbing.

She screamed, suddenly, flung to the left, as I drew the two-strap and three-strap at the same time, the tarn veering to the right. It was responsive. I then tested it in a dozen ways, to speeds, to flights, to turns. The girl was beside herself with fear. She sobbed, moaned, gasped, cried out, whimpered, and screamed, in turn, in the darkness of the blindfold, clutching the pommel, as the bird, obedient to the obligations of the harness, bent itself to his maneuvers. I was well satisfied. It was a warrior's mount, indeed.

"Please, please," wept the girl.

I had now returned the tarn to the vicinity of the Crooked Tarn.

I then made three passes near the Crooked Tarn, two over the palisade, over the tarn wire, and a third near its bridge and gate.

In the first pass I hovered the bird for a time, some fifty yards over a portion of the court on the top of the palisaded plateau, one rather behind and to the left of the main inn buildings, as one would face them, entering. There, sitting, heavily chained to a sleen ring, its plate bolted into the stone, wrists and ankles fastened quite closely to it, was a large, naked, bearded man, the burly fellow. I gathered he had not had the means wherewith to pay his bill. Seeing me, he seemed somehow agitated, even extremely so. He could do little more, however, than crouch, struggling, and pulling, at the ring, his head back, his face upward. He was howling something, but I could not well hear what he said. It is perhaps just as well. I did wave the pouch on its strap to him, cheerily, before proceeding onward, to make the second pass. He did not seem pleased with matters. I supposed I could not, in fairness, blame him.

In my second pass I hovered near the front of the inn building on the left, as one would enter. It was there that several sets of chains had enjoyed the possession of fair occupants, whose names, as I had learned in the paga room from the Lady Temione, were Rimice, Klio and Liomache, all from Cos, Elene, from Tyros, and Amina, a citizeness of Venna. These chains were now empty. I had taken the liberty early this morning, acting through my agent, a sutler, a splendid, if somewhat put-upon and long-suffering, chap, whose name was Ephialtes, to redeem them all, my expenses in the matter, 182 C.T. for the five of them, being considerably defrayed by means of the loot I had acquired from the gang of Andron the evening before.

Doubtless they were initially delighted to find that they had been redeemed. Perhaps they had laughed and clapped their hands with joy. Their delight, however, had doubtless been tempered somewhat by finding their necks were being put in iron collars, collars on a chain. As I briefly hovered there, over the court, I could see, too, partly to my irritation, and partly to my amusement, to one side, some additional evidence of the business acumen of the keeper. He had not simply permitted the women to be redeemed. He had gotten something of value from them, perhaps as a penalty fee, or as something in the way of compensation for the inconvenience they had caused him, over and above the amount of their unpaid bills. There, to one side, on a rack, long and lovely, hung pelts of female hair. Such, as I have mentioned, particularly in times of siege, though there is always a market for it on Gor, is highly prized for the making of catapult ropes. I had little doubt that the fellow, given my suppositions as to his probable thoroughness in such matters, would not even have had the graciousness to shear the heads of the ladies. In shearing, you see, one might lose a fifth of a hort or so of hair. Doubtless he had had their heads shaved.

Many girls will strive hard to please, for example, to be permitted to keep their hair, or to be permitted to let it grow out again. There were six pelts on the rack. The sixth was a lengthy and lovely auburn. I had also, by means of Ephialtes, redeemed Lady Temione. Her redemption had cost me a silver tarsk, five. This was expensive, but she would look well on her knees, collared. All told then, at the exchange rate of 100 C.T. per silver tarsk, the women had cost me two silver tarsks, 87 C.T. These women were now, if all had gone well, on their way to Ar's Station, probably chained behind, and attached to, the wagon of Ephialtes. The shaving of their heads would doubtless lower their value, but I did not object, because I was not particularly concerned with whether I made a profit on them or not. That was not their essential role in my plans. Indeed, if their heads were shaved, that might be just as well. That might suggest that they had come into the keeping of an exploitable fellow, one in desperate need of funds.

On the third flight in the vicinity of the inn I examined, hovering briefly, the area near the foot of the plateau, by the bridge. There were still some wagons there. I was particularly interested in one. At the side of it now, a stocky blond woman was kneeling. She was naked. A heavy chain was on her neck. It went back, under the wagon, where it was fastened. A fellow stood before her, holding a whip. I saw her put down her head, frightened, and kiss his feet. She was not the slender, dark-haired slave beauty who had been under the wagon last night, huddling in the tarpaulin, in the storm.

That one Ephialtes, if all had gone well, had purchased this morning. She would be made first girl over the coffle of "free women," the Lady Temione, and the others, that she might teach them something of discipline and the basic arts of giving pleasure to men, lessons which might soon make a serious difference not only with respect to the quality of their lives, but to the very existence of those lives, as well.

The canvas covering of the wagon had been drawn back, probably to air the contents from the dampness of the storm. No one seemed to be within the wagon, or about it, other than the pair at the side of it. I had little doubt, accordingly, that the blond woman kneeling before the fellow with the whip was his free companion, or former free companion. The girl who had been beneath the wagon last night, and whom Ephialtes had, hopefully, purchased for me this morning, had been formerly purchased, and primarily purchased, I had suspected, in an attempt, and perhaps a somewhat foolish, and somewhat misdirected attempt, I thought, by the fellow to encourage his companion to take her relationship with him more seriously. She had apparently done so, at least to the

extent of treating the slave with great cruelty. But now the
slave was gone, and there was a chain on her neck. He had
apparently now gone to the heart of the matter. If she were
still his free companion, it seemed she would now be kept in
the modality of bondage, but perhaps she was now only his
former free companion, and had been reduced to actual bondage, now being subject to purchase by anyone. I recalled how
she had bent in terror to kiss his feet. There was no doubt that
she would now take her relationship to him seriously.

It is difficult not to do so when one is owned, and subject
to the whip. The woman would now discover that her companion, or former companion, a fellow perhaps hitherto taken
somewhat too lightly, one perhaps hitherto accorded insufficient attention and respect, one perhaps hitherto neglected
and ignored, even despised and scorned, was indeed a man,
and one who now would see to it that she served him well,
one who would now own and command her, one who would
summon forth the woman in her, and claim from her, and
receive from her, the total entitlements of the master.

I then turned the tarn, and brought it to a suitable cruising
altitude. Below me now lay the Vosk Road, and we flew
north. It would take a regiment of Gorean infantry, in normal
marches, given time for the fortification of a camp in the late
afternoons, and so on, three days to reach Ar's Station from
the Crooked Tarn. I supposed that the wagon of Ephialtes,
particularly if he let the girls ride, as he probably would,
later, would make the same time. The common marches of
Gorean infantrymen, for example, are usually accompanied
by wagons, those of their supply train, proper, and vehicles
such as those of sutlers and masters of camp slaves.

I did not know what the name of the girl whom I had used
under the wagon last night had been. It did not really matter,
as she was a slave. I had not bothered to inquire. Now,
however, if I were to own her, I should probably give her a
name. It is better, I think, for a girl to have some name to
answer to. It is more convenient, too, for the master, I think,
to give her a name. It is thus, for example, easier to refer to
her, and to summon her and command her. Too, that she has
a name put on her by your power, and that she understands
the meaning of this, has a good effect on her. "Who obeys?"
"Tina obeys!"

I suppose, too, one has upon occasion seen a lovely woman and wished that she might have a certain name, for one might think that an excellent name for her. If she is a slave, of course, and one owns her, one can give her any name of one's choosing, indeed, perhaps that very name which is, at least in your opinion, ideal for her. Too, she might beg a name she has always wanted, and, if it is acceptable to the master, he might put it upon her. Names, too, of course, may be used to humble and punish a woman, and such names, humbling names, and punishing names, are as much real names as the most beautiful of names. That is, then, who she is. Perhaps in the future she will try much harder to be pleasing, that she might be given a better name. I considered the lovely girl whom I had enjoyed last night under the wagon, in the storm. I thought she looked rather like a "Liadne." That was a beautiful name. I thought I would give it to her. I decided upon it. She was now, although she did not yet know it, Liadne.

I looked down at the Vosk Road, below. There were fewer refugees on it now than last night. Perhaps many had passed through the area last night. Perhaps now, for most practical purposes, the route was cut off.

My attention was then drawn to the girl on the saddle before me. She was bent low, cowering over the pommel, sobbing, grasping it with both hands. She had had a very difficult time of it. There was no gainsaying that. I took her by the hair and straightened her, and, turning her head, twisting her body, looked upon her. The blindfold was still well in place. She moaned. Her cheeks, under the dampened blindfold, were run with tears. These, too, had run upon her body. I then turned her about again.

We flew northward, in silence.

She sobbed.

I considered feeling pity for her, and then dismissed the thought, for it was weakness. She was a woman. Her wrists, too, were in my bracelets.

We flew further, in silence.

She wept.

I saw that she, though slender, was well curved, and beautiful.

"You may beg," I informed her.

"What?" she said.

"You may beg to be caressed," I said.

"You're mad," she said.

"Is it your intention to be difficult?" I asked.

"Do not beat me," she said.

"You may now beg to be caressed," I told her.

"Have I fallen into the hands of a monster?" she cried.

She was a legally free woman, but she was now before me, half naked, blindfolded and braceleted, my captive and servant. Indeed, she had even purchased her captivity and servitude. I wondered if she regretted what she had done. She now, at any rate, understood it more clearly.

"Beg," I said.

"I am not in the mood," she cried.

I laughed. How amusing are free women! Slaves learn to be in the "mood" instantaneously, at so little as a glance or a snapping of the fingers, and a pointing to the floor.

"Please," she said. "Please!"

"Beg," I said.

"I beg to be caressed," she said, weeping.

I then began to caress her, she before me, weeping, trying to resist, captive and servant, clinging to the pommel.

"Monster," she moaned. "Monster." Then she sobbed, suddenly, partly with surprise, partly with sensation.

I chuckled. Her legs looked well, split, squirming, over the glossy saddle.

"Monster!" she wept, her head back.

Her hands jerked, the fingers moving. She could not reach me. I heard the small sounds of the links, jerking taut, then relaxing, then jerking taut again, joining the bracelets.

"Perhaps you are now more in the mood?" I asked.

"Do not stop!" she begged.

"I shall call you 'Phoebe,' " I said.

"Do not stop, please!" she begged.

"And what shall you call me?" I wondered.

"Oh," she moaned. "Ohhh!"

"Surely you are curious to know what you should call me," I speculated.

"Yes!" she cried. "Yes! Yes! What shall I call you? Oh! Oh!"

"You may call me 'master,' " I said.

"Yes, *Master!*" she cried.

I then held her still, trying to calm her for a time.

"I called you Master!" she cried. "Am I yet legally free?"

"Yes," I said, "but I think it will be well for you to accustom yourself to calling free men Master."

"Yes!" she said.

I decided that I would not yet grant her the collar, ripe for it though she might be. She was a free woman. I would make her wait longer, in frustration, for it.

"Please touch me again," she begged.

"You liked it?" I asked.

"I have now felt it," she said. "I now desperately need it."

"Even to the surrender of all you are, and have been?" I asked.

"You have tried out your tarn," she said. "Now, try me out!"

I regarded her. I thought she would look well, naked, tied absolutely helplessly, on her back or belly, over the saddle of the tarn.

"Master?" she asked.

It was a fitting tie for such as she.

"Perhaps later," I said.

I then folded my cloak about her, to protect her from the wind.

We continued northward.

# 9
# THE CAMP OF COS

"Who is it?" she asked, kneeling in the darkness of the tiny tent, the large sack covering most of her body.

"It is I," I said, reassuring her.

I crouched beside her and unfastened the drawstrings of the sack which I had tied under her body and about her thighs, to hold it on her. I then pulled it from her and unbraceleted her hands from behind her back.

"Were you successful?" she asked, shaking her head, loosening her hair.

"Cook," I said.

I then sat, cross-legged, in the tiny tent. We were just within the fringes of the Cosian camp. There were, in this vicinity, clouds of tiny tents and shelters, some of them belonging to soldiers, most to civilians, sutlers, merchants, slavers and such. The nearest investment trench was a half pasang away. One could see the walls of Ar's Station from where we were. The girl busied herself, preparing food. It seemed peaceful here. It was difficult to believe that fighting took place daily in the vicinity of the walls, indeed, sometimes at night.

"There is little but porridge," she said.

I nodded.

There would be even less, I supposed, in most homes in Ar's Station.

"Have you heard anything?" she asked. She was putting

twigs and leaves in a small pit outside the entrance of the tent.

"It is said the city will soon fall," I said.

"The defenses cannot be long maintained?" she asked.

"It is thought not," I said.

"You wish to gain entrance to the city," she said.

"Yes," I said.

"Why?" she asked.

"I have business there," I said.

"Your accent is not of Ar," she said.

"I would hope not, in this camp," I smiled.

She used a tiny fire maker and set fire to the leaves and twigs. She blew on the small flame, encouraging it.

We could smell cooking fires about. It was near dusk.

"Your plans have not proceeded as you hoped?" she asked.

"I do not complain," I said. "Things might have proceeded better than they have, but they have gone much as I expected they would."

She added sticks to the small flame.

The first portion of my plan had been to reach Ar's Station as swiftly as possible, which meant, in effect, to do so on tarnback, and in such a way as to gain immunity from the attentions of Cosian tarn patrols. That I had managed. The patrols, which were thick in the vicinity, given my habiliments and accouterments, and my brandished pouch, presumably a diplomatic one, had taken me for a courier. Also, although I had not planned it, the presence of the blindfolded, braceleted girl before me, apparently a capture, presumably picked up enroute, and doubtless soon to be collared, added to the effect. The ears of the delicate Phoebe must have burned as she heard the snapping of wings near us and the shouting of ribald, raucous jests, of which her beauty and its probable disposition were the subject. At times I had even received an escort, which happily, at their patrol limits, had been suspended.

I had hoped, of course, somehow, ideally, to be able to enter Ar's Station on tarnback. As I had feared, however, this had not been possible. Even my garb as a courier had not permitted me access to the airspace over Ar's Station. I had been immediately pursued and fired upon by flights of Cosian tarnsmen.

I had made the attempt in the afternoon and again in the evening of the first day I had arrived in the vicinity of Ar's Station. Had it not been for the strength of the bird and my start I might have been downed over the city. I had escaped the second time only with considerable difficulty, by taking my way over the citadel and harbor, past the chained rafts closing the harbor, and across the Vosk itself, eluding my pursuers only after a long run, under the cover of darkness.

In these attempts I had, of course, not taken Phoebe. I had no wish to risk a quarrel's penetrating that beauty, which, properly refined and improved, would, in my opinion, not have shamed even the central block of the Curulean. Too, her weight, slight as it was, might have made the difference between falling to pursuers and eluding them.

I had, accordingly, before these excursions, sat her down, closely, before a small tree, her legs on either side of it. I had then tied a rope on her left ankle, looped the rope about another tree, a yard or so away, and brought it back, to tie about her right ankle. I did this in such a way, adjusting the length of the rope, that though her legs were forced to be rather extended, they were also permitted to flex enough for comfort. I then pushed her belly against the bark and braceleted her arms about the tree. The extension of her legs, of course, was such that she could not reach the ropes on her ankles with her braceleted hands. It also, of course, made it impossible for her to rise to her feet. I had sat her down there, and she would remain there, sitting, and as I had placed her. The location of the tree was close enough to the road that she might, if I had not returned by morning, call out, attracting attention to herself, thus saving herself, even if, at the same time, making it almost certain that soon thereafter her thigh would know the fiery kiss of a slave iron, and her neck the clasp of a master's collar.

She built up the fire.

I watched her.

She unfolded and adjusted a single-bar cooking rack, placing it over the fire. From this she suspended a kettle of water. The single bar, which may be loosened in its rings, and has a handle, may also function as a spit.

"And what did you do today?" I asked.

"I knelt in a body hood," she said.

"It was only a sack," I said.

"It served," she said.

The sack I had drawn over her was an improvised body hood. There are several varieties of body hoods on Gor, which is not surprising in a society in which slavery, and particularly female slavery, is an essential ingredient. Most body hoods are made of leather or layers of stout canvas. I have seen at least one in which two layers of canvas were sewn about a lining of linked chain. They may be fastened by means of such devices as cords, straps and laces. They may be tied shut or locked shut.

The prisoner is entered into some body hoods from the back, her legs being placed through openings in the lower portion of the hood, the hood then being pulled up and, from the back, laced shut. Most of these hoods do not have openings for the arms, but some do. In most hoods the arms are confined within the hood, either free within the hood itself or bound or braceleted within it. Some hoods are open at the bottom, and fastened on the prisoner by means of thongs or straps, often looped about the thighs. Others are constructed in such a way that they may be opened at the bottom, for the master's convenience. Sometimes the hood is thrust up and fastened about the prisoner's waist.

The typical hood provides hand and arm security with the advantages of the blindfold. Most body hoods, unlike many common slave hoods, do not have provisions for an internal gag. The prisoner, of course, may be gagged before being hooded. The body hood, like the slave hood, tends to keep a female docile. This may be a particular advantage early in her training, when she may not yet fully understand her new nature and its meaning. Another advantage of the body hood is that it is intriguing and attractive on a woman, baring her legs but usually, unless the arms are also intriguingly bared, concealing the rest of her, this sort of thing exciting male interest, and yet in virtue of the predominant concealment afforded, making her seizure less likely than if she were lying about more exposed in common bonds.

Slavers, in moving their wares through the streets, sometimes place them in body hoods. To be sure, it is more common to throw a cloak or sheet, which might be of various lengths, over their heads, this usually being fastened on them by means of a cord or strap looped once or twice about the neck and fastened under the chin. In many cities free women object to the marching of naked slaves through the streets. Still, even though the girls may be covered with cloaks or sheets, the men will usually come to watch, and call out to them, and jeer, and such. It is understood, of course, that the girls, beneath those cloaks or sheets, are slave naked. It is sometimes very trying, though also perhaps very instructive, for a new slave, perhaps a woman of a conquered city, to be marched thusly through the streets, stung with pebbles, pinched and slapped, subjected to the most intimate forms of raillery, jocosity and abuse.

"Do you object?" I asked.

"No," she said, suddenly, quickly. Then she put herself on her belly, on the dirt floor of the small tent, before me. She lifted her head, looking up at me.

"When," she asked, "may I use the word 'Master' truly to you, in all honesty?"

"But you are a free woman," I said to her.

"I beg the collar!" she said.

"Is that not an unusual request for a free woman?" I asked.

"My freedom is now a mockery," she said. "After what you have done to me these past two nights, how could I even think of being free? Do you think that that delusion can be meaningful to me any longer?"

"You have then learned something about yourself," I said.

"Yes," she said. "I have learned that I should be branded, that I should be in a collar!"

I smiled.

"Do not frustrate me," she begged. "Let me be what I truly am, in all honesty!"

"The porridge water should be salted," I said.

"Yes, Master," she said, and crawled to the front of the tent.

"Salt it lightly," I said. She was learning to serve.

"Yes, Master," she said.

The days I had spent here had not been fruitless. I had muchly reconnoitered. I had thought that perhaps I might have been able to ascend the walls of Ar's Station on one of the scaling ladders, in a morning attack, but I had soon thought the better of it. Resistance was still such that few Cosians could reach the parapets, and those who did were usually driven back. Whereas I supposed it was possible that I might enter the city in this way this modality of ingress seemed dubious at best. It was difficult to see how my projects would be furthered if, while attempting to identify myself and explain my mission, I were to be cut open with a boat hook. Similarly I was not interested, in the midst of friendly overtures, in receiving a bucket of flaming oil in the face or, say, being struck from a ladder by a roofing tile brought from the interior of the city. I had also considered trying to enter the city through its main gate, in the confusion, when it opened for sorties by the defenders. There had been no sorties, however, for twenty days. That in itself was an index of the straits of the defenders, their will and numbers. Also, it did not seem to me practical to try to enter the city during the daylight hours from the harbor side because of the besiegers. Similarly, during the night hours, it seemed the defenders might be unusually alert.

I did not, of course, know any appropriate signs and countersigns. One might well be set upon as soon as one tried to haul oneself unto a wharf. Indeed, they probably patrolled the pilings and such in small boats. An additional problem, at least to a swimmer, I had gathered, from talking with some of the soldiers, were Vosk eels. These often lurk in shadowed areas, among the pilings beneath piers. Whereas they normally feed on garbage and small fish it is not unknown that they attack swimmers. In the last few weeks, too, given the fighting at the rafts, and in the harbor, predictably, river sharks, usually much farther to the west, had made their appearance.

My second plan, or the second portion of my plan, involved the women from the Crooked Tarn. Late this afternoon, as I had expected, they, in the keeping of the sutler, Ephialtes, had arrived. I had made contact with him away from his wagon and I had had him blindfold the women, with the exception of Liadne, the first girl, and the only slave among them, before I inspected them. Liadne, who was delighted with her name, showed them off to me, proudly.

She had done a good job with them, in only three days. The free women knelt very straight, their bellies sucked in, their shoulders back, their breasts thrust forward. Too, they knelt back on their heels, their knees spread, as those of slaves. They were all there, Lady Temione, Lady Amina, the Vennan, Lady Elene, from Tyros, and Ladies Klio, Rimice and Liomache, all from Cos. All of them had, or had desired, to exploit men. Now they knelt before me, not knowing who it was before whom they knelt. I regarded them. Once they had been haughty, proud free women. They now knelt within the fringes of a military camp, frightened, confused, chained, blindfolded, shaved-headed prisoners. They did not know in whose power they were, or what their fate might be. I had plans for them, or some of them. They, or some of them, would learn soon enough what these might be.

I watched Phoebe pour some meal into the boiling, salted water.

Temione and Klio had had marks on their bodies. Perhaps they had dared to be initially recalcitrant, at least to some small degree. Perhaps, incredibly enough, they had even had some reservations, free women, to being handled and treated as slaves, being stripped, and chained behind a wagon, for example, or to having to obey promptly and perfectly the orders of a slave, Liadne, who had been put over them, as first girl, kneeling before her, addressing her as Mistress, and such. Perhaps, free women, they had dared, at least initially, to think that they might be above such things. They had learned differently. Too, their treatment might, in some trivial ways, perhaps smooth, or make a bit less traumatic, the transition to bondage, which was a likely, as well as suitable, disposition for them. To be sure, there is probably no fully adequate way for one to anticipate, or prepare for, psychologically, the actual transition to bondage, even if one eagerly seeks it, even if one welcomes it joyously, for with it comes a new and profoundly different understanding of one's self and nature; by it, you see, a categorical and radical transformation of one's realities is effected; in it one realizes, suddenly, that one is now no longer what one was before, that one is now something absolutely different, that one is now no longer a free person, but a property, subject to buying and selling, an animal, a slave.

Phoebe knelt near the fire, back on her heels. Occasionally she would kneel, up, off her heels, and stir the porridge.

"Keep your back straight," I told her.

"Yes, Master," she said.

Her body was slim, her hair was long, bound behind the back of her head with the black cord.

Others about, too, were cooking.

She still wore the garmenture so much like the curla and chatka, the cord at her belly and the long, single strip of cloth, the latter passing over the cord from the outside to the inside in front, and then up, and over it again in the back, moving from the inside to the outside, the whole then, above the cord, pulled up and adjusted, snugly.

She stirred the porridge.

The bottoms of her feet were dark with dirt.

There was a scuffling sound outside and, looking up, we saw a stumbling woman, naked, a rope on her neck, her hands tied behind her, being dragged among the tents. She cast us one wild, desperate glance, and then was dragged past.

Phoebe knelt even straighter.

"I think it is a good thing that I kept you covered in my absence yesterday and today," I said.

"Master?" she asked.

"Do you know why I did so?" I asked.

"That I may learn discipline?" she said. "That I may learn that I am truly your servant, and what it is to be the servant of a man such as you? And that I may learn to be a good servant?"

"Such things," I said, "but there is, too, another reason."

"What is that?" she asked.

"That it is more likely that you will be here when I get back," I said.

"I would not run away," she said.

"I was not thinking of that," I said.

"I do not want to run away," she said, "but, too, I would be afraid to run away."

"But you are a free woman," I said. "It is not as though you were a slave."

"But if you caught me," she said, "you would punish me, would you not, and terribly?"

"Yes," I said. "But still it would not be as though you were a slave."

She shuddered. "If I were a slave," she said, "if I were branded and collared, I would not even dare to think of running away."

I nodded. Gorean, she was not unacquainted with the severities typically inflicted upon wayward slaves, slaves foolish enough to attempt escape. Too, escape, in effect, is impossible for the Gorean slave girl. The law, the culture, and such, are not set up to permit it.

"But why then?" she asked.

"That it would be less likely that you would be stolen," I said.

"Really?" she asked, pleased.

"Yes," I said.

"Do you really think a man might want to steal me?" she asked.

"Of course," I said.

"Would you?" she asked.

"I might consider it," I said. "I think you would look well on all fours, bringing me a whip in your teeth."

"Phoebe has gathered, the last two nights," she said, shyly, "that she may not be without attractions to master."

"Perhaps," I said.

"Even though I am a free woman?" she asked.

"Most slaves begin as such," I said.

"I want to live for a master," she said, suddenly, looking at me, "and to give him pleasure. I want it to be the meaning of my existence!"

"I see, free woman," I said.

" 'Free woman'!" she said. "I am free in name only! You know that in my heart I am a slave!"

"True," I said.

"I want a master to be everything to me," she said, "even if he scarcely notices me, or cares if I exist."

"I see," I said.

"But you have not imbonded me!" she chided.

"No," I said.

"If I were stolen," she said, "I wager that that oversight would soon be remedied."

"Probably," I said. "Particularly if it were done by a professional slaver."

She hummed a little tune.

"Surely you fear the whip," I said, "and the hazards of the collar?"

"The whip is good for us," she said. "Perhaps it is hard for you to understand that, as you are not a woman. It makes our womanhood a hundred times more meaningful. The essential point here is not being whipped, of course, which hurts, but being *subject* to the whip, and being *truly subject* to it. You see the distinction, I am sure. We know that men are by nature sovereign over us. That comprehension requires no great insight. Accordingly, men must then either fulfill their nature, or deny it, and in denying their nature, deny us ours, for ours is the complement to theirs. Accordingly we despise men who surrender their natural sovereignty. Surely we would not be so stupid, would not be such weaklings and fools as to do that, if we were men. It would be too valuable and glorious a thing to give up. Its surrender would be a tragedy. But we are not men! We are women, and want, truly, with everything in our hearts and bellies, to be women, and we cannot be women truly if men are not truly men! Lay down the whip, and we will attack you, and undermine you, and use your own laws, institutions and rhetorics to destroy you, inch by inch. Lift it, and we will lick your feet in gratitude. Own us, dominate us! Enslave us, properly, so that we may love you as women are meant to love, wholly and irreservedly, totally, without a thought for ourselves!" She looked at me, tears in her eyes. "Is it so wrong to want to be ourselves?"

"But there are hazards in slavery," I said.

"I accept them," she said, "and would try to please my master."

"You would be well advised to do so," I said.

"I know," she smiled.

"Attend to the porridge," I said.

She removed it from the fire and covered it, to let it stand for a bit. She then set out two bowls, with spoons, and two trenchers, for some bread.

She served, deferentially.

I considered her flanks, and breasts. They were excellent.

Although her garmenture was assuredly scanty, she was more extensively clothed than many of the women in the camp. There were men here.

She spooned the porridge into the bowls and set the bread, wedges, from a round, flat loaf, on the trenchers, and knelt back. She would wait, of course, until I had taken the first bite.

Considering the size of the besieging force there were not as many women in the camp as might have been expected. I hoped this would work in my favor. The paucity of women, relatively, rent slaves even bringing a copper tarsk a night, had largely to do with the coming and going of the slave wagons, which tended to carry off most of the captures, apprehended refugees, women who had fled from Ar's Station for food, giving themselves into bondage for a crust of bread, and such, to a dozen or so scattered markets, markets such as Ven, Besnit, Port Olni, and Harfax.

I bit into the bread and Phoebe then, too, began to eat, taking a small spoonful of the porridge.

It had become dark now.

We could hear the pleasure cries of a woman a few tents away.

"Do you think she is free?" asked Phoebe.

"Probably," I said. "There are not too many slaves in the camp now."

"What do you think he is doing to her?" she asked.

"Mastering her," I said.

"Do you think she is tied?" she asked.

"Probably," I said.

She looked down, shuddering, blushing. The intensification of sexual pleasure, both physically and psychologically, by the application of selected restraints is well known.

"The women I have seen in this camp," she said, "do not appear to be overdressed."

"They are the prisoners of strong men," I said.

She listened to the girl's cries.

"She is passionate," said Phoebe.

"She has probably been given little choice," I said.

"Nonetheless," said Phoebe, "she is passionate."

"Her destiny is doubtless to be the collar," I said.

"So, too, I would were mine," said Phoebe, boldly.

"You are already a captive and servant, a full servant," I said.

"I would go beyond that," she said, "to my ultimate meaningfulness, that of the slave."

"Eat," I said.

"Yes, Master," she said.

I considered, again, the women from the Crooked Tarn. They had knelt well, their knees spread as those of slaves. Liadne had done well with them. I had wanted them to learn, of course, not only discipline, but something of the arts of pleasing men. Liadne, herself, was not an experienced slave, for, I recalled, she had been startled to find herself utilized, with her ankles chained, but she would still, presumably, be worlds of sensuousness beyond the simple free women in her charge. What could she have shown them in three days? Something, I supposed. Perhaps little more than how to make slave lips and do a little squirming, naked. That might be enough, however, for my purposes. The Cosians in the front trenches, and behind the earthworks and hurdles, who would have borne the brunt of the sorties in the past, and had doubtless contributed more than their share to the assaults, would not, I thought, be averse to finding a woman among them, particularly one naked and on a chain.

"She is quiet now," said Phoebe.

"He is probably letting her subside," I said.

"What is that?" she asked, suddenly, lifting her head.

"War trumpets," I said. I rose up and went outside the tent. She followed.

Others, too, about, from others of the small tents, had emerged.

From Ar's Station came the sounds of trumpets, far off. "It is a night assault," I said.

We looked toward the city.

We could see lights there. These were probably bundles of sticks set afire by defenders, and thrown, suspended on chains, over the walls, to illuminate them.

"There must be many women left in Ar's Station," she said.

"Doubtless," I said.

"How they must be afraid," she said, "hearing such alarms."

"Perhaps," I said.

"There are many encampments of slavers, and slavers' men, and cages, and slave wagons about," she said.

"Yes," I said.

The women of a city are, of course, among its prize loot. The women in Ar's Station, even the youngest and most beautiful, might now be pale, and drawn and scrawny, but water, and slave gruel, forced down their throats if necessary, could bring back their color, and fatten them for the block. Females, of course, make superb acquisitions, and gifts.

We listened for a time to the distant trumpets, watched the small spots of light in the distance.

Those about us, one after another, returned to their tents. It was only another attack, far off.

"Men are dying there," I said, looking toward Ar's Station.

"I am afraid," she said.

"Go into the tent," I said.

We reentered the tent and finished our meal, in silence.

"Do not try to enter the city," she said.

"Your thigh would probably look well, roped to a post, awaiting the branding iron," I said.

"Master?" she asked.

"Do not move when the iron presses into you," I said.

"Am I to be enslaved?" she asked.

"My remarks are general," I said.

"You are planning on leaving me!" she said.

"I do not know if I will see you again or not," I said.

"Do not try to enter the city!" she said.

"Come here." I said. "On your knees."

She approached me, as commanded. She then knelt there, slimly, beside me.

"Clasp your hands behind the back of your neck," I said, "and do not interfere."

"What are you doing?" she asked.

"Kneel up, off your heels," I said.

"What are you doing?" she asked.

"This garment you are wearing," I said, "what is, in effect, a chatka, I am shortening and transforming into two slave strips." I drew the long strip before the cord in front back over the cord so that it would no longer hang midway, or about midway, between her knees and ankles but was now about eighteen inches long. The garment then looped below her body. I then cut the garment a bit behind and below the cord in front. I then moved her about and treated the garment similarly in the back, drawing the strip back over the cord so that it was now only about eighteen inches long, and then cutting it off a bit below and behind the cord. She now wore two slave strips, each about eighteen inches long, one over the cord in front, one over it in back.

"Face me," I said.

She obeyed.

"What have you done?" she asked.

"Exactly what you think I have done," I said.

"You have removed nether shielding from me!" she said.

"Yes," I said.

"Restore it," she said. "Quickly! There is enough left of the cloth! Please!"

She gasped.

I had thrown the remaining portion of the cloth into the fire.

She watched it burn, in dismay.

"Do you feel vulnerable?" I asked.

"Yes!" she said.

"In such ways may one increase the passion of a female," I said.

She shuddered.

"You are aware, of course," I said, "that these pieces of cloth might be pulled away, easily."

"Yes!" she said.

"Keep your hands clasped behind the back of your neck," I said.

"Now what are you doing?" she cried.

"In the future," I said, "the cord will be tied in this fashion, or in some equivalent fashion."

She moaned, looking down.

I had refastened it in a simple bowknot, a sort of knot which on Gor, in certain contexts, as in the present context, is spoken of as a slave knot. It is called that, I think, because it is sometimes prescribed by masters for the fastening of slave garments. Its advantage, of course, is that it may be easily undone, by anyone. It is fastened at the left side of the girl's waist, where it is handy for a right-handed male, facing her. "Now," I said, "it is possible not only to remove the pieces of cloth singly, but, if one wishes, one may easily, with a casual tug, remove the cord and, with it, both cloths together, simultaneously, expeditiously."

"Stripping me!" she said.

"Keep your hands clasped behind the back of your neck," I said. "Yes."

She looked at me, tears brimming in her eyes.

"Do you object to your new garmenture?" I asked.

"Surely I am entitled to object!" she said.

"Turn about," I said.

She obeyed. "Oh!" she said.

"You may again face me," I said.

She turned about, again, quickly, on her knees. She looked in dismay at the strip of cloth which I had taken from the back of the cord, as it now flared, and then turned black and crumbled, in the fire.

"Do you still feel that you are entitled to object?" I asked.

"No," she said. "No!"

"And why not?" I asked.

"I am your captive, and servant, your full servant!" she said.

I removed my hand from the strip of cloth tucked behind the cord, at her belly.

"Keep your hands behind your neck," I said.

"Why are you doing this?" she moaned.

"You still have more to wear than most women in this camp," I said.

She choked back a sob.

"Tomorrow morning," I said, "your neck will be in a coffle collar."

She looked at me, wildly.

"You will be on a chain, with other free women. You will be in the keeping of my friend, and agent, Ephialtes, a sutler. He will take care of you, or sell you, or whatever, as seems appropriate. It was my intention that you be put in slave strips in order that your sense of vulnerability, and your passion, suitably, might be increased. Too, in this fashion, I am, to some extent, preparing you for the terrors and exposures of the coffle. I have removed one slave strip as a punishment, and a sign of my power over you. To be sure, this will even further increase your sense of vulnerability, and your passion. Too, it may also better prepare you for what you might experience on the coffle, the scrutiny and attentions of men, for example. The other women, incidentally, will be stripped, totally, and their heads have been shaved. As you will, at least for a time, have a slave strip, and your hair, you will be regarded as the 'first' of the free women. All of you, however, will be subject to Liadne, a slave. She will be first girl over you. She has whip rights, and so on, over you, and behind her is the power of men."

"I understand," she said.

"She has also been given a slave tunic," I said.

"How often," smiled Phoebe, "did I, as a free woman, feel repulsion and horror at even the sight of such scanty, revealing garments, in which slaves were put. Now I would be grateful for so much."

I smiled. The tunic, in its way, put Liadne a thousand times above her charges.

"But she is a slave, is she not?" asked Phoebe.

"Yes," I said. Thus Liadne, tunic or not, was infinitely far beneath her. Indeed, they were not even comparable. They were not even on the same scale. One was a person, the other was an animal.

"I would that I were as she," she said.

"Perhaps, someday, you will be," I said.

"My arms are weary," she said. "May I lower them?"

"No," I said.

"May I confess something to you?" she asked.

"Yes," I said.

"When in Cos, and elsewhere, as a free woman," she said, "I saw slaves in slave tunics I told you that I felt horror and repulsion."

"Yes?" I said.

"But even more," she said, "I wanted myself to be put in such a tunic, and be similarly subject to men!"

"I understand," I said.

"As I am a free woman," she said, "I am shamed, keenly, to wear what I now wear, but, if I were a salve, I do not think I would be shamed. I think, rather, I would be grateful, for I might as easily have been accorded nothing. Similarly, I do not really think I would object, if I were a slave, and not a free woman, to being naked on a chain. I think, rather, I would feel very grateful, and very proud, that men had found me attractive enough, and exciting enough, to put me there.''

"There are many aspects to slavery," I said.

"I think I am aware of aspects, from the point of view of my female fulfillments, that you, as a man, may not fully understand," she said.

"Perhaps," I said. "I do know that women make excellent slaves."

"Have you never wondered why?" she asked.

"Perhaps because they are slaves," I said.

"Yes!" she said.

"Such as you?"

"Yes!"

"Yet, even so," I said, "I suspect that there are senses of slavery, and aspects of slavery, that one can never fully fathom or anticipate until the experience is real for one."

"Doubtless," she said, shuddering.

I regarded her. She was lovely, kneeling before me, in the slave strip and cord, her hands clasped behind the back of her neck.

"May I lower my arms now?"

"No," I said.

"You are training me, aren't you?" she said.

"Perhaps," I said.

"I am afraid," she said.

"Do you know why I had you kneel as you are?" I asked.

"That you might busy yourself with my garmenture, without interference," she said.

"Are you modest?" I asked.

"Of course," she said. "I am a free woman."

"But when you first presented yourself before me, at the inn," I said, "you had bared your breasts."

"I think I have pretty breasts," she said.

"You do," I said.

"I bared them," she said, "because I did not wish to risk rejection."

"So that is the sort of woman you are," I said.

"Yes," she said.

"So now," I said, "how you could possibly object if you must display them again, and as I see fit, even as a slave?"

She put down her head.

"You may lower your arms," I said.

She lowered her arms, and knelt back, on her heels.

"Knees spread," I said.

She complied.

"The slave strip looks well, fallen between your thighs," I said.

"Thank you," she said.

"Your thighs are pretty," I said.

She blushed.

"Yes," I said, "and your belly and breasts, and the rest of you."

"Thank you," she said.

"Yes, you are remarkably lovely," I said. "Yes, I think you would make a lovely slave."

She trembled.

"What is wrong?" I asked.

"I am afraid," she said.

"Why?" I asked.

"I do not know anything of being a slave," she said, "should it be done to me! I know nothing of pleasing men! I do not even know the draping of tunics, the tying of slave girdles!"

"Should you become a slave," I said, "submit yourself to your sisters in bondage, not as one who was recently a free woman but as one who is now the lowest and most ignorant of slaves, the humblest of tyros and novices. Watch them. Learn from them. Serve them. Bring them small treats which you might earn. Beg them to help you, to teach you their ways, their arts and secrets. Even such small things as the use of the tongue can make a great difference in whether you survive or not."

She trembled.

"Reach now," I said, "to the cord at the left side of your waist."

"I do not even know how to strip myself before a man," she said, in misery.

"There are a thousand ways in which it may be done," I said.

She touched the cord. Her fingers were on it. Then she looked up at me. "How might a slave do this?" she asked.

"In one of a thousand ways," I smiled.

She moaned.

"A typical way might be as follows," I said. "The girl might stand or kneel before the master. She might say, 'Your property begs to be permitted to reveal herself to you.' Then, if the permission is granted, she does so."

"Your property begs to be permitted to reveal herself to you," she whispered, softly.

"But," I said, "as you are a free woman, you are not my property."

She regarded me.

"And so I do not grant you permission."

"Are you angry?" she asked.

"No," I said, angrily. The slave was so visible in her, so near the surface, that it was maddening. How it strove to emerge, and become her, totally! That she, such a woman, should still be free was an outrage to all justice and rationality. Her thigh should bear a brand! She belonged in a collar!

"Master?" she asked.

I forced myself to remember that she, fittingly or not, absurdly or not, was, at least at this moment, free.

"Master!" she pleaded.

She was not now a slave. I must accord her dignity and respect!

"Collar me!" she begged.

I seized her by the arms.

I held her.

But then, in the distance, we heard the trumpets, the horns.

"What is it?" she asked.

"It is the recall," I said. "The assault has been terminated."

"The city has not yet fallen," she said.

"No," I said.

I released her.

"Shall I build up the fire?" she asked.

"No," I said.

I went outside the tent and scuffed some dirt over the remains of the fire and then reentered the tent, and, from the inside, tied shut the flaps.

"It is dark," she said.

"Lie down," I said.

I removed my belt, and tunic, and crouched beside her.

I put my hand down, into her hair, and lifted her head a bit, and turned it, in the darkness. With my other hand, I touched her neck.

"Collar me," she begged.

It would have been easy enough to do so, there in the darkness of the tent.

"No," I said.

I then put her back, on her back in the dirt.

"Lift your body," I said.

She obeyed.

"Shall I free the cord?" she sobbed.

"I shall do so," I said.

"Do not leave me tomorrow," she begged.

"I must," I said.

I laid aside the cord and strip. "Do not lower your body," I said.

"It is now lifted to you, as though it were that of a slave," she said.

I put my hand on her, gently.

"Oh!" she said, squirming.

"Excellent," I said.

She sobbed.

"I think," I said, "you might bring a high price in a slave market."

"Do not leave me," she begged.

"I must," I said.

# 10
# THE TRENCHES;
# THE WALL

"Behold Klio, the free woman," I said, whipping the sheet from her.

She was on all fours in the trench and looked up, about her, with alarm, at the men.

There was raucous laughter.

I put a leash on her neck.

"She has already made her contribution to the success of Cos," laughed a fellow.

"But not of her own free will, I wager," laughed another.

"You have leashed me!" protested Klio, looking back at me.

There was more laughter from the men.

"Keep your head down," one of the fellows advised me.

"There is not so much need now," said another fellow. "They seldom fire now without a clear target."

"Where am I?" asked Klio.

"You are within two hundred yards of Ar's Station," I informed her.

She trembled. This was the most advanced of the Cosian siege trenches. Even the openings to the mines, now gated, and closely guarded, were further to the rear. The only closer entrenchments were sapping trenches, partly covered with wood, leading directly toward the walls. These were used not only for attempting to undermine the walls, but also for providing cover to men advancing for assaults. The sapping trench, of course, requires much less labor on the part of the besiegers but, too, it is less difficult to detect and stop than the mines. The mine, of course, need not stop at the wall, but can proceed within the city and when opened, pour soldiers out, behind the walls. The wall mine is usually terminated at the wall, which is then undermined but kept temporarily in place with a system of supports. Then later, concerted with an attack, these supports may be burned or, more dangerously, struck away. The coordination between the collapse of the wall and the attack can be sharpened when the supports are struck away, the same signal, say, the blast of trumpets, initiating both actions.

"Where is Elene?" asked Klio. When we had left Ephialtes this morning I had taken both Elene, from Tyros, and Klio, from Telnus, along. Elene had been the third woman of the debtor sluts. She was the only one who had been a blonde. Klio had been second at the wall.

"I sold her, a hundred yards or so back," I said.

"What!" cried Klio.

I had redeemed her, by means of Ephialtes, at the Crooked Tarn, for thirty-five copper tarsks, the cost of her bill, but I had sold her for forty, a modest, almost irresistible price, considering the value of women here, at least prior to the city's fall. A squad had chipped in and bought her. She would serve them all. Later they would probably play stones, or roll dice, for her. I had conveyed to the men, as though by inadvertence, that I suspected she might have little value as she had had her head shaved. I had suggested, too, I think, that I might be in need of money. As it was I made a profit on her which, when I had left the Crooked Tarn, I had never really counted upon, nor even anticipated. To me she had not been so much a property on which to make a profit as an instrumentality in my plans. Still, in her way, she was a property, and, accordingly, I was not displeased to be able not only to utilize her in my plans but also make some money on her.

Her blond hair would in time grow out again and the soldiers would discover that she had an additional loveliness. Eventually I had no doubt she would bring a high price. Auburn hair is generally thought to be the most prized hair on Gor, but I myself generally prefer brunets. This is not to deny that blondes, suitably enslaved, and desperate to please, are not without interest. Blondes sometimes bring higher prices as their hair color is rarer, but once they are home, in the collar, they are, of course, no more than any other slave. In the end, in my opinion, the crucial factor is the individual girl. Everything depends on the individual slave.

"Yes, sold," I said, answering Klio's look of disbelief. There was laughter from the men.

"And before I sold her," I said, "she performed well."

"No, please!" said Klio.

I had, as though looking for a good price first on Elene, made my way through the network of trenches toward the walls of Ar's Station. A trench back, one of the siege trenches, I had sold her. Some of the fellows from this trench, the forward trench, had come back to watch. There had been no difficulty in moving through the trenches in my guise as a mercenary with one or two women to sell. I had followed them back, at their own behest, through one of the connecting trenches, to the lead trench. We had herded Klio before us, under the sheet, on all fours, encouraging her occasionally with a foot or the blow of the looped slave leash, not yet on her at that time.

"Did you already sell the best one?" asked one of the men.

"You might think so, or not," I said. "I do not know. I think, from my own point of view, that I would prefer this one."

Klio looked back at me, frightened.

"I think I would prefer this one, too," said one of the fellows who had come back with me.

"She is a well-shaped beauty," said one of the men.

"Sirs!" protested Klio.

"We should have the best," said a fellow, "as we are the closest to the enemy."

"Keep a lookout," said one of the men to another, one standing on a low wooden platform, at the forward edge of the trench.

"I think I would prefer her, too," said another.

"Yes," said another.

Klio looked about. I could see she was pleased to be so approved of, in her basic elements, as a naked female, but, too, she was alarmed, having some inkling as to what might be the entailments of such preferences.

"Have her perform," said one of the men.

I shook the slave leash, now on her, This movement was transmitted through the leather, until it jerked and snapped at the ring, on the leash collar.

"No," said Klio, "please!"

"What?" I asked, puzzled.

"Sirs," cried Klio, "soldiers of Cos, warriors for truth and justice, redressers of wrongs, kinsmen from across the sea, I am Lady Klio, of Telnus, of Cos! I am a free woman! I beg your kindness, your indulgence, your protection! Rescue me from this barbarian! Clothe and honor me! Return me in dignity to freedom!"

"Many of these fellows," I said, "are not of Cos, but are mercenaries in the service of Cos."

She looked about the faces, frightened. On many faces there was amusement.

"I am of Telnus," said a fellow.

"I, too," said another.

"Free me!" she cried. "I demand it!"

They smiled.

"Some of these fellows have not had a female in a long time," I said.

" 'Had'?" she stammered.

"Yes," I said.

These men were front-trench fighters, most of them. Probably in defense, and in support of assaults, and in assaults themselves, they had been muchly employed and risked. The siege had been long, and bitter. Those who were not of Cos, and were mercenaries, fighting only for their fees, and some loot, perhaps a female or two, and gold, would presumably not be much moved by appeals to Cosian heritages or patriotism. Their loyalties would be less to Cos than to their captains and comrades. In some cases, they might be loyal, as well, to their word, to their oaths and pledges, and, if they understood what they were marking at the recruitment tables, their contracts. And the fellows from Cos itself, and from Tyros, and their close allies, were surely by now, if they had not been before, hardened veterans, men unlikely to be swayed by the self-serving appeals of beautiful women, men accustomed to seeing such women, of whatever city, in terms of the collar and chain.

"Why are you not in Telnus?" asked a fellow.

Klio was silent, in consternation.

"She lived from men, following them and exploiting them," I said. "She was a debtor slut. I paid her bills and thus came into her *de facto* ownership, through the redemption laws."

"But he did not free me then!" she cried.

"No," I said.

"Where did you pick her up?" asked a fellow.

"South, on the Vosk Road," I said, "at the Crooked Tarn."

"I know the place!" said one of the men.

"I, too," said another.

"I was once well taken at the Crooked Tarn," said the first man, "by a wench whose redemption cost me three silver tarsks, plus travel money, supposedly to get her back to Cos. For all this I received not so much as a kiss, she informing me that that would demean our relationship, putting it on a physical basis. She only laughed at me, from a fee cart, moving rapidly away, with my purse, waving the redemption papers, signed for freedom, in her hand. I was a fool. Often since I have dreamed of her in my power, naked and in a collar, my slave! I would use her well! Her name was Liomache."

I was interested to hear this. Had I known it I would have brought Liomache along. It seemed to me quite possible that the Liomache I had on the chain of Ephialtes might be the same woman. If so, she would be doubtless delighted to renew her acquaintance with the soldier. Certainly he, at any rate, would be delighted. Even if she were not the same woman, she had been making her living in the same way, and had had the same name. That might well have been enough to interest him in buying her. If she were the same woman, I did not think I would envy her, to find herself in the possession of her former dupe. She might, too, I supposed, discover that their relationship might then have, indeed, something of a physical aspect. Indeed, it would then be a totalistic relationship, the most totalistic relationship possible between a man and a woman, that in which she is total slave, and he absolute master.

"This woman, in effect," I said, "made her living in the same way as your Liomache."

"Kill her," said a man.

"Do not kill me, please!" said Klio.

The eyes of many of the men were hard upon her.

"She exploited men," said a fellow.

"I will not do it again!" cried Klio.

She looked from face to face, but found little to comfort her in those countenances.

Too, besides their anger, these men were Goreans, and many of them regarded women in terms of the perfection of the collar. Too, many had been frustrated by free women, and free women in their own city. It was a rare fellow who did not, from time to time, regard the women of his own city as quite as suitable for collaring as those of other cities. Were they not all women? Many Goreans, for example, rejoiced in the situation in Tharna, where almost every female is a slave.

"I will not do it again!" whispered Klio.

"You may attempt to do it, as you please, in the future," I said, "but I think you will do it within the limits of the collar."

"Oh, please, no!" she wept.

"I have shaken the leash, once," I said. "You did not then perform. Fortunate it was for you then that you were a free woman, and not a slave. Even so, I was not pleased. Do you understand?"

"Yes!" she said.

"Now, when I shake it again, you will perform."

She put her head down, trembling.

"Do you understand?" I asked.

"Yes," she whispered.

"You must remember, gentlemen," I said, "she is only a free woman."

I shook the leash and Lady Klio, naked, attempted to perform.

Some of the men laughed.

"Surely you can do better than that," I said.

She sank to her stomach, in the dirt, at the bottom of the trench, weeping.

"Whip her," said a tall fellow, watching her, with his arms folded.

She looked up at him, frightened.

His eyes suddenly glinted. I had not seen what passed between them but I suspect that he had seen in her eyes something swift, some flash of sudden fear and recognition, that she had seen him as her master.

Then she put down her head again and there, in the dirt, shuddered.

"On your knees," I said. "Now."

She cried out, and rose quickly to her knees.

"Knees spread," I said.

She knelt there, her knees spread. She blushed crimson. It seemed she could not take her eyes off the tall fellow.

"Perform," I encouraged her. "Move. Call attention to your charms."

Again Lady Klio began to perform, as she could.

"It may not be much, gentlemen," I informed them, holding the leash, "but surely for such a woman it is an unusual activity. I suspect that she is not accustomed to doing it. Perhaps in the future she will be better at it. Look, gentlemen. Little as it may be, I suspect this is far more than was provided for the many chaps who paid for her meals, her lodging, her wardrobe, her transportation, her luxuries, her claimed needs, her numerous bills.

"Continue to perform," I said. "You may leave your knees, but do not rise to your feet."

She regarded me, in wild protest.

"Yes?" I said.

"Do not make me do these things," she begged. "Do not make me dance and writhe so. I am a free woman!"

"Your freedom will soon be a matter of the past," I told her. "How well you do now could influence the quality of your life in the future.

"Do not fear," I said. "I know you are truly a slave. I learned it in your kiss, when you were shackled at the wall at the Crooked Tarn. I think that perhaps, in the same kiss, you learned it."

The men laughed. She sneaked a glance at the tall fellow, and then, hastily, put down her head. He smiled.

"Lady Elene, of Tyros, your friend, whom you remember from the Crooked Tarn, and the coffle," I said, "is even now in a slave collar." It had been put on her within moments of her sale.

Klio looked back at me.

"In her performance," I said, "the slave, unrestrained, emerged quickly and in moments the woman discovered that it was she. It pleased the men abundantly. It brought a good price. It is now collared."

Klio sobbed.

"Frankly," I said, "I had not expected you to be inferior to her."

She looked at me, angrily.

"But perhaps the women of Tyros," I said, "are superior to those of Cos?"

"I think not," said a man, rather angrily.

There was laughter from the others. I supposed he must be Cosian, natively.

"But then," I said, "it is said, I have heard, that those of Port Kar prize Cosians as slaves."

"Show us what a Cosian can do," said a man.

"Thus," I said, "it seems that it is not, really, that the women of Tyros are superior to the women of Cos, but merely that, in your particular case, you are inferior to the Lady Elene."

She looked at me, again angrily.

"But that is only to be expected, upon occasion, I suppose," I said, "that some woman of Tyros would be superior to some woman of Cos. Too, it is no disgrace to be inferior to the Lady Elene, who is quite attractive and, in time, might even make a dancer."

"I am not inferior to Elene," she said, angrily.

The men laughed at her vehemence.

She looked at the tall fellow.

I quickly then, that she would feel the authoritative signal of the leash and collar rings while she was looking at the tall fellow, shook the leash.

"Ah!" said a fellow.

I was quite pleased then with Klio.

My expectation, I then felt, that she would prove to be the most exciting and desirable of the two, was borne out. That was why I had saved her for last, of course, for use in the trench closest to Ar's Station. To be sure, I might have been somewhat prejudiced, for I remembered Klio's lovely dark hair, and I tend to be partial to brunets. Who, eventually, would prove to be the best slave I did not know. Let such women compete desperately with one another, and with other slaves, each striving to be the best.

One of the men cried out with pleasure.

That had been an excellent leash move, to be sure. Klio displayed herself brilliantly on the leash. Such things seem very natural for a woman. Perhaps they are, to some extent, like slave dance, instinctive, the biological template, or genetic dispositions for them, having been selected for thousands of years ago, the most pleasing of captive women, perhaps those squirming best on their tethers, or in their bonds, tending to be utilized for sexual conquest. Perhaps, however, they are associated, in their way, with something even deeper, something clearly selected for, the biological need of a woman to belong, to be approved of and to love.

"Superb!" said a fellow.

I wondered if Klio, sensing these deep, dark, wonderful, frightening things within her, the rightfulness of the destiny of submission to men for her, and such, had not, perhaps in the privacy of her own chambers, before her mirror, put the leash on herself. Perhaps she had then, there, before the mirror, in the privacy of her own quarters, moved similarly. It is not unusual for women to do this sort of thing, alone, often in bonds and chains, expressing plaintively therein their longing for a master.

"Superb! Superb!" cried another fellow.

Klio, I recalled, had chosen a dangerous way of life, one which she must surely have realized, on one level or another, might lead to the collar.

" 'Klio'," I said to the men, "might be an excellent name for a slave, do you not think so?"

"Yes!" said more than one.

Klio flushed with pleasure. Somehow it seemed she became even more sinuous, more sensuous, then.

I saw that she was paying a bit too much attention to the tall fellow.

"On your belly," I said to Klio. "There, that fellow," I said, indicating a grizzled sapper to one side, his tools near him, "address yourself to him, about the feet and legs."

He grinned.

"No!" said the tall fellow.

I had thought this move on my part might bring him into action.

Klio stopped, and turned, from her knees, to regard him.

"I will buy her!" he said.

"She is not cheap," I said. It seemed to me I might as well get what I could for Klio. I fear I must admit occasionally to a streak of opportunistic greediness.

"A silver tarsk!" he cried.

"Done!" I said. I had not really expected anything like that. Klio, redeemed through Ephialtes, had only cost me thirty copper tarsks. Perhaps I should have held out for more, seeing the eagerness of the fellow, but, after all, I was taken by surprise by the splendid offer, and even opportunistic greediness has its limits, particularly when surprised.

"On all fours," I said to Klio.

Immediately she went to all fours.

"A silver tarsk," I said.

It was placed in my palm and I put it in my pouch. I then removed my leash and collar from her neck. I had not even returned the leash and collar to my pouch before I heard a decisive click and a small cry from Klio. She looked up, collared, a slave, at her master.

"She dances the leash dance well, does she not?" I asked.

"I will improve her in it," said he, grimly.

Klio quickly bent her head, unbidden, to his feet, and kissed them.

"Share her," said a fellow.

"Let her dance again," said another, "not in the leash."

"Proffer her to the arms of each of us," said another, "in turn."

"She is mine," said the fellow.

"We are your comrades in arms," said another.

"True!" said another.

"Have no fear," said the tall fellow, "I will share the slave, and my good fortune, with you, but do not forget that in the end it is I alone to whom she belongs, that it is mine alone whose slave she is."

The men had crowded about Klio now, and I could hardly see her among them. Even the fellow from the low wooden platform, which gave him a vantage over the top of the trench, had joined them.

I backed away, unnoticed, toward the nearest sapping trench. In a moment I had then turned and was making my way rapidly toward the walls. In places the sapping trench was covered with planking, which might protect workers, or soldiers in their advance. In an Ehn or so I had come to its end, some twenty yards or so from the wall. Boulders lay about there, probably rolled from the height of the wall. Some were lodged at the trench, having crushed in the timber cover. The trench had not been taken around these obstacles. My heart was beating rapidly. I emerged from the trench, and waving a piece of white cloth, which on Gor is a truce cloth, as it is on Earth, climbed, slipping, up the rather steep incline toward the base of the walls.

"Ho!" I cried. "Do not fire! I am a friend. I have come here at great risk! I have a message for Aemilianus from Gnicus Lelius, Regent in Ar! Admit me!"

There was silence from the height of the wall.

There were no posterns here, and the great gate was hundreds of yards away. Too, in such a time, it would surely not be opened for one man.

I waved the white cloth vigorously.

That such a cloth may be used upon Gor as a truce cloth may have a direct historical connection with the similar device on Earth. Certainly many Gorean institutions and practices would seem to have Earth origins. On the other hand, its relationship to the Earth device may be merely a coincidental one, a white cloth, in effect, a blank flag, seeming to be a reasonably natural device to signify neutrality. Blank standards, too, or, more commonly, standards draped with white cloth, sometimes serve similar purposes. There are other devices, too, pertinent to such matters, particularly in formal contexts, such as the symbolic laying aside of arms, but I was certainly not, in this context, about to lay aside any arms.

"Admit me!" I cried.

Was there no one on the wall?

I looked back, toward the trench. I saw no unusual activity there.

"Ho!" I called, waving the cloth. "Ho!"

There was silence.

"Is there no one there?" I called.

For a wild, irrational moment I wondered if the city might have been deserted. But that would not be possible, of course. The garrison and population could not have withdrawn unnoticed. The land side was invested. The countryside swarmed with Cosians, and their mercenaries and allies. The harbor was closed with ships and rafts. What was more likely, of course, was that there were few men on the walls. What defenders there were would presumably be summoned by alarms to threatened points. I feared my position might be noticed at any moment by Cosians, and that I might be trapped against the wall.

"Is there anyone there?" I called. I assumed that at the distance I could not be heard in the Cosian lines.

Suddenly a basket, on a rope, was flung over the wall and lowered.

I hurried to it. In it lay a golden tarn disk.

"You are mad to come in daylight," called a voice from above. "Put your food in the basket, quickly, and be gone! Hope that no one has seen you!"

I stepped back a few yards.

I thrust the white cloth in my belt.

There would be no point in climbing the rope as it could be cut or dropped, or, if I were not welcomed at the height of the wall, I could be cut from it there.

"I am Tarl, of Port Kar," I called, "a city enemy to Cos."

"Do you have food?" called a man. I could see his face now, in one of the crenels at the height of the wall, some eighty feet above the embankment at the foot of the wall. It was gaunt, and hard.

"I come from Gnieus Lelius, regent in Ar," I called. "I bear a message for Aemilianus! Admit me!"

I saw part of a crossbow at one of the other crenels. These crenels, like many, were wider on the outside than inside, constituting embrasures. This affords a wider range of fire by missile weapons.

"Do you have food?" called a voice.

"No!" I said.

"Go away!" it said.

The basket, on its rope, maddeningly, drew upward some yards.

"Admit me!" I called. "Look! I have a diplomatic pouch, too, taken from a courier of Artemidorus. It may contain matters of moment! Admit me."

"It seems you offer us many inducements to admit you," called a fellow.

"Admit me!" I cried, urgently. "Do not fire!" I called out to the fellow with the crossbow.

"Go away!" said one of the voices.

"You would be mad to enter this place," said another voice.

"He is a spy, who would see behind our walls, who would inquire into our defenses," said another.

"No!" I said. "Blindfold me, if you will. Take me to Aemilianus!"

"You have been seen," said another fellow, the voice drifting down to me. I saw his hand, pointing out, toward the Cosian lines.

I turned about. I could see one or two fellows standing at the height of the trench.

"Your friends call to you," said a voice. "Make it back to them, if you can." I saw the crossbow move. Then, in another crenel, I saw another.

"Do not fire!" I called.

"Spy!" called one of the fellows.

"No!" I said.

"If you were not of Cos, you could not have come through their lines," he called.

. "No!" I said.

"How came you through the lines?" called another.

"By trickery," I said.

I heard laughter, unpleasant laughter.

"Admit me!"

"Return to your friends," laughed another fellow.

"I am of Port Kar!" I cried. "I am a courier for Gnieus Lelius. Summon Aemilianus, if no other can admit me!"

"Your friends are in the trench," called a fellow. "They come to support you! Perhaps you can make it to the trench. Run!"

I made no move to approach the trench. I looked back. To

be sure, there seemed to be movement in the trench. I could see it here and there, from the embankment, in the openings between the wooden coverings.

"Admit me!" I cried. Then I raced, suddenly, to the foot of the wall. Two quarrels struck into the embankment where I had stood.

"Admit me!" I cried upward, from the foot of the wall. It would be hard to be struck from the wall in such a place.

"If you are a friend, show yourself," called a fellow.

"Come out where we can see you, friend," called another voice, enticingly.

A quarrel then, suddenly, from the direction of the sapping trench chipped the wall, beside my head.

"They are firing on him!" said someone, from above.

Even before he had spoken two answering quarrels from the wall had leaped toward the trench, one skittering off one of the boulders there, then bounding oddly away, end over end, to the right, another passing half through some of the planking spread over the trench.

I heard the basket, scraping against the wall, dropping down, on the rope.

I saw a fellow rise up, in the trench, his bow leveled. I moved, faster, then slower, laterally, watching him, toward the rope. His bolt struck the wall, flashing against it, ahead of me. He had overled his shot. I then had my hands on the rope, above the basket. I swung wildly, kicking away from the wall, and was then, for a moment, half climbing, half being drawn upward. "Fire!" I heard from the trench. Two more quarrels struck near me. "Fire!" I heard from above. I continued upward, sometimes climbing hand over hand, feverishly, as I could, the rope momentarily arrested, at other times then, the rope moving rapidly upward, doing little more than clinging to it, sometimes, again, both climbing and being drawn upward. I swung as I could, too, and kicked away from the wall, that the target of the men in the trench would move in more than one plane. More quarrels struck about me, bursting chips from the wall, some striking me like stinging pebbles, then, at last, after a seemingly endless ascent, hands burning and raw, I was at the height of the wall, some eighty feet above the embankment, and hands reached out, seized me, and pulled me inward, through a crenel.

"My thanks!" I gasped.

I was flung to my stomach on the walkway behind the parapet. Hands held me down. My weapons and pouch were removed.

"Strip him and chain him," said a voice.

In a moment, lying on my stomach, on the walkway behind the parapet, I was stripped and chained, my hands manacled behind me, a chain running from the manacles down to join another chain, one strung between the shackles on my ankles.

"I am Tarl, of Port Kar," I said, "a courier, from Gnieus Lelius, regent of Ar!"

"Hood him," said a voice. "Use that white cloth."

The white cloth I had brought with me, as a truce flag, apparently doubled, or folded, was put over my head and tied under my chin.

"Kneel him," said the voice.

I was dragged up, to my knees.

"Here are the things he had with him," said a fellow.

Inside the improvised hood I could see very little. I could make out shapes about me.

"Put a rope on his neck," said the voice.

A shape bent toward me. I was neck-roped.

"Release me," I said. "Take me to Aemilianus! The message in my pouch is for him. He may be, too, interested in the contents of the diplomatic pouch. I do not know. I took it from a courier of Artemidorus, south of here, on the Vosk Road, at an inn, the Crooked Tarn!"

"Hooded, and on a rope, I do not think you will learn much of our defenses," said a voice.

"Take me to Aemilianus," I said.

"Silence, spy," said a voice.

"I am not a spy!" I said, angrily.

"Let us hang him," said a voice. "Let us show the sleen of Cos that we do not waste time with spies."

"I am not a spy!" I said.

"Good," said another voice, approvingly.

"Fasten the rope here," said a fellow, to my left, "and

show them that their spy is thrown over the wall, hanging against the stone, within Ihn of his entry into the city."

"Excellent," said another.

I felt the rope jerked on my neck.

I felt hands on my arms.

"They fired upon me! You saw it!" I said.

"But they did not hit you," said a fellow.

"Would you rather that they had?" I asked.

"It might have been better for you, had they done so," said another, grimly.

I was pulled to my feet.

"The rope is secure," said a voice.

"I came under a flag of truce," I said. "Is this how those of Ar's Station respect the conventions of war?"

The hands of the men were tight upon my arms. I could feel a breeze through the crenel to my left. Through the whiteness of the hood I could make out the opening.

"Hold," said a voice.

I heard the rope being unfastened. It was now, again, a tether.

"We had almost forgotten our honor," said the voice. "We are grateful to you for having recalled it to us. To be sure, it shames us that this should have been done by a sleen of Cos. Yet it does not matter. That it should be remembered is what is most important."

"I had not realized until now," said a man, "that we had suffered so much. I had not realized until now that we had been so deeply hurt, that our wounds were so grievous."

"Behind the trenches I think the Cosians are forming," said a fellow.

"It is the morning assault," said another fellow, wearily.

"Stranger," said the voice which had first spoken of honor to me, "know that you have been spared now, in your entry into the city, because of the flag you bore. And tragically, I confess, nearly it was not so. But, now, beneath its aegis, beneath its shelter, guarded within its folds, you are as safe as though ringed by walls of iron. The honor of Ar's Station has it so. I give you thus the option, if you wish it, to return to those of Cos."

"Take me to Aemilianus," I said.

"I think you are a spy," he said.

"I am not a spy," I said.

"You understand that if you go now to Aemilianus," he said, "that you forfeit the protection of the flag you bore."

"I understand," I said.

"Take him to Aemilianus," he said.

"Give me something," I said, as I was turned to the side, "if even a shred of my tunic, to cover myself."

"There are many Cosians forming," said a fellow, near the wall.

"You came as a spy," said the voice. "It is to Aemilianus as a caught spy that you will go."

Hands closed tightly on my arms.

"Take him away," said the voice.

# 11
# AEMILIANUS

"There," said a voice.

I was forced down, on a hard surface, tiles, I thought, on my knees.

The white cloth I had used as the truce flag was removed from my head. I blinked, looking about myself.

I knelt, on tiles, to be sure, before a curule chair, on a stepped dais.

To one side of the curule chair, kneeling below it, on one of the broad steps, collared and briefly tunicked, was a pale, blond slave.

"You may leave us, Shirley," said the man on the chair.

"Yes, Master," she said. Her head had been turned to the side, and her eyes had been averted. I was a free man and, had she looked upon me, without permission, she might have been punished. Slave girls do, upon the streets, occasionally look upon stripped free prisoners, sometimes even taunting them, and such, but they are not likely to do so, without permission, beneath the very eyes of their masters.

The name 'Shirley' is an Earth-girl name but I suspected that she was not an Earth girl. Her accent, at any rate, did not suggest it. She might have been of Earth, of course. After a few months on Gor it often becomes very difficult to distinguish Earth girls from Gorean girls, at least without a careful examination of their bodies, for example, for fillings in the teeth, or an inquiry, they kneeling before you, into their

specific antecedents. Goreans sometimes give Earth-girl names
to Gorean girls, as they think of them as excellent slave
names. To a Gorean ear names such as 'Jean' or 'Joan' have
an exotic flavor, and are regarded as fit names for slaves
brought in from such far-off, mysterious places as "Tennes-
see" or "Oregon." Some girls, too, coming to understand
the sensuous connotations of their names on Gor come to
regard them then no longer as common, or plain, names, but,
like the Goreans, as thrilling, beautiful names, and come to
revel in them, and try to live up to them, as superb slaves. To
be sure, they know they wear them now only as slave names,
theirs only by the will of a master.

It is true that Earth girls are regarded as slave stock by
Goreans, but I think, at least these days, that there is nothing
special about this, really. As the girl left I watched her. She
was quite thin. Once, I thought, she would probably have
been much more fully bodied in her beauty. Once she might
have been luscious, perhaps even voluptuous. By such signs I
conjectured the paucity of rations in Ar's Station. I supposed,
however, that she, and others like her, might be quickly
enough returned to a former condition of desirability by so
simple a means as the restoration of a proper diet, both with
respect to quantity and quality. By such means do dealers
prepare women, grateful for the food, to bring higher prices
upon the slave block. Her blond hair, too, had been cropped.
In these times, I suspected there would be few unsheared
slave girls in Ar's Station, and probably, too, few unsheared
free women. In the case of the slave girls, of course, their
hair would simply be taken from them. The hair of the free
women, on the other hand, would presumably have been
donated, as a contribution to the defense of the city.

"Yes," said the fellow sitting on the curule chair, a strongly
built man, though one now seemingly weary, one with a
bloodied bandage about his head, "she was once quite
beautiful."

I turned my attention to the man. He had, with him, on his
lap, the diplomatic pouch, opened, and the letter cylinder,
taken from my pouch. It had been sealed with wax and
ribbon, the wax bearing the seal of Gnieus Lelius, regent of
Ar.

"Are you Aemilianus," I asked, "commander in Ar's Station?"

"I am," he said, looking at me.

I glanced toward the retreated slave, who had turned to regard me.

The fellow on the curule chair smiled. "She has dared to look upon you?"

"No," I said.

"They are so curious," he said.

I did not respond.

"Shirley!" he called, without turning to look at her.

"Master?" she answered, from near a side door in the back.

"Remind me, tonight," he said, "to whip you."

"Yes, Master!" she sobbed. She turned, then, and fled from the room.

"They are women," I said. "They cannot help themselves."

"I do not object that she did what she did," he said. "It is only that, as she has done it, she is to be whipped."

"I see," I said.

"Even in hard times," he said, "it is good to maintain discipline."

"Doubtless," I said.

"Do you know where you are?" he asked.

"No," I said.

"You are in the citadel," he said.

"I thought I might be," I said. It seemed a likely place to house the headquarters of the city.

"You are Tarl, a fellow of Port Kar," he asked, "as you told my men upon the wall?"

"I am Tarl," I said, "of Port Kar."

"And you claim to be the regent's courier?" he asked.

"I am the regent's courier," I said. "Why am I still stripped and chained?"

"Does it not seem odd to you that the regent should employ as a courier one from Port Kar?"

"Perhaps," I said. "I had delivered letters to him from Dietrich of Tarnburg. Perhaps it then seemed plausible to him that I might similarly serve Ar."

"Dietrich, the tarn of Tarnburg?" he asked.

"Perhaps some call him that," I said. "I have never heard

him use that expression of himself, nor have I heard it used by those most close to him. I do not even think he would care for it.''

"And how does he think of himself?" asked Aemilianus.

"As Dietrich," I said, "Dietrich, of Tarnburg, a soldier, a captain."

"Dietrich, of the Silver Tarn?" he asked.

"His standard, it is true," I said, "is that of the Silver Tarn."

"He is a mercenary," said Aemilianus, bitterly.

"He now holds Torcadino," I said, "to halt the advance of Cos to the south."

"I do not believe that," said Aemilianus.

I then realized the degree of isolation of those in Ar's Station. Aemilianus was ignorant of something so basic as the action of Dietrich at Torcadino.

"Surely there is something to that effect in the letter, or letters, from Gnieus Lelius, which I have delivered."

"You, too, are a mercenary," he said, bitterly.

"I have served for fee," I said.

"Anyone's gold can purchase your steel," he said.

"Perhaps not anyone's," I said. Some mercenaries chose their causes with care.

"Do you know the contents of the diplomatic pouch, for, indeed, it seems to be such."

"No," I said. "As you must have seen, its seal was unbroken."

"Perhaps you were apprised of its contents before it was sealed?"

"No," I said. "I took it from a courier for Artemidorus at the Crooked Tarn, an inn, south on the Vosk Road. I told your men this."

"Do you expect me to believe that?" he asked.

"Where else would I have obtained it?" I asked.

"Perhaps from the hands of Artemidorus himself," said Aemilianus.

"I do not understand," I said.

"I am prepared to believe that you might well not have known its contents," he said.

"Why?" I asked, puzzled.

"If you did know its contents," said Aemilianus, "I do not think you would have dared to bring it here."

"What are its contents?" I asked, not much pleased at hearing this.

"Its contents are not even in cipher," said Aemilianus. "Does it not seem unusual to you that Artemidorus, a tarnsman, an astute commander, should transmit military documents in so careless and open a fashion?"

"Perhaps he is overconfident or arrogant," I said. "I do not know."

"Does it not seem strange to you?" asked Aemilianus.

"Yes," I said, "it does."

"I think," said Aemilianus, "this was intended to come into my hands."

"I doubt that," I said. "What does it say?"

"It is an intelligence report," he said. "It gives the numbers, and positions, of the forces of Ar."

"May I inquire where they are?" I asked. I had pondered this many times.

"I will tell you where they really are," said Aemilianus. "They are moving by forced marches to our relief."

"By what route?" I asked, puzzled.

"North on the Viktel Aria," he said.

"No," I said. "I came by the Viktel Aria. They are not there. No one has seen them for hundreds of pasangs from here."

Aemilianus smiled.

"May I ask where the report claims them to be?"

"The report claims they are in winter quarters at Holmesk, one hundred pasangs south of the Vosk."

"In winter quarters?" I asked. "While Cos is at Torcadino, and Ar's Station under siege?"

"You see the absurdity of the report," said Aemilianus.

"Yes," I said, awed.

"Had you known the contents of the report perhaps you would have declined to carry it," he smiled.

I almost rose in the chains, but I was pushed down, back onto my knees.

"I submit, Captain," I said, urgently, "that incredible though it seems that the report may be accurate." The situation had suddenly begun to assume an alarming shape in my mind. I was confident, as Aemilianus was not, that the report was authentic, even if, in some respects, it might not be reliable.

Aemilianus laughed, and, so, too, did several of the men about.

"Where are the relief forces of Ar?" I asked. "Where?"

Aemilianus looked at me, angrily.

"Even though you are isolated here, and invested," I said, "surely you must understand that the siege of Ar's Station can be no secret. You must realize that a relief force would have been dispatched, that it should have arrived by now. If you are so sanguine about your prospects, I suspect that your men, those out on the walls, are not. I have been among them. They are hungry. They are gaunt and drawn. They are not buoyed by optimism. I suspect that they, even if you do not, realize that any relieving force should have been here by now, and long ago!"

I heard a sword, half drawn, behind me. Then it was returned, angrily, to its sheath.

"The report is inaccurate," said Aemilianus. "It is not even intelligently conceived. It gives such numbers for Ar's troops at Holmesk as would mean that the main might of Ar is in the north, which is unthinkable. Such forces would not be needed to raise the siege. Ar, too, in such a case, would be in effect undefended, her territories, if not herself, at the mercies of Salarians, Travians, Tharnans, even men of small cities like Tarnburg and Hochberg."

"There could be treachery," I said.

There was an angry murmur from those behind me.

"You have been abandoned," I said.

"Let me cut his throat," said a man behind me.

"All that stands between Ar and Cos," I said, "is the presence of Dietrich at Torcadino, where he has seized Cosian supplies and engines."

"He could not take Torcadino," said Aemilianus. "He has too few men."

"It was done by stealth, through the aquaducts," I said.

"He would have too few to hold it," said Aemilianus.

"The Cosian siege train was captured within Torcadino," I said. "The city itself, as last I heard, though invested, has not been attacked. Indeed, the Cosian main forces, which I assure you are not inferior in numbers to those of Ar, are probably now in winter quarters, perhaps a tenth of them in the vicinity of Torcadino. The situation of Cos was clear. She could not proceed without the siege train and it would take some months to replace it."

"And what do you suppose will eventuate?" asked Aemilianus.

"I do not know," I said. "Once Cos has engines again she might attack Torcadino, if only to punish Dietrich. If I were Myron, Polemarkos of Temos, he in command of the Cosian forces on the continent. I would myself turn toward Ar, wasting no time at Torcadino, a subsidiary objective. Dietrich would then escape, but he would not have the forces necessary to do more than harry the Cosian advance to Ar, and, once those forces are out of Torcadino, they might well be hunted down and dealt with, with only a fraction of the might of Cos."

"Why would Dietrich of Tarnburg risk this perilous intervention?" asked Aemilianus.

"There are valuables, women, and such, in Torcadino," I said.

"And such may be found in a hundred towns and cities," said Aemilianus.

"He has no love for either Ar or Cos," I said. "He prefers the victory of neither. Any such victory, with its achieved hegemony, might end, and would surely threaten, the existence of the free companies. Too, many would fear in it the destruction of social openness, of pluralism and freedom, as it now exists on Gor."

"And do you share such sentiments?" asked Aemilianus.

"I would not look forward eagerly to a world dominated by either a Marlenus of Ar or a Lurius of Jad."

"Such would bring peace," said Aemilianus.

"The peace of chains," I said.

"Is not peace more important than anything else?" he asked.

"No," I said.

"I find it hard to believe that your own interests in these matters is so abstract and elevated."

I did not respond to him. He need not know the secret motivations, which I could confide to few, underlying my original journey to Ar, that journey in which I had been detained at Torcadino. He need not know, for example, the contents of the secret papers which I had obtained at Brundisium last Se'Kara, papers which I had swiftly burned. In those papers had been made clear the treason of one who currently stood high in Ar.

"I shall now explain to you the situation as it actually exists," said Aemilianus. "The main Cosian forces are here, at Ar's Station. She lacks the troops to penetrate south. She wants power in the Vosk Basin, that is the best for which she can hope. Torcadino is an ally of Ar, and has never fallen. There is no southern invasion force from Cos. The story about Dietrich of Tarnburg is a fabrication. This pretended intelligence report, absurdly conceived, is intended to lead us to despair. It is a ruse to bring about the surrender of the city. Do they really think we would believe that this report just happened to fall into our grasp, at this time? Do they intend for us to take it seriously? It is not even in cipher. The implicit absurdity of this document, suggesting that Ar would stand about with almost the totality of her might while we are under attack, that we have been, in effect, abandoned, makes it clear that the relieving forces of Ar must actually be quite close, perhaps only a day or two away."

There were sounds of agreement, perhaps rather desperate ones, behind me.

"I do not know the location of the main body of the might of Ar," I said, "but I suspect it is exactly where this report states it is, and that this report is apprising Artemidorus of the situation. I do not know why it is not in cipher. Perhaps this information is not really that secret, at least to Cosians. After all, it is not easy to conceal the whereabouts of thousands of men from a foe with tarn scouts. I would also suggest to you that there is indeed a Cosian invasion force in the south, and one that makes the one here look like a squad. Your conjecture that Cos could not field such land forces assumes that these forces must consist of her own troops. That is not true, of course. You must realize that even here the majority of the men who face you are not Cosian regulars but allies and mercenaries."

"Do you realize the cost of supporting such forces?" asked Aemilianus.

"Lurius is willing, I suspect, to gamble the gold of Cos on victory, and recoup his investment a thousandfold in the future."

"There is not so much gold in Cos and Tyros," said Aemilianus.

"It may not all be from Cos and Tyros," I said.

"From whence then?" asked he.

"From cities interested in a Cosian victory," I said, "and, too, I suspect, from Ar herself."

I felt a knife at my throat, above the rope tether there.

Aemilianus made a small, negative gesture. The knife was pulled back.

"You do not know the message in the letter cylinder," he said.

"No," I said.

"Did you see the regent close the cylinder, and affix his seal upon it?" he asked.

"No," I said. "It was handed to me by a subordinate, in the condition in which you received it."

"It is a little joke on the part of the regent," said Aemilianus.

"A joke?" I said.

"Yes," said he, "your allegiances and treachery were discovered in Ar, long before you came here."

"I do not understand," I said.

" 'The bearer of this cylinder, who calls himself Tarl, of Port Kar,' " read Aemilianus, " 'is a Cosian spy. Deal with him as you please.' "

"No!" I cried. I tried to rise but I was forced down, again, on my knees. I was held there. One fellow had his foot on the tether about my neck, keeping my head low. I put back my head, as I could, to look at Aemilianus.

I heard grim laughter about me.

"It is a trick!" I said.

"And you are the one who has been tricked," smiled Aemilianus.

There was laughter.

"Did you truly think we might surrender the city?" asked Aemilianus. "Do you really not know how long and bitter has been this siege? Do you not know how lengthy and terrible has been the fighting? Do you not know the losses of

Cos, as well as ours? Do you really think we do not know what fate would await us if we opened the gates?''

I was then held even more sternly, and the tether, under the fellow's foot, was shortened further.

"But where," asked a young fellow in the back, the first time he had spoken, "are the relieving forces of Ar?''

"It is my hope that they are on their way here," said Aemilianus.

"But why have they not arrived?" asked the young fellow.

"Do not forget your age," said a man.

"I have been on the wall as much as you," he said.

"I do not know," said Aemilianus.

"It is possible, is it not," asked the young fellow, "that they might arrive too late?''

"It is too possible," said Aemilianus.

"The safety of the city is in your hands, Captain," said the young fellow. "The security of her citizens is your responsibility. I think that in the light of the events that have taken place you should consider an alternative.''

"Who would do this?" asked Aemilianus.

I did not understand their discourse.

"I would," said the young man.

"No!" cried an older fellow. "We would die to the last man before we would have recourse to such an action!''

"They would laugh at us!" said another.

"You were not on the river," said Aemilianus.

"With your permission, Captain?" said the young man.

"Go," said Aemilianus, resigned.

"No!" cried another man, but the young fellow had turned, and was already taking his way from the room.

"He will never make it from the city," said a fellow.

"He will be dead by dusk," said another.

"Listen," said a man. "The trumpets.''

"The morning assault has begun," said another.

Aemilianus rose up, unsteadily. "Gentlemen," said he, "let us to our stations." Then he looked down, wearily, upon me. "I understand," he said, "that on the wall, you were nearly hung.''

I looked up at him, as I could, but said nothing.

"Perhaps it is just as well that you were not," he said. "Hanging is too swift a death for a spy."

I struggled, futilely.

"Put him with the other spy," said Aemilianus.

# 12
# THE CELL; THE SPY

The tether on my neck was removed.

I stood before an opened iron door.

"Remove his shackles," said an officer.

My hands and ankles were freed. I was covered by two crossbows. Any suspicious or sudden move, I was sure, would result in the entry into my body of those two stubby, heavy iron bolts.

I was then thrust through the door and it shut heavily behind me.

I heard it locked.

I stood in a cell, on huge, flat stones, strewn with straw. There was more straw piled in the corners of the cell. It was not a small cell. It was perhaps twenty feet square. It was lit by a shaft of light, descending from a window high in the wall. This window was barred. The bars appeared to be some two inches in thickness and were set about two inches apart.

I tried the door. It was sturdy. The hinges were on the other side. It had an observation panel in it, which, latched, as it was now, could be opened only from the outside. There was also a narrow paneled opening in the bottom of the door, also locked now, through which, when it was opened, a pan, say, of water, or bread, or dampened meal, might be inserted. I looked about the cell. I checked the floor, the walls. It was a sturdy cell. It was the sort of cell in which inmates, to their dismay, soon discover that they cannot escape, that they are helpless, that they are truly prisoners.

I then turned to face the other prisoner.

She shrank back, naked in the straw. She was at the side of the room. She knelt there, frightened, her knees clenched closely together. When I had been entered into the room she had cried out in protest and cringed. She had moved her head and her hands for an instant in such a way as to suggest she wished to bring her hair forward, before her, to use it to partially cover her breasts and body, but then she moaned. She could not do so. Her hair, as she had recalled, almost immediately, had been cropped short. She did pull straw up, about her thighs and waist, to help hide herself. She now looked at me, wildly, kneeling, huddling in the straw, covering her body, as she could, with her hands.

"Why have they done this?" she asked.

"What?" I asked.

"Put you in with me!" she said.

"I do not know," I said.

Then she bent down further, making herself even smaller in the straw, looking up at me.

"Are you a gentleman?" she asked, plaintively.

"No," I said.

She moaned. "They must hate me so," she wept. "They have done this deliberately! Is it not enough that they have removed my clothing and incarcerated me?"

"You are a spy," I said.

"So, too, then must you be," she cried, "that you have been put in with me!"

"It seems they think so," I said, irritably.

"I was caught!" she cried. "What will they do to me?"

"Are you a free woman?" I asked.

"Yes!" she said. "Of course!"

"I do not think it will be pleasant then," I said.

She moaned.

I looked up at the high window. There was nothing in the room which made it possible to reach it, even to look out.

"They hardly feed me enough to keep me alive!" she exclaimed.

"You are probably fed as well as others in Ar's Station," I said.

"Look," she said. "They took my hair!"

"In that way," I said, "they have seen to it that you have done your bit for Ar's Station."

"The city must soon fall," she said. "We must then be rescued!"

"The citadel," I said, "can be held long after the walls. They would have time to deal with us."

She put her head down, weeping bitterly.

"When are we fed?" I asked.

"At noon," she said, lifting her head, looking at me, angrily.

"Do they make you perform for your food?" I asked.

She looked at me, in fury.

"I see that they did," I said.

"No more," she said. "There is a woman warder now. The men were needed on the walls."

"Full usage?" I asked.

"No," she said, angrily, "such things as dancing, and posing, before the panel. They never entered the cell."

"Did you dance and pose well?" I asked.

"When I did not, I was not fed," she said, bitterly.

"Still," I said, "you escaped easily."

"Undoubtedly," she said, bitterly.

"Did you enjoy dancing, and posing?" I asked.

"Are you mad?" she asked.

"Perhaps," I said. I smiled inwardly. I had noted a tiny movement about her, and a fleeting, frightened expression, before she had answered so belligerently. I saw that she was female.

I glanced toward the door.

"There is a woman warder?" I asked.

"Do not rouse your hopes," she said. "She does not enter the cell."

"Who are you?" I asked.

"Claudia, Lady of Ar's Station," she said.

"Where were you caught?" I asked.

"On the parapet," she said. "I did not even know I was suspected until I felt the rope on my neck."

I sat down in the straw, facing the door. "Tell me of these things," I said.

"Doubtless my story, in its way, is not much different from yours," she said.

"Perhaps," I said.

She spoke more freely, not under my eye.

"I did not receive the promotion and advancement which were my due here," she said. "I wanted even missions to Ar herself, but others were chosen in my place. How wrong this was!"

"Continue," I said.

"I am a beautiful and brilliant person," she said. "Yet my perfections were insufficiently rewarded."

"Perhaps you are only a pretty mediocrity," I said.

"My talents were ignored," she said, angrily.

I thought she might, if only latently, have excellent woman talents.

"Then the Cosians were upon us," she said. "We were all in fear of our lives. It became clear, after weeks, that Ar was not coming to our rescue. It would be everyone for himself. The clever must save themselves. I would be clever. Sometimes at night the women go to the parapets, to lower baskets with money, for food. Some women, as you probably know, particularly those without money, stripped themselves and lowered themselves over the wall, surrendering to the first Cosian they met, selling themselves into slavery for so little as a crust of bread or a handful of gruel."

There was still food, though it seemed not much of it in the city. For example, even she, a caught spy, was still being fed. The women who did this, I suspected, lowering themselves naked over the wall, their bodies brushing and touching the stone in their descent, had had motivations deeper than hunger. Hunger, however, might have provided a convenient and excellent rationalization for their action. The nudity of the suppliants, of course, was only to be expected. Stripping themselves, baring their breasts, and such, is natural for female suppliants before men. The nudity, too, would make clear their intent, and make it less likely that they might, in the darkness, be slain as mere fugitives. Nudity, too, makes it difficult to conceal weapons. For example, sometimes, when slaves are taken to Ubars, and such, they are stripped and wrapped in a scarlet sheet, if they are "red silk," and in a white sheet, if they are "white silk." They are then placed in the master's chambers, often through a panel in the door, the sheet remaining behind. A girl normally makes the journey only once in a white sheet, of course. Nudity, all in all, is not uncommon in women surrendering to men. It is also not uncommon, of course, in slaves presenting themselves before masters.

"I see," I said.

"But such was not for such as I," she said. "I had no wish to risk being hooded and chained in a crossing stall in Tyros, being used to breed quarry slaves for Chenbar, the Sea Sleen."

I rather doubted that she, who was slight, delicious and well-curved, would have to fear that fate. Too, most women would spend very little time in a crossing stall. How long, after all, she placed there without slave wine, at the exactly ideal moment in her breeding cycle, does it take to impregnate a slave? Most such slaves are used in this fashion only once or twice, and then they are assigned other duties.

"I formed the habit of going to the wall with the other women, 'fishing,' as we spoke of it. I made certain, of course, that I went to the same place on the wall at the same time each night. The first few times I put money in the basket. Later, when I increased the amount of money, I received some bread and vegetables. Can you imagine? A silver tarsk for a few suls?"

"The prices are higher now," I said. I recalled there had been a golden tarn disk in the basket which had been lowered to me at the foot of the wall.

"Then," she said, "I began to put messages in the basket, innocent ones at first, asking questions about the position of the relieving forces, and such."

"I understand," I said.

"But my intent seemed quickly grasped," she said, "for shortly thereafter, with food, concealed under the cloth, in the bottom of the basket, were questions pertaining to conditions in the city."

"Did you respond to these?" I asked.

"Yes," she said.

"You were at that point a spy," I said.

"I did not think so, yet," she said. "Such information was surely general knowledge."

"Not necessarily to those outside the city," I said. "To be

sure, there are usually informers, if not traitors, sometimes several, who can be relied upon for such details."

"The next time I drew up the basket," she said, "there was a very specific question, concealed in a wedge of Sa-Tarna bread. 'Are you for Cos?' it asked. The next night I lowered the answer, 'Yes.' "

"You were then a traitress," I said.

"Ar's Station had betrayed me!" she said. "It had not given me what I wanted! It had not even given me missions to Ar. Too, do you think that I, a person such as I, wanted to remain out here, on the Vosk River, all my life?"

"What happened then," I asked.

"I then made clear my position, that I would bargain, and bargain severely."

"You requested food?" I asked.

"I had food," she said. "I had hoarded it from the beginning of the siege, even buying it up when it was cheap, early in the siege, when it was still thought that Ar, any day, would arrive with her banners fluttering in the wind, dispelling the Cosians like the sun the fogs on the river!"

"For gold then?" I asked.

"Yes," she said, "for gold, and jewels!"

"It seems you have little gold and few jewels now," I said.

I heard her move angrily in the straw.

"Once you had declared for Cos," I said, "I think you would have been wise not to begin bargaining for monetary returns."

"Why not?" she said.

"Because you had declared for Cos," I said. "Cosians, like those of Ar, or elsewhere, expect those whose allegiance has been freely given to serve as those who have given their allegiance freely, and not as merchants or mercenaries."

"What difference does it make?" she asked.

"Occasionally such things mean the difference between riches and a collar," I said.

"I protected myself in my bargaining against such possibilities," she said, "demanding, as conditions of my cooperation, not only riches but my safety and freedom."

"That you not be made a slave, for example."

"Yes," she said.

"But, suppose," said I, "that in the meantime, perhaps by others, you had been made a slave."

"Then that," she said, "would be the end of it. I would then be a slave. A slave is a slave."

"True," I said. The Cosians had agreed not to make her a slave, not to free her, if she had already been made a slave. As she had said, a slave is a slave.

"I, too, demanded power in Ar's Station, should the city not be destroyed, for there were those here, those who had not granted me preferments, on whom I would have my vengeance. I even wanted some of the women consigned to me as slaves, so that I could sell them to men."

"You were thorough," I said.

"Yes," she said.

"You needed then only count on the honor of Cos."

"Men are honorable," she said.

"So, too, are some women," I said.

"My allegiance is to myself," she said, angrily.

"There are dispositions for women such as you," I said.

"I do not understand," she said.

"Proceed," I said.

"My terms agreed to," she said, "I received extremely specific instructions. These instructions pertained to the supply of information on various topics, matters pertaining to supplies within the city, the condition of the gates and walls, and which were the weaker and less defended points, the numbers of the active garrison, civilian and military, the relative distributions and dispositions of these components, the numbers of the ready militia, the posting of guardsmen, the timing of their watches, and such. I could not find such things as the signs and countersigns. Too, I understand they are changed daily."

"Generally," I said.

"Bit by bit," she said, "I parceled out such information, as I could acquire it, each night. To be sure, some of the things I could not learn. In return I now received gold and jewels."

I smiled.

"Did you make your name known to your confidant, or more likely, confidants, at the foot of the wall?" I asked.

"I was too clever for that," she said. "I did, however,

demand, and receive, a letter of safety, and an acknowledgement of services rendered, made out to the bearer.''

"You are a clever woman," I said.

"I am extremely clever," she said.

"How came you then to be naked in a cell?" I asked.

She made a tiny, angry noise.

"Continue," I said.

"Perhaps I had excited suspicion," she said. "Perhaps guardsmen had noted my appearance frequently on the wall, at the same time and place. Once I had to strike another girl away from my place, fighting her for it. She did not understand my intensity. She had thought it perhaps only an excellent place for fishing. But it was my place! Perhaps my inquiries in the city, or my going about, examining places, had been noticed. Perhaps suspicions had been cast upon me by enemies. Perhaps some were angry that I had not had my hair cut for catapult cordage. Perhaps they were jealous of my beautiful hair! But I was a free woman! They could not make me have my hair cut, make me cut my beautiful hair!''

Her hair, now, of course, had been cropped.

I heard a small sound outside the cell, perhaps someone passing in the corridor outside. It must be, I thought, in the neighborhood of noon.

"Continue," I said.

"I grew bold," she said. "I would be rich. I saw Ar's Station, to my satisfaction, grow weaker each day. But when it fell, I would be safe! Too, I would have my vengeance on my enemies!''

"The city, of course, would be likely to be destroyed," I said.

"Either way I would have my vengeance," she said.

"I see," I said.

"Too," she said, "as you may recall, I had reserved my pick of certain women, to be consigned to me as slaves.''

"Personal enemies?" I said.

"Of course," she said.

"Whom you might then sell to men?"

"Yes," she said. "And that pleasure would presumably remain mine even if Ar's Station were burned to the ground, and salt cast upon the ashes!''

"Of course," I said.

"And so I went again to the wall, as I had so many times," she said. "This time the papers hidden in my basket pertained to the defenses at the great gate, the posting of guardsmen, the arrangement of their watches, and such. I put the basket over the wall, through the same crenel, and had begun to lower it. I had even feigned some weakness on the parapet, stumbling a little, as though I might be faint with hunger. I thought that I had acted skillfully. My attention was on the rope and basket. Then I felt the loops of a rope put about my neck, closely, tightly, and I was drawn backward. 'Do not make a noise,' said a voice. But I could not have made a noise, had I wished, so tight was the rope. I had wanted to drop the basket but I had had no opportunity to do so. There were three men. As one man had put his rope on me, making me his prisoner, another had taken the rope from my hands. A third, standing back, had a dark lantern. I had not even heard them approach. It took them only a moment, in the unshuttering of the dark lantern, to rifle beneath the cloth and money in the basket and find the papers. Their nature was immediately determined. I was immediately stripped. The rope which had made me its prisoner was then fastened on my neck as a tether. My clothing was put in the basket and lowered. I gathered that the nature of its message would not be lost on him, or those, below. The rope was then drawn up again and removed from the basket. My arms were then bound tightly to my sides with it, in what seemed a hundred coils. It is hard for me to make clear to you how helpless I felt. I was then drawn to my home, where my money and jewels were found, notes of my next reports and the letter of safety, with the acknowledgement of services. I was then conducted as I was, bound and naked, on a tether, before Aemilianus. I was knelt before him, so. The evidence pertinent to my case, both from the parapet and from my home, was presented before him. That very night, I was put in this cell, as I am."

"And you now await the pleasure of those whom you betrayed," I said.

"Yes," she said. In her voice there was terror.

I heard a sound behind the door, the placing of a pan on a stone.

"And what is your story?" she asked.

"I am a courier of Gnieus Lelius, Regent of Ar," I said, "mistaken for a spy." I was sure that there was significant treachery in Ar, and in high places. The regent's message, I was sure, had been removed from, or had never been inserted in, the letter cylinder. A substitution had been made, doubtless, of the contents of the cylinder or of cylinders themselves. I had not, of course, seen the regent place the message in the cylinder and seal it. There would be nothing unusual in that, of course, for it is not required that couriers be present at such times. Seldom are they privy to the councils of state. Normally they simply receive the sealed letter or closed cylinder, or such, from a subordinate, later, and are on their way.

"No!" she said. "You are lying! You are trying to save yourself! You, too, are a spy!"

"Perhaps," I said.

The observation panel in the door slid back. Lady Claudia quickly hurried forward, to kneel a few feet before the door, back from it, thusly, but in easy view from the panel. "Kneel beside me," she whispered, tensely. "We are fed but once a day!" I saw no one in the observation panel. I remained sitting, as I was. "Kneel beside me," begged Lady Claudia. I then heard something like a stool or platform scrape on the stones outside the door. A moment later I saw a small head rise up behind the panel, that of a child or woman. I could see little, but it seemed to be a delicate head, covered closely with a white, scarflike turban, and I saw deep eyes, and a bit of veil, over the bridge of a fine, delicate nose.

"I see, Lady Claudia," said a woman's voice, from behind the door, amused, "that you will not be so lonely now."

"Glory to Ar!" cried Lady Claudia, frightened, Then she turned to me. "Kneel beside me," she begged, "or we will not be fed!"

I knelt beside her, and the woman behind the door laughed. Then she snarled, "Spies!" I did not think I could get my hand through the panel, it was too narrow. "Glory to Ar," said the woman behind the door.

"Glory to Ar! Glory to Ar! Glory to Ar!" cried Lady Claudia. Then she turned, distraught, to me. I had been silent. "Please!" she begged.

"Glory to Ar," I said, three times.

The woman behind the door laughed.

I wished I had a way to get my hands on her. Her small, turbaned, veiled head then disappeared from behind the opened panel and, a bit later, the low panel slid back and a pan of water was slid partway beneath the door. Lady Claudia went to it and took it back to the right, where she emptied it in a small, shallow cistern in the cell. She then slid it back under the door, and returned to kneel where she had been before. It did not seem probable I could get my hand well through the low portal, to seize an ankle or wrist. It was worth consideration, of course. A male warder, taller, could see through the observation panel, and determine that we were kneeling in our proper places, at the same time that he might shove pans beneath the door with his foot. The woman would, however, would not be tall enough for that.

Her head again appeared behind the panel.

"Food pan forward," she said.

Lady Claudia immediately fetched a shallow pan from the side and put it about five feet in front of where she now again knelt. I gathered she had been well trained in these feeding procedures. Presumably to have put the pan forward earlier, before receiving the order, or permission, would have been regarded as presumptuous, and perhaps have resulted in its remaining empty for the day.

"You are pretty, naked, Lady Claudia," said the voice.

Lady Claudia choked back a sob.

"Glory to Ar!" said the voice behind the door, sternly.

"Glory to Ar!" cried Lady Claudia, three times. I repeated this formula, as well, three times.

The head then disappeared again from the panel. At the same there was a tiny scrape, as of wood on stone, probably from a platform on which she had stood. There was then silence, no sound of pans, or such. I quickly, to the consternation of Lady Claudia, moved to the observation panel and looked through it. I saw the warder going down the corridor. She was barefoot, and wore tatters which barely covered her calves. These tatters appeared to be the remains of what had perhaps once been a double dress, now shortened. The hems of both the inner and outer skirt, doubtless in their shortenings, had been deeply serrated, each in a series of some seven or eight large, triangular points. These points were alternated in such a way that those of the inner skirt appeared between those of the outer skirt. Thus, though the general appearance of the garment suggested rags, they were, in their way, contrived rags. In a way, though she perhaps did not understand this, they invited a man to their removal. Perhaps it was her hope that if the city fell such a garment might save her life, sparing her for the collar. The white, scarflike turban on her head, I supposed, was a vanity, to conceal shortly cropped hair. The veil, of course, was appropriate for a free female. I observed her calves, her bare feet, the cleverly contrived rags she wore. Perhaps she had already rehearsed how she would surrender herself to a man. If the time came, I was sure, stern warder though she might pretend to be, she would submit herself quickly enough and appropriately enough, ending her farce, accepting nudity and a collar, to a master. She bent down and picked up a bucket, and, before she turned back, I left the observation panel and returned to my place.

"Do not leave your kneeling position at such a time," begged Lady Claudia, tears in her eyes.

The head reappeared behind the observation panel and found us in our places. As soon as it left the panel this time I bent down to see if it might be possible to seize her somehow from under the door. But, to my irritation, a pan, into which had been ladled some meal and a piece of bread was thrust beneath the door with a rod. Lady Claudia rushed to the pan and placed the meal and bread in the cell's food pan some five feet in front of her and then replaced the delivery pan half under the door. It was pulled back with the rod. The warder, given that she was a female, had been well taught suitable alterations in the common routines of warders. Doubtless, too, somewhere there were men about, to back her up, if need be. I was angry. I then straightened up in time to be in place when she looked through the panel again. The use of the two pans is not primarily for security as one pan could be used, or an exchange of pans, provided suitable distances between the prisoners and the warders are maintained, but rather to keep pans localized to given cells. This helps to prevent the spread of infections and makes each cell responsible for its own hygiene.

"Please give us more to eat!" cried Lady Claudia.

"You are too fat now," said the warder.

"Please!" begged Lady Claudia.

Lady Claudia, in my opinion, was certainly not fat. On the other hand, it was probably true that she had been better fed than most in Ar's Station, at least prior to her incarceration in the cell, given her former hoarding and the additional food she had obtained at the wall, in the basket.

"Are you afraid your pretty complexion will suffer?" asked the warder.

"Please!" said Lady Claudia. "Please!"

The panel slid shut.

"The she-sleen!" cried Lady Claudia. "How I hate her!" She clenched her fists. "I hate her! I hate her!" she said. She pounded her fists on the stone, the blows softened by the intervening straw. Then she looked dismally, angrily, at the bit of meal and the crust of bread in the pan. "Surely it is their intent to starve me!"

"Us?" I asked.

"Yes, us," she said.

"You are probably being fed as well as most in Ar's Station," I said. The men on the walls, hopefully, would receive more. Yet those I had met had seemed half starved. "Too," I said, "it is not unlike the rations given to new slave girls early in their training period, when they are being taught their dependence on men for their food."

She made an angry noise and stood up. She made as though to move to the pan, but stopped short. "Oh!" she said. My hand had closed about her ankle.

"Get on your belly," I told her.

"What are you doing?" she exclaimed, angrily. She could not advance toward the food.

"Now," I said.

Angrily she went to her belly and I drew her back a foot or two by the ankle. She put out her hands but could not reach the food. I then got up and went to the pan. I picked it up and took it back, toward the back of the cell, where I sat down, cross-legged, the pan before me. She turned about, not daring to leave her belly, to look at me.

"You may approach," I told her. "But do not come close enough to touch the food."

She squirmed forward, desperately.

"Are you hungry?" I asked.

"Yes!" she said.

"Would you like to eat?" I asked.

"Yes!" she said.

"Perform," I said.

"No!" she cried. "I am a free woman!"

"Very well," I said. I paid her no more attention. I fingered some of the meal into my mouth. It was in a glutinous, semisolid glob. It was neither sugared nor salted.

"Please!" she cried. She had not risen from her belly.

"Do you think you are still alone in the cell?" I asked.

"Please!" she begged.

I fingered more of the meal, a good two fingersful, into my mouth.

"I will perform!" she said.

"Stand up," I said, "back a bit, where I may see you." I put the pan to one side, on the straw, on the stone, and looked at her. She was not a woman of Earth. She was a Gorean female, and knew the men of Gor. A woman of Earth, if not beaten, and swiftly forced to learn her womanhood, would doubtless have held out for a time, confident that Gorean men, like those to whom she had become accustomed on her native planet, would prove to be weak, that they would yield to her. They learn, soon enough, however, that the average Gorean male simply does not share the conditioned political conceptions of the female which in so many cases have succeeded in crippling, weakening and demasculinizing the men of Earth. She finds that she is viewed rather in the context of biology and nature. She quickly learns, too, that where women are concerned, and thus where she is concerned, the average Gorean male has a will of iron. She also quickly learns that he has, personally and culturally, the power to enforce this will.

"Stand straight," I said, "the palms of your hands on the sides of your legs."

She did so.

The spy was lovely, though there was a kind of hardness, and nastiness, about her.

"Perform," I said.

"For such performances," I said, "it is hard to believe that the guards would have fed you."

She looked at me, angrily.

"Now," I said, "perform for me, as you did for them."

"Not bad," I said, fingering more of the meal into my mouth. I was, after all, hungry, too. I had not eaten since early morning, at the small tent I had shared with Phoebe. To be sure, Lady Claudia would not have had anything since noon, the day before.

"Please!" she said.

"But I," I said, "am more demanding than the guards. Do you understand?" I put more meal into my mouth.

"Yes!" she said. She then began, again, to try to please me, this time even more desperately. She did not do badly. Then, after a time, I helped her, giving her detailed instructions, putting her, here and there, and about the cell, through detailed woman paces. Then she lay on her belly before me, gasping, covered with sweat. I motioned that she should kneel near me, and I placed her hands on her thighs. I rubbed my hand on her head. The short-cropped hair was wet with sweat. I then, having her lean forward, keeping her hands on her thighs, bit by bit, as I chose, fed her by hand. She would lean forward, eagerly. Sometimes I made her stretch, holding the food just a little out of her reach. Sometimes I had her lick and suck my fingers, too, which she did eagerly enough, that none of the meal would be lost. Then we had finished the bit of meal and bread between us. She knelt back, regarding me reproachfully.

"Stand," I said, "back a bit, where I can see you, straightly, with your hands on the sides of your legs, as you did before."

I then rose up and went to her, and looked at her, walking about her. Then I stood again before her.

I put my hands on her upper arms. "Look at me," I said. She lifted her head.

"You are hard, and petty, and nasty," I said.

She looked up at me, angrily.

"But you are pretty," I said.

She did not respond.

"Yes," I said. "You will do."

" 'Do'?" she said.

"Yes," I said.

"I do not understand." she said.

"Do not tire me," I said. I then flung her back, behind where we had stood, to the straw, and put her to my purposes.

# 13
# FOOD

"My hair," she said, "is grown out more now."

"Yes," I said, rubbing the brush of it near my thigh, where her head rested.

"I want my hair to grow out," she said.

I did not respond.

Chloe looked up at me, from where she lay, beside my thigh. "You have made me soft, and female," she said. "You would have it so, and have had it so. Now I can be no other than that, nor do I desire to be other than that."

"Kiss me," I said.

She did so, softly, obediently, much as might have a slave.

I had given her, for my purposes, the name 'Chloe'. Technically, of course, as she was still a free woman, she was still Lady Claudia of Ar's Station. She had, however, however deceitfully, several days ago upon the wall, lowering her message in the basket, declared for Cos. Accordingly I had given her a Cosian name. It was a lovely name. She responded well to it, psychologically, socially and sexually. Further, she understood the propriety of its having been put on her.

Five days ago the walls of Ar's Station had been breached. Cosians were now within the city. The defenders, sometimes fighting street by street, and building to building, and those who could reach it, had now withdrawn to the citadel, bringing with them what belongings and supplies they could. In the citadel now, hungry and miserable, besides the defenders, were crowded hundreds of women and children. Ar's Station was in flames. Smoke drifted even to our cell.

"What was that?" cried Chloe, leaping up.

I, too, leaped up.

There had been a rumbling crash from somewhere outside the citadel.

"I am not sure," I said.

Later that afternoon there were several more such crashes, all on the land side of the citadel.

"There is another," said Chloe, toward dusk.

"It is Cosians," I said. "They are clearing the ground outside the citadel, destroying the buildings, that they may bring their engines within range."

We heard, from somewhere outside, the long, wild scream of a woman, perhaps from among the buildings, outside the wall.

Chloe looked at me.

"She has been caught," I said.

It had had a sudden wild ring about it, as though she might suddenly, to her dismay, have felt ropes settle about her body, and draw tight.

"I, too, was caught," said Chloe. "And then, later, you, too, caught me. I do not mind having been caught by you. I am pleased to have been caught by you."

I pulled her up beside me, and kissed her. She snuggled into my arms, frightened.

"The slavers are out there, somewhere, aren't they?" she asked.

"Yes," I said.

"With their cages, and chains, and wagons," she said.

"Yes," I said.

"For hundreds of pasangs about," she said, "women will be cheap for months."

"Perhaps," I said.

"I envy them their chains," she said, "especially with what I have learned in your arms."

I put my hand gently on her head. She was still a free woman, and in the keeping of those she had betrayed. Well might she envy those whose fate would be merely a brand, a

collar and the absolute helplessness and submission of Gorean
bondage.

"Many of those captured," I said, "might be shipped to
the islands, Cos, Tyros, Tabor, Asperiche and so on. If that
is the case, they might not depress the market as much as you
feared."

"You are kind," she said.

"Do you wish to be beaten?" I asked.

"No," she said, quickly.

"And many, most, I suspect, of those women of Ar's
Station who had not managed to flee earlier, at the approach
of Cos, or somehow escape the city, are in the citadel."

"There must be hardly room to move in the citadel," she
said.

"Our quarters are doubtless among the most luxurious," I
said.

"Why do they not take us outside and chain us to a post?"
she asked.

"Perhaps that the people not tear us to pieces," I said.

She shuddered. The cell door, now, it seemed, so stoutly
locked, might be serving as much to protect us as confine us.
On the other hand, perhaps most of the people outside did not
even know why we were here. If they did, perhaps they
would have been at the door, trying to force it open.

"The Cosians must not bring their catapults into action, at
this range," she said.

"Why not?" I asked.

"The people," she said. "The crowding. It would be
terrible."

"I see," I said.

"Surely they would not do so," she said.

"I would conjecture that the engines will be in place by
morning," I said.

"But they will not use them!" she said.

"I would expect them to do so," I said, "with stones, and
oil, and javelins."

"There must be little food in the citadel now," she said.

Our rations, small though they were, had been halved. We
were both weak.

"Why do they bother feeding us?" she asked.

"I do not know," I said. I had some idea as to why they

were probably feeding her, at least. I did not, however, want to speak to her of this.

The observation panel in the door slid back. I saw the head of our warder rise up, behind the slot, as she stepped up, onto her platform. She still had the white, scarflike turban and veil. "Prisoners, forward," she said. "Kneel."

We obeyed. It was toward dusk. It was not time to be fed.

"You, Claudia, slave girl," she said. "Kneel behind him and to his left." A slave girl, in heeling her master, commonly follows on the left. That she follows indicates that she is subservient, that he is master and she slave; that she follows on the left is a cultural matter probably indexed to the fact that most Goreans are right-handed. Her presence on the left, thus, is not likely to interfere with his draw or the movements of his sword arm.

"You are pretty, slave girl," snarled the warder to Lady Claudia. "How natural you look there!"

"Yes!" said Lady Claudia to her. "I am a slave girl! He has taught me that I am a slave girl! I know it now!"

"Slave! Slave!" snarled the warder.

Lady Claudia, of course, was not a slave, not a legal slave, at any rate. She was still, legally, a free woman. I had seen no point in imbonding her. Similarly, I had ordered her not to submit herself to me, of her own free will, even when she had begged to do so. In either case, she could have been taken from me easily enough by force, and then freed, to be made again legally susceptible to whatever punishments they wished to visit upon her. To be sure, they might, if they wished, make her a slave themselves, or let her be a slave, either by my action or her own, and then, if she were a slave, do anything they wished with her.

I found it hard to understand the warder's hatred for Lady Claudia. It surpassed anything which seemed rationally connected with her culpability in the matter of espionage. The first time I had used Lady Claudia, the first day I had been in the cell, flinging her to my feet in the straw, I had taken little time with her. Later that afternoon, after I had slept, I had awakened and snapped my fingers. She was over against the far wall, awake, wide-eyed, half covered in the straw, lying on her side, watching me. At my signal she had crawled across the floor, through the straw, and then knelt before me,

her head down, submitted. I had taken her by the arms and
thrown her again to the straw. I had not expected the intensity
and helplessness of her response. Within the Ahn she had
become, in effect, my slave.

That night I gave her the name 'Chloe'. A transformation
had soon become visible in her, over the next two or three
days, in her entire body and personality. The hardness, the
selfishness, the nastiness, the smallness, the pettiness, the
meanness which had so characterized her began to melt away.
In its place she was becoming soft and feminine, delicate and
attentive, eager to please and serve, and loving. At first the
warder was much amused by the imperious and uncompromising treatment to which my fair cellmate found herself
subjected, taking great pleasure in her fate. Sometimes, in the
first day or two, the warder would even watch us, encouraging me and jeering at the helpless, lovely spy. Soon, however, as it became clear that the Lady Claudia was becoming
happier, and more fulfilled and more beautiful her attitudes
changed, dramatically. The warder now began to castigate
her, and subject her to incredible verbal abuse, of the sort to
which free women often subject slave girls. The Lady Claudia, on the other hand, though not even enslaved, did not
seem to mind. She was beginning to understand, dimly, it
seemed, what the nature of bondage might be for a female.
The sterner I was with her the more she seemed to enjoy it.
The stricter I was with her the more she loved it. When I
would cuff her from me she would crawl back to my feet,
kissing them. Treated as a woman, and finding herself in
male power, she would look up at me, with love, awe and
gratitude in her eyes. I scarcely dared conjecture what her
responses might have been, had she known herself truly,
helplessly, imbonded. I had little doubt that she would bring
an excellent price on the slave block.

"Slut! Slut! Slut!" screamed the warder at her. Her hostil-
ity was clearly directed at the Lady Claudia and not me. She
could not stand it, it seemed, that the Lady Claudia, almost
before her eyes, had become beautiful. I regarded Lady Claudia, the "Chloe" of my uses. She had indeed now become
beautiful, wholly and through and through beautiful. She was
now very different from her former self. She could not now
even dream of betraying Ar's Station, or men. Yet her former

self had done so, and her new self, whether in true justice or not, could be held accountable for the action.

"Yes," said Lady Claudia, softly, humbly, then adding, meaningfully, somewhat maliciously perhaps, for she was still a free woman, "—*Mistress*."

The warder cried out in fury and smote on the cell door with her small fists.

"For what purpose have you interrupted us?" I asked the warder.

"I am not speaking to you," she said.

"But I am speaking to you, female," I said.

The head moved angrily, behind the slot. I wished I could reach the veil and pull it away from her, face-stripping her. I wondered if she would be pleasing.

"Do not think that you can escape punishment by pretending to be a slave!" said the warder to Lady Claudia.

"Do not fear, my dear," said Lady Claudia. "I know that I am a legally free woman. I may be in my heart a slave, and I may be kept in this cell, and serve here, as a slave, but I know that I am legally free."

"Do you think the citadel will fall tomorrow," I asked, "or the next day? And do you still wear artful rags, and go barefoot, and display your calves and ankles?"

Her eyes widened. She realized then I must have spied on her through the slot. I knew these secrets about her, whose import must be clear enough to any strong man. Her small brows knit in fury.

"Do you think you will have an opportunity to surrender to a man?" I asked. "Have you practiced how to tear your robes from your breasts, the words with which you will beg to be spared?"

"Sleen!" said the warder.

"I see that you have," I said, "noble free woman."

"Sleen!" she cried.

"Perhaps you would look well, naked," I said, "in a coffle."

"Sleen! Sleen!" she cried.

Lady Claudia laughed merrily.

"Laugh now!" she said. "But I will tell you why I have come. You, Lady Claudia, traitress and slut, have been sentenced by Aemilianus. Tomorrow, at noon, you are to be displayed above the wall, as an act of defiance, impaled!''

Lady Claudia turned white.

"As for you," said the warder, addressing me, "I do not know what is to become of you. Aemilianus, for some reason, seems hesitant about you." The observation panel then slid shut, with a snap.

I caught Lady Claudia, that she not fall.

"I am sorry," I said.

"Is impalement swift?" she asked.

"It need not be," I said.

"I cannot move," she said.

I then lifted her and took her back, and put her gently on the straw.

I was not surprised that Aemilianus was less certain what to do with me. My own case, in his mind, must seem somewhat ambiguous. Why, for example, would I not have been dealt with directly in Ar, if they were convinced that I was truly a spy? Too, there was the matter of the documents in the diplomatic pouch. Were they really spurious, and had they really been intended to bring about the surrender of Ar's Station why would they not have been more realistically conceived, that they might have been more likely to achieve such a purpose? For example, why would they not have been in some cipher, one which might, after a reasonable effort, be broken? Too, why would such a purportedly authentic document contain information which must surely, at least to the officers at Ar's Station, seem militarily implausible, if not preposterous, for example, that Ar should have forces in the numbers named in the north, and unengaged! No, Aemilianus, weary and confused as he might be, was no fool. Doubtless he had begun to suspect that the report, though perhaps absurd or false, was authentic. Too, days had passed and the hoped-for relief from Ar, the advance of which he had speculated might have precipitated so desperate and foolish a ruse, had not materialized.

"It is terribly painful, impalement, is it not?" she asked.

"It depends on how it is done," I said.

"I am a traitress," she said.

"Once," I said. "No longer."

"I am afraid," she said.

I kissed her, gently. I wished I had something to cover her with.

"There is no hope," she whispered.

"There is always hope," I said.

"You are kind," she said.

"Do you wish to be beaten?" I asked.

"No," she smiled.

"There is hope," I said.

"How?" she asked.

"It is quiet outside," I said.

"Yes?" she said.

"You have not now, for some time, heard the crashing of buildings," I said. "Cos has the city now. There is nothing to keep them from undermining the foundations, firing the buildings, clearing paths through debris."

"I do not understand," she said.

"They have finished their work," I said.

"I do not understand," she said.

"The engines are probably in place," I said.

She looked at me, frightened.

"I would expect the attack to begin in the morning," I said.

"I am afraid," she said.

"I will defend you, as I can," I said. "They will have to enter the cell to fetch you out."

"Do not risk your life for me," she said.

"Why not?" I asked.

"Because I am really only a slave girl," she said.

"It is for such that men most cheerfully risk their lives," I said.

"Oh?" she smiled.

"Certainly," I said. "You would not expect them to go to all that trouble for a mere free female, would you?"

"Monster," she said.

"And if you save her," I pointed out, "you can often keep her."

"I see," she smiled.

"The slave girl, after all," I said, "is good for something. She has her uses. You can even sell her."

She laughed.

"Enough free women, too, in their time," she said, "have doubtless been sold."

"Yes," I said. "They can be captured, bound and turned over to a slaver, and such."

"Had you captured me, somewhere, as a free woman, would you have sold me?" she asked.

"I might have kept you that evening in my tent," I said, "to see what you could do."

"I wish that we had met under different conditions," she said, "in the fields, or in my own bed."

I did not speak.

"If you had first met me in a slave market, I on a slave shelf or bench, chained there, a property, waiting to be purchased, would you have considered buying me?"

"Certainly," I said.

"Am I that attractive?" she asked.

"Yes," I said.

"That pleases me," she whispered. Then she shuddered. "But woe," she said, "I am a free woman."

"Yes," I said.

"I am afraid," she said.

I held her more closely to me.

"That is why they have been feeding me, isn't it?" she asked. "For tomorrow?"

"I think so," I said.

She sobbed, against me. I felt her tears on my chest. Then, suddenly, she looked at me, concerned. "But what of you?" she asked.

"Do not concern yourself with me," I said.

"No," she said, "what of you?"

"Willful free woman," I chided her.

"What of you?" she pressed.

"I do not know," I said. "I am not sure."

She put her head back, against my shoulder. The moonlight streamed in through the high, barred aperture. It was quiet outside. I held her in my arms, for a time, the naked spy, in the straw.

"Am I to be beaten tonight?" she asked.

"Is it necessary?" I asked.

"No!" she whispered.

"You are eager to serve, and be pleasing?" I asked.

"Yes!" she said.

"Then it does not seem that there would be much point in it," I said.

"No!" she hastened to assure me. "But if you were not pleased, you would, wouldn't you?" she asked.

"Yes," I said, "or if I wished to do so."

She shuddered against me, with pleasure. "I wish," she said, her voice soft, thrilled, vibrant with soft, frightened emotion, "that I had met a man such as you, long ago."

"Had you done so," I said, "you presumably would not be here now."

"I do not regret having known you, and having served you, and as you have made me serve you, even under these circumstances."

"You enjoy serving," I said.

"Yes," she said, "I do, and had I the choice I would choose to have no choice but to serve, and serve as you have made me serve, totally."

"It is time to go to sleep," I said.

"Can you sleep at this time, on this night?" she asked.

"Yes," I said.

She then lay down in the straw, next to me. I heard her sob.

"I do not know if they will feed you in the morning or not," I said, "before they come for you, near noon. They might. In the event they do, do not eat the food. Give it all to me."

"All of it?" she asked.

"Yes," I said.

"You would take the food, that food?" she asked.

"Yes," I said.

"You could do that?" she asked.

"Yes," I said.

She looked at me, puzzled.

"Surely you recognize that I would get more good out of it than you would," I said.

"Undoubtedly," she said, shuddering.

"Certainly," I said.

"I do not think I would be able to eat it, anyway," she said.

"Good," I said. "Then there is no problem."

"No," she said. "There is no problem."

"Excellent," I said. I then, in a moment or two, I cannot well remember it, was asleep.

# 14
# MORNING

"They are going to come for me before noon," she whispered.

The cell was in darkness.

"I know," I said. "I heard."

A few Ehn ago I had awakened instantly, hearing the movement of the observation panel. The warder had lifted a small, tharlarion-oil lamp to the aperture.

"Prisoner Claudia, forward," she had whispered.

Lady Claudia had gone forward to kneel, before the door, dimly illuminated in the tiny bit of light coming through the aperture.

I had pretended to be asleep.

I conjectured it was something like an Ahn before dawn.

"Glory to Ar!" whispered the warder.

"Glory to Ar," moaned Lady Claudia. I do not think she had slept.

I then saw, in the light of the lamp, which had then been set on the floor outside the lower panel, the water pan put beneath the door. This was emptied into the small cistern by Lady Claudia, and the pan returned to the warder.

"Is he awake?" inquired the warder.

"I do not think so," said Lady Claudia.

"Food pan forward," said the warder.

In a moment Lady Claudia knelt behind the cell's food pan, brought forward.

"Glory to Ar!" whispered the warder.

"Glory to Ar," sobbed Lady Claudia.

I think that the whispered tones of the warder were motivated primarily by her desire that Lady Claudia obtain her food and finish her feeding before I might awaken. In this fashion I might not take the food from her, or force her to share it. Perhaps she even expected her to be drawn out of the cell before I awakened, that I might awaken and simply find her gone. That might be easiest for them. Still I expected they would send two or three men to fetch her.

Lady Claudia was now again kneeling before the cell's food pan, and the head of the warder, again holding the tiny lamp up, reappeared in the observation aperture.

"See?" asked the warder, whispering. "There is much more food there than usual, and meat!"

Lady Claudia looked down at the pan, in the dim light.

"Spread your knees!" suddenly hissed the warder.

Lady Claudia, startled, frightened, did so.

"There now," said the warder, amusement in her voice, "that is like the slave girl you are!"

Lady Claudia, interestingly, made no move to draw her knees back together. Rather she knelt there in that profoundly meaningful, indicative and vulnerable position, looking up at the warder. The food pan, which for once seemed amply filled, was before her, now almost as though framed between her knees.

"You and I know that you are really a slave, don't we?" asked the warder. "But we will not tell the men, will we?"

Lady Claudia said nothing.

"Do you know why you are fed so heartily?" she asked.

"It is a kindness to me," she said.

"No," laughed the warder. "It is to build up your strength so that you will squirm well on the impaling spear."

Lady Claudia looked at her, doubtless with horror.

"We want you to put on a good show for your Cosian friends," said the warder. "You may even last two or three Ahn."

Lady Claudia shuddered. In such an impalement, the female is usually simply set upon the spear. It is not necessary to bind them, as, straightened, they cannot reach the spear nor obtain any leverage for removing themselves from it. They are held upon it, helplessly, by their own weight.

Usually such a fate is visited only upon a free woman. It is thought that it gives them time to consider and repent their ways. A slave girl, on the other hand, would be more likely, like meat, to be thrown to sleen.

"I heard them talking," said the warder. "They are going to come for you before noon, too. Perhaps they will come as soon as it is well light. I do not know, nor do you. Do you have six Ahn, or three, or two? Tremble within your cell, waiting to hear them come for you! When you hear the small sounds outside the door you will know they are here. When you see the door open you will know they have come for you! Eat well, naked spy!" The observation panel then slid shut with a click. I also heard the small latch drop into place, securing it, so that it could not be opened from the inside.

"They are going to come for me before noon," she had whispered, having crawled to my side.

"I know. I heard," I had told her.

"I wanted to bid you farewell," she said.

"Bring me the food," I said.

"Of course," she said, bitterly.

She turned about and crawled back toward the center of the cell where, feeling about, she located the pan of food. She then lifted it and rose up, and came back, slowly, feeling her way with her feet, through the straw.

"Why will they not wait at least until noon?" she asked, in misery.

"It is a good sign," I said. "It is a very good sign." I did not explain this to her, but from so small a detail I gathered some estimate of the straits of the defenders, and the numbers and positions of the Cosians, and the menace of their engines.

"I do not understand," she said.

"We are on the cityside of the citadel, are we not?" I asked.

"Yes," she said. Even had we been brought to the cell blindfolded, there would have been no difficulty in making this determination. It was clear in the patterns of sunlight in the cell, that the cell faced south, the city. Too, even more obviously, we could hear the sounds of the city, and not of the harbor. Indeed, of late, we had even heard the sounds of collapsed buildings, some of them perhaps within a hundred yards of us.

"That is it," I said.

"I do not understand," she said.

"It is possible that you will soon be in greater danger from Cosians than from your compatriots of Ar's Station."

"You're joking," she said.

"That is why they will not be waiting until noon."

"I do not understand," she said.

"I do not even know if the citadel can stand until noon."

"That is absurd," she said. "It is impregnable."

"No," I said. "The defenders are worn and half starved. The buildings about the citadel have been brought down. The engines can fire at almost point-blank range. All the might of Cos in the north will be focused on this one small point, the citadel."

"What will happen?" she asked.

"The women and children will already have been moved to the harbor side of the citadel," I said.

"What will happen!" she said.

"The citadel will be taken," I said. "Cosians will enter, with fire and sword. The noncombatants, the able-bodied men, the soldiers, the garrison, what's left of it, will then be forced to withdraw to the wharves and piers. Then they will be driven from them. I fear there will be great slaughter in and about the harbor. Perhaps few will escape."

"Surely terms will be sought," she said.

"The Cosians have waited long for Ar's Station," I said. "Doubtless they never guessed the resistance they would meet. They have lost many men. Their patience is at an end."

"It is my fault," she said. "Better that I had been what I rightfully should have been, a slave girl."

"It is not your fault," I said. "I doubt that your pittance of treachery made any difference whatsoever. It is the fault of Ar."

"But I am guilty," she said.

"Yes," I said, "and for your crime perhaps a reduction to bondage would be fitting. Too, given what you are, I think that such a fate would be quite appropriate for you."

"It is true," she whispered, "—Master."

I then turned my attention to the pan of food. "There is much food here," I said, "and meat. I doubt that even those at the central crenels, those on the towers, those defending the gate itself, feed as well this morning."

"But you are only putting it to your lips," she said.

"I am tasting it," I said.

"Why?" she asked.

"It seems good," I said.

"What is your concern?" she asked.

"It is nothing," I said.

"What?" she asked.

"I thought they might have entered something into the food," I said, "in kindness, a painkiller, something with an analgesic effect, to ease your pain."

"If they have," she said, "I would appreciate a little food."

"But they have not," I said. "Apparently it is true, as our charming warder told you, that they want you to squirm well on the spear."

She shuddered.

"They see no reason in encouraging espionage," I said.

"No," she whispered.

I then fed lustily. Strength flooded into my body. I had not eaten so well for days. Too, I had the girl, in effect, my girl, bring me water.

"That was good," I said.

"How is it that you can eat at a time like this?" she asked.

"You must keep up your hope," I said.

"I am a naked female," she said. "Men can do with me what they want."

"True," I said, "but it may not be the case that every man wants to do exactly the same thing to you at exactly the same time."

"I suppose not," she said.

"And therein lies your hope," I said.

"What hope have I," she asked, "other than they might put me on the spear a little later, rather than a little sooner?"

"I think you have more than you know," I said.

"How?" she asked.

"You have unexpected allies," I said.

"Who?" she asked.

"Outside," I said. "Cosians."

"How can they help?" she asked.

"Perhaps they can't," I said. "It is only a possibility."

"I think it is near dawn now," she whispered. There seemed a narrow fringe of lightness in the darkness, at the edge of the high window. We looked up at it. We could not reach the window, even if she were to stand on my shoulders.

"I think you are right," I said.

"Oh!" she cried, startled, and threw herself into my arms. She looked up at me, wildly, frightened.

"It is the trumpets," I said. "They signal the attack."

There were answering trumpets from the walls.

There had been a great, ringing blare of trumpets from outside, perhaps hundreds of them. The response from the wall, in comparison, brave though it might have been, had seemed frail, indeed. When the trumpets had rung out there had been, too, from before the citadel, raised the war cries of thousands of men. These cries, too, had been answered, by a ragged cheer from the walls. She looked up at me, half kneeling, half lying in my arms, in the darkness of the cell. A naked woman feels good in one's arms. I wished I owned her. They feel even better when you own them, and they know you own them.

We then heard a dull impact, from a distance.

"What is that?" she asked, alarmed.

There were then two more sounds, much like the first.

"Come here," I said, and pulled her, on her side to the outside wall, and lay in the straw on the floor there. It is safer there, where the floor, like a buttress, reinforces the wall. You are safer there, too, from showering stone, bursting inward.

"It is the artillery," she said.

"Yes," I said.

We could hear, too, from time to time, the sound of the kick and rattle, and vibration of cordage, of a catapult above us, on the walls. They are often roped down. Otherwise they can radically change their position, spinning half about, or even, literally, flinging themselves back off the walkway. They are easier to manage on softer surfaces, where the wheels can be dug in.

"You are covering my body with your own," she said.

"Be quiet," I whispered to her.

"You are protecting me," she said. "You are sheltering me. You are a true gentleman! You pretend not to be, but you are a true gentleman! Oh! No! What are you doing? I am on my belly! Only a slave is had in this position! No! Oh! Oh!"

"Do you still think I am a gentleman?" I inquired.

"No," she said.

"What am I then?" I asked.

"My master," she said.

"But you are a free woman," I reminded her.

"Yes," she wept. "I am a free woman."

I continued then, for a time, to shelter her body. I was pleased that I was now more relaxed. I had enjoyed myself, but, too, my use of her, and as one might make use of a slave for such a purpose, had been a calculated one, to combat the waiting, the fear, the worry, the anticipation, the expectation, spread over Ahn. That sort of thing can gnaw at you. There is an optimum point for readiness and action. It was at that point that I wished to be when the door opened. We heard, more and more frequently, the impact of stones about us. Two assaults were forced back from the walls. When it grew lighter, and I feared they might soon come for her, I left her at the outside wall, and went to my former place in the straw, and lay there. The food pan I put back, a few feet before the door, where it could be seen through the observation panel. Its contents were now gone. I myself lay in the straw, perhaps too weak to move.

# 15
# WE LEAVE THE CELL

"Come, come, little vulo," said the man, "do not be shy."
He beckoned, coaxingly, to Lady Claudia, who was still near
the outside wall, crouching there now, in the straw, numb
with fear. I did not even know if she could stand. In his left
hand he carried several coils of rope, and a leash and collar.
She regarded him with horror. "Come, come," he said,
advancing past me, lying in the straw. There were two others,
with set crossbows, in their hands, standing within the cell,
rather to the right of the door, as one would face it from the
inside. At the door stood our warder.

I did not think the fellow with the rope really wanted to
approach the far wall, the outside wall, or weather wall, too
closely. From time to time we could hear, and sometimes
feel, through the floor, the impact of the Cosian projectiles,
the great stones, some of which would weigh a thousand
pounds or more, flung by mighty catapults, some the size of
houses. We could hear, too, as though far off, the rhythmical
shock of the battering ram at the gate, where men toiled at the
hundred ropes, beneath the long shedlike roof which protected them and the ram.

"We do not want to stay here too long," said the warder to
the fellow with the rope. "It is dangerous on this side.
Hurry!"

"Come here," said the fellow to Lady Claudia. "Kneel
here, straightly, up, off your heels, your arms at your sides."

"Please!" begged Lady Claudia.

"Hurry!" snapped the warder.

I think the fellow did not much care to be the object of adjurations by such as the warder. I think he would have preferred to have found her not in a position of authority, small though her authority might be, but rather in a position more fitting for her, one more appropriate, too, to her sex and nature, say, naked on her belly, at his feet, subject to his kicks and whip. He said nothing, however. Rather, angrily, summoning up his courage, he went quickly to the Lady Claudia, seized her by the scrub of her hair and drew her, she half crawling, half being dragged, to the center of the cell, and knelt her there, in the position he had specified.

The warder laughed.

Did the fellow not know the Lady Claudia was a free woman? It seemed to me he handled her rather roughly, given that she was free. She was not, after all, a slave girl.

The rope, then, in coil after coil, was wrapped about the Lady Claudia. It was in this fashion, I had gathered, from her own account of her capture, that she had been bound on the wall, and brought before Aemilianus. This touch was doubtless intended to remind her of the events of that evening.

"Make it tight!" said the warder.

Lady Claudia winced as the ropes were drawn about her.

"Now the leash and collar!" said the warder.

In a moment, then, the leash and collar were fastened on her. She then knelt there, in the center of the cell, heavily bound, collared, the leash dangling down before the ropes bound about her.

"Splendid!" said the warder.

Tears ran down Lady Claudia's cheeks. She looked at me, and smiled. She pursed her lips a little, kissing softly, almost imperceptibly, at me. I watched, lying in the straw, my eyes half closed. I did not respond to her tiny, pathetic gesture. It interested me, however, that she bore me no ill will. Had I not led her to believe that I might be of assistance to her? Had I not tried to keep up her courage? But I realized now she had never expected me, really, in the moment of truth, so to speak, to act. It would be pointless.

"How touching!" said the warder.

I made as though to try to rise, to my knees, my head down. It seemed I could not manage this.

"Remain where you are," said one of the fellows with a crossbow.

"He is too weak to do anything," said the warder. "He cannot even stand." She then went to stand before Lady Claudia. "The spear, my dear Claudia," she said, "is a single piece of solid, polished metal. It is very long, and less than a hort thick. It is tapered to a point. It fits in a mount."

Lady Claudia knelt there, with her eyes closed.

I made as though, again, to try to rise. One of the guards looked at me, and then looked away.

"Glory to Ar!" snarled the warder.

"Glory to Ar," wept Lady Claudia.

"Do you know what we are waiting for?" asked the warder of Lady Claudia.

"No," whispered Lady Claudia.

There was then a sudden impact somewhere on the wall, perhaps not seventy-five feet from where we were.

"That was close," said one of the guards, uneasily.

As I had expected they would, they had more to worry about than what went on in the cell.

Again I struggled to my knees. This time I remained there, head down, as though unable to move.

"Stay where you are," said one of the guards. I was about seven or eight feet from him.

"We are waiting for the executioner to come for you," said the warder, delightedly. "He will come to fetch you, and take you to the wall, to the spear."

Lady Claudia put down her head.

"Glory to Ar!" cried the warder.

"Glory to Ar," said Lady Claudia. She had her eyes closed. That, I thought, was fortunate. The nearest guard looked at me, and then glanced back to the two women. The guards had been in the cell some time, at least a few Ehn. This, I had thought, would put them at their ease. The expectation of resistance, of course, is at its height early. If it were to rise again, which I did not really expect, or not significantly, under the current circumstances, presumably that would be shortly before their departure from the cell. They were now awaiting the arrival of the executioner, who was to fetch Lady Claudia to the spear. Their expectation of resistance, now, I thought, might be at its low. To be sure, that is an excellent time to be particularly prepared. Yet it is impossible to maintain an attitude of full alertness for an extended period of time. It is psychologically impossible. This meant that the initiative, in this situation, was mine. If they had expected resistance, of course, they might have thought, appropriately enough, that I might choose to act before the arrival of the executioner, as that would mean an additional fellow to deal with.

I had not, of course, realized that the executioner would come to the cell. If I had given the matter much thought, I would have supposed that he, or they, would wait on the wall. Such customs, I supposed, would differ from city to city. I was not pleased to hear about the pending arrival of the executioner, of course, as that might set me an additional problem, one I had not anticipated and one I certainly did not welcome.

It was not a mistake that I had lain in the straw where I had. I had, the day before, found a ridge in the stones there which would give me leverage, something to push away from. Too, I was barefoot. I would not slip. I lifted my head, dully, as though groggily, to look at the guards. They were half starved. Their reflexes, I was sure, would be slow. They would not have their full strength. The nearest guard looked at me, again, and I returned his gaze, dully. He then glanced back at the women once more.

"He is very skilled at his work," said the warder to Lady Claudia. "He will put you on the spear so gently that you will last a long time."

Lady Claudia kept her eyes closed, and she shuddered.

"But if he wants to hurry a little," said the warder, "he will tie weights on your legs."

Lady Claudia sobbed.

"How pretty you look, kneeling there, my dear, all tied up, and in your collar," she said. "Do not fret. He will be here soon! You will then be taken to the spear! You do not have long to wait! You will look amusing, wriggling on it! Glory to Ar! Glory to Ar!"

"Glory to Ar!" wept Lady Claudia.

At that instant I lunged forward and the nearest guard had

barely time to turn his head before I caught him, and his fellow, taking them together, striking them with great force, I sprinting, thrusting, they off balance, and blasted them back, one loosened, sprung quarrel skittering about the room like a frightened animal, the other smote from the guide into the straw, against the wall, and I snarled, the noise not in that moment seeming human, and it was the terribleness of the warrior's exhilaration that was that instant in my heart, nostrils and mouth, and, one with each hand, struck back their heads against the stone. Had they not been helmeted their brains would have been on the stone.

In the same moment I had freed the sword of one of them and I turned, crouching, snarling, to face the man near Lady Claudia. His face was white. Perhaps I seemed then to him more beast than man. I did not take my eyes from him. I was one who had fought Kurii and lived. I was between him and the door. The warder, cut off, too, from the door, had fled behind him. He weakly half drew his sword but before it could clear the sheath I was upon him, within his guard. He released the hilt. The blade fell back, into the sheath. I turned and kicked back and he grunted, collapsing. The warder bolted for the door but I caught her at the portal by the back of the neck and lifted her up and turned, and then flung her stumbling back toward the far wall. I then returned to the fallen warrior, and bent over him. He was gasping. His eyes were wild. Not taking my eyes from the warder, who now crouched down, against the outside wall, her eyes wide with terror over the veil, I seized him by the back of the neck, below the helmet, and lifted his head a few inches from the floor. He could offer no resistance. I then struck his head, back, in the helmet, on the stones.

"You have killed them, you have killed them all!" said the warder.

"No," I said. The first two had been in the greatest danger, but their helmets had saved them. It was not that I had lost control of myself in the rush of that first moment. I had not. It was rather that, in the exigencies of the situation, it had not been my intention to take any chances with them. But their helmets had saved them.

"Lie down," I said to the warder, "on your belly, in the

straw, your head to the wall. Spread your legs as widely as you can. Cover your head with your hands and arms."

She sobbed, but did so. In this fashion she could not see what might transpire behind her, she could not easily rise, and she would have some protection from debris, if the outside of the cell wall should be struck.

I then stripped the clothing and accouterments from the fellow I had just struck, and donned them. I did, however, exchange swords, removing his from its scabbard and placing therein the one I had taken from the other guard. It was a looser fit, which pleased me.

There was an impacting on the side of the citadel, some hundred or so feet away. I could feel the jar, however, through the floor. The warder, over by the wall, moaned, her hands and arms over her head. I then put the three guards together, in a corner of the cell, and heaped straw over them. They could not be seen from the observation panel.

I then turned to the Lady Claudia who still knelt as she had been placed. Her eyes were wide. There must have been fifty coils of rope wound tightly about her fair person. On her neck was the collar; from it dangled the leash.

"Greetings," I said.

"You must flee!" she whispered. "Save yourself! I am known! Do not concern yourself for me!"

I removed the leash and collar from her.

"Do not stop for me!" she begged. "Flee!"

I began to remove the rope from her.

"The executioner may arrive at any moment," she said, miserably.

"He is more likely to think I am binding you, than unbinding you," I said.

She moaned.

Then she was free of the rope. I looked at her, closely, as a master at a slave, and she shrank back. I saw that, indeed, she would bring a high price in a slave market.

"You must leave me behind!" she said.

"You are too pretty to leave behind," I said.

She looked at me, wildly, elatedly.

"Yes," I said.

She laughed, and smiled at me, through tears. "I am pleased if master finds me pleasing," she whispered.

"Where did you ever hear talk like that?" I asked.

"I once heard a slave girl speak so to her master," she said.

"And what did you do then?" I asked.

"I ran home to my bed," she said, "to strike it with my fists, and to weep and squirm with frustration."

"Such words are appropriate for you, too, to say," I said.

"I know!" she said. "I know!"

I looked in the fellow's wallet, which I now wore at my belt. There was, as I had hoped, a crust of bread in it. Such things, in Ar's Station, in these days, might be kept in such places. It might be his secret horde, or day's ration. It was probably worth more to him than gold. I gave it to Lady Claudia and she, with two hands, gratefully, thrust it in her mouth, crumbs at the side of her mouth. "Look in the pouches of those other fellows, too," I said. "They might have some food. If so, eat it. Then come join me."

Quickly she did as she was told. It amused me to see with what alacrity she sprang up to do my bidding. It was as though, suddenly, she was a new person.

I then went to stand near our warder, lying on her stomach in the straw, her head to the wall, her legs spread, her head covered with her hands and arms. Aware of my approach she widened her legs further. This pulled her artfully contrived rags, with their points, higher on her legs. I noted that she had excellent calves and ankles.

"There is food here," called Lady Claudia, softly, elatedly, from where she crouched, near the guards.

"Good," I said. "Eat it."

She thrust the bit of food into her mouth, feeding on it like a voracious little animal. She fed with the eagerness of a half-starved slave girl.

I looked down at the warder. "Put your legs together," I said, "and your arms at your sides, palms up."

She obeyed.

I then crouched down, beside her.

She moved, uneasily, but kept position.

"These rags," I said, "are doubtless contrived in such a way that they may easily be removed."

She squirmed in anger.

I did not touch them, however.

I pulled back the warder's scarflike turban which, I had assumed, was worn to cover and hide a closely cropped head. "Oh!" she said. To my surprise, however, her hair, loosened from under the turban, would have, had she been standing, fallen well beneath her shoulders.

"Oh," said Lady Claudia, interested, come now to my side, a piece of crust in her hand.

"Yes," I said. "Her hair has not been cropped."

The warder squirmed a little, angrily.

"As I recall," I said to Lady Claudia, "you had not had yours cut either."

"No," said Lady Claudia, smiling. "I did not want it cut. I was too vain. I was too proud of it. I thought it too pretty to cut. Too, I did not want my appearance impaired. I did not want to look like one of those girls who carries water in a quarry, or works in a mill or laundry, in the heat. Let other women sacrifice their hair, not me. But when I was caught on the wall it was cut quickly enough."

"Then as a punishment," I said.

"Doubtless," she said, "but, too, they had need of catapult cordage."

"What is your name, prisoner?" I asked our warder.

" 'Prisoner'?" she said.

"Yes," I said.

"Publia," she said.

"Are you free?" I asked.

"Of course!" she said.

"You will forgive me," I said, "but the most common brand sites are covered by your rags."

"Do you think," I asked Lady Claudia, "that Lady Publia's motivations in the matter of keeping her hair were similar to yours?"

"I suppose so," said Lady Claudia, finishing the bit of bread.

"And you are probably correct," I said, "but there was one other, too, perhaps, which had not occurred to you?"

The prisoner moved a little, angrily.

"What was that?" asked Lady Claudia.

But I addressed a question to our prone captive. "What is your caste?" I asked.

"The Merchants," she said.

"That, on the whole, is a quite well-to-do caste," I said.

"It is mine, too," said Lady Claudia.

I jerked the pouch from the prisoner's belt, breaking the strings. It was a weighty pouch. I tossed it to Lady Claudia, who examined its contents.

"There is much gold here," she said.

"Put it in my pouch," I said.

Lady Claudia did so.

"How is it, Lady Publia," I asked, "that you, a member of the Merchants, and one who until a moment ago had a heavy purse, are barefoot, and clad in rags?"

She did not respond.

"And such artful rags?" I asked.

She did not answer.

I fingered them. "I doubt that you sewed these yourself," I said. "They were probably done by a Cloth Worker. Consider the stitching, the tightness of the stitches, its regularity and fineness. It seems very professional. Doubtless though it was done according to your directions. The outfit is calculated to give the appearance of rags but, upon close examination, we discover it is more in the nature of a costume." I smiled inwardly. Slave girls, too, I knew, occasionally practiced such wiles with their brief, scandalous ta-teeras, supposedly mere rags, befitting their degraded status. Yet I knew they often labored on such rags in such a way as to show an inch here, and conceal an inch there, in such a way that a masterpiece of sensitivity, vulnerability and provocation was achieved. By such means and many others do the luscious, loving, collared little brutes save themselves many a beating and drive their masters half mad with passion and desire.

"I congratulate you," I said. "The entire ensemble, the points and such, and the varying lengths thusly achieved, and the consequent, now-and-then baring of your calves, and such, is extremely well done. The entire essemble reveals marvelous imagination and exquisite taste."

The prisoner made a small, pleased noise.

"The question remains, of course, as to why you might do such a thing."

She lay very quietly, not moving.

"The question may be easily enough decided, of course," I said, "by seeing whether or not these garments, unlike the garments of free women, can be easily, swiftly and provocatively removed, and, say, whether or not, in the typical fashion of free women, even of the lower castes, you are wearing underrobes.''

Her small fists clenched in fury.

''Accordingly,'' I said, ''rise up on your knees, and turn and face me.''

She did so, in fury.

Then her fury turned to fear, timidity and docility as I held her veil. I drew it toward me, gently. Instantly she fell forward, to all fours, to relieve pressure on the veil, to keep it on her. Her eyes were now wild over it, it held out from her. ''No,'' she said, ''please do not take my veil.''

''I shall not do so,'' I said.

She gasped with relief.

''Lady Claudia will do so,'' I said.

Tears brimmed in her eyes.

''Surely you have looked upon her, unveiled,'' I said.

The prisoner sobbed.

''Stay on all fours,'' I cautioned her. In this way she would be unable to interfere. Too, she could not put her hands before her face.

The prisoner sobbed, and trembled.

''Remove the veil, carefully,'' I cautioned Lady Claudia. I had my reasons for not wanting it damaged.

''Please, no!'' begged the prisoner.

The veil was fastened with a string and Lady Claudia, with two hands, lifted it gently from the head of our prisoner.

''She is beautiful!'' said Lady Claudia.

''Please do not look at my lips!'' sobbed the prisoner. But my hand was in her hair, holding her head up.

''She has excellent lips,'' I said. ''Properly trained, she could probably kiss well.''

''How beautiful she is!'' breathed Lady Claudia.

''No more beautiful than you,'' I said.

''Truly?'' asked Lady Claudia.

''Yes,'' I said.

Lady Claudia caught her breath for an instant, suspecting then, perhaps, how attractive she herself might be.

''You may kneel back,'' I told the prisoner, releasing her hair.

She lost no time in scrambling back to her kneeling position, and put her two hands before her face.

"Put your hands down," I said.

"I do not have my veil!" she said.

Her lips, her mouth, her features, in all their expressiveness, with all their delicacy, sensuousness and beauty, it was true, should she lower her hands, would be bared. They would be exposed. One could look upon them, even idly. She had been face-stripped. Her face was now naked, as much so as that of a slave.

"Now," I said.

She lowered her hands, sobbing.

I had denied her the delicacy, the modesty, the shield and defense of the veil, just as it is denied to slaves.

"Did you not expect to tear off your veil before Cosians?" I asked.

She looked at me, angrily.

"I see you did," I said.

"One grows used to being without the veil," said Lady Claudia.

"Slave!" cried Lady Publia.

"I am as free as you!" retorted Lady Claudia.

"In the south," I said, "the women of the Wagon Peoples, even the free women, do not wear veils."

"Slave!" cried Lady Publia again to Lady Claudia.

"My face is no more naked than yours!" retorted Lady Claudia.

"Naked face!" cried Lady Publia.

"Naked face!" responded Lady Claudia.

"On the other hand," I said, "the free women of the Wagon Peoples do wear clothes."

Lady Publia looked at me, suddenly, sharply.

"Those are pretty rags," I said.

She said nothing.

"Remove them," I told her.

Angrily Lady Publia removed the belt from her waist. It was a sturdy belt, flat, white, woven of ropelike material, quite capable of supporting the purse she had carried. It was, however, a hook-fastened belt. And she had unhooked it in an instant and, thus, freed, it fell back, behind her. She then, angrily, put her hands to the sides of her garment, up about the neck. It was a wraparound garment. She undid one hook there and, in fury, with her two hands, swiftly, easily, insolently, gracefully, slipped the garment away.

"Ah," said Lady Claudia, softly, admiringly.

Lady Publia straightened her body, pleased.

"Did you notice how she could do that, on her knees?" I asked Lady Claudia. "The garment is designed to allow that. You could perhaps imagine the difficulty of getting out of the customary robes of concealment while on your knees."

"She is so beautiful," said Lady Claudia.

"You removed your garment well, Lady Publia," I said. "Doubtless you have practiced it many times. If I were a Cosian, however, I think you would have done it somewhat less insolently."

"Doubtless," she said.

"Under different circumstances," I said, "and if we had more time, it might be interesting to put you in a bit of slave silk, and teach you how to disrobe properly before a man."

She tossed her head.

"What formulas had you in mind to use to the Cosians?" I asked.

"I do not know what you are talking about," she said.

"Doubtless you rehearsed them well," I speculated.

She looked at me, angrily.

"Yes," I smiled. "I am sure you did."

"Formulas?" asked Lady Claudia.

" 'I bare my breasts before you. Make me a slave,' 'I surrender to you, naked. Spare me. I beg bondage,' 'I have endeavored to conceal my true nature from men, that I am a slave. Visit justice upon me,' 'I have stripped myself before you. Let me live, that I may serve you as the most abject and loving of slaves,' and such sayings," I said.

"Such sayings stir my belly," said Lady Claudia.

"That is because it is the belly of a slave!" snapped Lady Publia.

"It would be easy enough to tell," I said, "if your belly, too, is that of a slave. I need only place my hand on you, and have you say such things, slowly, deeply and with feeling."

She regarded me with horror.

"But you are, of course, a free woman," I said.

"Yes!" she said. "Yes!"

I saw then the nature of her belly, that she feared it would betray her.

"Had you never considered such sayings?" I asked Lady Claudia.

"Yes," she said, smiling, "often, but I had never really thought of them in such a formal way."

"But you never dared to kneel naked before a man, and say such things?"

"No," she said, shyly. "I was much afraid. Bondage is a great step for a woman. It is so absolute, and different. It is natural for her to fear it. And now that I long to do so, he who is to me as master has forbidden it. It seems he wants to keep me as a free woman, at least for a time, for some reason."

That was true. I had my reasons.

"What did you expect to do," I asked, "if, say, Cosians, or others, in darkened buildings or flaming streets, came upon you?"

"I had thought I would have had my letter of safety," she said.

"Do you think looting soldiers would have stopped to read your letter?" I asked.

"Perhaps not," she smiled.

"So what would you have done?" I asked.

"What I suppose most any woman would do," she said. "I would have stripped myself and knelt, begging to be kept as a slave. Then, if I were fortunate, I suppose I would soon thereafter, my hands bound behind me, be following my master, on a cord and nose ring."

"It is not unlikely," I said.

"Slave!" hissed Lady Publia.

We then regarded Lady Publia, kneeling there, naked, in the straw, her rags back over her calves.

She had beautiful eyes and hair, and features. She had a marvelous belly, breasts, and thighs, a luscious love cradle. Women are so incredibly, so inutterably beautiful! They have been made for seizing in one's arms, and owning and collaring.

"She is very beautiful," said Lady Claudia.

I studied Lady Publia closely, to her acute discomfort, as she looked away, frightened, not wanting to meet my eyes. Yes, I thought, it is true, she is very beautiful, and those small, white limbs would look well in shackles, and that face, those breasts and thighs would exhibit well on the block, under the torches of an auction.

"Very beautiful," said Lady Claudia.

"No more so than you," I said.

"Am I truly so beautiful," asked Lady Claudia.

"Yes," I said.

Lady Claudia put down her head, shyly.

I supposed it would not do to tell Lady Claudia, as she was still a free woman, but she was actually, at this time, at any rate, far more beautiful than Lady Publia. This was because she had now begun to get in touch with her womanhood. In the past few days in the cell she had begun to discover herself; she had begun to learn her femaleness.

"But you are a slave," snarled Lady Publia.

"Yes," whispered Lady Claudia, speaking not her legal status but her truth.

Lady Publia laughed, scornfully.

Lady Claudia lowered her head, shamed.

I wondered if Lady Publia thought her own truth was different. She, too, after all, was a female.

"Slave!" sneered Lady Publia.

Lady Claudia did not respond.

In general physical characteristics, such as their height and figure, their eyes and hair, their complexion and such, they were rather similar.

Lady Publia regarded Lady Claudia scornfully.

Lady Claudia did not meet her eyes.

I thought they might look well, particularly if Lady Publia were improved, as a brace of slaves. Sometimes one can get more for two girls together, as a brace, each reinforcing or enhancing, or setting off, the other in some way, than one could get for them both, sold separately. To be sure, many buyers, when they buy more than one item, expect a discount on one or both of the items.

"Turn about now," I said to Lady Publia, "and go to your stomach, as you were before, with your arms at your sides, the palms up."

She did so, and now lay as she had before except that now she was stripped.

"You are a free woman, as I understand it," I said.

"Yes!" she said.

I put her hair behind her back, over her shoulders.

"And what, then," I asked, "would you have done, if Cosians had come upon you?"

"I am a free woman!" she said. "I am not a slave! I would never have surrendered!"

"I do not like her, Master," said Lady Claudia. "And I would not be as she. I would find that disgusting and terrible, as well as ultimately barren and miserable."

"I am not sure there are free women," I said, "except in a trivial legal sense."

"I am such a woman!" cried Lady Publia.

"How such women shame women such as I, who are weak and needful, and loving," said Lady Claudia.

"In your weakness and need, and love," I said, "in your honesty, and truth, you are a thousand times stronger, and greater, than such caricatures of women, than such travesties of women, than such pseudomales and facsimile men, denying themselves and their feelings, holding themselves rigid, not daring to feel or be themselves."

"But men keep women such as I powerless," she said, touching her thigh.

"Yes," I said, "and you love it."

"Yes," she whispered, frightened, looking down, trembling with emotion.

I gathered together the scarflike material she had had wrapped turbanlike about her head, her veil and her "rags," and handed them to Lady Claudia.

"What are you doing?" asked the prisoner.

"Put these over there, by the rope, and the leash and collar," I said to Lady Claudia.

She obeyed. She then returned, to be beside me.

"There are trumpets outside," said Lady Claudia, suddenly.

"It is another assault," I said. Almost simultaneously there were raised thousands of cheers.

"There are your friends, the Cosians," I said to Lady Publia.

"They are not my friends!" she said.

If there was a response from the walls, it was hard to make it out.

"But yet you were preparing yourself quite carefully, hoping to be permitted to belong to one as a slave."

"Liar!" she cried. I saw her small fingers move, but she did not dare to clench her fists. The fingers moved helplessly, but the palms remained facing upward, exposed.

"You were bearing much gold," I said, "which, foolishly, you thought to offer to Cosians, that they might spare you and keep you as a slave. But that was stupid. For they would take the gold and then do what they wanted with you, putting you to the sword or not, as they pleased."

She cried out in anger.

"But if your thoughts in this matter had been correct," I said, "it might have been too bad, might it not, for many of the other women of Ar's Station, women less fortunate, less rich, than you, who lacked the means wherewith to purchase their lives?"

"That could not be my concern," she said, angrily.

"But I assure you, Lady Publia," I said, "the pertinent determinations in such matters, when the women are stripped and stood against a wall, are not made on the basis of gold."

"I suppose not," she said, bitterly.

"Why, too," I asked, "did you, a wealthy woman, of the Merchants, choose to wear artful rags, as though you might be a simple low-caste maid?"

She was silent.

"There were two reasons," I said. "The first is that you feared that the high castes and the richer castes, such as the Merchants, might be less likely to be spared by the enemy, that they might be the subject of more resentment, perhaps because of envy, or perhaps that they would be particularly sought out for vengeance, on the supposition that they, presumably the more powerful castes in the city, might be most responsible for the prolongation of the siege. You, on the other hand, by your disguise, so to speak, might hope to escape such a fate. Cosians would see you, you hoped, not in terms of politics, but merely in terms of loot. The second reason is more interesting. You wanted to be seen in terms of something well worth hunting and capturing. Thus the artful rags, apparently so inadvertently but excitingly, displaying your calves. You did not wish to be brought down with a quarrel at a distance but to find yourself at close quarters with captors. Then you would surrender to them."

"No!" she cried.

"It is for such a reason," I said, "that your rags were designed to be removed swiftly, so easily and gracefully, and on your knees."

"No!" she said. "No!"

"Lie quietly," I said. "And most interestingly, and objectionably," I said, "you had not had your hair shorn."

Lady Publia did not respond.

"To be sure," I said, "you wished to give the impression that you had done so. That was the purpose of the cloth you wore about your head. It was intended to make it seem as though you, perhaps in understandable vanity or embarrassment, wished to conceal shortly cropped hair. Certainly I, at first, assumed your hair had been shorn."

"I, too," said Lady Claudia.

"Do you recall," I asked Lady Claudia, "that I earlier suggested that there might be a reason, other than reasons of your sort, for not having her hair cropped?"

"Yes," said Lady Claudia.

"Do you now suspect such a reason?" I asked.

"Yes," she said.

"Yes," I said. "With such hair, such lovely hair," I said, toying with it, behind Lady Publia's back, "she would be more likely to be spared."

Lady Publia tensed, angrily.

"Let other women have their hair shorn," I said, "donating it to the defense of their city. Not she. It, like the artful rags, their length, their ease of removal, and such, had its clever, calculated part to play in her plan. She would thus, retaining her hair, it enhancing her beauty, if captured, stand out like a paga slave among mill sluts. If selections were to be made, it then seems that surely she would be among the first chosen, not for the sword, but for the chain."

Lady Publia's small fingers moved wildly, angrily, but she dared not close her hands. The palms remained up, exposed.

"There are the trumpets again," said Lady Claudia.

"It is the recall," I said.

"But they will come again, will they not?" she asked.

"Yes," I said, "and, if necessary, again, and again."

I looked down at Lady Publia.

"Does it seem fair to you," I asked Lady Claudia, "that Lady Publia should have such an advantage over the other women of Ar's Station?"

"I do not know," said Lady Claudia.

"It does not seem fair to me," I said. "When you were going through our friends' pouches over there, did you find any small knives, such as a hook knife or a shaving knife?"

I had a belt knife myself, which was sheathed on the sword belt, to the right, but at the moment I preferred something lighter-bladed, smaller and sharper, if it were available.

"One fellow had a shaving knife," said Lady Claudia.

"Bring it to me," I said.

"What do you want it for?" said Lady Publia, anxiously.

In a moment Lady Claudia had returned with the implement.

"What are you going to do!" cried Lady Publia.

"Hold still," I said.

"No!" she wept. "No!"

In a few moments I discarded the small knife, throwing it to the side. Lady Publia was lying in the straw, bawling. She clutched her head wildly, in dismay, in disbelief.

"Kneel," I said, "facing me."

Weeping, Lady Publia obeyed, her hands still on her head.

"Now," I said, "if Cosians come on you, you will be on the same footing as the other women of Ar's Station."

Tears filled her eyes.

I had left her enough hair so that I could get my hand in it, in the scrub of it, so that I might use it as the guard had earlier the hair of Lady Claudia, to control her. Too, thusly, it was now of a convenient length for a Cosian to seize it, should that eventuality occur. It was of about the same length as that of Lady Claudia.

Lady Publia, half hysterical, kept her hands on her head. This lifted her breasts nicely. Then, seeing my eyes on her, she wept and put down her head, kneeling low, her hands still over her head.

"Prisoner," said I, harshly, "on all fours."

She assumed this position.

"Go to the place where you put the clothing," I said to Lady Claudia, "by the rope, the leash and collar, and wait there."

Lady Claudia hurried to the place.

I then stood up and looked down at Lady Publia.

"Lift your head, prisoner," I said.

She did so.

"Lift up one end of the rope," I said to Lady Claudia.

She did so.

I then, abruptly, seized Lady Publia by the scrub of her dark hair and pulled her, she crying out, half crawling, half being dragged, over to where Lady Claudia waited. It was precisely so that the guard, earlier, had treated Lady Claudia.

"Kneel here," I said to Lady Publia, indicating the same spot where Lady Claudia had knelt, "up, off your heels, your arms at your sides."

Frightened, Lady Publia complied.

It was exactly in such a position that Lady Claudia had been knelt by the guard.

I then took the free end of the rope from Lady Claudia's hand and, exactly as she had been tied, with the many coils, beginning near her waist, began to bind Lady Publia.

"What are you doing?" moaned Lady Publia.

"Put on her clothing," I said to Lady Claudia. "Hurry." The most recent assault force, the third of the morning, had been recalled. This meant a lull. At such a time men could be freed from the walls. Too, it was now late morning.

"What does she think she is doing!" demanded Lady Publia, outraged. "Oh!"

"As I recall," I said to Lady Publia, "you recommended that the ropes be made tight."

"Oh!" she said. Then suddenly, again, "Oh!" Then, "Please," she begged, "do not make them so tight!" Then, "Oh! Oh!" she said.

Then she was trussed.

"Your calves and ankles," I said to Lady Claudia, "are as attractive as hers."

Lady Claudia flushed with pleasure at my compliment. Then she said, delightedly, touching the garment, "I have not worn clothes in days!" I smiled to myself. I thought she might as well enjoy clothes, while she was permitted them.

"Now put on the veil, and wrap the cloth about your head, quickly," I said, "as she had them."

"What is the meaning of this outrage!" demanded Lady Publia, squirming in the ropes.

"That is very good," I said to Lady Claudia. She, like Lady Publia, had dark brown eyes. If one did not know Lady Publia personally, or if one did not know her all that well, I did not think there would be any difficulty in Lady Claudia's being taken for her.

"What is this all about?" asked Lady Publia.

"Go to the fellows over there by the wall," I said, "and cut free one of their tunics. I need some cloth."

Lady Claudia did so, using a belt knife, taken from one of the guards.

"What is this all about?" said Lady Publia, again, insistently, angrily.

I then put the collar about her neck. Its leash was already attached. She then knelt there, as had Lady Claudia, leashed and collared.

"I do not understand!" said Lady Publia, angrily.

I stood up, and looked down at her. She was on her knees, bound. She trembled. Women understand that position.

In a moment Lady Claudia had rejoined me, carrying a good bit of cloth.

"Release me," demanded Lady Publia.

"You are going to help us leave the citadel," I told her.

"Never!" she said.

"I have a plan," I said.

"Doubtless you think she can pass herself off as me," she said, scornfully.

"I think so," I said.

At that moment there was a great impact somewhere, perhaps a hundred feet away.

Lady Publia, bound at our feet, winced. There was a noise as the leash ring moved on the collar ring.

"It is the artillery," said Lady Claudia, shivering. "It has begun again!"

"She is pretty," I said. "Perhaps Cosians might spare her."

"I think so," said Lady Claudia.

"Why do you speak so explicitly of Cosians?" asked Lady Publia suddenly, apprehensively. "Am I not beautiful?"

"Yes," I said. "You are."

"Then would not anyone spare me?" she asked.

"Perhaps not just anyone," I said.

"You understand, do you not, Lady Publia." I said, "that there are many ways, behavioral and psychological, in which one can determine whether or not a woman's bondage is meretricious?"

"Yes," she said, frightened.

"Even so," I said, "one might be found who might not choose to spare you."

"What are you waiting here for?" asked Lady Publia, frightened. "Why do you not run? Why do you not flee?"

"We are waiting for a caller," I said.

"Who?" she asked, apprehensively.

"Surely you have not forgotten," I said. "He was to have been along in a few Ehn. I expect him in a bit, the assaults now having abated."

"If she is to be me," said Lady Publia, suddenly, frightened, looking at Lady Claudia, wearing her former rags, veil and scarf, "what then is to be my role in this farce?"

While we had been talking I had taken the cloth which Lady Claudia had brought from the side earlier, that which she had cut from the tunic of one of the guards, and had been tearing it here and there, and working with it.

"Can you not guess?" I asked.

"No!" she cried. "No!"

"Perhaps," I said. I was now wadding one of the pieces of cloth into tight ball.

"Are you not a Cosian?" she asked.

"No," I said.

"What is your city?" she asked, frightened.

"Port Kar," I said.

She suddenly turned white.

"Glory to Port Kar," I said.

"Mercy!" she cried.

"Glory to Port Kar," I said, regarding her, evenly.

"Glory to Port Kar!" she cried, desperately, fervently.

"Three times," I said.

"Glory to Port Kar," she cried, thrice.

I then thrust the small ball of tightly rolled cloth into her mouth, where, instantly, as it was actually a rather large piece of material, it expanded.

"Those may be the last words you ever speak," I said.

She looked at me wildly, tears in her eyes, squirming, shaking her head, protesting, making tiny noises, but I then secured the wadding tightly in her mouth, with two rolled strips of cloth, pulled back tightly between her teeth, and tied in back of her neck.

"When the executioner arrives," I said, "who do you think he is going to find, waiting for him?"

She turned white, squirming, shaking her head.

"You were not really very pleasing," I said. "Perhaps you would like to be more pleasing now?"

She nodded, desperately, tears bursting from her eyes.

"Hold her leash, close to the collar," I said to Lady Claudia, who was white-faced, too.

This would keep Lady Publia from plunging her head to the floor, at our feet.

She threw her head back, in misery.

But I pulled it forward, by the hair, and covered it, with a large piece of cloth from the guard's tunic. I then, with a knife, and a cord of rolled cloth, put through holes in the bottom of the cloth, made it into a rough hood, and tied it on her, fastening it behind the back of the neck.

"Perhaps if you had been more pleasing," I suggested.

She then began hysterically, piteously, to squirm and moan.

I rose to my feet. I gestured to Lady Claudia to release the leash. It seemed she could hardly open her fingers but she did so. Lady Publia, as I had expected, as soon as the leash was released, put her head, secured in the darkness of the crude hood, wildly, piteously down, searching, groping, for my feet, to press her covered, parted lips and stopped mouth against them. I let her search for them for a moment, and not find them. Then I took the leash back between her legs, crossed her ankles, and bound them together with it. She was thus, having herself assumed this position, now, at my convenience, fastened helplessly down, bent over, on her knees. I stood up. I looked down at her. Yes, it was also a position of obeisance.

"See if anyone is coming," I said to Lady Claudia.

She hurried, distraught, to the cell door.

In a moment she had returned.

"Doubtless he will be along presently," I said.

Lady Claudia looked down, horrified, at our helpless warder.

I crouched down by the prisoner. "The spear, as I understand it," I said, trying to recall the words of our warder earlier to Lady Claudia, "is a solid piece of polished metal, very long, and less than a hort in width. It is tapered to a point, and fits in a mount."

Lady Publia squirmed on her knees hysterically. She uttered tiny, wild, protesting noises.

Lady Claudia looked at me wildly, over the veil. There were tears in her own eyes.

At that moment there was a hideous impact some forty feet or fifty feet from us and on the other side of the interior wall to the left, as one would face the cell door, in what, presumably would have been the cell adjoining ours, there was a bursting inward of brick and stone. In a moment there was a cloud of dust in the corridor, some of which drifted into our cell. I put my arm before my face. Lady Claudia's veil and Lady Publia's hood doubtless afforded them some protection.

We heard a cough in the corridor outside.

In a moment a tall fellow entered our cell. He wore a black hood, which, save for a narrow, rectangular opening for the eyes, covered his entire head. The hood and shoulders, in particular, were covered with dust. He struck some dust from his clothes and body. "The wall weakens," he said to me. "In a few Ehn they will be coming again. They are forming. We can no longer keep them back. Their engines are almost climbing the walls."

I nodded.

"You are Lady Publia, the warder?" he asked Lady Claudia.

"I am," she said, boldly.

"I do not approve of woman warders," said he. "It is a task for men."

She tossed her head.

"Perhaps you regret having accepted the position," he said.

"Perhaps," said Lady Claudia.

At our feet, Lady Publia, kneeling, bent over, small, hooded, the leash tight against the back of her neck, unable to raise her head, squirmed and uttered wild, tiny noises. We paid her no attention, as she was the prisoner. I supposed, however, that perhaps she did, now, upon reflection, regret having accepted the position of warder.

"You have pretty legs," said the fellow to Lady Claudia. She did not respond.

"What is your caste?" he asked.

"The Merchants," she said.

"Why are you not in the white and gold," he asked, "on this, of all days?" White and gold, or white and yellow, are the caste colors of the Merchants.

She did not answer.

"You are not even in the Robes of Concealment," he said.

"They are not appropriate here," she said.

"You do not wear them here because it is not appropriate for them here," he asked, "or is that why you are here, because it is not appropriate to wear such things here?"

"There are many places where they would not be appropriate," she said.

"Yes," he said, "for example, on a Cosian sales block."

"I meant other places," she said.

"It is true," he said, "for example, in climbing the rubble, carrying stones to workmen on the walls, in tending the wounded, and such. Thus I wonder why it is that you chose to be here."

"It is cool here," she said.

"And perhaps you could feel more like a man here," he said.

"Perhaps," she said, as though angrily.

Lady Publia, in the hood, tied at our feet, made a small, wild noise, as of understanding, acknowledgement, dismay, regret, misery and pain. The fellow's question had apparently seemed profoundly meaningful to her, for some reason. At any rate, if she had had secret, internal pretensions to manhood, or to similarity to men, or something along these lines, it seemed unlikely she now retained them. I thought that she probably now realized she was something quite different, and in my opinion, something quite individual, authentic and wonderful, a woman. At any rate, she would know something that was indisputable, that she was at our feet, a helplessly bound female.

"From the look of it, woman," said he to Lady Claudia, "I do not think you have underrobes beneath those rags."

"That is my own concern," she said, loftily.

"By nightfall you will probably be in a collar, licking the feet of a Cosian," he said.

"Perháps," she said, angrily.

"And what of you, my little vulo," he said, not unkindly, crouching beside Lady Publia. "I wager that you, too, would like to have the opportunity to prostrate yourself before Cosians."

Lady Publia began to squirm and wriggle wildly, making piteous sounds.

"You must have fed her very well," said the fellow, looking up at Lady Claudia, whom he took for Lady Publia. "She has a great deal of energy."

Lady Publia struggled wildly, trying to pull her head up, against the thick collar and heavy strap. But, in the end, she was exactly as she had been before.

"Why is she gagged?" asked the fellow.

"That she not be able to make her identity known," I said.

Lady Publia stopped moving, startled.

"I do not understand," said the fellow.

"It is the orders of Aemilianus," I said. "He was not certain whether or not there were more than one spy of such a nature in the city. Accordingly, in this fashion, if there should be more than one such agent, Cosians would not know which of them was mounted on the pole. The hood, of course, has a similar purpose. To some extent, it might, though it seems a little late now, impair the functioning of their intelligence network in the city. Similarly the other agents, if there are such, might be intimidated or terrified, not knowing which of their number had been captured, how much was known, who might be next, and so on."

"The commander is a clever man," said the fellow.

"Yes," I agreed. I did have respect for Aemilianus as a commander.

Lady Publia squirmed, and wept. The hood was wet with her tears.

"Do not fret, little vulo," he said to her, putting his hand on her head, "you will soon be on the spit, cooking in the sun."

She wept and struggled.

"It seems there will be little difficulty in getting this one to squirm on the spear," said the fellow.

Wild, tiny, piteous noises emanated from Lady Publia's hood.

"Sometimes they wriggle well," he said, "perhaps because they are afraid, or because they think they can get off the spear somehow, or because they are trying to end it. Sometimes they try to hold themselves as still as possible. Sometimes then we use the whip on them, and sometimes not. If we let them take their time about it, of course, the penetration is sometimes as little as a hort an Ahn. The end result, of course, is the same."

Lady Publia squirmed hysterically. She uttered desperate, piteous, pleading sounds.

"Usually they are not this agitated," said the fellow. "Usually, by this time, they are numb with fear and dread, and offer no resistance. Many cannot even walk."

I recalled that Lady Claudia had been much that way earlier.

"It is time to go, vulo," said the fellow, getting to his feet.

Lady Publia, at his feet, shook her head wildly, feverishly, piteously, desperately, as she could, in the constraint of the collar. It must have burned the back of her neck. Because of the coils of rope I could barely see her back.

"She begs for time, for mercy," said the fellow.

"Perhaps," I said.

She whimpered, piteously.

"Filthy spy," he said. He then, angrily, spurned her with his foot, thrusting her to her side.

Lady Claudia, wide-eyed, frightened, looked at the prisoner, lying on her side, helpless, and looked then, too, at the fellow. Perhaps she had never before seen a woman so treated, or at least a free woman so treated.

The fellow then freed the ankles of Lady Publia, and brought the leash forward, between her legs. He then coiled it, to the leash ring. Then, one hand on her arm, the other on the leash coils, he pulled her to her knees.

Lady Publia whimpered piteously before him. I think she was now beginning, better than before, to understand her unenviable position. I feared she might collapse or faint. I was not certain she could even stand now.

"Think now on Cosian gold," he said, bitterly.

She shuddered.

"Let us show your Cosian friends how pretty you will look on the spear," he said, angrily.

She shook her head, numbly.

"I am now giving you tether," he said. He shook out the leash. "When I pull twice on the leash," he said, "you will rise and follow me, responsive to, and conducted by, the leash."

But before he could draw twice on the leash, giving the prisoner her signal, she thrust her head down, to his feet, reaching for them, as she had earlier for mine. He let her find them, for a moment, and press, and rub, her face, her head, her gagged, covered mouth desperately, piteously against them.

"You seem to have the dispositions, and makings, of a slave," he mused.

She lifted her head to him, in the darkness of the hood, pathetically, hopefully.

"And surely your body," he said, "so trim and excitingly shaped, is much like those that are found in slave markets." She whimpered affirmatively, beggingly.

"But unfortunately," he said, "you are a free woman."

She shook her head.

"You seem to have forgotten your brand," he said.

She made a small, begging sound.

"But perhaps all you free sluts are truly slaves and belong in collars," he said. He looked at Lady Claudia. "Your friend, Lady Publia, the warder," he said to the prisoner, "has pretty calves and ankles. Doubtless those are displayed for the interest and delectation of Cosians, and masters."

Lady Claudia stood back, not answering.

I wondered if the fellow saw that Lady Publia was thinking of running.

"Traitress," said the fellow to Lady Publia.

Lady Publia then, suddenly, leaped to her feet and tried to run, but, in an instant, expertly, with a turn of the leash, she was flung to her side before him. He held the leash. His foot on it, near her neck, kept her head down. Lady Claudia's hand went before her veiled lips. She looked down at the helpless, prostrate Lady Publia. I supposed that perhaps Lady

Claudia had never seen a woman subjected to leash control before.

"That was stupid," said the fellow. "Now, shall we begin again?" He took his foot off the leash. He shook the leash once, to alert the prisoner that a leash signal was imminent. Then he drew on the leash twice. "Stand," he said. "Follow."

Lady Publia struggled to her feet, then her legs gave out, under her, and she collapsed.

"Be warned," he said. "If I carry you, I shall carry you as a slave is carried."

But I think Lady Publia, now, truly, could not stand. I think that her bonds, the security of her gag, her inability to dislodge the hood, its effectiveness in concealing her, the ease with which her attempted escape had been dealt with, had all combined to make clear to her her utter helplessness, that she could not, in the least, by her will or action, alter the course of events. We had seen to it. Now she could scarcely move.

With a thong he addressed himself to her ankles.

"What is wrong with you?" asked the fellow, looking up at Lady Claudia. She stood there, frightened. It seemed she herself could hardly stand.

Lady Claudia looked at him. She put out her hand a little, piteously.

"Do not concern yourself with her," said the fellow, finishing with the knot, jerking it tight, on Lady Publia's ankles. "She is a spy."

Lady Publia struggled weakly, her ankles now thonged.

"It is a pity that such lusciousness must be destroyed," he said. "Such shapeliness has slave value."

Lady Publia whimpered.

As he considered the prisoner, Lady Claudia hurried to my side, keenly distressed, half beside herself. "You cannot let her go to the spear!" she whispered.

"I suppose once you were a haughty free woman," he said to Lady Publia. "You do not seem so haughty now. Doubtless once, too, you thought yourself very clever, when you betrayed your city and accepted Cosian gold. Now, however, I suspect that you are less sure of your cleverness."

I motioned that Lady Claudia should return to her place.

"What is wrong with her?" asked the fellow.

"She pities the prisoner," I said.

"Spare her!" cried Lady Claudia, suddenly.

Her outburst was greeted by a frenzied squirming, and a renewal of tiny, pathetic noises from the prisoner.

"Do not take her to the spear!" begged Lady Claudia. "What can it matter? The city, I am certain, will soon fall. What difference will it make!"

I wished Lady Claudia would have kept her lovely face shut.

"Why do you think we have waited until now?" he asked. "Let that be the irony, if you wish, that today, of all days, when the citadel surely must shortly fall, when she is so close to rescue by her Cosian friends, but so far, that she, today, of all days, in full view of the foe, in justice and defiance, is placed upon the spear!"

Lady Publia shuddered.

Lady Claudia shrank back, horrified. She looked at me, wildly.

"Would you like a hand with her?" I asked. This would bring me close enough to deal with him.

"I can manage," he said. "Where are the others?"

"What others?" I asked.

"Usually there is a squad of three, with the warder," he said.

"Doubtless they are about somewhere," I said.

"The other two are doubtless on the wall," he said.

"Perhaps," I said. That surely seemed a likely supposition on his part, given his information.

"It was wise of them," he said, "to move the other prisoner out, if they could bring only one man here this morning."

"That would seem to make sense," I said.

"He would probably, in any case," he said, "have been too weak to do anything."

"Perhaps," I said.

"Doubtless a child could have handled him by now," he said.

"Perhaps," I said.

"We are all weak," he said, irritably.

"Are you certain that you would not care for my assistance?" I asked.

"No," he said. "This filthy, treacherous little vulo's weight is nothing."

He turned about then and bent to pick up the quivering Lady Publia, to hoist her to his shoulder. Suddenly he stopped. He had then, apparently for the first time, detected the bodies, muchly concealed with straw, which we had hidden at the side of the cell. I moved quickly toward him but then it seemed, suddenly, as though the world had burst apart, and I spun about, covering my head with my hands, and it seemed in that instant that the cell was filled with bursting stones and bricks, and there was a great sound, and Lady Claudia screamed, and one could hardly see or breathe for an instant, the dust in the air, the white, bright dust, and we were coughing, and my eyes stung, and there was debris all about, and it seemed half the cell wall was gone, and I squinted against the light, so bright, the dust glittering in it, flooding the room. The fellow had lost his footing. The floor, where he was was crooked, buckled. Some of the great stones tilted upward. He seemed half in shock. He turned, in the dust, pointing back to the wall, startled, that he would apprise me of his discovery, not even seemingly suspicious, and met the stone in my hand, part of the wall I had seized up, and sank to his knees. Lady Claudia crouched down, shuddering, her hands over her head. Lady Publia lay prone among the buckled tiles, perhaps in shock. Both were covered with dust.

I scrambled up an embankment of debris to the great opening in the wall.

There, spread before me, in the bright morning sun, under the clear blue sky, bright with glittering spear blades and shields, with nodding plumes, with the standards of companies and regiments, dotted with engines, here and there a tharlarion stalking about, tarnsmen in the sky, in serried ranks, some stretching back to buildings still standing, even crowding streets in the distance, most on an artificial plain extending for three hundred yards about, created from the flattened ruins of burned, razed buildings, the debris sunk in cellars, and basements, and leveled, or hauled away, was the marshaled might of Cos in the north!

I motioned eagerly for Lady Claudia to climb the rubble, that we two, together, might stand in that opening and regard the grandeur of war.

"Do you see how it is, that men can love it?" I asked.

"It frightens me!" she gasped.

"Look at them," I said, "the soldiers, their glory, their strength!"

"It terrifies me!" she wept, the wind moving the veil against her lips.

"How splendid it is!" I cried.

"I belong naked in chains!" she suddenly cried.

"Yes," I said, seizing her arm, "you do!"

Had I not held her arm, I fear she might have swooned on the rubble.

We then heard, from all about, before us, the notes of trumpets.

"The men are moving!" she said.

"It is the attack," I said.

"They are silent!" she said. Hitherto the trumpets had been followed by great cheering.

"They have had their fill of shouting, and such," I said. "They come now to finish the matter."

Light-armed troops hurried forward, slingers and archers, and javelin men, to keep defenders back, as they could, from the crenels. Under their cover the ladder brigades followed and the grapnel men; behind these came scalers, crouching, protected under the shield roofs of infantry men.

"The wall will be attacked at several points," I said, "to spread the defenders."

She suddenly gasped.

"What is wrong?" I asked.

"I thought I saw a building move," she said, "back by the other buildings."

"Where?" I asked.

"It does not matter," she said, "it was only an illusion, a ripple in the air, a matter of the waves of heat rising from the stone, the debris."

"Where?" I asked.

She pointed. Then she gasped, again.

"It is no illusion," I said. "It is moving. There is another, too, and another."

"Buildings cannot move!" she said.

"I count eleven," I said. "They can be moved in various ways. Some are moved from within, by such means as men thrusting forward against bars, or tharlarion, pulling against harnesses attached to bars behind them, such apparatuses internal to the structure. Some, on the other hand, look there, there is one, are drawn by ropes, drawn by men or tharlarion. That one is drawn by men. See them?''

"Yes," she said.

There must have been at least fifty ropes, and fifty men to a rope. They seemed small yet, even in their numbers, at this distance.

"Even so, how can such things be moved?" she said.

"They are not really buildings as you think," I said, "made of stone, and such. They are high, mobile structures, on wheels. They are heavy, it is true, but they are light, considering their size. They are wooden structures, frameworks, covered on three sides with light wood, sometimes even hides. The hides will be soaked with water as they approach more closely, to make it difficult to fire the structure. They overtop the walls. Drawbridges can then be opened within them and men can pour out, preferably down, this giving them momentum for the charge, over the walls, others following them up the ladders within. There are many types of such structures. Some are even used on ships. We call them generally castles or towers. As they are used here, one would commonly think of them, and speak of them, as siege towers."

"They are terrible things," she said.

"Even one of them," I said, "from the platforms and landings within, and by means of the ladders, bringing men from the ground, may feed a thousand men into a city in ten Ehn."

"They are like giants," she said.

"There does, indeed, seem to be stately menace in them," I said.

We stood framed in the great, jagged hole.

"Come away," I said, then, suddenly. I dragged her back, behind me, down the rubble into the cell. I went to the executioner and drew away his mask, drawing it then over my own head. I went to Lady Publia, who lay in the debris, covered with dust. I brushed her with the side of my foot, and she did not move. I then kicked her with the side of my foot, and she still lay still. I did not think she was dead. She had been the most sheltered of all of us when the wall had burst in. There was no blood about the hood or ropes. I did not even think she was unconscious. It was my surmise that she had been hoping against hope to be ignored, or not to be noticed.

I did not know, but I doubted that she, lying where she was, confused and frightened, down amidst the rubble near the door, had even heard us, high in the aperture, above her, across the cell. If she had heard us, I did not think she would have been able to make out our words, or, probably, even whose voices she heard, or their location, except with respect to her, she doubtless by now helplessly disoriented in the hood. Perhaps she had hoped that she might be the sole survivor of the strike. I did not know. In any event, she, hooded, and helplessly bound, would have at best only a very imperfect understanding of what had occurred. Presumably she would not know, for example, who might have survived and who not. Gagged, too, of course, she could not even beg for information. This amused me.

I motioned that Lady Claudia should be silent. I looked down at Lady Publia, lying so still. I supposed now she was pretending to be dead, or, at least, unconscious. There are numerous ways in which such fraud may be terminated, for example, to throw the woman into water, to hold her head under water for a bit, to see if she tries to free her head, sputtering and begging for mercy, to put her under the whip, to use the bastinado on the soles of her feet, to claw unexpectedly at the soft flesh behind her knees, even to lightly caress the soles of her feet, and so on. I wanted something, rather, which would prove to Lady Publia, even if to her profound humiliation, what she was. First, I separated the ropes a bit on her upper body and put my ear to her heart. It was beating, so she was alive, as I thought. I also heard the heart rate increase, excitedly, she frightened, and knowing I was making this determination. Still she pretended to unconsciousness.

I then lifted her up a bit, supporting her with my hand behind her back, and put my other hand to her belly. She tried to pretend to be unconscious. She tried to hold herself still. But soon the very physiology of her body, almost autonomically, became active, and I felt the gathering heat, and the oil and openness of her, her vitality, readiness and need. Then, surrendering, she moaned and squirmed. Then, piteously, abandoning all effort at deception, she thrust herself against me, offering herself to me, whoever I might be, for use as a slave.

I then withdrew my hand and, as she moaned piteously, helplessly, threw her to my left shoulder. This keeps the sword arm free. I carried her with her head to the rear, as a slave is carried. She would think herself, I was certain, on the shoulder of the executioner. Too, she could feel the hood I wore, against the left side of her waist. I then, followed by Lady Claudia, carried her from the ruins of the cell.

# 16
# I ASSUME COMMAND

"Where have you been?" called a fellow outside the cell, approaching. "They are moving forward even now! The ram will be at the gate again in Ehn!"

I lifted my right arm, acknowledging his words. We had not seen the ram from the cell. It had been perhaps obscured by the main gate's west bastion. He turned about and I followed him through the corridor, presumably to the height of the forward wall.

Lady Publia then began to squirm madly on my shoulder, considering such might be her last opportunity perhaps to draw attention to herself. She did call attention to herself, but mainly to find herself the butt of jeering remarks, which, even hooded, she could hear well enough; too, several of the men, and women, struck her as we passed, she reacting, startled, and in pain. By the time we reached the wall I did not doubt she would be well bruised. Lady Claudia followed, closely, frightened, miserable. It seemed she cried out, softly, as the blows struck my moving, helpless, well-curved burden, almost as though she felt rather they should have been hers to endure. She even sobbed. If Lady Publia heard these tiny noises, and associated them with Lady Claudia, presumably she thought that Lady Claudia was accompanying the executioner to the wall, doubtless as she herself would have. She had been quite cruel to us, I recalled, as our warder, and had much mocked Lady Claudia in her distress, when Lady

Claudia, rather than she, had worn the ropes. Now, to her horror, she found that it was she herself, unknown to her compatriots, who was being carried to the wall. She herself, doubtless, had the situation been reversed, would have followed the executioner eagerly, and, later, with sardonic amusement, as the spectacle unfolded, done her best to increase Lady Claudia's misery. That being so, perhaps she could not understand the sobs, and the sounds of commiseration, she heard behind her. But she, unlike Lady Claudia, had not yet been taught her form of humanity and her sex. She was, however, learning something of the preciousness of life.

Then, after a long, spiral climb, we emerged through a guard station, and onto the wall. It was bright and windy there. Lady Publia, feeling the cool air and wind, emitted a long, helpless, miserable groan.

"There," said the fellow we had been following. He pointed to the battlements over the main gate, higher than those on the wall generally. On that creneled, raised platform, already in its mount, I could see the long, slim, polished impaling spear. He then left us.

I looked over the wall and noted that the long, rolling, shedlike structure was quite near, beneath which the battering ram, on its ropes, was slung. It had not been visible from the cell, as I had speculated, as it had been obscured by the gate's west bastion. Some of the ladder men and grapnel crews were already probing the walls. The siege towers were still some hundreds of yards away.

A quarrel sputtered against the interior of an embrasure, chipping it and glancing away, upward.

As I went toward the gate's battlements a grapnel looped over the wall gracefully and fell behind the walkway. Considering the arc, its width and height, I assumed it had been lobbed there by an engine. It was drawn forward and one of the hooks caught and the rope sprang taut. Such things are generally not much good in this form of fighting except for secret ascents, say, at night, when they are not noticed, or there are too many of them to deal with. They are much more useful, in my opinion, at sea, as in, say, drawing ships within boarding distance of one another, the ropes then usually being attached to chains some ten feet or so behind the hooks. This makes it hard to cut them free. Boarding hooks, on poles, are often used, too, for such purposes, when one can get close enough. These are sometimes sheathed with tin near the points, again to make it harder to cut or chop them away. Pikes for repelling boarders, it might be noted, are often greased near the blade end. This makes it harder for boarders to grasp them, wrenching them away, forcing gaps in the pike wall, and so on.

I will append one qualification to these observations pertaining to grapnels which is to acknowledge the giant, chain grapnel, and its relative, the grapnel derrick. The giant grapnel is hurled by an engine and then, either with the second arm of the engine, or by the same arm, reversed, drawn back with great force. This can rip away the crests of walls, tear off roofs, and such. If Cosians used them here they might have created gaps in the battlements. The effectiveness of such a device, however, given the weights involved, and the loss of force in the draw, is much compromised by the necessity of extreme proximity to the target. Also the defenders may be expected to free or dislodge the grapnel if possible.

The derrick grapnel is much what the name suggests. It is used from walls, dangled down, and then drawn up with a winch. If the wall is a harbor wall it can capsize a ship. If the wall is a land wall, it can, with luck, topple a siege tower. This device also, however, tends to be ineffective except under rather optimum, special conditions. For example, very few captains are likely to get their ships within range of a derrick grapnel. Would you?

I watched the rope on the grapnel for a moment and noted that although it was taut it did not exhibit the differential tensions which it would if it were being climbed. I pulled it loose then and, letting its tautness do the work, let it fly back over the walkway and the crenelation. Had I more time or been of Ar's Station, perhaps I might have waited until it was being climbed and then, after a while, cut the rope. This sort of thing, as you might imagine, tends to be somewhat frustrating to the fellows who are climbing the rope, particularly if they are some seventy feet or so up the wall at the time. It takes great courage, incidentally, to climb such a rope in daylight under battle conditions. I did not doubt but that one or two of the fellows on the other side of the wall were probably just as pleased that it had come back as it did. It also takes great courage, incidentally, though it is much easier to do, to climb a siege ladder, particularly when the walls are heavily or stoutly defended. It is better, I think, for the individual attacker, particularly if the walls are high, over twenty feet, say, to try to enter over the bridge of a siege tower or, even better, through a breached wall or gate.

I looked through the crenelation again, standing back from it. The siege towers were still at least two hundred yards away. It takes time to move such cumbersome objects. Their progress forward was steady, but so slow, it seemed sometimes almost like watching the hands of a clock move.

I passed a lad standing behind one of the embrasures with a crossbow. He was too young to be on the wall. One quarrel reposed in the guide of his bow. Beside him, leaning against the inside of the parapet, were some more quarrels, only two of which were crafted, one feathered, one with light metal fins. The others were little more than filed rods, neither feathered nor finned. With these, too, there were some wooden quarrels, blunt-headed, such as boys sometimes use for bringing down birds. I did not think they would be effective. Perhaps, ideally targeted, launched from within a yard or so, one might cause a fellow to lose a grip on a ladder. More likely they would serve as little more than irritants.

I smelled hot oil on the parapet, and a cauldron of it was boiling, which I passed. Buckets on long handles could be dipped into this, the oil fired, and then poured on attackers. The oil tends to hold the fire on the object. I passed two catapults on the walkway. They were quiet now, not even manned.

I proceeded on toward the raised platform over the main gate, where the impaling spear, flashing in the sun like a polished needle, was mounted. I passed another lad, too, also, in my opinion, too young to be on the wall. Better these fellows had been running about the windy corners of the markets, looking for the veils to blow about the faces of free women or pursuing slave girls, pulling up their brief skirts, playing "brand guess," or busying themselves playing stones or hoops behind the shops. He was crouching beside a pile of stones, building stones, and tiles. It is hard to throw these with accuracy without standing above the crenelation. This exposes the caster, of course. He seemed lost in his thoughts.

I wondered if he had been on the wall before. I supposed he had a mother, who loved him.

When I passed him, he looked up. I saw then that he had been on the wall before, and that, though his age might indeed be that of a boy, that he was a man. He then put down his head again, returning to his reflections, whatever might have been their nature. Near the steps to the raised platform I passed two men with long-handled tridents. These are used to thrust men and ladders back from the wall.

Turning, about fifty yards behind me, I saw the upright of a single-pole ladder jut from the outside over the wall. The two men, gaunt and weary, paid it no attention. Back there, however, a cluster of defenders sped to the place. The ringing of swords came to my ears. More than one fellow leapt over the crenelation but the ladder itself was thrust back. This isolated the Cosians who had attained the wall. Men swarmed about them. Two were cut down and a third climbed back over the wall and leapt away, plunging to its foot, preferring to risk the consequences of such a fall rather than face certain death on the walkway. The bodies of his two comrades, stripped of weapons, half hacked to pieces, were flung after him.

I hurried up the broad stone steps to the surface of the platform over the main gate. This area, at least at the moment, perhaps because of its height, and its position over the gate, the ground below soon to be blocked by the ram, the men working it protected by its sturdy shed, was empty. It would have made an excellent command post for Aemilianus, I thought, but, I gathered, he must be below, in the vicinity of the gate. Perhaps he thought, and rightfully, for all I knew, that there lay the greatest danger. I supposed that by now tons of rock would have been piled behind the gate. Still the ram might attempt its entry there, pounding through the brass facing riveted into the thick beams of the gate, punching, driving it back, snapping the crossbars, forcing back, blow by blow, even the rock and sand behind.

I placed Lady Publia on her back at our feet, near the mount for the spear.

I then dismissed her from my mind, for the moment.

I considered the approaching towers, the thousands of men I could see in the field, the ladders being carried, the supporting engines. I then regarded the walls. There were too few men there. The results of the battle were a foregone conclusion. The Cosians had waited long for this day.

I looked up to my left. There, on a pole, defiantly, snapped a torn flag, bearing in yellow the single letter 'Ar' on a red background with, beneath it, a wavy yellow band. This was the flag of Ar's Station, signifying the power of Ar on the Vosk. I did not think it would be there long.

I then lifted the tall impaling spear from its mount, laying it, with a sound, beside the supine, bound figure. She tried to rise but, her ankles thonged together, she fell. She tried to scramble back, but I reached out and took her ankle, and then pulled her where I wanted her, closer, across the stones.

"Please, no!" wept Lady Claudia, putting out her hand. I brushed her aside.

I then addressed myself to Lady Publia. "Would you care to confess yourself a slave?" I inquired.

She thrashed about, uttering wild, affirmative whimpers, nodding her head in the hood, vigorously.

"You recognize my voice, do you not?" I asked.

Again she nodded. This was the first she would have realized, for certain, I supposed, that she had come to the height of the wall, to the foot of the impaling mount, on my shoulder, and not on that of the executioner. Hope would be springing up wildly within her, for the executioner not knowing who she was, and thinking she was the Lady Claudia, would presumably have simply put her on the spear and went about his business, probably, pulling off his mask, to some post on the wall. I, on the other hand, she knew, knew well who she was. Too, my words must have given her some hope that she might have, at my hands, at least some slim chance for life, albeit that it might have to be purchased at so alarming a cost as consigning herself by her own words to a fate no less than the degradation and categoricality of uncompromising Gorean bondage.

Lady Claudia put out her hand and touched me on the shoulder, gratefully.

I pulled Lady Publia to her knees.

"Are you a slave?" I asked.

She nodded, vigorously.

Lady Claudia clapped her hands with delight, she herself no better.

"Do you beg permission," I asked, "to legalize the matter, to speak appropriate words of self-enslavement?"

She nodded, vigorously, again.

I then loosened the hood and pushed it up, about her head and forehead. I had not remembered she was so beautiful. I then loosened the two ties of the gag and pulled the wadding out from her mouth, letting it hang over the loosened cords, putting the whole by her throat. She looked at me, wildly, gratefully.

"Speak," I said.

"I am a slave!" she said.

"She is a slave!" said Lady Claudia softly.

The prisoner shrank back, frightened, shuddering, helpless, thrilled, now knowing herself slave.

"You are now a slave, Publia," said Lady Claudia, wonderingly.

"She is no longer Publia," I said to Lady Claudia. "She has not yet been named."

The slave looked at me, in awe.

Then she cried out, suddenly, as I replaced the wadding in her mouth, tightening it in again, with the cords.

"What are you doing?" asked Lady Claudia, frightened.

I saw the slave's eyes regarding me, wildly, just before I drew the hood again, over her beautiful features, securing it in place, tying the cord at the back of her neck.

"What are you doing?" cried Lady Claudia.

"She has got us this far," I said. "This is as far as we could expect to get with her, unchallenged, she in her guise as you. She has done as much for us as she can. She has thus served her purposes."

"What do you mean?" whispered Lady Claudia.

I reached for the impaling spear.

"No," said Lady Claudia.

I pressed the point of the spear against the interior of the slave's thigh. She threw back her head, and moaned.

"You knew she would declare herself a slave!" said Lady Claudia.

"She is a slave," I said. "It was fitting."

"I am no less a slave than she!" said Lady Claudia.

"That is true," I said.

"And now," she cried, "that you have won from her her confession that she was slave, and she has said the words themselves, enacting imbondment upon herself, you would put her, now, not even in the dignity of the free woman, but in the misery and degradation of a shamed slave, upon the spear!"

"Do you not think this slave, when she was a free woman," I asked, "would not have enjoyed seeing you on the spear?"

"No matter!" cried Lady Claudia. "No matter!"

"Those of Ar's Station," I said, "will expect to see her on the spear. If she is not there, I do not think we will get very far. When we leave the platform here, let them think our work has been done. Then we will draw away somewhere, I removing this mask, you retaining your rags and veil."

"No!" said Lady Claudia.

"It may be our only hope at escape," I said, "you falling to Cosians, I perhaps managing to mingle with them."

"You are a brave man," she said. "I admire you. You have been strong with me. You have been kind to me. You have risked much for me. I want you to escape. I see your reasoning. But if there must be a body on the spear, let it be mine. It is I who am guilty of treason, not she. Thus, it is I who should be impaled, not she."

"But you are a free woman," I said. "She is only a slave."

"You know, truly," she said, "she is no more, if as much, a slave as I. Surely in the cell, often enough, I gave you ample evidence that my fitting destiny was to give my entire being to the selfless love and service of a man!"

"You pity her because you are yourself no better than a slave," I said.

"I would pity her if she were a free woman," she said, "and I pity her now, that she is a slave."

"Because you, yourself, are a slave," I said.

"Perhaps," she wept. "I do not know."

Within the hood, I smiled. Slaves, as is well known, are on the whole far more loving and compassionate than free women. That is probably because they are so much more female than the free woman.

"We must hang her on the spear," I said, jocularly.

Suddenly Lady Claudia flung her body across that of the slave, as though she would protect her from me. It was a touching gesture, I thought. To be sure, it was a little silly. I could fling her a dozen feet away at my will, or. if I wished, with a judicious blow, little more than a quick tap on the diaphragm, have her instantly on her back helpless, gasping for breath. If necessary, I could bind her, or, if I wished, in an instant, strike her senseless.

"You would protect her, wouldn't you?" I asked.

"Yes!" she wept.

"She is perhaps your worst enemy," I reminded her.

"It does not matter," she wept.

"You have incredibly deep feelings and emotions," I said. "You would make a superb slave."

She looked up at me, puzzled. Her veil was wet with tears.

"Well, we had better hang this slave on the spear," I said, removing my sword belt.

"You have been joking," she said, suddenly. "You never intended to put her on the spear!"

"She is going to hang on the spear all right," I said. I then removed the sword from the sheath and thrust the sheath up, between the slave's back and the ropes, and then forced the point of the spear up, high, into the sheath. This did not do the sheath any good, distending it, but then it was not one, I reminded myself, for which I had had to put out my own tarsks. I then buckled the sword belt, making a new hole in the belt with my knife, tightly about the slender waist of the slave, up a bit, so it, too, was hidden behind the thickly coiled ropes. The spear's point was now entered into the sheath, the sheath held in place behind the slave by her ropes, and the slave's body held against the sheath and spear by the ropes and belt. She could not slip down the spear because of the spear's insertion in the sheath. In this way, when the spear was placed in the mount, it would appear, I hoped, that the slave had been mounted on the spear. To see that this was not so, I thought one would probably have to be rather close. There is not much blood, incidentally, with the sort of impalement which, I had gathered, they had intended for the prisoner, as the spear itself, in such an impalement, packs the wound.

"You are sparing her!" breathed Lady Claudia.

"Of late," I said, "she has been concerned to be pleasing."

The former Lady Publia shuddered, realizing what might as easily have been her fate.

I then lifted the spear up and inserted it, down, into its mount.

We heard some cheers from down on the wall, a handful, presumably greeting the appearance of the impaling spear, seemingly burdened. Most of the fellows, though, I suspected, had other things on their mind. Behind the slowly approaching towers, partly in their cover, advanced hundreds of men. The towers themselves were now little more than seventy-five yards from the wall. They had now aligned themselves, and the dropping of the bridges, when the towers were in position, would be simultaneous. Surely men should be drawn up from below to help defend the wall. The smaller probes, now, those of the scattered grapnels and single-pole ladders, had ceased. There were dozens of supporting grapnel and ladder crews, however, now approaching between the towers.

"Wriggle," I commanded the new slave, bound on the spear. "Wriggle well, and deliciously, or I shall set you on the spear properly!"

She then wriggled, and writhed, helplessly.

"Could you really put her on the spear?" asked Lady Claudia, softly.

"Certainly," I said. It was true.

We heard laughter from down on the wall, and, I think, even from Cosians below the wall. They, too, had little respect for traitresses.

Lady Claudia shuddered.

"Not too much," I cautioned the new slave, "mostly at first, then less. Then hold yourself tense, trying not to move."

The new slave, hung in the ropes, moaned her acquiescence.

"What is wrong?" I asked Lady Claudia.

"It could have been I, truly impaled," she said.

"But it is not," I said.

"The ram pounds the gate," she said.

We could feel the vibrations, even here.

"Let us leave," I said to Lady Claudia.

"There is no safety," she said.

Down on the lower walkway we looked back to the battlements over the gate. It did look as though the former Lady Publia were on the spear.

The towers were now but thirty yards away. There was no way their discharge, their rushing, armed effluxes could be stayed by the men here.

"If she is rescued," said Lady Claudia, looking back at the lovely, nude figure, seemingly mounted upon the impaling spear, "doubtless she will deny she is a slave."

"But even so," I said, "she would still be a slave, and would know it in her heart."

"Yes," said Lady Claudia.

The slave cannot free herself. She can be freed only by an owner. The condition of slavery does not require the collar, or the brand, or an anklet, bracelet or ring, or any such overt sign of bondage. Such things, as symbolic as they are, as profoundly meaningful as they are, and as useful as they are for marking properties, identifying masters, and such, are not necessary to slavery. They are, in effect, though their affixing can legally effect imbondment, ultimately, in themselves, tokens of bondage, and are not to be confused with the reality itself. The uncollared slave is not then a free woman but only a slave who is not then in a collar. Similarly a slave is still a slave even if her brand could be made to magically disappear or, if she has been a made a slave in some other way, if she has not yet been branded. Indeed. some masters, somewhat foolishly, I think, dally in the branding of their slaves. Indeed, some, perhaps the most foolish, do not brand them at all. Such girls, however, when they come into the keeping of new masters, usually discover that that oversight is promptly remedied.

"The slave who lies about her slavery," I said, "is not thereby the less a slave. It is only that she is then a lying slave."

"I have heard that bondage is difficult to conceal," said Lady Claudia.

"That is particularly so," I said, "if one has been a slave for a time. It can be given away in many ways, by the movements of the body, by certain timidities, and deferences, dispositions to kneel, slips of the tongue, and such. Slavers, and others, it is well known, can often pick out a slave from among women all clad in the Robes of Concealment, by simply having her walk, or speak, or by looking in her eyes. She is then disrobed, the brand revealed, and given over for punishment.''

She looked up at me.

"I spoke of legal bondage, of course," I said. "Perhaps you meant natural bondage, that of the woman who is by nature a slave?"

She looked down.

"That," I said, "is independent of the proprieties of legal bondage, of course."

"Yes," she whispered.

"To be sure," I said, "the condition of the natural slave, like that of the legal slave, can be difficult to conceal, particularly under certain stimulus conditions. It need not remain, however, simply a guilty secret locked in the heart of a frustrated, unfulfilled free woman, not yet in the keeping of her master. It can be shown by such things as her profound psychological dispositions to selflessly serve and love, her desire for, and response to, male domination, her understanding of chains and the whip, the quickening, deepening and intensification of her sexuality under conditions of bondage, her happiness and fulfillment when she finds herself placed in her proper relationship to the male, her joy in fulfilling her biological role, her joy in obedience, submission and love, her elation in knowing herself owned and mastered, subdued and conquered, a condition manifested in acts as disparate, and yet strangly akin, as the tying of her master's sandals and slave writhings in the furs, being forced to thrash helplessly in the orgasmic ecstasies he chooses to impose upon her."

She trembled.

"There are women who understand such things," I said.

"All women understand such things," she said.

"Perhaps," I said. "I do not know."

Again she trembled.

"But we were speaking of the former Lady Publia," I said. "She now knows herself a slave, having said the words. Too, she knows that she, a slave, can be freed only by a master. What will she make of these things? That, I take it, is your question?"

"Doubtless she would pretend she had never said the words," she said.

"That she would, in one way or another, attempt to conceal her true condition?"

"Yes," she said.

"Perhaps," I said. "But, of course, she would still, in her heart, know the truth, that she was a slave."

"Yes," she said.

"And that only a master could free her?"

"Yes," she said.

"Surely it might be difficult to live with such a hidden truth," I said. Perhaps it, irrepressible, insistent within her, might finally require some resolution. She must then take action. She might turn herself over to a praetor, hoping for mercy, as she had surrendered herself. Or perhaps she might solicit some person to make active claim upon her, such a claim, after certain intervals, superseding prior claims. Although there are various legal qualifications involved, which vary from city to city, effective, or active, possession is generally regarded as crucial from the point of view of the law, such possession being taken, no other claims forthcoming within a specified interval, as conferring legal title. This is the case with a kaiila or a tarsk, and it is also the case with a slave. In such a case, presumably the woman would expect the master who has then put claim on her to free her. That would presumably be the point of the matter. Otherwise she could simply submit herself to him as an escaped or strayed slave. Thus, in this fashion, she could reveal her hidden truth, thereby alleviating her acute mental conflicts, and her sufferings, attendant upon its concealment, and by another, as she has no legal power in the matter herself, be restored to freedom. To be sure, there are risks involved in this sort of thing. For example, when she kneels before him, his slave, perhaps he will then simply order her to the kitchen or to his furs. No promise made to her has legal standing, no more than to a tarsk. In this way, she, ostensibly seeking her freedom, may find herself plunged instead into explicit and inescapable bondage, and will doubtless, too, soon find herself properly marked and collared, to preclude the possible repetition of any such nonsense in the future."

"Yes," whispered Lady Claudia, not taking her eyes off the small figure suspended on the spear, on the battlements over the gate.

I looked over the wall. The towers had now stopped, aligned, some twenty yards or so from the wall. They would overtop it. When they advanced, they would do so, together.

"You had best go now," I said.

"I do not want to leave you," she said.

"When the towers spill their troops onto the wall," I said, "I do not think they will be stopping to make slaves. Go, hide. Perhaps later, when the citadel is burning, when resistance is ended, when the blood lust has to some extent lessened, you may receive an opportunity to strip yourself for captors."

"What of her?" she asked, pointing to the former Lady Publia.

"The slave?" I asked.

"Yes," she said.

"She is already stripped," I said.

"True!" she laughed.

"You had best leave," I said.

"You never intended to impale her, did you?"

"Not on the spear of execution," I said.

"I see," she said.

"Unless perhaps she might prove displeasing or in some way uncooperative."

"I understand," she said.

"There are, however, many other forms of impalement quite suitable for such as she," I said.

"Doubtless!" she laughed.

"And for you," I said.

"Yes," she said, "for me as well!"

"Go," I said. "The towers will advance at any moment."

"Why did you let us believe you would impale her?" she asked.

"Surely the genuineness of her terror added to the effectiveness of our disguises," I said, "as did your own authentic concern."

"You manipulated us as women, and slaves!" she said, her eyes flashing.

"And you are a clever woman," I said, "biding your time here against my will."

"I am a free woman," she said. "I think I shall remain here, by your side."

"Free woman or no," I said, "I wish I had a slave whip. I would teach you docility and compliance quickly enough."

"And I would offer them to you without the whip," she said, "—Master."

"Fortunate for you that you are not a slave!"

She laughed, merrily.

"I would you were naked at my feet, in a collar," I said, angrily.

"Ah," she said, "I would that I were there, too, my master, but I fear that that pleasure, if pleasure it be, seeing me so, having me so, will go not to you. but, if luck be with me, to a Cosian."

"That is not unfitting," I said. "You are a traitress. You declared for Cos. It seems not unfitting, then, that you should belong to a Cosian."

She tossed her head, angrily.

"Go," I said.

"I do not want to go," she said.

"I will not be able to protect you here," I said, "nor, in a few moments, will these others."

"I will remain here," she said.

"Here you will be in the way," I said. "You would jeopardize others, concerned for you."

She looked at me, her eyes angry.

"Go," I said. "You do not belong here."

"And do you?" she asked. "You are not of Ar's Station. You are not even of Cos!"

"Go," I said. "The work of men is soon to be done in this place."

She knelt down before me, though she was a free woman, and lifting her veil, pressed her lips to my sandals.

She then lifted her head to me, tears in her eyes. "I would that I were at your feet as a true slave, my master," she said.

"Go," I said.

Her eyes regarded me, piteously.

"Go," I said. "I would, if I were you," I said, "while any of Ar's Station are about, with a sword in their hand, keep my veil."

She nodded, frightened. She then looked once more at the former Lady Publia, now a roped slave, suspended on a spear, and then again at me, and then hurried from the wall.

I then turned to look across the twenty yards or so of space between the somber, looming towers, aligned, and the wall of the citadel. I could see cracks in the wood. Through some of these I could see numerous shapes, on various levels. The hides hung profusely about the outsides of the towers, especially on the frontal surfaces, were dark with water. The ram was still pounding at the gate.

The men on the wall, others coming up to join them from below, prepared to meet the onslaught. Groups bunched before each tower. Others scattered down the wall to meet the grapnel crews and the scalers, with their ladders. Weapons were unsheathed. Tridents were readied. Buckets of oil on the long poles were ignited.

I would have thought Aemilianus, commander of the citadel, would have come to the wall, but I did not see the helmet with the crest of sleen hair.

It occurred to me that I had not much business here, really. This was not my fight. I was no lover of Ar nor of Cos.

The trumpets would surely sound any moment.

The sky was calm enough, oblivious of a pending tumult beneath. The clouds would be indifferent to the blood that would be spilt beneath, dark in their racing shadows. What occurred here would surely be insignificant in the face of the universe. What small expanse of meaning was this, compared to the magnitudes of space? How tiny the disturbances and exertions of the afternoon must seem, compared to the dissolution and formation of worlds, and the turmoils wrought in the depths of incandescent orbs? Yet there was feeling and consciousness here and they, flickering it seemed in the darkness, tiny and frail, seemed to me in that moment to blaze in dimensions unfamiliar to the physicist, and in their own world and way to dwarf and mock the insensate placidities of space. Should the eye which opens on the awesomeness of the universe not apprehend as well the awesomeness of its own seeing? In man has the universe not come to self-consciousness, surprised that it should exist?

Where then was Aemilianus?

It was not my fight. I should go below. Surely in the citadel, somewhere, I could find other garments. My accents could not be confused with the liquid accents of Ar or those so similar, of Ar's Station. In the ingress of victors I should mingle with them.

It was not my fight.

Where was Aemilianus!

How dispirited seemed the defenders! How listlessly they stood! How resigned to their fate! What preparations did they make for the towers? Did they think they now faced only fellows on ladders, fellows climbing ropes, the clinging, climbing, creeping, shouting swarms, stinging with spears and blades, that they knew from a hundred trails in the past? They would be swept aside like dried leaves before the descendent blast of Torvaldsland. Were Cosians not to know their swords had been warmed and nicked in their romp?

"Ho, fools!" I cried, striding down the walkway. "The bridges will drop and you will think an avalanche of iron has spilled upon you! How shall you meet it? Let it spill on your heads? Clever fellows! Bring poles! Bring stones! You, fetch grapnels and ropes. The crews to the catapults, now! Yes, to the engines! You men there, you can see where this tower will come, there by the stairs. Break away the stone there! Open a great gap! You there, bring tarn wire!"

"Who are you?" cried a man.

"One who holds this sword!" I said. "Do you want it in your gut?"

"You are not Marsias!" cried another.

"I am assuming command," I said.

Men looked at one another, wildly.

"The wall cannot be held," said a man.

"True," I said. "I do not lie to you. The wall cannot be held. But what will it cost the Cosians?"

"Much," said a man, grimly.

"Those who have no stomach to stay," I said, "let them hide themselves among the women and the children below."

"Life is precious," said a man," but it is not that precious."

Suddenly there was a blast of trumpets from the foot of the wall and the eleven towers, with a lurch and groan, began to creep forward.

"Hurry!" I cried.

"Bring stones, poles, tarn wire!" cried men.

# 17
# BATTLE:
# WE WILL WITHDRAW
# TO THE LANDING

The bridges of the towers were still raised. These bridges were each about eight to ten feet in width. The towers themselves, which taper on the sides and back for stability, but are flat on the approaching surface, to make it possible to come flush with the wall, at that height were about fifteen feet in width. They were out from the wall, back from it, some seven feet. The lower sills of the bridges, from whence they would swing down, clapping, thundering, on the crenelation, were about four or five feet above the height of the wall. This permits a considerable momentum to the attackers without being so steep as to endanger the surety of their footing. There was no accident about the height of the towers. A simple geometrical calculation gives the height of the wall. We could now hear little movement within the towers, scarcely the clink of arms. They were, however, crowded with men.

"It is the waiting I do not like," said a fellow near me.

I lifted and lowered my sword. Men tensed along the wall. Fires were lit.

It had taken the towers at least five Ehn to move the twenty yards or so to the wall.

They were now here.

There are many ways of meeting such devices. The most effective, but generally impractical, as it consumes much time and materials, is to raise the wall itself, building it higher, so that they can serve as little more than ladder platforms. What is more often done when time permits is to build portable wooden walls, some fifteen feet, or so, in height, with defensive walkways and loopholes for missiles, which are then moved in the path of the towers. Sorties, the object of which is to fire the towers, are less practical than it might seem at first glance. Such towers are usually well defended, and are often not brought into play until such excursions are for most practical purposes beyond the resources of the defenders. Too, it is difficult to fire such objects, and the fires began on them by, say, small task forces are generally quickly extinguished.

At a single blast of trumpets, the eleven bridges were loosened, rattling, to the crenelation.

As soon as the bridges struck down on the stone, at eleven points along the wall, from each of the somber, giant, looming, hide-hung towers, scores of men packed within rushed forth, spewing forth, erupting, like lava or steam and water breaking from the side of a cliff, racing, sprinting, descending the bridges, shields set, hurling themselves downward. Poles, and pikes, and stones, and wire, and steel and fire met them. At two of the towers great poles were used. One, a foot thick and twenty feet in length, managed by ten men with ropes, mounted at an angle of some twenty degrees on an improvised pivot of heaped stone, swept the bridge an instant after it struck the crenelation, then tumbled off, used once, to fall behind the parapet. Men, before its movement, were struck screaming to the ground, but others followed them, pouring over the wall, to plunge into coiled tarn wire, to stumble, to fall, to wade in it bloodied, to meet stones and steel. The second great pole was tied on two crosspoles and, by ten men on each crosspole, was thrust in place as soon as that bridge fell, and was held at an angle, like a railing, its sturdy barrier diverting the stream of attackers, causing many on the outside edge to be buffeted by their comrades to the ground below, a hazard in crossing such a bridge at any time under the conditions of battle. Many clung to the pole, as they could, and many strove to slip under it or climb over it. In the cleared angle of the bridge, the defenders mounted to the bridge itself and there, behind the barrier, and about it,

stanched the flow of men upward, holding them on the
planking of the bridge, between the tower and the wall.

At two of the bridges tiles and bricks, some two feet in
length and six inches in height and width, met the attackers,
not so much to stay the force of the attack as litter the bridge
itself, that rushing men, not suspecting them, might stumble
and fall. And in such cases there was always the press of men
from behind, ascending the ladders, pushing the others forward. Tarn wire here, too, was set to enmesh those who came
over the wall. I had had the rear portions of the two catapults
propped up, that the angle of fire could be flattened. This,
given the height of the openings, revealed by the dropped
bridges, made it possible to fire at point-blank range, the
shovel of one catapult containing a thousand bits of rock and
metal, the shovel of the other a large boulder, weighing
perhaps fifteen hundred pounds, requiring five men men for
its loading, trundling it up the ramp.

The first catapult slung its storm of missiles into the charging men, blinding them, denting shields, cutting clothing
from bodies. The second catapult cast its load, its boulder,
into the midst of startled men and had it not been for their
smitten bodies, dashed back, cushioning the blow would have
torn its way free through the back of the tall, shedlike tower.
In both cases defenders then climbed to the bridges to meet
the foe, driving him back, thrusting him down to the lower
level, stopping the ascent at the ladders. At the termination of
another bridge we had broken away an opening in the walkway, enlarging a gap about stairs. Here charging foes leaping
from the wall found no footing but only an opening beneath
them, half pit, half stairs. Men waited below for those who
still moved, with axes. Another charge, rushing forth from
the tower, unable to stop, pushed on by the masses behind
them, plunged into flames, where we had heaped bundles of
tarred sticks in their path, the sort that on wires and chains,
flaming, are hung over the walls at night to illuminate ascending foes.

At another bridge, Vosk fishermen, from the vicinity of
Ar's Station, fought, perhaps men who had merely been
trapped in the city when the Cosians had taken their positions, and, at another bridge, huntsmen, from the interior,
perhaps similarly detained. The fishermen had a net with

them, doubtless brought up from their small boat in the harbor. Such devices are rich in war uses. They can discommode scalers and grapnel crews. They can block passages. From behind them one may conveniently thrust pikes and discharge missiles. In the field they may serve as foundations for camouflage, for example, effecting concealments from tarnsmen. Questioned, eagerly had I assented to its use, pleased to have the unexpected and welcome aid of such an object. Nets, too, of course, are used at sea in the repulsion of boarders. Similarly, nets, often small and silken, but sturdy and cunningly weighted, are used in the taking of women. At both these bridges the charge was arrested by the bristling points of a braced, pike wall, two men to a pike. At the fishermen's bridge the net was cast, but its weights were not now stones. Rather was it weighted with two logs which, as it settled upon its catch, were toppled over the parapet.

At the bridge of the huntsmen loops of tarn wire were cast over the armed, halted efflux which the foe, to his horror, trying to extricate himself, felt draw tight and then he, too, snared, was dragged from the bridge. Huntsmen are skilled in the stringing and weighting of such devices. The wire, in its wide, supple loops, had settled about its victims, their legs and bodies. Its two free ends were weighted, secured about heavy posts which were then toppled over the parapets, this causing at one time the tightening of the loops and the dragging of the catch not now into the air, where it dangles helplessly, upside down, awaiting the convenience of the huntsman, perhaps to have its throat cut, but from the bridge. As with nets, with snares there is a great variety of types and uses. Some are fine enough to set for field urts and others stout enough for tharlarion.

At both bridges, following the success of the devices of the fishermen and huntsmen, the temporary consternation of hesitant successors permitted defenders to take their place, too, on the shaking bridge, where, in moments, they had pressed their way back even to the edge of the flooring, that of the highest level, beneath the roof, at the back of which would be located stairs or ladders, depending on the structure of the particular tower. At the last tower a simple garrote of tarn wire, almost invisible, had been thrust forth, secured between two poles. Such wire is usually handled with gloves. It can cut to the bone. It can take a wing from a tarn. I do not think the first fellows hurrying down the bridge even saw it. Their bodies, lacerated, impeded the flow of their fellows. Pikes thrust forth from behind the parapet, and at the sides, and over the planks, of the dropped bridge, where it projected beyond the crenelation on which it rested. While these things were going on hundreds of grapnels had looped over the wall and the ropes on them strained with swiftly climbing men, and the uprights of hundreds of ladders, like a forest, set themselves against the walls. Between the towers men hurried cutting ropes, and, where they could, thrusting back the ladders with the long-handled tridents. Oil was poured on screaming men ascending. Bodies aflame leapt from wood and rope. But Cosians came over the wall.

"We cannot hold them!" cried a man.

Fellows came then from below. The walkways behind the parapets were swarming with men.

In two of the towers defenders had won the top level and poured flaming oil about the floor and down the ladderways. On two others some, with axes, literally chopped away at the bridge, behind their fellows.

I saw quarrels discharged at point-blank range.

Blades rang.

A Cosian, twisting, fell back from the wall.

I saw one of Ar's Station run through, and slip to one knee, and then disappear back, over the interior edge of the walkway, probably to plunge to the rubble there, and then roll down to the court, behind the wall.

I saw a defender leap back from a tower, a torch in his hand. Smoke flowed from behind him, out of the opening. Such structures are easier to fire from the inside than the outside. I saw other fellows carrying bundles of flaming sticks and tar on their pikes into a tower. It was aflame.

Some defenders leapt back to the wall, and the bridge, cut in pieces, sagged behind them.

Cosians, sweating, their eyes wild in their helmets, reaching out from ropes, and ladders, struggled through, and over, the crenels.

The crew of one of the engines had set another great stone into its shovel. Their backs strained, turning the windlass, winding that huge torsion-powered device taut. I saw one of them, a quarrel in his back, fall away from the windlass. Then, suddenly, a lever thrown, the mighty arm of the engine went forward again and a great stone burst against one of the towers. It was half turned and tottered, but did not fall. The draw bridge hung down, leading now only to the air.

At one end of the wall I saw Cosians coming through a tower. No longer were they impeded by tarn wire. They crossed it now literally on the bodies of their fellows fallen in it, and strewn over it, as one might cross a river on stones or a bog on planks. I dispatched the few reserves I had to seal off that portion of the walkway. On such a narrow path I hoped twenty men might hold against a thousand, for there the thousand could put against them no more than twenty. But the thousand were nourished and strong, and soldiers, not an aggregation of half-starved scions of a hundred castes, not one in ten of the warriors, not one in five trained in arms.

I had taken up my post above the main gate, on the higher battlements, where the impaling spear was mounted, and the flag of Ar's Station still snapped defiantly. This seemed to me the likely place for a command post. It was the most central location on the land wall. It was where I would have expected to have found Aemilianus.

More Cosians came over the wall. There were pockets of them, embattled, here and there along the walkway. The men I had sent to the west end of the land wall, past the west bastion, had actually sped by them. There are in battle, I have found, often oddities, which seem inexplicable, and yet they occur. I have sometimes seen a man walk among combatants, threading his way here and there, almost as though among crowds in a market, no one bothering to challenge him or pay him the least attention. But if eye contact is made, then there is not unoften a fight to the death. Also, I have seen two pairs of men fighting, those of each pair side by side, as though fellows, and yet they are enemies, and each engages another foe. The riderless tharlarion or kaiila, like the riderless horse in battles of Earth, can sometimes be seen whirling about, obeying the trumpet calls for charging, and retreating, and such, just as though his master were still in the saddle. Too, sometimes such animals may be found calmly standing about, or grazing, while the fiercest of fighting surges about them. I have seen, too, wounded men being carried to the rear, their bearers unmolested, through clashing ranks, and other fellows pausing to loot a body, blades flashing about them. Sometimes, too, in a moment's lull, one notices little things, to which one has perhaps hitherto paid scant attention, the movements of an ant, how rain water irregularly stains a rock, moving and spreading, depending on the texture of its surface.

I remember one fellow telling me about a man who had died near him, in a field. The man had been lying there, on his back. The last thing he said was, reportedly, "The sky is beautiful." My informant told he, however, that the sky then had looked much the same as it usually does. This is a hard story to understand. Perhaps then the dying man had seen it differently, or perhaps only then seen that it was beautiful. I now saw a fellow from Ar's Station on top one of the towers, on its roof. He was just standing there. He seemed to be admiring the view. I had little doubt it was somewhat spectacular. He waved to me. I lifted my sword to him, in salute.

Suddenly, on the approach from the right, a fellow, breaking away from a knot of embroiled fighters, raced up the stairs, toward me, sword drawn. It was his intention, I gathered, rather after the moment, to have had the honor of slaying the commander on the wall. This occurred to me as he spun about, blood gushing from beneath his helmet, falling back down the steps.

On the east, and nearer the center portions of the wall, four of the towers were aflame.

Not seventy feet away, a rope severed, men plunged screaming to the earth below.

Along the wall, at two of the towers, men chopped away at the housings for the chains which controlled the bridges. Some of the bridges, but most not, were raised and lowered by ropes. One whose ropes had been cut had its bridge hanging down. against the front of the tower, useless. Cosians were trying to run planks out from the tower, to span the crevice between the tower and wall. I did not doubt but what, sooner or later, the towers might be brought flush to the wall. This is commonly not done, however, for various reasons. It more exposes the tower to the defenders, who might then tear the hides from it and smear it with flaming tar, or enter and attack it at their own choosing. Too, it makes it much easier to prevent the dropping of the bridges, by blocking them with beams or poles, or, in some cases, by fouling one or both of the chains, usually with metal pins. It is better for the attackers, usually, to have the tower isolated, back from the wall, and to be able to control its bridge without concern for the defenders. Thus they may lower it when they will and raise it when they will, perhaps after a retreat, transforming the tower then into what, in effect, is a small, inaccessible, impregnable keep, with its moat of space, a keep, however, whose bridge might then, suddenly, at any moment of the day or night, drop again, once more disgorging its onslaught of attackers.

I saw a fellow, aflame, running below, beyond the wall, then he fell and rolled in the dirt.

The pounding of the ram below continued. It had a different sound now than before. I did not understand why.

Men leaped back from towers to the wall, their work done on them. Two swung back on ropes and climbed through the crenelation, almost as though they might have been Cosians.

I thought I heard the scraping of a ladder against the wall near me. This startled me, as the battlements here, in the vicinity of the gate, were higher, surely, than even the long, bending single-pole ladders used along the wall.

I saw more Cosians spew forth from a tower, over its bridge, and fall into tarn wire, and meet the pikes of defenders. From where I stood I could see, outside and below, hundreds of Cosians, and their mercenaries and allies. These fellows were back about a hundred yards. Many seemed at their ease, watching the walls, the ladders, the grapnel men, what they could see of the fighting.

In places along the wall defenders sought to get their poles under the bridges, between them and the crenelation, and, using the wall as a fulcrum, to lift the bridges back up. Sometimes Cosians and defenders, fighting, were on the very bridges being pried upward. At two towers the poles had thrust the bridges up and back. Men tried to hold them braced. But other men, Cosians, within, dozens, some with axes, half breaking the bridges apart, from the inside, forced them down again.

I heard the bellowing of an agonized tharlarion from below, and saw some led from burning towers, their harnesses cut. One, tearing itself free, heedless of the cries and blows of its keeper, ran blindly back toward the city, the men among the engines breaking apart, or climbing on the engines, to let it pass.

To my amazement then I saw two uprights of a ladder, a two-upright ladder, not one of the single-pole ladders, suddenly appear but feet from me. I ran to the place and thrust through the crenelation at a fellow, his hand already half over the wall. He tumbled back, into space. The next fellow had his shield before him. I could not get at him, nor he, because of it, at me. I crouched in the crenelation, bracing myself with my left arm. He climbed another rung and I kicked out, turning the shield to the side. He was half pulled from the ladder by the shield straps but he slipped down a foot or two, recovering himself. He looked up. I could not reach him. Something, slipped past, hardly sensed, like a snake, leaving a thread of sound in the air. Another thing cut the mask at the side of my face, like a knife.

One fellow was trying to climb past the nearest fellow on the ladder. This fellow, in one hand, grasped a spear. He was then on the same rung with the fellow with the shield, and then one rung higher. The spear blade thrust up, scratched the inside of the crenel. I seized the shaft behind the head. He held it with both hands. I wanted the spear. I could not get leverage from where I was, to move the uprights. He would not release it. Then he was pulled free of the ladder and hung in the air. A quarrel struck the outside of the wall a foot or so from my face. It was like an ice pick suddenly driven into ice, but what burst forth was not ice but stone. He hung tenaciously to the spear. Did he not truly, in that moment of terror, I wonder, comprehend what was supporting him, that it was not the spear, but I? Despairing of gaining the spear I released it. His hand reached out wildly then, belatedly, for the ladder, but his hand could not close on it. I drew back. Another movement sped past, like a puff of breath passing my ear. Below I heard yet another fellow trying to climb higher, and another. There were shouts. I looked through an adjacent crenel. The fellow with the shield hung half off the ladder. Another fellow had passed him and was almost up. I returned to my original place to meet him, but suddenly, just as he was coming within reach, I heard a sound like a fist striking leather, it came from his back, and he looked surprised, and then stiffened on the ladder and threw back his arms and head, and, twisting, plunged downward. I caught sight of a quarrel's fins protruding from his back.

Another fellow was behind him, and I met him. He blocked my blow with his blade. He blocked my blow again with his blade. Then he did not block my blow. Clutching the uprights, grimacing, coughing, spattered with blood, he slipped back some rungs, until he was a few feet below me. I looked about, wildly. I thrust my sword through my belt, to which were attached my pouch and knive sheath, both on the left side. I raced to the impaling spear, hoisted it up, some five feet, from its mount. The slave who had been Lady Publia, its burden by means of the ropes, the sheath and sword belt, twisting wildly, throwing her head about as though bewildered, as though she would try to see through the hood, uttered a tiny, terrified, questioning, miserable, helpless noise, her oral orifice. of course, remaining subject to the closure I had imposed upon it. I leveled the spear, then cast it to the ground. I was in a hurry. She was a slave. I then, lifting the spear up a bit, her head down, thrust her with my foot, in her ropes, with the sword belt and sheath, from the spear.

I then hurried back to where the ladder was. Another fellow had just appeared in the opening in the crenelation and I pushed out at him with the long impaling spear. Its point is a dull one, designed for an unpleasantly lengthy penetration. Even so with the force I slid it across the stone it jammed between his ribs, entered his body, and carried him out from the ladder. He dangled on it and then slipped from it, unable to cling to it with his hands. I think he struck the ladder again, some feet further down. I heard another man cry out, a few feet below. There was then a scream.

Armed with the spear, which is some fifteen feet in length, like a third- or fourth-rank phalanx spear, I reached over the wall and managed to get it behind the top rung of the ladder. No one was close to me then. The highest fellow was the man with the shield, who had withdrawn earlier. He looked up, discarded his shield, started to climb madly toward the spear, then stopped. The ladder leaned out, a yard or so from the wall. I pried back further, and the ladder straightened, and then it leaned back further, held in place only by the friction with the spear. Some men leaped from it. Others tried to throw their weight against it, to force it forward again. Some dared not move. I slid the spear back and up. The ladder tottered. It must fall backward! But it did not. It crashed forward, against the wall. I pried at it again, and the top rung broke. I wished that I had had one of the tridents or one of the sharpened, steel crescents fixed on a metal pole, useful in such work. The fellow who had had the shield now climbed toward me. This time, however, the ladder leaning out from the wall, I managed to get the point of the spear free from under a rung and on one of the uprights itself. I could now push back. He tried to dislodge the point from the wood but I shifted and caught him under the arm and pushed back more. I hoped to use his own fear against him, his unwillingness to release the ladder, but before I could push back enough, past the center of balance, he released one hand and twisted, hanging to a rung with his free hand. But then, again, I managed to get the point on an upright. The ladder straightened, and I thrust out another foot, and then another, moving my hands on the spear, my hands sweaty, and then the ladder seemed, for an instant, to lean oddly back, away. For an instant I was not clear that it would fall. But then men were screaming and leaping from it, up and down its length, and I saw it turn on one upright, doubtless more from their movements and the shifts in weight than from anything of my doing, and then it fell back, and I heard it snap and break. At the same time I drew back, as a pair of quarrels flashed past. I think it probable that some had been fired at me when I had struggled with the spear for I saw at least one new, irregular scratch in the stone near where I had labored. Yet, oddly enough, though there must have been noise, I had not even noticed it at the time. It was only now, oddly, in recollection that it seemed to me I might have heard something there, cutting at the stone, and other things, too, like hissed whispers about me.

A young fellow, one of the two of an age to be lads whom I had seen on the wall, appeared on the steps leading to the upper battlements. He had only two quarrels left, one in the guide, the other grasped in his hand, with the bow, not really quarrels even, only sharpened rods. Even the blunt-headed wooden quarrels, suitable for stunning birds, were gone. I had used him, and the other, he between the command post and the west, the other between the command post and the east, as messengers, hoping in this way to keep them within the semblance of interior lines, out of the thickest fighting. "They cannot hold on the west walkway!" he cried. "They give way!"

I issued orders and he raced back. My plan, even if successful, would keep the walkway, nearer the command post, only for a few Ehn. I looked to the east. There more Cosians leapt from the bridge of a tower, clambering and stumbling over the bodies of others, tangled lifeless and wounded in the wire. Men struggled to meet them, with pikes and axes. I became aware then again of the blows of the ram below. The sound had been different for the last few Ehn. How had the ladder I had repelled managed to reach the height of the wall? I went to my left and bent over the crenelation, leaning over the wall. I saw then that the roof of the ram shed sloped upward. A hill, literally, of debris, of sand, rock and bodies, had been built there, before the gate, and the shed thrust up this incline. This brought the blows of the ram high on the gate, presumably over the rocks and sand, and such, which had been heaped behind it by the defenders. That accounted for the difference in the sound of the ram. What effort it must have taken to force the long ram shed up this incline, how much more arduous must be the labor of those within the shed, hauling on the ropes, swinging the great ram upward! I could hear, too, between the heavy, periodic strokes of the ram, the blows of hammers and axes, and the smiting on punches and chisels, and the sounds of creaking metal, as men sought to cut and punch openings in the facing on the gate, then twisting and prying it back. Plates of facing buckled and were torn away. It was on this artificial hill, built before the gate, that the ladder which had reached to the height of the battlements had been mounted. From where I now stood, because of the shed, I could not see the remains of the ladder.

I went to my right then to survey what might be the case on the west. I watched. Then, suddenly the defenders there, holding the west walkway, withdrew. They had been fighting behind a breastwork of fallen bodies, those of both Cosians and defenders. The Cosians seemed for a moment bewildered, but then, with a great cry, swarmed over the bodies in

pursuit. Scarcely were the defenders drawn back than the
great cauldron of oil, its oil now ignited, now aflame, into
which the buckets on long handles had been dipped, was
overturned with poles and flooded the walkway behind them.
The bulk of the Cosians stopped at this wall of flames some
forty feet in width. Some, however, raced into it. Of these
some perished in the flames. Others, half afire, screaming,
turned about, fleeing back to their fellows. Some crossed it,
and were cut down on the other side. This retreat, though it
surrendered the western walkway, decreased the amount of
area to be held, and, with these new numbers, increased the
defenders there. The Cosians then within the wall, in the
center, were much harder pressed. Some withdrew, even, to
the towers, some of which were aflame. I saw the bridges,
burned through, collapse beneath some of them, plunging
them to the ground.

I went again to my left. There, on the east, I saw that the
Cosians had gained yards, and that they were now beyond the
wire. The defenders, foot by foot, were being pressed back.
More Cosians leapt from the bridge of a tower, down onto the
bodies and wire, climbing over them, hurrying to join the
fray. The east walkway could not be long held.

I went, wearily, to where the roped, ankle-thonged, naked,
gagged, hooded slave lay, on the stones. With my foot I
turned her to her back. I unbuckled the sword belt from about
her, and then, crouching beside her, turned her to her stomach. I withdrew the sheath from between her back and the
ropes. It was distended, where it had received the spear,
almost to the bottom. I pressed it as flat as I could, with my
hands and foot. The blade then, again, but not well, fitted
into it. I rebuckled the belt and put it about me, the strap over
my right shoulder, the sheath at the left hip, as one wears it
on the march. That is a stabler carry. The advantage of the
left shoulder carry, the sheath at the left thigh, is the ease of
discarding the belt and sheath, thereby ridding oneself of a
possible encumbrance.

The young fellow with the crossbow climbed to the upper
battlements. He now had only one quarrel left. "The flames
on the west walkway are lessening," he said. He looked
down at the slave. "She is still alive," he said, puzzled.

"Yes," I said.

"How can it be?" he asked.

"How do you think?" I asked.

"A trick?" he said.

"Yes," I said.

"But I saw her on the spear," he said.

"She was hung on it," I said, "not mounted upon it, not impaled with it."

"Are you going to kill her now?" he asked.

"No," I said, "at least not immediately, unless perhaps she should be in some respect displeasing."

"You speak of her as though she were a slave," he said.

"Are you a slave?" I asked the girl. "Whimper once for 'Yes,' twice for 'no.' "

She whimpered once.

"Do you desire to please men?" I asked.

She whimpered once.

I patted her. "Show us," I said.

She lifted her behind, piteously, placatingly.

"That is not Lady Claudia!" said the young fellow.

"No, it is not," I said. But I smiled to myself as I said it. Did he not know that Lady Claudia would have been quite as quick, if not quicker, to lift herself, hoping to please?

"Who is it?" asked the lad.

"I have not yet named her," I said.

"Who was it?" he asked.

"Do not concern yourself with the matter," I said.

"Where then is Lady Claudia, the traitress?" he asked.

"I do not know," I said.

"It is as Caledonius said," he said. "You are not Marsias."

"No," I said. "I am not Marsias."

"Who, then, are you?" asked he.

"One whom you have acknowledged as your captain," I said.

"Yes, Captain," said he, lifting his bow in salute.

I issued orders, with the injunction that he should, when they were delivered, return to the upper battlements.

He hastened down the stairs to the right.

I then returned my attention to the slave. I unknotted the thong by means of which her small, fair ankles had been so securely bound, the one to the other. I looped the thong in and about the ropes at her back.

At that moment the other young fellow, who had seemed so mature, who was serving as my messenger to the eastern walkway, gasping, ascended to the upper battlements.

"We are giving way!" he said.

I had been waiting for him.

He, too, seemed startled to see the slave. "It is not Lady Claudia," I said. "It is only a nameless slave."

"They are calling up from below," he said, paying the female no more attention. "The gate is being sundered!"

I issued him orders, orders parallel to those I had given the other young fellow, with the injunction that he, too, after their delivery, return to the upper battlements.

I then went to the wall and looked out, once more, on the vast panoply before me, across the burned, leveled ground, at the engines, the troops, the hulks and shells of buildings in the distance. In the eastern part of the city there was still smoke. There had been fires in the city for days. I could even see the outside wall, far off. It seemed a long time ago, now, that it had been breached. I then, slowly, drew down the flag of Ar's Station from the citadel. That would not be done by Cosians. I did not raise another cloth in its place.

"We have withdrawn to just west of the west gate stairs," said the young fellow, reporting from the western walkway.

"Take the slave," I said, "and put her on the central walkway, behind the upper battlements. You will find slave rings there, in the wall. Fasten her to one, kneeling, by her leash." Such things are common conveniences in Gorean cities, in public places, and such. Even when the slave is seldom attached to one, she sees them, and this has its psychological effect with her. She knows that they are for the tethering of such as she. Here, within the citadel, of course, such rings, though usually called slave rings, could serve a large variety of purposes. They are not merely for girls chained there on furs in the moonlight, for the use of strollers, off-duty guards and such. They may be used, for example, for such purposes as anchoring war engines, to keep them, in their reaction, from backing off the walkway, restraining guard sleen, and securing prisoners. "Then return to your fellows, and watch for my signal. It will be delivered from the central walkway, behind the upper battlements."

"Yes, Captain," he said.

"On your knees, woman," he said.

The slave struggled to her knees.

"On your feet, woman," he said.

She who had once been Lady Publia rose unsteadily to her feet. It was hard for her to stand. She had not stood for some time, and her ankles, for some time, had been closely bound.

The young fellow, seeing her difficulty, took her leash close to the collar, that he might, if necessary, steady her, and keep her from falling. He then drew her along quickly, she stumbling, after him. He was in age no more than a lad and she was a mature, fully grown, beautiful woman but in accord with nature's decisions, given the differential parameters involved, those of his size and strength, contrasting so markedly with hers of slightness, delicacy, softness, and beauty, he handled her with ease.

I watched them descending the steps to the central walkway. She half fell once, losing her footing, striking against the right side of the stone stairwell, but he kept her upright, his hand then literally about her thick leather collar, and then, in a moment, now again on a short leash, I saw her drawn about the corner, toward the line of rings below and in back of the upper battlements.

I turned about and the other youg fellow, he who was my messenger to the eastern walkway, climbed to the upper battlements from the eastern stairwell.

"The flag!" he cried.

I handed it to him.

"Keep it," I said. "One day it may fly again."

There were tears in his eyes.

"Return now to your fellows," I said, "and watch for my signal. It will be given from behind the upper battlements."

He hurried away.

I looked to the western walkway and saw the other young fellow with the fellows there. He was behind their lines, facing the central walkway. His presence there informed me that the slave, her upper body so wound about with ropes as to almost conceal her beauty, would be at a slave ring, behind and below the upper battlements, kneeling there, hooded and gagged, fastened to it by her leash.

I looked to the eastern walkway. I saw the other young

fellow there now, clutching the flag in his arms. He, too, was looking back, toward the central walkway.

It was important to me to coordinate the withdrawal of both wings, to keep balance in the positions, to prevent flanking movements. Too, I thought I might buy some time for them by seeming to offer the Cosians an enviable prize, the capture of the wall commander. I thought this might be of particular interest to them, given the losses they had suffered this afternoon.

From below, in front of the wall, I could hear the buckling and tearing of plate on the gate, the pounding of the ram, the groaning and cracking of wood.

I then descended to the central walkway. There were bodies there, as elsewhere about the walkway, those of Cosians, those of defenders. A Cosian, wounded, seeing me, tried to struggle to his feet. He was a mass of blood. It was dried in his beard. His helmet was gone. He could hardly lift his blade.

"How are things in Cos?" I asked him.

"Well," he said.

"Put down your blade," I suggested.

He thought for a moment and then shrugged. He could scarcely hold it.

I then kicked it away from him.

"It seems the day is yours," I said.

"That it is," he whispered.

"Rest," I said to him.

He slumped back against the rear of the upper battlements, not far from one of the rings there.

I could hear the ringing of swords, the clash of metal on shields, from both the right and left.

I then went to the slave, kneeling on the walkway, facing the stone backing of the upper battlements, tethered there. Her head was actually turned sharply to the left she was fastened so closely to the ring by the leash. I saw that the young fellow, though he might be young, had an instinctive sense for the handling and owning of women.

I took the thong which had originally bound her ankles, which I had earlier removed from them on the upper battlements, and looped in and about the ropes on her back, and put it beside me on the stone. I then, holding her wrists, and by means of them, moving them back and forth, as she whimpered, and drawing them more closely together, slowly worked her arms more behind her under the ropes. I then, when I could, crossed her wrists and tied them with the thong, her arms still under the ropes. I then loosened one end of the long rope bound about her body and tied it to the ring. I then loosened the other end, too, and tucked it loosely in among the lower coils, near her waist. She whimpered piteously, questioningly. I then freed her leash from the ring, where her neck was held so closely to it. I then drew her to her feet and, turning her a few times, unwrapping some of the rope, stood her near the courtyard edge of the walkway. She stood unsteadily.

"If I were you, I would not wander about just now," I said. "Do you understand?" She whimpered once. "Stay," I told her, making certain of her compliance, giving her a command common to slaves. This informs them they are to remain where they are until moved, or given permission to move. She whimpered once, once again. She did not know it but she stood but a foot from the drop to the courtyard. To be sure, now, with the interior debris below, the drop there was only about forty feet, but then there was another distance, longer, given the angle, down to the courtyard, down the hill.

I then turned to the left and right, and made certain that I had the eye of my messengers, the young men on the left and right. I then lifted and lowered my sword. Immediately following this signal the defenders on both the left and right began an orderly withdrawal, rear lines first, front lines backing, fighting, down the stairways closest to them, the two gate stairways, one to the west of the gate, the other to the east of the gate. The stairways, of course, were much narrower than the walkway, and could be held by fewer men in the retreat.

"Ho!" I called to the Cosians to the left and right, lifting my sword.

I saw men pointing to me. I had little doubt that some of them, at least, would have seen me on the upper battlements, and would realize I had been commanding on the wall. Too, I stood next to a well-roped woman who, though hooded, and much covered in the upper body by ropes, would be likely to intrigue them. She had lovely legs and the contours of the ropes about her upper body would not leave much doubt that luscious slave curves were the helpless prisoners of their coarse, serpentine coils.

I sheathed my sword.

It must have appeared to most of them that my escape was cut off, that I was somehow trapped between the two stairways.

Doubtless we would seem prizes in diverse ways to the Cosians. the commander of the wall and a female who might hopefully, when unhooded, be found to have a face to match the excitements of her figure. Too, if she were in the keeping of the wall's commander did this not, in itself, suggest that she might be worthy a cord and nose ring?

Too, my sword was sheathed. Did this not suggest that I might regard myself as trapped, as I seemed to be, that I might regard my position as untenable, that I thus might choose not to offer resistance, that I might be prepared to surrender?

Almost at the same time one or two score of fellows, from both sides, began to race toward me. Others stood back, near the heights of the stairs, to watch. These things, I assumed, would draw much pressure from the stairways. My defenders would probably be able to withdraw more easily, close portals and block passages.

I thrust the slave to her right and she tumbled off the walkway. There was suddenly, she losing her footing, knowing herself unsupported, her head jerking wildly in the hood, her legs moving wildly, treading on nothing, beginning to turn to her side in the air, starting to plunge downward, a wild, tiny, terrified, prolonged noise from within the hood, what perhaps a shrill, terrified scream might have been, if it were to be compressed within the latitudes permitted by a Gorean gag, emerging then as a small, helpless noise, one not likely to disturb masters. But in an instant she had gasped and was jerked up short by the coils of rope, her plunge arrested, but then, again, almost instantly, the rope began to uncoil from her body and she, spinning, the rope unwinding, in a series of wild jerks, awkwardly began to descend, riding the uncoiling rope downward. In an Ihn or so she had struck the hill of debris and then, still moving, still descending, the rope still uncoiling, turning over and over, tumbling, rolled toward the bottom, toward the courtyard. For an instant it had been hard to get my hands on the rope, it was moving so, over the edge of the walkway, but, a moment or so after she had struck the hill of debris, I had it in my hands and began to descend it, rapidly, hand over hand. I would not slide down the rope, incidentally, because I did not have protection for my hands. Sliding down such a rope for even forty feet or so can burn the flesh from one's hands. One can be crippled for weeks. Under certain conditions, this may be an acceptable cost, but it is not likely to be so if one expects to have use for the sword in the near future.

As soon as I reached the hill of debris I had my feet under me and then, even more rapidly, half sliding and jumping, holding the rope, hurried down the hill. When I reached the bottom of the hill I turned and looked upward. Mainly I wanted to see if there were any crossbowmen on the walkway. There were none. One or two fellows looked as though they might be thinking about following me down the rope, but they did not do so. On the hill of debris they would have poor footing. At the foot of the rope they would be in the courtyard, perhaps isolated. They could come down only one at a time. All in all I did not blame them.

"Well done," said a young voice.

I turned about. It was the young fellow who had the crossbow.

"I thought this might be your plan," he said, "when you had me put the slave at the ring."

"You are a clever fellow," I grinned.

"And so I came to cover your descent," he said.

I smiled. I had not realized this additional reason for not following me down the rope. The fellows on the walkway had seen him. I had not. It was true, of course, that he had only one quarrel for his bow. Yet who, still, would wish to be the first down the rope?

"You are a brave young fellow," I said, "to have come here, for such a purpose, with but a single quarrel for your bow."

"I shall find others elsewhere," he said.

"Thank you," I said.

"It is nothing," he said.

The other young fellow, he who had been my messenger to the eastern walkway, emerged into the courtyard. He looked up at the walkway. The Cosians were now leaving the central walkway, and hurrying to the stairwells, those to the east and west.

"The citadel is being evacuated," said the newcomer.

"We shall withdraw to the harbor area," said the fellow with the crossbow. "Then the slaughter will take place."

"We have fought a good fight," said the second fellow.

"I think so," said the first.

I went to the slave. She lay on the lower slope of the hill of debris, her head down, her legs higher, up the hill, her right leg flexed. The end of the rope was a few feet above her, on the hill, where she had come free of it, and then rolled further downward. Her hands were thonged behind her. There were rope marks on her body, the signs of her spinning, jerking plunge to the hill, and then her tumbling downward, rather to her present location. She was trembling, uncontrollably. I supposed it had been frightening for her, she helpless in the hood.

I took her by one arm and drew her to the level, at the foot of the hill, and knelt her there.

I then bent her back, one hand on a thigh, the other on the back of her collar, in a slave bow, for the inspection of the young fellows.

"She is pretty," said the first.

"Yes," said the other.

I released her. "You are in the presence of men," I told her.

Swiftly she bent forward and put her head down to the ground.

"Take this slave," I said to the fellow without the bow, "and put her with the women and children. If you meet Cosians throw her to them. If they stop to take her in tow you may escape. Similarly, in the vicinity of the women and children, she might serve similar purposes, being used for a diversion or something."

"We would rather stay with you, Captain," said the fellow with the bow.

"The women and children will need you," I said.

"What of you?" he asked.

"I would see what is going on by the gate," I said.

The young man with the bow lifted it in salute.

"Stand, slave," said the other fellow to the girl. She stood and her leash was taken in his grasp. She could not see, of course, confined in the hood, but he had looped the end of the leash. It was long enough, thusly, to serve as a disciplinary lash. In a moment the two young men, and the slave, had disappeared through an interior portal at the far side of the courtyard. I myself took one of the smaller portals at the side, to follow an interior corridor to the vicinity of the main gate. The great interior gate, leading into the courtyard, like the outer gate, in the wall, from which it was separated by a covered way, some forty feet in length, had been backed with debris. This was, indeed, the debris to which we had descended by means of the rope. Provisions had been made, too, I supposed, for closing the corridors. In the corridor I met retreating defenders.

"We are abandoning the gate, Marsias," said one of them. "Come with us!"

I nodded. It was only later that I realized that he had called me "Marsias." One of the fellows on the wall, I remembered, had asserted that I was not Marsias. Yet they had followed me. Marsias, then, surely, was the name of the fellow whom I was impersonating.

I then emerged into the closed area between the outer and inner gate. There there was a huge hill of sand, rock and such, packed against the lower portions of the outer gate. The ram could not be well turned within the covered way.

In this covered way, men passing him, from various parts of the citadel, taking their way through the sheltered corridors, presumably to the harbor area, on a piece of stone, broken from the inside of the way, his head in his hands, sat Aemilianus, bleeding.

There was a great splintering of wood from above us and, over the hill of sand and such, packed behind the door, suddenly, bursting wood apart, there protruded, black, over five feet thick, and of solid iron, like some mythological monster, a great form, with curled-back horns, cast in the likeness of an adult verr ram.

I had never seen such a thing closely. I drew my sword and scrambled up the debris behind the gate to examine it, but, as I approached it, it, in its rhythm, swung back. I caught sight of figures on the hill outside, just movements, parts of bod-

ies. I, now on the summit of that small, artificial hill, suddenly drew back, shielding my eyes, as the huge form smote
again through the gate, splintering wood about. It was then,
at the height of its swing, but a foot from me. I put out my
left hand and touched it. This time, as it swung back, I could
see, along its shaft, the interior of the inclined shed that
housed it, and how it was fifty feet long and slung in leather
cradles, and the many ropes that controlled it, and the men
drawing on the ropes, surely more than a hundred of them
under that long shed, men stripped to the waist, sweating,
and as it drew back this time a figure suddenly leapt forward,
to enter and I parried and slipped my sword into him perhaps
as startled as he was and he was pulled back, bleeding, and I
heard shouts outside, and then, again, I drew back, covering
my eyes, and the great head splintered inward again.

I stood near the opening but this time, following its retreat,
none rushed through. Again I saw along the shaft of the ram,
the shed, the men, the ropes. A quarrel sped past. I heard a
tumbling of stone behind me and the western corridor was
closed, props struck from beneath a scaffolding of masonry.
Aemilianus, with two retainers, remained where he was,
below and to the left, he bleeding, sitting on the piece of
stone. "Hurry!" I heard someone call, I suppose to Aemilianus.
"We are going to close the east corridor!" I heard a trumpet
from somewhere toward the harbor. "It is the recall!" cried
one of the fellows with Aemilianus. "It sounds by your own
command. Come, Commander!" The citadel then was being
abandoned. But Aemilianus did not move. I could smell
smoke from somewhere. Another fellow from outside suddenly appeared in the opening, high in the ruptured gate. We
crossed swords in the opening three times. Then he stiffened
in the opening, his guard down. I flung myself back and the
ram smote through again. Another fellow then, flanked by
two others, appeared in the opening. Steel struck steel, sparks
leaping forth. He tried to climb over the jagged portal. "Look
out!" cried someone from the outside. I could see as my
opponent could not the coming forward of the ram. He must
have realized the danger but had not anticipated being held in
the threshold. He turned away from me, and his two fellows
leaped from him, but too late, and the ram, as I drew back,
caught him and carried him, on its snout, tearing him against

the side of the opening, for five feet, until he tumbled from it, to roll to the bottom of the hill. Two bodies now lay there, or a body and a part of a body. The head of the ram now was spattered with blood, as was, too, the side of the portal. I saw other men marshaling outside, to enter.

"Hold the ram!" I heard. A spear thrust at me through the opening. But the ram came forward again. I seized the spear behind the point. Then it was splintered like a twig as the huge head burst again inward. I threw the bit of a spear away. The head of the ram was so constructed, and the horns on it so curved back, that it was unlikely, given the forces involved, that it could become lodged in the door. I could not, thus, in any simple fashion, even with the beams and planks about, in the rubble, thrust anything behind it, crosswise, say, behind the horns, to prevent its withdrawal. The sand was useless. The rock, however, suggested a temporary expedient. "Hold the ram!" I heard, from outside. But it must come again, at least once! Men hesitated to rush forward. I then saw the great iron head seemingly become smoothly larger and larger as it swept forward. The bloody metallic configuration burst through again and this time, as soon as it had entered, before it could swing back, I rolled a rock from the debris between it and the lower edge of the rupture. There was a grinding of iron and rock as it swung back and then reared up, against the top of the rupture, and was still. The men on the ropes had not the leverage to swing it back, though they could try to pull it back. They would, of course, attempt to swing it in further, gain leverage, and then try to draw it back again. In this, however, they would lack the momentum generated by the full movement of the ram, utilizing the full arcs of the leather cradles.

A blade thrust through between the head and the wood, and then a spear thrust through, similarly. I saw the great head inch forward and then back, and again stop. Spears tried to force the rock from its position. There seemed to me no point in staying where I was. As soon as the ram was free of the opening, it would presumably be held back, in place, and then men would come through the portal, one by one, or in twos and threes. I could not well defend it, not indefinitely, not against quarrels, as well, with no shield. I saw the head move again, and again stop. I then sheathed my sword and half slid, half ran, down the slope of the debris and reached the stone flooring of the covered way. Aemilianus looked up at me, dully. There were men at the props of the scaffolding holding up the masonry that, when it fell, would block the east corridor. I did not care to be trapped here, between the gate and the rubble in the corridor, when the Cosians entered.

"Assist me," I said to the two fellows loyally with Aemilianus.

"Go," said Aemilianus. "I will stay here."

"I shall carry him, or you shall support him," I said to the two fellows.

"Who are you?" asked Aemilianus.

Just then there was a cry from above and the huge stone, forced from its place by spear butts, rolled down into the covered way. At the same time the great head drew back.

"Stop!" cried Aemilianus, but his two fellows had seized him, one by each arm, and, putting his arms about their shoulders, hurried him toward the east corridor.

I looked up and saw some four or five Cosians creep through the opening at the height of the artificial hill.

I backed toward the eastern corridor.

"It is dark here," said one of the Cosians.

But two men pushed past him, squinting into the dim covered way, from the height of the hill within the gate.

I heard the sound of mallets on wood behind me, heavy blows.

"Do not let them escape!" called a Cosian pointing downward.

"Take them from the sides!" I shouted, as though to men ensconced in an ambuscade.

The ten or twelve Cosians now through the gate crouched-down, suddenly, arrested, looking wildly about.

I then backed quickly through the portal of the eastern corridor.

As I did so the final blows were struck at the props supporting the scaffolding of masonry and with a tumble of dust and stone the rocks fell.

I had hardly gone ten paces down the corridor, following the others, when I heard the rubble of masonry being torn away from the outside. Undefended I did not think it would take them more than a few Ehn to open a passage through it.

In an Ihn or two I had caught up with the others, Aemilianus, the two fellows supporting him, and the two who had waited behind to block the passage.

Suddenly swords were drawn for men blocked the passage, come doubtless from the walls.

These men I saw, however, did not wear the blue of Cosian regulars but only armbands of blue.

"Ho, lads!" I called to them. "Behold the glint of gold!" I took from the pouch I wore golden coins. These were the coins which had belonged to the former Lady Publia when she was free, when she could still own things. I had relieved her of the burden of their weight in the cell. She had intended to use them to bargain for her life with Cosians, begging to purchase it from them, even at the frightful cost of Gorean bondage. I then cast the coins behind the fellows, and to my left, into a side passage.

"Gold or steel?" I inquired.

"Why not both?" asked a man, stepping forward.

Then he was dead in the corridor.

"Gold," said one of his fellows, grinning. Then he, and the others with him, backed down the passage down which I had flung the coins. Then, in a moment, they had turned, and were scrambling in the dim light for them.

I wiped my blade on the tunic of the fellow who had opposed us.

"You are not Marsias," said one of the men with us.

"No," I said. I also relieved the fellow of the contents of his purses. He had carried three.

One of the men with us closed the door of the passage down which I had flung the coins.

In a place such as the citadel, under the conditions of war, one is normally very careful about closed doors. One usually either opens them very carefully, or flings or kicks them open, standing back from them, waiting. One does not burst through. One does not know what is on the other side.

"Let us continue," said another man.

"I smell smoke," said one of the fellows supporting Aemilianus.

"There are looters behind us," said the other.

There was a movement in a side passage.

"Wait," I said.

A fellow there swiftly leapt up from a naked woman, one with richly blotched skin and helplessly erected nipples.

"Kneel," he said to her.

She scrambled to her knees.

Her eyes were wild. She could not move her hands together. They were held apart, by her waist. The current positon of her left hand was just above her left hip, and of her right hand, just above her right hip. A single narrow cord bound her. The tie is accomplished as follows: One wrist is tightly encircled by the cord and bound within it, about eighteen inches in from one end of the cord. The longer length of the same cord is then taken about her belly and the other wrist is then tied within it, on the other side of her body, leaving some eighteen inches of cord on the other side of the tie. The cord is then drawn back about her belly and the two free ends tied together behind her back, this being done in such a way that the bond is quite snug. The result is that her hands are held apart, on opposite sides of her body, and that neither hand can reach a knot, either at a wrist or behind the back. This tie, it might be noted, positions a girl's hands quite near areas of likely predation by a captor. But, too, because of it, perhaps to her acute frustration, so near, and yet so far, she finds that she is absolutely incapable of interfering with any attentions to which he chooses to subject her. The waist tie, too, of course, in a female, given her marvelous beauty, the flaring excitements of her hips and breasts, cannot be slipped. It is a common capture tie. She looked up at us, gasping. A circular, overlapping pin had been spread and one end inserted through her septum, drawn through and allowed to spring back, forming a nose ring. From this dangled a looped, closed cord, the loop about eighteen inches in length.

The fellow, crouching, now faced us, sword drawn. "I took her fairly," he said.

She squirmed in the bonds.

"Was she a free woman?" I asked.

"Yes," he said.

"Did she submit herself to you?" I asked.

"Yes," he said.

"Keep her," I said. "Of what interest to us is a slave?"

We then continued on our way.

"There is light at the end of the hall," I said. "The gate is open there."

"That is the gate to the landing, and thence to the walk-way, leading to the piers," said one of the men.

I did not think about it at the time, but if he had thought me of Ar's Station I do not think he would have said this. I would have known it.

I suspect now that more than one of these fellows suspected who I might be.

"You should have left me to die by the gate," said Aemilianus.

"Would you not rather die in the sunlight," I asked, "in the fresh air, under the blue sky, the clouds, in sight of the harbor, the river?"

"I would rather die in sight of the walls of Ar," he said, "that I might spit upon them."

"The reinforcements were never intended to arrive," I said.

"Let us continue on," said the fellow, he who had also spoken earlier. "I hear the press of pursuers."

"I hear women and children," said another.

"It is shame that I should die before them," said Aemilianus. "Leave me here, that I may for a time, while I can hold a sword, detain our pursuers."

"Bring him along," I said, and continued toward the gateway.

"And who are you?" asked a fellow.

"One, at least," I said, "who may be thinking a bit more clearly than others this afternoon."

"And why should that be?" asked a man.

"Perhaps I was better fed," I said.

# 18
# THE LANDING

"Hail, Captain!" called the young fellow with the crossbow, near the gate leading out onto the landing, from which a walkway gave access, across a stretch of harbor water, some two hundred yards in width, to the piers. Beyond the piers, and beyond the wall of rafts, chained together, with which they had closed the harbor, the Cosians had their ships, five of them. In the harbor, within the wall of rafts, there was the burned wreckage of ships, and in some places masts emerged from the water, of ships of Ar's Station, burned in port.

"Hail, Captain!" called the other young fellow who had been with us on the wall.

"Hail, Captain!" called others, lifting their swords.

The landing was crowded with women and children. Some, too, already, had made their way out to the piers.

"Hail Commander!" then cried the fellows there, spying Aemilianus.

"Why do they call you 'Captain'?" asked Aemilianus.

"He commanded on the wall!" cried a man. I remember him from the wall. He had been there.

"It was you who held the wall so long?" asked Aemilianus.

"I and a couple of hundred of your stout fellows, like these," I said, indicating the elated young men at my side.

"There are Cosians on the interior walls, overlooking the landing," said a man.

I looked up. I saw them. Some had their helmets off,

cooling their heads in the breeze, more to be felt at that height.

"They can fire into the crowd," said a man.

"But they have not done so," said another.

"They are waiting for the camp commander," said another.

"I will not go to Cos, naked in a cage," said Aemilianus to one of his men, one of the two who had stayed with him. "At the end, then, you know what to do."

"As you will, Commander," he said, his voice thick with emotion.

"How many are here?" I asked one of the fellows about. The landing was packed with women and children. More were out on the piers.

"Who knows?" he asked. "I think there must be two to three thousand women and children, and perhaps some four to five hundred men. I do not know."

"Of all the people of Ar's station?" I asked.

"Some fled months ago," he said, "some even when it was learned the Cosians had landed at Brundisium, others when it was rumored they were marching on Ar's Station. Many escaped before the investment lines were closed. Some bought their way out, which you could do, in the early days, before the Cosian casualties were high."

"Still," I said, "there must have been thousands in the city when the investment lines were closed."

"There were," he said, bitterly.

"And this is all that is left?" I asked.

"There were desertions," he said.

"Still," I said.

"Many perished of hunger or disease," he said. "Doubtless, too, many perished in the fires."

I regarded him.

"Many could not reach the citadel," he said. "Many streets were cut off, even districts."

"I understand," I said.

"Why did the relief from Ar not come?" he asked.

"I do not know," I told him, though I thought I knew.

"It is said the Cosians did much butchery in the city."

"Perhaps," I granted him.

"Beneath the walls of the citadel," he said, "they paraded

loot carts and lines of our women, stripped, and trussed as slaves.''

I nodded. I had not been able to see this from the cell, of course, but I did not doubt but what it was true. It was a touch not untypically Gorean.

"Doubtless even now hundreds of them are packed behind the bars of cage wagons, being taken to Brundisium, there to be shaved, and then shackled on the tiered shelves of slave ships, to be embarked for Cos and Tyros.''

"Perhaps," I said. In actuality, of course, I surmised that many would be distributed to continental markets, if only to take a quicker profit on them and avoid deflating the market on the islands. I did not doubt, however, that many of the most beautiful would indeed find their way to Cos and Tyros, if only as examples of prize loot. Such, too, might well grace the triumphs of victors. Beautiful, naked women look well being marched in golden chains before the war beasts of masters. Doubtless many would march before Lurius of Jad, Ubar of Cos, in some grand triumph, though in the fighting he would not have stirred from his palace in Telnus.

"Still," he said, "there are many here."

"Yes," I said, looking about, at the crowded landing, and the piers out toward the river. "There are.''

"It will be a terrible slaughter," he said.

Aemilianus was sitting on the landing near me. A man supported him, holding him about the shoulders.

I looked up at the interior wall.

"Commander," I said to him, "many of your people are within missile range from the wall.''

Indeed, it would be hard to fire into that crowd without scoring a hit.

"I am tired," he said.

"Many are afraid to go to the piers," said a man. "They are afraid of the Cosian ships, that the wall of rafts will be opened, that they will attack. They fear to leave the landing, the shelter of the wall of the citadel.''

"What shelter?" I asked, angrily.

"Many others," said a fellow, "fear to tread the walkway.''

"There are sharks about," said one man.

"See the fins in the water," said another. "There, there are two!''

"Blood has carried down to the delta," said another bitterly. "River sharks have come from as far west as Turmus. The bodies of delta sharks, leaving the salt water of the delta, bloated, litter the shores between the delta and Ven."

"There is even a greater reason to avoid the walkway," said another man, bitterly.

"What is that?" I asked.

He did not explain himself.

Suddenly Aemilianus looked at me. "What did you say?" he asked.

I crouched down beside him.

"Move your people out to the piers," I said. "The walkway can be destroyed behind them. Then the Cosians can approach only by water."

"There is no food there," said a man.

"There is none here either," I said.

"It makes no difference," said Aemilianus, wearily.

"It is the militarily appropriate action," I said.

"It is hard to see," he said, suddenly.

"Make a litter," I said. "Carry the commander to the piers."

"I have a net," said a fellow.

Two spears were thrust through the net, about two feet apart, and Aemilianus was placed on it.

He opened his eyes.

"There are Cosians on the wall!" he said.

"They have been there," I said.

"Why have the people not been withdrawn to the piers?" he asked.

"The orders have not been issued," I said.

"Where is Marcus Tulvinius?" he asked.

"Here," said an officer.

"Withdraw to the piers," he said.

"It cannot be done," he said.

Aemilianus struggled to focus his eyes on him.

"The walkway has been interdicted," he said. "The people on the piers made it there earlier, before the Cosians came to the inner wall. You can see the bodies of some of those who tried it later. Make a move toward it, and it will be covered by a hundred crossbows."

"It seems," said Aemilianus, "that we may choose to die here, or there."

"I would choose to make matters less convenient for Cosians," I said.

Aemilianus smiled.

"The situation is hopeless," said the officer. "I shall treat for terms."

"With Cosians?" smiled Aemilianus.

"Look!" cried a fellow. "On the wall!"

We now saw a tall figure there, behind the ramparts, one whose helmet was surmounted by a crest of sleen hair. There were standards held behind him.

"It is the camp commander!" cried a fellow.

"Commander?" asked the officer.

"Do as you will," said Aemilianus, wearily.

The officer turned about and, drawing from beneath his cloak a white sheet, which he had apparently concealed there, lifted it, and approached the base of the wall.

This action seemed to be greeted with derision from the Cosians. One could see no reaction from the fellow with the helmet, with its crest of sleen hair.

"Aemilianus asks terms!" called the officer, up to the wall.

I saw the fists of Aemilianus, in the improvised litter, clench.

There was laughter from the wall.

"Let your women strip themselves stark naked," called a fellow down from the wall, "and present themselves one by one at the gate for our appraisal."

"Perhaps some will be found pleasing," said another fellow.

"The throats of the others can be cut!" laughed another from the height of the wall.

The tall figure on the height of the wall, the standards behind him, betrayed no emotion. He surveyed the scene below him. Smoke was rising from somewhere in the citadel.

"Aemilianus himself agrees to surrender his person into your hands!" called the officer.

Aemilianus lay back on the litter, on the stone of the landing, his eyes closed.

"Terms!" called the officer. "We ask terms!"

The figure on the height of the wall lifted his hand, a small gesture.

"No!" cried the officer below.

He stepped back, the hand which held the white sheet lowered. "No!" he cried.

At the gesture of the commander on the wall two of the fellows flanking him, crossbowmen, had set quarrels into their bows.

"No!" cried the officer below, backing away.

I saw the two quarrels leave the bows like metal birds. The snap of the cable and its vibration carried even to the landing.

"Shield wall!" I cried. "All with shields here! Form the wall!"

Men with shields hurried to where I stood, lifting the shields, overlapping them.

I forced my way among them, sometimes literally thrusting shields into position. Quarrels struck about me. I saw in one wild instant the officer who had addressed the wall now facing us, he having turned about. He had a look of dismay, of disbelief, on his face. Then he fell, the two quarrels in his chest.

"Back!" I cried to the screaming women and children. "Get as close to the wall as you can! Back! Back!"

But many fled toward us.

I saw a fellow tumble from the wall, a quarrel in his chest, though it was not finned. It had apparently been only a sharpened rod. I saw the young fellow who had had the crossbow lower his weapon.

Quarrels rained down at us.

I detailed men to assist, as they could, shielding them, women and children running toward the walkway.

There now seemed hundreds of bowmen at the height of the wall. The nearer portions of the walkway seemed to be growing quarrels like grass. Many of the bowmen had apparently received orders to seal off the walkway, as they could, this penning the people below between the water and the wall, holding them there, like verr for the slaughter.

I crouched down behind the shield wall. "Take the commander, shielded," I said, "to the piers."

"I will remain here," said Aemilianus.

"You will command," I said, "from interior lines."

"I will stay here!" he said.

I gestured to the bearers of his litter, who lifted it, the two fellows with the spears thrust through the net, Aemilianus on the net between the spears. Aemilianus stretched his hand toward me, and I clasped it. The bearers, then, crouching down, behind four fellows holding shields between them and the wall, hurried toward the walkway.

The women and children closest to the wall were in little immediate danger from quarrels. It was hard to strike them with quarrels from the height of the wall.

I looked wildly to the height of the wall. The commander was no longer visible.

I then sent forth men from the shield wall singly, and in squads, to ferry the women and children, one at a time, or the women carrying children in their arms, beneath the cover of their shields, to the walkway. Once they were beyond quarrel range they hurried back to conduct still others to temporary safety.

There were cries of rage from the wall.

I saw the young crossbowman, under the cover of a shield, held by his friend, the other young fellow from the front wall, harvesting quarrels from the walkway. These were fine quarrels, crafted by metal workers, not sharpened rods, not blunt sticks, fit for stunning birds. He distributed these to cohorts behind the shield wall, neglecting not to retain some for himself. He was young but his aim was fearsomely accurate. He had been trained on the wall, in a hundred assaults.

I looked at the gate. It was at the end of the corridor we had followed, which had led out, to the landing. Some men were guarding it. Naturally it opened inward, to the advantage of the citadel. We had no adequate way, given the time and materials at our disposal, of barring it from the outside.

Now some of the fellows on the wall were hurling stones and tiles down on the figures huddled below.

I saw one fellow doing this suddenly pitch back, his hands clutching at the shaft of a quarrel. Its passage upward through his head had been arrested by the back of his helmet.

The young fellow with the crossbow set another quarrel to his weapon.

I sent some men forward, to try to shield the huddled noncombatants, before they could be conducted away from the wall, but it was of little use.

Many of the noncombatants broke and ran.

Many were cut down before they could reach our shield wall.

"Stay closer to the wall!" I cried. "Get closer to the wall!"

I saw another fellow, his hands on a large stone, it held over his head, turn and fall within the rampart, struck by a quarrel.

The young crossbowman set yet another quarrel to his weapon.

"It is harder for them than they would like," said a fellow.

"They will be pouring through the gate in a moment!" said a fellow.

"And over the wall," said another grimly.

He had hardly spoken when the interior gate, leading out to the landing, swung inward, and a stream of Cosians waiting within, a moment later, helmeted, with shields, thrusting with spears, slashing with swords, pressed out against the defenders. At the same time a hundred ropes, along the wall, were thrown downward and men, one after the other, began to lower themselves to the landing. The women and children then, suddenly, screaming, panic-stricken, fled away from the walls. The shield wall was disrupted, the frightened women and children rushing through it, tearing at it, plunging toward the walkway behind us. As shields were turned and lifted quarrels sped down from the walls and men screamed, twisting, hit.

"Forward!" I cried, seizing up the shield of a fellow fallen. "To the wall!" Behind us we heard the screams of women and children, crowding toward the walkway. We heard, too, the sounds and screams of those swept, as by a flood, from the landing, and from the sides of the walkway, striking into the water. In the panic most of the women and children had fled from the wall. Whereas this more exposed them to the fire from above it also, for us, cleared a killing space. A fellow dropped from a rope before me, and before he could regain his feet, he was dead. Another screamed, his legs hacked. Another leapt from the rope onto the spear of a fellow near me. He was kicked from it. The spear was then driven into another. Butchery at the foot of the wall occurred. Some tried to descend with one hand, fighting with the other. Sometimes two men seized an end of the rope and swung it out and back against the wall, dashing men from it. Cosians feared then to lower themselves into the waiting blades, like steel teeth, waiting for them. Some tried to press down, past others who, seeing what awaited them below, clung ever more desperately to the rope. Men fell to the foot of the wall, to be cut to pieces. Some tried to climb back up the rope but could not do so for the others above them. Some, reaching the crenelation again, were struck back by the jabbing spears of their own men, screaming at them. In their fall they not unoften took others with them, the some seventy feet or so, to the landing, the wall lower on the harbor side than the land side.

Others clung wildly to the ropes, unable to move. Of these flighted quarrels, at the leisure of calm marksmen, took bloody tolls. Some men below stood even on bodies trying to reach men above them on ropes. More stones and tiles rained down. I saw a fellow struck to one knee by a tile hitting on his shield. For a moment he seemed in shock. Then he struggled up, again, unsteadily, to guard his yard of wall. More quarrels were flighted over us. They hit the walkway like hail. I heard women screaming. "To the wall!" many screamed. "Back to the wall!" I supposed that many of the bowmen on the wall, from the safety of the crenelation, were continuing tenaciously, following their original orders, to seal off, as they could, the walkway, keeping the pen closed, so to speak. A child ran screaming past me to press himself against the wall, cowering there. In a moment he had been overtaken by a woman who crouched down, wrapping him in her cloak. We were buffeted by women.

"Get out of the way!" cried one of our men. A Cosian slid down a rope, shielded by the women. He thrust one aside, putting his blade into a fellow. Another, though, from the other side, caught him, and he backed against the wall, then turned, scratching at it, spitting blood. The child wrapped in the cloak, soothed by the woman, watched him as he sank to the foot of the wall. The woman was weeping. A glance about showed that the danger was at the gate where the Cosians, in their hundreds, were pressing out, swelling forth, onto the landing. I hurried along the wall, to the left of the gate, as one faces it from the landing.

"To the gate!" I cried to every other man. "To the gate!" Their swords bloodied they turned and sped to the vicinity of the gate. I hurried about the fighting there and detailed men from the right, as well, to the gate. In the layered leather of my shield bristled quarrels.

I returned to the wall. Few descended now the ropes. It could be seen from the wall even more clearly than from the landing, I suppose, the steady, blade by blade, stroke by stroke, expansion of Cosian territory below, its burgeoning from the gate. When it reached the walkway the walkway would be indeed closed. That was what I wanted most desperately to prevent. I was not interested in holding the landing itself, except in so far as it protected the walkway. My primary objective was to evacuate the landing and withdraw to the piers. Indeed, I myself would wish to close the walkway once this evacuation was complete. I seized two fellows and issued orders. I was surrendering the wall. One raced to the wall to the left, the other to the right. Two lines were formed, one on the left, one on the right, of fellows with shields. These two lines, converging, the fighting in the center, by the gate, between them, led to the walkway, and then out on the walkway, for better than forty yards.

The men in these lines crouched down, their shields between themselves and the wall, creating an open fence of shields, a poor, broken cover, given the paucity of their numbers, but better than none. Some fellows near the wall urged the women and children to stream behind these, trying to reach the piers. Crouching down many did, and, it seemed, all with children. I saw the one woman, still clutching the child in her cloak, darting from shield to shield. Other women chose not, either from fear or prudence, to risk this dangerous run. I saw some looking up, in fear, at the ropes, still dangling there, and pull away their veils, thrust back their hoods and put their hands to the collars of their robes.

A woman clutched at me, then sank to her knees beside me, holding me. I looked down, angrily. Her eyes, over the veil, looked up at me. It was Lady Claudia, in the provocative rags that had been designed by the former Lady Publia, that she might hope to be of interest to Cosians. A free woman, bundled in the robes of concealment, spit on her as she passed. "Slave!" she hissed. Lady Claudia looked up at me, clutching me. I pressed her away with my foot, to the landing. "Traitress!" I said to her. She crawled back to me and brushed aside her veil, to press her lips piteously to my feet. "To the piers!" I said to her. She leaped up, sobbing, and fled toward the walkway.

Now that the wall was freed I saw more Cosians descending on ropes. I saw, too, happily, some small boats from the piers, manned apparently by fishermen and others, fellows who had made it to the piers earlier, making their way toward the landing. I had little doubt that these were the results of the commands of Aemilianus, now out on the piers somewhere, hoping that they might, in their small way, aid in the evacuation of the landing. To be sure, for the quarrels, it would take great courage to bring these to the landing. I could see, too, the backs and fins of sharks crowded about the lower edge of the walkway, near the landing. They were so thick there it seemed they constituted a surface. It was almost as though one might walk upon them. Yet I would not have cared to tread that shifting, treacherous, churning surface. The water, close to the landing, by the walkway, was white with their thrashing. I think perhaps they attacked one another as often as those in the water.

I saw more than one woman, struck from the walkway, reaching out, seizing the walkway, pulled again, screaming, to its safety, even in the midst of the frenzy at its edge. Among the free women running to, and on, the walkway, under the partial cover of the shields, I saw slave females, too, barefoot and bare-armed, in their tiny skirts, their necks in their light steel collars. The heads of the women who were not hooded I could see were shorn and those of the slave females cropped the shortest of all. Among those hastening on the walkway I then saw a naked figure, stumbling, being dragged by a free woman behind her on a leash. The naked figure's wrists were thonged together behind her back. Her head was covered by a hood, improvised from a part of a man's tunic. The gag would still be in her mouth. It was she who had been Lady Publia. I recalled that she had not had her hair shorn until I had done it, with a shaving knife, in the cell. One could not see it under the hood, but I had made it slave short.

It seemed to me then that most of the women who wished, or dared, to attempt the walkway had done so. It was well for the men were being beaten back, almost to the beginning of the walkway. I saw the snout of more than one shark rising from the water. Cosians pressed about. More swarmed through the gate to the landing. More descended on the ropes. I issued orders, dispatching the fellows nearest me to convey them to their respective destinations. The two lines which had to some extent protected the women and children now withdrew to protect the flanks of the center. Then I, standing at the walkway, man by man, as was opportune, sent fellows back along the walkway, retreating to the piers. These mostly backed along, protecting their retreat with their shields, making their way in a file between the fellows still in position on the walkway, on each side of it, those I had placed there to afford protection to the women and children. The lines thinned to the sides of me, and before me, and the Cosians pressed in, yet more closely.

I held my ground, as men of Ar's Station, one by one, backed past me, onto the walkway. I had been behind the fighting, directing it. Now I was but a line or two from the front ranks. There were screams from near the wall. Some of the Cosians, many just coming forth from the citadel, not yet entered into the fighting, indeed, not being readily able to reach it, for their fellows, had turned aside to attend to the females there. "They are taking the women!" cried one of the fellows, a few ranks in the Cosian press. He, and some others, then back, turned back. There was a momentary hesitation in the Cosian advance. I took advantage of this to pull in the flanks and send them back over the walkway, and then drew the fellows before me closer, freeing some, the lines then being shortened, to follow their fellows back. I myself withdrew some ten feet or so. There were more screams of women from the wall, women being seized to be made slaves. Again the Cosians hesitated. "The women are being taken behind you," I cried to the Cosians, "taken by those who have not even nicked their steel!"

"Forward!" cried a Cosian officer. "Forward!"

"You are losing slaves!" I cried to the Cosians.

"There are more slaves before you lads, on the piers!" cried the officer.

"See them strip themselves, eager to be made your slaves!" I cried.

Some of the Cosians in the rearward ranks turned about. I ordered more of my men back. We did not press them.

"They are pretty," I cried, "begging for their nose rings!"

To be sure, many of the women had torn away their clothing, and were now kneeling on the landing, by the wall, some with their hands clasped, others with them piteously extended, in various attitudes of petition and supplication. Among them strode men, some with bloodied swords. I saw small wrists being tied together and roes being put on lovely necks. Those who were slaves were picked first, as most desirable, surely at least at the moment, before the disciplining and training of the others.

I saw one free woman backed against the wall, a sword at her belly. Then she pulled her robes away from her shoulders and breasts, and then, a moment later, at an impatient movement of the sword, which made her wince, thrust them down over her hips, and let them slip to her knees. Then she straightened up. The sword was then again at her belly, only now it was bared to the sharpened steel. She turned her head to the side, in misery, in terror, being assessed. Then, at a movement of the blade, and ordered, doubtless, she looked at the fellow. It seemed then she was suddenly startled. Then she began to tremble. I had little doubt she had seen in him her master. It is an interesting moment for a woman, the first time she finds herself looking as a slave into the eyes of her master. She quickly knelt, as though fearful of displeasing him. I saw her turned about, rudely and thrust up, closely, against the wall. Her hands were bound behind her. She was leashed. I saw more than one female slave, kneeling before a Cosian, her hands fastened behind her, put her head far back, to facilitate the insertion of the nose ring. I saw a free woman, similarly kneeling, similarly bound, watch this in terror, and then, quickly and exactly, imitate the action of the slaves.

Some of the women, in one fashion or another, were being marked, or tagged. Sometimes this was being done with a circular or oblong pin, rather like the temporary nose ring, put through the lobe of the left ear, from which a disk or tag dangled. Sometimes the disk or tag was affixed similarly but by means of a simple wire passed through the ear lobe, closed and twisted shut. Women so marked, of course, would later have their ears pierced. Some fellows fastened tags, or other devices, to the nose rings themselves, or to the looped cord dangling from the nose ring. With others, the cord itself is color coded. Some women were marked by as little as a tag on a thong, fastened about their neck, wrist or ankle. Others had their body itself.written upon, as with a grease pencil. The marking is usually on the upper portion of the left breast. Slavers, too, commonly mark women in this fashion, for temporary purposes, for example, with lot numbers for sales, and such. Permanent markings are usually done with hot irons.

"You are losing slaves!" I called out, again, to the Cosians.

"The distributions will be made later!" cried the officer to his men.

"To whom will they be distributed?" I asked. "To you fellows sweating in the front ranks, or to suppliers, officers, and agents? Who says there will be any distribution to you fellows, at all? If there is, will you get your pick? Will the best women be distributed? What of hundreds of wenches already on their way to Brundisium, and Cos and Tyros? Have they been distributed? Did you get your hands on them? I think you will have to bid on the leftovers in camp auctions! Is not that the way it has been before? You are fighting for Cos now, not in a free company, whose captain will look out for you, who will see that beauties figure in your pay!"

"He says true," growled a fellow, drawing back.

"Forward!" cried the officer. "Forward!"

"Get them while you can!" I cried. "Some are still clothed, others have not yet been seized! They cower with their sisters by the wall, half hidden, waiting for you!"

"Do not listen to him!" called the officer.

"Some are doubtless quite attractive. They have not yet been marked or tagged!"

"Do not heed him!" said the officer.

"Woe!" I said. "The fellows who have not fought are advancing on them even now!"

The Cosians wavered.

Few quarrels fell now at the entrance to the walkway, for those upon the wall must now fear the striking of their own men.

There were more screams of women from the wall.

"Forward!" urged the officer.

Now clearly came to the walkway the moans, the weeping protests, the wailing lamentations of beauties finding tight bonds being placed on their bodies.

"Back, back," I said, softly, to the men about me. "Behind me! Back!"

"There are less than two hundred left there now, lads," I called to the Cosians.

I had the men of Ar's Station then, to my elation, on the walkway, drawing back on either side of me. I spoke softly. Those who had much fought withdrew up the walkway, between those who had shielded the women. These other men then, fresh, came forward, flanking me.

I saw a brunet, out from the wall, her wrists thonged behind her, weeping copiously, uncontrollably, as the spread prong of a nose ring was pressed through her septum, the ring then springing back into shape. She, nose-ringed, looked up at her captor, its cord looping up then to his hand. At the slightest of tugs she leapt to her feet, weeping, to follow him with perfection. I saw her being led away. Others, too, I saw being pulled to their feet, doubtless to be taken to improvised holding areas.

"Even now they are being led away, fellows!" I said.

"Draw back," said the officer, angrily.

He had seen the vacillation of his men, that we had gained the walkway, that fresh troops now flanked me.

Cosians, mercenaries mostly, broke free from their rearward ranks and ran to the wall, to claim females. So, too, then, backing away, then turning, did several in the forward ranks. The officer rallied enough regulars about himself to assure that we would not attempt to press forward.

"You use our own women as a diversion," growled a fellow near me, "as though they might be slaves!"

"Look at them," I said.

"Aii!" he said.

"Draw back with me," I said, softly, backing away. The Cosians, regulars and mercenaries, responsive to the orders of their officer, advanced some yards onto the walkway. They did not follow us closely, however.

We saw a shark reach up to the landing, near the walkway, and drag a body, by the leg, back into the water.

"Go back, and tell Aemilianus that the evacuation is complete. He will know what to do."

The man beside me shuddered. It was no accident I had stopped where I had. From this point effective quarrel fire could not be directed to the piers.

"We will stay with you," said he young man with the crossbow, now beside me. His fellow, the other young fellow from the wall, the one with the shield, who had protected him in the fighting, was at his side.

"No," I said.

"Is that an order, Captain?" he asked.

"Yes," I said. "Obey it."

He and his fellow hesitated a moment, then turned, and went toward the piers.

"The rest of you," I said, "withdraw now."

"You cannot hold the walkway alone," said a grizzled fellow.

"Go," I said. I would not order, nor did I think Aemilianus would either, any to stand here beside me, not given what must be done.

"You will need skilled swordsmen," said the grizzled fellow, "preferably those of the scarlet tunic."

"Go," I said.

"Four or five will do," he said.

"I have four here, including myself," said a voice behind me.

"And I am the fifth," said the grizzled fellow.

Men were hurrying back down the walkway, toward the piers.

I turned about, startled.

"It would be an honor to die in the company of Marisas," said a tall fellow.

"I am not Marsias," I said to him.

"That is a relief," he said, grimly, "for I was growing

confused about the matter. You see, I had thought that I was Marsias."

"I recognize you now," I said.

"That is flattering," he said.

"How is your head?" I asked.

"Considering that it was struck with a large piece of building stone with great force at close range, splendid," he said.

I Looked at one of the other fellows. There were three behind him. "I see that you have managed to find a tunic," I said to one of them.

"Yes," he said, "mine was stolen, in a cell."

"That is where I found mine," I admitted.

"We were roused by a guard," said Marsias, "who was checking the walls for ruptures which might allow access to Cosians. He found an excellent example of such a breach in a certain cell, as you might perhaps remember."

"Yes," I said.

"It was our intention to come looking for you immediately, as you might well suppose," said Marsias, "to settle accounts, so to speak, but Cosians, as seems their wont these days, interfered. We had to defend that break in the wall for Ahn. When the recall was sounded, we learned, somewhat to our surprise, as you might suppose, that I was a hero on the wall, at least according to some, and later, too, at the gate. These fellows, and I, decided to look into this, and now have done so."

"You have found me now," I said.

"And will fight beside you," said Marsias.

"I am grateful," I said.

"The small boats are coming," said one of the fellows.

"The Cosians, too, have seen them," I said. There was considerable excitement on the walkway near, and at, its end, and on the landing. I could now see, again, too, the standards over the wall of the citadel. The camp commander, he in charge of the Cosian forces at Ar's Station, had resumed his coign of vantage. In the boats, approaching from the piers, the same boats which had come earlier to help evacuate the landing, there were men with torches and axes. There were some small boats, too, at the landing, some perhaps captured,

others which may have been there earlier, or perhaps within
the citadel walls somewhere.

"I gather, from reports of those who were on the wall,"
said Marsias, "that you impaled the traitress, Lady Claudia."

"Perhaps," I said.

"Or was it our pretentious, nasty little warder, Lady Publia?"
he inquired.

"Do not concern yourself with the matter," I advised.

"That would have been an irony," he remarked.

"Doubtless," I said.

"And a waste," he said.

"Doubtless," I said.

"Many think that both Lady Claudia and Lady Publia
needed to learn their womanhood."

"Lady Claudia," I said, "had already begun to learn
it."

"Like those women on the landing," said a fellow beside
us.

"Yes," I said.

The Cosians there must have taken at least four hundred
women on the landing. At least two hundred of these were
still there. Many were pushed up against the wall, in some
groups facing it, in others with their backs to it. I had little
doubt that the delicious loot even now was learning masculine
domination. On the landing many were kneeling, or bellying.
There was much licking and kissing. More than one had been
put in a display position, and forced to hold it. I saw one girl
cuffed, and another, one who had perhaps been slow to obey,
lashed with a strap. Swiftly then, and eagerly, did she begin
to lick and kiss her captor about the feet and ankles. Some
were still being tied and tagged. Others were being lined up,
their hands tied behind their backs, to form coffles, ropes
being put on their necks. Some, among these many others,
were serving even now on the landing, being put to use by
impatient masters. We could see their squirming bodies, their
subdued, thrashing limbs, hear their cries, cries with which
they responded to, and registered and recorded, their ravish-
ments, cries mostly, at this point, of protest and lamentation,
but, too, in instances, of astonishment and wonder, and
sometimes, even so soon, of sudden, frightened acquies-

cence, of eager acceptance, of grateful yieldings, dreams coming true in thongs.

"Yet, too," he said, "many claim, interestingly, to have seen the same female, she who was supposedly impaled, whoever she was, later on the wall's walkway, and later, too, with the women and children."

"Surely that seems unlikely," I said.

I noted one girl on the landing. From the way she held her hands behind her back I could tell that she was in thumb cuffs. These are handy devices. They are light and take up little space in a warrior's pack. I myself, thinking sometimes that thumb cuffs are perhaps a bit cruel, generally prefer, if slave bracelets are not available, a simple thong or a short length of binding fiber. A woman, of course, may be bound in a large variety of ways and with a large variety of materials. For example, one might use strips, cut and rolled, from her own clothing, particularly as one will probably be removing that garb from her anyway. If she is naked, she might even be bound with short lengths of her own hair. Two or three horts of hair suffice to tie her thumbs behind her back, and another two or three will suffice to tie her two large toes together.

I might mention two possible reservations pertaining to thumb cuffs. First, many feel that they are much less secure than, say, slave bracelets, because of the diverse ratios involved, of wrist to hand, and of upper thumb to the thumb joint, at their location points. To compensate for this, of course, one can make the thumb cuffs tighter, but this produces greater discomfort in the wearer. It is harder for her to attend to her lessons, naturally, if she is in pain. I generally feel that pain, at least generally, should not be inflicted on a slave unless it is meaningful. There can, of course, be a point to generalized discomforts, even of a rather trivial nature.

For example, when a woman has been slept naked on a hardwood floor without covers, she is likely to come to a much better understanding of the value of a slave blanket. Second, if the woman is in thumb cuffs, and she becomes hysterical, it is much easier for her to hurt herself. Accordingly, just as one would not wish to secure a sleen or a kaiila in a way in which it might inadvertently hurt or injure itself, so, too, one might not wish to secure a slave in such a manner. The slave, too, is a domestic animal, and like other domestic animals, has a specific value. Accordingly, thumb cuffs, if used on a slave, in my opinion at least, should be used only under close supervision. To be sure, under such supervision, they might be helpful.

Certainly it is hard for a woman to wear thumb cuffs and not understand her helplessness. Some masters favor them early in a girl's training, thinking that it hastens their progress. Whereas I have occasionally introduced a woman somewhat rudely into the realities of bondage, I generally prefer to ease them into it, giving them time to develop and gradually understand their new feelings and sensations, giving them time to accomodate themselves to their new life and destiny. Accordingly, though I might put a girl into thumb cuffs for an Ahn or so, perhaps early in her training, perhaps in the process of informing her as to the nature of various bonds, their textures, and such, I generally do not use them. I think of them, like close chains, more as a punishment than a restraint. That she knows they exist, and could be put on her, by my will, like close chains, in itself has its salutary effect on her. And that seems to me generally sufficient.

The major point of the restraint is to restrain, not hurt. Indeed, pain can interfere with many of the diverse subsidiary values of restraints, physical and pyschological. It can be distractive. Pain is a bit like the whip. The slave is subject to the whip, and truly subject to it, but this does not mean that she is necessarily whipped; that she could be whipped, and will be whipped, if she is not pleasing, is what is important, not that she need be whipped. Why should one beat a pleasing slave? To be sure, there are no bargains, contracts or arrangements in these matters, and the slave may be beaten whenever the master pleases, with or without a reason. She is, after all, a slave. Similarly, along these lines, to be perfectly honest, I have upon occasion used thumb cuffs on females, when it has seemed to me there was a point in doing so, or when it pleased me to do so.

"She was naked, hooded, and thonged, and on a leash, in the keeping of one or another free person," he said.

"That sounds like a slave," I said.

"Yes, it does," he said.

We heard the small boats behind us, drawing up, near the pilings beneath the walkway.

"It is my supposition," he said, "that no female was impaled."

"That is an interesting supposition," I granted him.

"If it is true," he said, "Lady Claudia, whom I suspect is somewhere about, probably in the rags of Lady Publia, is still entitled to look forward to her impalement."

I saw that the woman in thumb cuffs was now on her knees on the landing, and that her head was pushed down to the stone. The cord from her nose ring was lying beside her head on the stone. She was then put to use. I saw her wrists lifting, her fingers, beside her confined thumbs, jerking, opening and closing. Then she was pulled to her feet by the cord on the nose ring and hurrying after her master.

"Do you not think so?" he asked.

"They are marshaling at the end of the walkway," I said.

I heard axes behind us, attacking the pilings of the walkway.

"Do you not think so?" he asked.

"You are certainly a zealous fellow," I said. "I have seldom encountered so single-minded a devotion to duty."

"Obviously, if you did not impale her," he said, "you did not wish her impaled, and you have done service to Ar's Station, whatever may be your own Home Stone. That is one reason I am beside you now, that I may guiltlessly evade, if possible, my very unpleasant duty, but clear duty, in that matter."

"I did not understand," I said. "I am sorry."

"But if we should survive," he said, "you understand that we must attempt to apprehend the prisoner and see that the sentence is carried out upon her, even if it means only weights on her ankles and a sharpened pole on a pier."

"The Cosians!" I cried.

Then, with shield and sword, with the ringing of metal,

with shouts, with cries of war, the six of us, I, Marsias, the grizzled fellow, and the three who had come originally to the cell, struck by charging Cosians, almost swept back, struggled to hold the walkway.

# 19
# THE WALKWAY

It was on the long walkway leading out to the piers that we fought.

Behind us, some fifteen yards back, the walkway was afire.

Portions of it, hewn and chopped from the small boats, sank into the water. Most of these boats were of Ar's Station, those which had been out at the piers. Other boats trying to flank our position, for using their crossbows, were met and turned back by those of Ar's Station. Indeed, the walkway for a dozen yards, closer to the landing, was covered by these boats, until the camp commander sent his own crossbowmen out on the walkway, to keep them their distance. Fourteen times did the Cosians assault us. In the fifth assault Marsias was grievously wounded, and one other, one who had come originally to the cell. At that time the walkway was still intact, though flaming, behind us, and they could be withdrawn through the fire and smoke to the piers. Their places were taken, to my amazement, by other stout fellows of Ar's Station. Behind us it seemed men vied to join us. Then, in the seventh assault, two others of our original band, the other two who had come originally to the cell, were forced back, bleeding, unable to stand. They were lowered by fishermen into waiting small boats. From these two others climbed to the walkway, to take their place. Of the original band this left only myself and the grizzled fellow.

Fins slid through the water circling the boats, and back and forth beneath the walkway, among the pilings. Sometimes, converging, they suddenly knifed toward a splash in the water, as one fellow or another lost his footing, or fell, bloodied, from the walkway. There were screams from the water and extended hands, and wild eyes. Then there would be churning froths, and blood swirling up, and reachings out, graspings with nothing to grasp, and then we would see bodies drawn under the water. Sometimes we could see them being drawn under the walkway, being taken into its shadows. Sometimes we could see, too, less easily, the long dark shapes, a yard or so beneath the water, conducting them, and the movements of the powerful, vertical tails. Often the fish fought for their prey, sometimes under the walkway itself. We could sometimes feel the movements of their bodies against the pilings beneath us. I saw one fellow of Ar's Station, standing in a small boat, scream with hatred and strike down at one of the shapes with a pike. I think he cut its back. I saw another fellow, a fellow of Cos, spend a quarrel on a fish that was scouting his boat. It descended rapidly, as though stung, the metal fins of the quarrel disappearing under the water with the dorsal fin.

In between the assaults we gasped for breath and crouched behind our shields, resting their rims on the walkway. To lift such a device for Ehn at a time, and receive blow after blow upon it, bearing up under them, in time makes the arm desperately tired and sore. It is little wonder warriors often train with weighted shields. In the early Ahn of battle a common cause of casualties, particularly with young warriors, is recklessness, and the failure to use the shield properly to protect oneself. In the late Ahn of a battle, however, an even more common cause of casualties, interestingly enough, is the simple inability to lift, control and maneuver the shield. There is a great temptation to lower it, to ease the pain of the screaming muscles. This compounds, of course, with arm weariness, the result of wielding the sword, and the slowing of reflexes and reaction time, resulting from general fatigue.

The same problems, of course, normally afflict one's enemy. When one understands these factors, and that battles often last several hours, and are sometimes renewed for two or three days, it is easier to understand certain things which might otherwise seem anomalous in this form of warfare, for example, the respites between assaults, the fluctuations of lines, the occasional, apparently incredible truces which can occur by mutual consent here and there in the pockets of a battle, men standing about, looking at one another, sometimes even conversing, and the great importance of the judicious distribution of, and application of, reserves.

For those who are interested in such matters, it might be pointed out that factors such as these seem to be playing their part in the gradual replacement of the phalanx with the square in Gorean warfare. It is not simply that the squares are more tactically flexible, being capable of functioning on broken terrain, and such, but also that they facilitate substitutions in the front lines, permitting the swift injection of fresh troops at crucial points. The success of many generals, in my opinion, is largely a function of their intelligent use of reserves.

Deitrich of Tarnburg, for example, though one often thinks of him in terms of innovations such as the oblique advance and the use of siege equipment in the field, is also, in my opinion, based on my studies of his campaigns, for example, in the commentaries of Minicius and the "Diaries," which some ascribe to Carl Commenius, of Argentum, a military historian, a master of the use of reserves. Some claim, incidentally, that Commenius was himself once a mercenary. I do not know if this is true or not, but his diaries, if, indeed, they are his, suggest that he was not a stranger to the field. I do not think it likely that all the incidents in them, in their detail, are merely based on the reports of others. His accounts of Rovere and Kargash, for example, suggest to me the fidelity, the authenticity, of a perceptive eyewitness. It seems to me, for example, that a common soldier would not be likely to supply a detail such as the loosing of water by a confused, terrified tharlarion in the field. The common soldier would be aware of such things, and, indeed, would even take them for granted, but they are not the sorts of details which he would be likely to include in his accounts of battles. Too, one wonders how a simple scholar could have come by the numerous beautiful slaves and fortresslike villa of a Carl Commenius. I suspect that at one time, perhaps long ago, he may not have been a stranger to the distributions of loot.

"They are drawing back," said a fellow near me.

"They have nothing more to gain here," said another.

We looked behind ourselves, wearily. Much of the walkway was now gone, or burning. Great lengths of it, some half submerged, tilting, others at, or almost at, the surface, floated in the water. Some of these lengths had turned, and hewn pilings, in an inch or two of water irregularly moving about over the now-upturned undersides of the lengths, like heavy, coarse wooden points, jutted up.

"We have held the walkway," said a man.

"Yes," said another.

We stood on the blood-stained boards.

It was true, we had held the walkway.

It was the middle of the afternoon. I looked about. It seemed odd, where we were, at the new end of that walkway, at the end of what now seemed a meaningless, eccentric bridge leading out from the landing but stopping abruptly in hewn, charred wood. The walkway had been cut behind us. Some of the fellows in the small boats had even drenched the boards behind us with water, to keep the fire from us, while others had hacked away at the pilings. Even so we had felt the heat of the flames at our back. There had been smoke, too, but not enough to affect what occurred on the walkway. Twice, when the wind had turned, it had drifted past us. There was far more smoke from the citadel, which, given the prevailing winds, the force of which had much diminished since the late morning and early afternoon, drifted out over the harbor, toward the river.

"Shall we now swim for the piers?" asked a fellow.

"Certainly," said another.

"I, myself," said another, "will prefer waiting for the boats."

"And why might that be?" inquired another of our number.

"I do not like getting my feet wet," responded the first.

We watched the fins moving about in the water. Here and there there was a stirring at the surface, as though there might be violent agitation some feet beneath. Too, in places the harbor water suddenly muddied, the mud from the bottom rising to the surface. These upswirling discolorations marked places, I supposed, where, below, unseen, a few yards beneath the surface, the long fish, pulling and fighting, snapping and tugging, stirred the mud.

A small boat struck gently against the piling near us, to the left.

There were now eleven of us on the walkway. Two were wounded. One of these was the grizzled fellow, who had been among the first to stand with me on the walkway. He had been wounded in the last assault, the fourteenth. So, too, had the other fellow. We lowered these two into the boat. Two others, too, joined them. The small boat rocked, and was almost swamped.

"Wait," said the fellow at the oars, alarmed, holding up his hand.

The rest of us, seven men, watched the small boat pull away from the walkway.

It made slow progress back toward the piers.

"There are fewer fish about now," said a fellow.

"Stay where you are," I advised him. To be sure, he was right. Many of the fish had apparently departed. Indeed, I was sure that many of them, with bodies, and parts of bodies, in their jaws, had sped away, toward the piers, or had gone out farther in the harbor, beyond them, or had even returned to the river, perhaps sometimes followed by several of their brethren. It was, however, I was sure, still dangerous. Sometimes river sharks, like Vosk eels, hang about piers and pilings, in their shade, and are, I am afraid, often rewarded by garbage, or other organic debris. One could still see, here and there, streaks of blood in the water.

"Look!" said a fellow. He pointed toward the landing. There it seemed that a number of small boats was being mustered and not a few raftlike structures, doubtless improvised from materials within, and about, the citadel.

"They will be coming out to the piers to finish their work," said a man.

"What we have done has been for naught," said another.

"The harbor is closed with Cosian ships and the chain of rafts," said another. "There is no escape."

"Apparently it is not their intent to starve us out, on the piers," said another.

"They are impatient fellows," observed a man.

"They have waited a long time," said another. "They would like to finish their business this afternoon."

"It should not prove difficult," said another.

"It will be a slaughter on the piers," said a fellow. "There is no shelter there. They are open, exposed. What can a handful of shields do there? Little, or nothing. They can do as they wish. They can pick their targets from boats, and rafts. They can attack in force."

"They will probably signal the other fellows, out where the harbor is closed," said a man, "so that they can attack on two sides at once."

"It is all finished," said another fellow.

"It will be done in two or three Ahn," said another.

"You two in this boat," I said to two of them, as another of the small craft touched against the piling. The oarsmen stood up, a fisherman, and extended his hand, to help the two fellows into the boat. We had overloaded the last boat.

We, the five of us remaining on the walkway, watched this second small boat pull away, moving slowly toward the piers.

"I would like to say goodbye to my companion," said one of the fellows.

"Perhaps she is still alive out there," said another.

"When do you think it will be over?" asked one of the fellows.

"By the fifteenth Ahn," said another, grimly.

"Good," said a fellow.

" 'Good'?" asked the other.

"Yes," he said, "then we will not have to miss another supper."

"How would you like to get your feet wet?" asked the grim fellow.

"Not I," replied the other.

In a bit another one of the tiny boats had come to the walkway and the two fellows embarked in it.

There were then three of us left on the walkway.

"It is the women and children I feel most sorry for," said the fellow beside me, looking back toward the piers. They were crowded with noncombatants. I suppose there must have been somewhere between two thousand and twenty-five hundred women and children crowded on the piers. By now there were probably not more than two or three hundred able-bodied men. In a few moments another small boat arrived.

"I will wait with you," said one of the fellows.

"No," I said. "Go."

The two fellows then stepped down, carefully, into the small boat.

I was then left alone on the walkway.

I saw a piece of the broken walkway, half submerged, off to the right.

I looked up, from where I crouched behind the shield. Then I rose up, lifting the shield once more.

A solitary figure, with no shield, but in helmet, and with sheathed sword, approached. It seemed a long walk, coming toward me, on the walkway. I could hear his steps when he came within a few yards of me. The water lapped about the pilings beneath the walkway. There was the cry of a Vosk gull overhead. I could see the smoke still lifting from the citadel, then drifting out, toward the river.

"Do not come closer," I told him.

"The day belongs to Cos," he said.

"Yes," I said.

"There remains to be accomplished only the slaughter on the piers."

I did not respond.

"Thus what you have done here has gone for naught."

I did not respond. What had been done here, however, had been entered into the annals of reality. The meaning of history is its own terrain, its own mountains and summits, here and there, wherever they be found. It is not all prologue to a last act, following which comes nothing.

"It is speculated that you are not of Ar's Station," he said.

I shrugged.

He did not attempt to come closer.

"It is speculated that you are a mercenary," he said. "Cos has use of such. I come on behalf of Aristimines, Commander of Cos in the north. He is pleased with your work, though it has been to his own cost. I have here a purse of gold. Contract your sword to Cos and it is yours." He dropped the leather purse, drawn shut with strings, to the boards of the walk. He then stepped back. "See?" he said. "We do not cut at your neck, as you bend to take it."

"I am not taking fee today," I said.

"You are, then, of Ar's Station, or Ar herself?" he asked.

"No," I said.

"With the gold," said he, "comes a command, and women,

slaves trained to please men in all ways, domestic and lascivious.''

"Aristimines is generous," I said.

"Your answer?" he asked.

"I am not taking fee today," I said.

"But what of the women?" he asked.

"I will take my own," I said.

He approached the gold, bent down and picked it up. He did not even watch me as he did this. I accepted this tribute to my honor.

He tucked the gold back in his tunic. "You are not a mercenary, then?" he said.

"I did not say that," I said.

"Choose for Cos," he said.

"Not today," I said.

"Yet today, I think," said he, glancing out to the piers, "would be a good day to choose for Cos."

"Why did not relief come to Ar's Station?" I asked.

"It was not the will of Lurius of Jad, Ubar of Cos," said he.

"I see," I said. How lofty then, I thought, must be the heights of treachery within the walls of Ar.

"And the will of Lurius has not yet been accomplished in the north," said he.

I did not understand this.

"I have brought you the gold of Cos," he said. "When I return, you understand, I must bring her steel."

"The walkway is meaningless," I said to him.

"Not to Aristimenes," he said.

"I wish you well," I said.

"And I, too, wish you well," said he. He then turned and walked rapidly back toward the landing. He had not taken more than five steps before a number of Cosians, who had been waiting on the landing, hurried onto the walkway. He was for a moment like a rock in the midst of their stream, and then he turned, facing me. At the same time some small craft set out from the landing. Two of the fellows hurrying toward me were too eager, separating themselves from their fellows. One's shield, he charging, I struck obliquely to the side, and he, in the grip of his own momentum, lost the walkway. I cut

at the other below the shield, above the knee, and he slipped
to the boards. "Hold, fellows," called the officer, behind the
men, he who had come with the gold on the walkway.
"Good," he said. "Together now, gently fellows, spears
down. Look for your chance. Forward, carefully. There is
only one man there. Swordsmen for flanking, behind spearmen.
To each side, fellows. Forward."

"Help!" cried the fellow in the water, grasping upward.
He was trying to climb the piling, but slipped on it. He could
not reach the surface of the remains of the walkway. The
piece of broken walkway which had been to the right was
now back, a few feet from the torn end of the walkway,
floating in the inner harbor.

"Stop!" I ordered the approaching Cosians.

They, puzzled, stopped.

The fellow whose leg I had cut was backing away, toward
his fellows, limping. Blood flowed down his leg, running
among, and over, the thongs of the high, bootlike sandal he
wore. His retreat could be traced in the trail of blood on the
walkway.

I put down my shield on the walkway, and extended my
hand down to the fellow in the water. There were fewer fish
about now, I was sure, but I did not think he would be likely
to thrash alone for more than a moment or two. I could
already see two dark shapes beneath him.

"Do not move," said the officer to his men.

The man in the water, frenzied with terror, his eyes bulging, seized my hand and I drew him to his stomach, to the
walkway. He lay there on the drenched boards, trembling. I
do not think I could have managed this as little as a quarter of
an Ahn earlier. I think it likely he would then have been
seized in the jaws of some fish or other, perhaps one of the
visitors from the river, drawn eastward by the traces of blood
in the water.

I then stepped back, and faced the Cosians, some yards
toward the landing.

The officer lifted his sword to me, in salute. I returned this
salute. The men with him smote with their steel on their
shields. I acknowledged their tribute as well.

"On my own authority," called the officer, "and at my

own risk, that of my life for yours, should this not be found meet by Aristimenes, I again offer you the gold of Cos!''

I sheathed my sword. "I am not taking fee today," I said.

"Lower spears," said the officer to his men. "Swordsmen, flank.''

I turned, suddenly, then, and ran to the end of the walkway. There I leapt from the walkway out, over the water, to the piece of half-submerged wreckage, cut from the walkway. It sank down a foot or two into the water, but then rose up, again. A moment or so later a dozen or so Cosians crowded the charred end of the walkway. None of them, as I had anticipated, cared to attempt the same leap. I had had a running start. I had known where the wreckage was. I had kept it in mind. I did not think that one of them, given the crowding on the walkway, would attempt the same leap. If he did, and managed to reach the wreckage, I would be waiting there, sword drawn. My ankles were under water. The force of my leap had thrust the piece of wreckage out further, toward the piers. The men on the walkway and I regarded one another. Several lifted their weapons in salute. I lifted my hand, too, to them. It was, I suppose, one of the odd moments that sometimes occur in war, one of those moments in which the rose of gallantry suddenly emerges from the background of danger and blood. A great, long body suddenly emerged from the water and lay half on the wreckage. With my foot I thrust it back into the water. I saw some small craft from the landing approaching, with crossbowmen in them. But then, too, I saw the rowers of these small vessels, rest on their oars. About the piece of wreckage on which I stood, then, were small boats from the piers. On one of them I saw the young fellow with the crossbow. No quarrels were exchanged. I stepped from the wreckage into one of the small boats. We then put about, and I was rowed slowly toward the piers.

# 20
# THE PIERS

I climbed from the small boat to one of the piers.

Men lifted their weapons, saluting me.

"Come with me," said a fellow.

I passed among wounded men. I saw there, Marsias, the grizzled fellow, the men who had originally stood with me on the walkway, and many others. I passed, too, among many women and children.

I was conducted into the presence of Aemilianus.

"You did well, to hold the walkway, you and others," said Aemilianus.

He was sitting on a pier, propped up against some boxes. These piers are the main harbor piers, between the inner harbor, that between them and the citadel landing, and the outer harbor, which leads to the river. The outer harbor, now, of course, was blocked, a few hundred yards out, with the chain of rafts and, behind them, five ships.

"These would be dead now," said he, gesturing about himself, "had you and those with you not done so."

I looked back to the walkway in the distance, across the inner harbor. "The standard of Cos now surmounts it," I said.

"You held it for the time that was needed," said Aemilianus, "the time required to seal off the piers."

It interested me that Cos would bother setting its standard there, at the end of that charred walk, jutting out toward the piers. Apparently we had made it mean something to them.

I looked back, too, to the citadel, and the city. The citadel was afire. Fires, too, still, after all these days, burned in the city.

"You are not Marsias," said a man to me. "Who are you?"

"Ar's Station is gone," I said to Aemilianus.

"No," he said. "Its Home Stone survives."

"It was taken from the city?" I asked.

"Yes," he said. "Weeks ago it was smuggled from the city, and sent south to Ar, where, if all went well, it must now be."

"So long ago," I said, "you did not expect relief from Ar?"

"I was right," he said, bitterly.

I nodded. One does not keep secret the siege of a city such as Ar's Station. It was one of the largest of the ports on the Vosk. Too, anyone can read a calendar.

"You maintained a brave front," I said.

"And what would you have done, had you been commander in Ar's Station?"

I shrugged. "Much the same, I suppose," I said.

"So," said Aemilianus, "though I did continue to hope, I would not risk the Home Stone. I sent it south."

"By tarnsman?" I asked.

"No," he said. "Cos controls the skies. I sent it south in the wagon of a tradesman, Septimus Entrates."

"It may have escaped notice, then," I said, "among the innumerable wagons, the carts, the strings of refugees, and such, fleeing south."

"That is my hope," he said.

It seemed to me that I might, somewhere, have heard the name, Septimus Entrates. But then one hears many names, thousands of names, here and there.

"Cos," said a man, "prepares to attack."

"From both sides?" asked Aemilianus.

"It would seem so," said a fellow. "The chain of rafts has been opened in three places. The ships of Cos now enter the harbor. Too, there are other rafts from the river. Rafts, and boats, too, are now coming out from the landing."

"The Cosians will spend time in barrages of fire," said Aemilianus, "from the boats, from the rafts. The sky will be dark with their metal. Use the bodies of the slain, and the wounded, as shields." He did not tell them to tear boards from the piers themselves, to construct makeshift hurdles and barricades. Perhaps that could be done later, but now this would, interestingly, have dismantled the very platform on which we stood, so crowded they were. Indeed, it would be difficult to use weapons here, except in thrusting. "When the Cosians ascend the piers themselves," continued Aemilianus, "we will meet them, with what men we still have, and make them pay for every board they cross. Carry me now to the side facing the inner harbor."

"But you are wounded," said his aide.

"Of course, you fool," said Aemilianus, angrily. "What do you think? Do you think I would have given an order I would not be willing, under similar circumstances, to obey? My body, as it is wounded, will serve as a shield in the fighting. It is all that it is good for now."

"We need Aemilianus, our commander," said a man, "not a body for a shield."

Aemilianus tried, angrily, to rise to his feet.

At the same instant, from beneath the bandage bound about his body there emerged a bright, fresh stain of crimson.

Aemilianus sank back, to a sitting position. "Surilius," said he. "The sword, use it now. Then there will be no more quibbling about bodies and shields."

"No, Commander," said he.

"I have never known you to refuse an order," said Aemilianus, puzzled.

"If there must be a body for a shield, use mine, instead," he said. He drew his own sword.

"No, old friend!" begged Aemilianus.

He called Surilius stood ready to pierce his own heart with his sword.

"You," said Aemilianus, lifting his hand to me. "Strike me with your sword."

"I am weary," I said.

"Draw my own sword," he begged. "Hold it, that I may throw myself upon it."

"No," I said.

"No?" said Aemilianus.

"I am not of Ar's Station," I said. "Do not presume to command one who has no fondness for either Ar or Ar's Station."

"But you have fought for us!" said Aemilianus.

"I saw things that did not please me," I said, "and I have fought, but so, too, might a tarn fly and a kaiila run."

Men shuddered. Warriors, it is said in the codes, have a common Home Stone. Its name is battle.

"Your word, Surilius," protested Aemilianus, turning again to the aide, his friend.

"My word is sacred to me," said Surilius, "but so, too, are the terms of my word, and they require only that I do not permit you to fall, when you yourself could not avoid it, into the hands of Cosians. Then, but then only, am I prepared to strike."

"You are a good soldier," said Aemilianus. "I beg your forgiveness, my friend." He then grimaced. Fresh blood appeared again beneath the bandage, running to his waist.

"Let him rest," I said.

A fellow lowered Aemilianus to the boards, amidst the feet about him.

Aemilianus lifted his hand to his friend.

"I will be at your side," said Surilius.

"They are coming," said a fellow. "There must be a hundred rafts and boats, from both sides."

"It will not be long now, will it, dear friend," said Aemilianus.

"No, dear friend," said Surilius, "I do not think it will be long now."

"Look off there," said a fellow, pointing toward the harbor. "I did not know they had so many ships."

"What!" I said.

"There," said the man pointing, out toward the river.

I could see, out beyond the wall of chained rafts, opened now in three places, a flotilla of sails, long and low, triangular, sloping, those of lateen-rigged galleys.

"They are coming for the kill," said a man.

"Where is a glass," I cried, "a builder's glass, a glass of the builders!"

Even as we watched we saw the sail of the first ship furled

to its sloping yard and the yard swung, parallel to the keel, and lowered. In a moment the mast, too, had been lifted, and lowered. The other ships followed suit. The hair on the back of my neck rose. These are preparations of galleys for entering battle. They would now be under oar power alone. It was hard now to even see the ships at the distance. Those were not round ships. They were long ships, ramships. They were shallow drafted, low, like knives in the water.

"Bring me a glass!" I cried.

"A glass!" called more than one man.

"One of the ships of Cos is putting about," said a man.

"I do not understand," said another.

"See them come," said another fellow.

"How many are there?" said another.

"Where could Cos find such ships?" asked another.

"The Cosians on the rafts and boats are approaching," said another. "In a moment they will open fire."

We saw a tarnsman streaking by, coming from the direction of the river, in flight over the piers, speeding toward the landing, or the citadel.

"Shields to the edges of the piers!" called out Surilius. He had drawn his sword.

Women and children huddled toward the center of the piers, crouching down. Many of the women had their heads down, clutching children, shielding them with their own bodies. There was very little noise.

"Here is a glass," said a fellow. I lifted the apparatus to my eye. In a moment or two I had adjusted it, and had it trained on the flagship of the approaching flotilla. I sought the flag tugging and snapping on the stem line, run between the bow and the stem castle. Then I lowered the glass, closing it.

"What are their colors?" asked a man.

"It is the blue of Cos," I said.

I saw Surilius, grasping his sword, look down at the unconscious figure of Aemilianus.

"Cos does not have such force on the river," said a man.

"Look at the fellows on the rafts out there," said another fellow.

"They seem to be in great agitation," said a man.

"May I look?" asked a fellow.

I handed him the glass.

Quickly he looked out at the mouth of the harbor. The ships were closer now. Now one could clearly see the blue fluttering at the stem line of the flagship.

"That is not the flag of Cos!" he cried.

"Surely then it is a variant of the flag of Cos," I said, "perhaps the flag of their forces on the river."

"It is the flag of Port Cos!" he cried. "It is the flag of Port Cos!"

"The flag of Port Cos!" cried others.

"What does it matter, then?" I asked. "Port Cos is a colony of Cos, the very citadel of her power on the Vosk."

"The topaz!" cried a man.

"The topaz! The topaz!" cried others, hundreds of voices.

Surilius was shaking Aemilianus, trying to arouse him. Tears were flowing from his eyes. "The topaz!" he cried to Aemilianus. "Marcus got through! It is Calliodorus, of Port Cos! It is the pledge of the topaz!"

"I do not understand," I said.

Suddenly I saw the flagship, knifing through an opening in the chain of rafts, literally sheer oars from the side of the Cosian ship put about in the harbor. I then saw another Cosian ship rammed amidships. The other three Cosian ships were trying to make a landfall at the sides of the harbor. I saw one run aground there, by a guard station. The fellows at the rafts were trying to close the chains, to close the harbor. I then saw four or five of the ram ships, their bows high, the rams out of the water, dripping water into the harbor, literally ride over, scraping and sliding, the rafts, and plunge into the harbor. The crews of the other two Cosian ships which had been in the harbor, those not injured, and not run aground, leapt over the sides, and, waist deep, waded to shore. I saw some other ships draw alongside the chains, and men swarm out onto the rafts. The Cosians that had been there fled before them. There remained the three openings, then, in the chain of rafts. Indeed, two trains of rafts now floated untethered in the harbor, and the other two trains floated loose, fastened only at one end, each still fastened to great pilings driven into the sand near guard stations, one on each side of the harbor. Out in the harbor itself the small boats and rafts of Cosians which had been approaching to attack were now hurrying to the shore, to one side or another, to take shelter near the most convenient guard station. One ship after another of the newcomers then entered the harbor. The flagship, even now, was easing itself against the outer pier.

"I do not understand what is going on," I said. "What is all this about a topaz?"

"You are then indeed a stranger to Ar's Station, and to the river," said a fellow. "The pledge of the topaz was originally an agreement between river pirates, a pledge of mutual assistance and, in crisis, alliance, between them, those of the eastern and western Vosk, between Policrates in the east and Ragnar Voskjard in the west. When the ports of the river, and their men, rose up against the predations, the tolls and tributes, of these pirates, the topaz fell into the hands of the victorious rebels. From such fighting came the formation of the Vosk League."

I knew something of the Vosk League. Its headquarters was in the town of Victoria, on the northern bank of the Vosk, between Fina and Tafa. Due to its patrols and presence piracy, and certainly large-scale, institutionalized piracy, had been largely removed from the Vosk, from east of White Water, near Lara, a town of the Salarian Confederation at the confluence of the Vosk and Olni, to the delta.

"But a topaz is a stone," I said, "a kind of semiprecious stone."

"And such a stone is the symbol of the pledge," said the fellow. "It was originally a quite unusual stone, one which bore in its markings and coloration a remarkable configuration, that of a river galley. The stone was broken, however, into two pieces. One does not see the ship in the separate parts of the stone for the isolated marks and colorings seem meaningless. When the parts are joined, however, the ship appears. One part of the stone was originally held by Ragnar Voskjard, chief of pirates in the west, and the other by Policrates, chief of pirates in the east. Each, when in need of counsel or support, would send his part of the stone to the other. They would then join forces."

"What has the topaz to do with the Vosk League?" I asked.

"It has nothing to do with the Vosk League itself," said

the fellow. "It is now a private pledge between Port Cos and Ar's Station."

"But the sympathies of Port Cos are surely with her mother ubarate," I said, "and those of Ar's Station with Ar."

I could see several galleys now drawing up at the piers. Men with shields leapt from them to the piers, hurrying to the sides facing the inner harbor. Cosians attempting to climb to the piers there would encounter fresh, dangerous armed men, in hundreds.

"Both Port Cos and Ar's Station fought on the river, in terrible and bloody battles, hull to hull. After the final victory over the pirates, which took place at Victoria in 10,127 C.A., the parts of the stone came into the keeping of Calliodorus, at that time acting first captain in Port Cos, and Aemilianus, who was at that time commander of the naval forces of Ar's Station. The pledge was renewed privately between them, I think, as comrades in arms, as Ar's Station was not permitted by Ar to join the Vosk League."

"Why was that?" I asked.

"I do not know," he said. "It is speculated that Ar feared such an alliance would compromise her claims in the Vosk Basin."

I nodded. That made sense to me. I had suspected as much earlier. The fellow, incidentally, had given the year of the aforementioned battle as 10,127 C.A. It was natural that he, of Ar's Station, would give the date in the chronology of Ar. Different cities, perhaps in their vanity, or perhaps simply in accord with their own traditions, often have their own chronologies, based on Administrator Lists, and such. A result of this is that there is little uniformity in Gorean chronology. The same year, in the chronology of Port Kar, if it is of interest, would have been Year 8 of the Sovereignty of the Council of Captains. The reform of chronology is proposed by a small party from among the caste of scribes almost every year at the Fair of En'Kara, near the Sardar, but their proposals, sensible as they might seem, are seldom greeted with either interest or enthusiasm, even by the scribes. Perhaps that is because the reconciliation and coordination of chronologies, like the diction and convolutions of the law, are usually regarded as scribal prerogatives.

"That is the *Tais*," said a fellow, pointing to the flagship of the newly arrived ships. "I would know it anywhere!" It was being moored at the pier. Its captain, who had been standing on the stern castle, issuing orders, now descended the steps, past the posts of the two helmsmen. In a moment, vaulting over the rail like a common seaman, he had disembarked. He was hatless and helmetless. A young fellow followed him. I recalled him from the audience chamber in the citadel. He was, I took it, the young warrior, Marcus. Men were cheering. Men clutched at them as they sought to make their way through the crowd. I saw them reaching out to touch even the swirling cloak of the captain. "Where is Aemilianus?" called the captain. In his hand, uplifted, about half the size of a fist, the sun catching its polished surface, was a yellowish stone, marked with brown. Men, seeing it, wept and cried out.

"Surely there are more ships there than would have been sent by Port Cos," said a man.

"Do not speak of them," whispered another.

His caution puzzled me.

To be sure, there must have been twenty-five ships in the outer harbor now, several of which had drawn up to the piers. On planks set out to the piers I saw women and children being ushered aboard.

I went to the inner side of the pier, that facing the inner harbor. There was a line of men there, come from the ships. They crouched there, with overlapping shields, their swords drawn. I would not have cared to essay the climb to the pier.

The captain and the young fellow, Marcus, made their way to the side of Aemilianus. He was sitting up, held by Surilius.

I stepped back a little, toward the center of the pier, that I might observe them. Then I was close to them. Men had made way for me.

The captain, whose name I had gathered was Calliodorus, he who had apparently fought long ago with Aemilianus on the river, when both were lesser officers, crouched beside him. He pressed the piece of stone he had brought with him into his hands. Aemilianus held it, tears in his eyes. Calliodorus then, as men observed, removed from his own pouch a similar stone. He then, steadying the stone in the hand of Aemilianus, who could scarcely hold it, fitted the two stones together. I was startled, for no sooner had the two pieces of stone been fitted together than it seemed there suddenly emerged, as now from a single stone, unriven, the image of a galley.

The fellow beside me was crying.

I saw a blond slave, thin and in rags, dare to crawl among the legs of free men, to lie on her stomach near Aemilianus. She put out her fingers to touch his leg. She, too, was weeping. It was she who had been called "Shirley," whom I had seen in the audience chamber of the citadel long ago. I recalled she had been ordered to remind him to whip her the same night, for having dared to look upon me, when I had been brought in, as a prisoner. Doubtless she had done so, and had received her whipping. She lay at his side, humbly. How helplessly was she his slave! I thought she would be luscious, when fattened up, for love.

Calliodorus put the hands of Aemilianus on the stone, and placed his own hands over them. Their hands were then together, over the two joined halves of the stone, the topaz. "The pledge is redeemed," he said.

"My thanks, Commander," said Aemilianus, softly.

"It is nothing, Commander," said Calliodorus.

Women and children were still boarding galleys. I heard the trumpets of recall from the landing. The small boats, and the rafts, in the inner harbor, turned about then, and began to withdraw to the landing. I saw the standard of Cos removed from the walkway. Not a quarrel had been fired.

"It took me days to reach Port Cos," said the young man, Marcus. "I was pursued closely. Once I was captured. I escaped. I moved at night. I hid in swamps. I am sorry."

Aemilianus lifted his hand to him, and weakly grasped it. "You reached Port Cos," he said.

"It took us time to fit and rig the ships," said Calliodorus. "I am sorry."

"Such things cannot be done in a moment," said Aemilianus.

"There was no problem with the crew calls," said Calliodorus. "Volunteers abounded. Indeed, there is no man with me who was not a volunteer. We had to turn men away. Most of these with me fought with us against Policrates and Voskjard."

Aemilianus smiled. "Good," he said.

"So far west on the river," said Calliodorus, "we had not realized your straits were so desperate."

That interested me. The major land forces of Ar, I had gathered, were somewhere in the west, south of the river. I wagered that the men there, those in the ranks there, at least, were no better informed than, apparently, had been those of Port Cos. There had been no dearth of intelligence as to the desperate situation of Ar's Station, however, in this vicinity, east on the river, and south towards Ar.

"How many ships have you?" asked Aemilianus, a commander's question.

"We have brought ten from Port Cos," said Calliodorus, smiling, "but as we came upriver it seems some unidentified ships joined us, from here and there."

"Unidentified?" smiled Aemilianus. "From here and there?"

"Yes," said Calliodorus, smiling, and speaking very clearly. "They are unidentified, absolutely. We do not know where they came from, nor what might be their home ports."

"How many of these came with you?" asked Aemilianus.

"Fifteen," said Calliodorus.

"These ships would not be under the command of one called Jason, of Victoria?" smiled Aemilianus.

"I certainly could not be expected to know anything of that sort," said Calliodorus.

"Praise the Vosk League!" said a man.

"Glory to the Vosk League!" whispered another man.

"It must be clearly understood, by all," said Calliodorus, standing up, smiling, putting his half of the topaz into his pouch, "that the Vosk League, a neutral force on the river, one devoted merely to the task of maintaining law and order on the river, is certainly in no way involved in this operation."

"Glory to the Vosk League," said more than one man.

I moved away from the crowd about Aemilianus and walked along the outer edge of the piers. I did count twenty-five ships at the piers, and out in the harbor. Ten of these flew the blue flag I had taken for that of Cos, or that serving for Cos on the river. From the stem lines of fifteen of the ships, as far as I could tell, for some were out in the harbor, and blocked by others, there flew no colors at all. Indeed, interestingly, as I walked along the piers I saw that canvases had been thrown over places on certain of the ships, at the stern, and on the sides of the bows, where one might be accustomed to look for a name.

On the way back, along the pier, I stopped by one of the unidentified ships, one wharfed adjacent to the *Tais*, the flagship. Indeed, it had been the second ship into the harbor, and the one that had rammed the Cosian ship amidships.

"You wonder where these ships are from?" asked a fellow near me, a fellow from Ar's Station, on the pier.

"Yes," I said. "I am curious."

"This ship here," he said, "is the *Tina*, out of Victoria. I have seen it often enough on patrols."

"That is interesting," I said. Victoria, of course, was the headquarters of the Vosk League.

"You must understand, of course," said the fellow, "that I do not know that."

"I understand," I said.

A tall, dark-haired fellow was on the ship, near the bow. He carried himself as one of natural authority, but he wore no uniform, no insignia. His men I gathered, knew well enough who he was, and others need not know. He had noted us standing on the pier, near the bow. It was there that one of the cloaks of canvas had been placed, perhaps to conceal a name. One was similarly placed on the other side of the bow.

"Tal," said he to us.

"Tal," said I to him. "If I were to remove this canvas would I see the name '*Tina*'?"

The fellow on board looked sharply at the man with me. Apparently he knew him, from somewhere. Certainly the fellow with me had seemed to have no difficulty in identifying the moored vessel. "Vitruvius?" he asked.

"He can be trusted," said the man with me. This trust, I gathered, I had earned on the wall, at the gate, on the walkway. Too, I think there was little truly secret about this ship, or the others.

"Do as you wish," said the fellow on board.

I lifted up the canvas a bit, and then let it drop back, in place. I had read there, in archaic script, the name '*Tina*'.

"Your ship, then," I said to the fellow on board, "is indeed the *Tina*."

"There are doubtless many ships with that name," said the fellow, smiling.

"And what is the port of registry of your ship?" I asked.

"It is registered west of here," he grinned.

"Victoria?" I asked.

"Or Fina, or somewhere," he said.

"Surely these ships with you, those surprisingly flying no colors, are not of the Vosk League."

"We are an innocent trading fleet," he said.

"One Cosian ship has been destroyed in the harbor," I said, "and another has been disabled."

"Yes," he said. "It seems two regrettable accidents occurred in the harbor."

"You are embarking women and children," I said.

"Passengers," he said.

"Some may think these are ships of the Vosk League," I said.

"What do you think, Vitruvius?" asked the fellow, leaning on the rail.

"It seems to me unlikely that these could be ships of the Vosk League," said the fellow beside me, "for the Vosk League, as is well known, is neutral. Does it not seem unlikely to you, as well?"

"Yes," said the man on the ship. "It seems quite unlikely to me, as well."

"What is your name?" I asked the fellow on the ship.

"What is yours?" he asked.

"Tarl," I said.

"That is a common name," he said.

"Yes," I said, "especially in the north."

"My name, too, is a common one," he said, "especially west, on the river."

"What is it?" I asked.

"Jason," said he.

"Of what town?" I asked.

"The same which serves as the home port of my ship," he said.

"West of here?" I said.

"Yes," he said.

"Victoria?" I asked.

"Or Fina, or somewhere," he said.

"I wish you well," I said.

"I wish you well," he said.

Women and children, and now men, were being taken aboard this vessel as well. Turning about, looking back to my left, toward the flagship, I saw Aemilianus being carried aboard. Some tarnsmen flew overhead, but none fired downward.

I watched the piers being emptied, women and children, and men, of Ar's Station, embarking.

I then saw, a rope on her neck, her hands thonged behind her back, still veiled, still clad in the provocative rags which had been those of the former Lady Publia, Lady Claudia. She had been caught among the crowds of women and children on the pier, perhaps noted by the wounded Marsias, or one of the others who had been with us in the cell, or perhaps by others still, alerted by one or the other of them, as to her probable disguise. The Cosians had not come to the piers. She had not received her opportunity to surrender herself to them, begging from them the desperate boon and privilege of reduction to absolute slavery. Among others boarding the flagship, too, in her improvised hood, naked, her hands, too, thonged behind her back, as I had fastened them earlier, being pulled on her leash by one free woman, being herded from behind, poked and jabbed, and struck, with a stick by another, stumbling, ascending the narrow plank to the flagship, was a slave, one who had once been Lady Publia of Ar's Station.

I saw her lose her footing once on the plank and fall, belly downward on it, her legs on either side of it. She must have been utterly terrified, in the darkness of the hood, helpless, unable even to cry out. The first woman tugged at the leash. The other beat her with the stick. She struggled to her feet, and then, obedient to the leash, and trying to hurry before the cruel incitements of the stick, she ascended the plank. Female slaves are seldom left in any doubt on Gor that they are slaves, and particularly when they are in the keeping of free women. I saw two of the oarsmen lift her from the height of the plank, down, between the thwarts, and then place her kneeling, behind them, amidships, on the deck. Other slaves already knelt there. Too, in that place, kneeling, too, a neck rope dangling before her, but in no one's keeping, knelt Lady Claudia.

The two free women who had had the former Lady Publia

in their care were courteously directed forward, where, before
and about the stern castle and even on the small bow deck,
were gathered several women and children. These, already,
were being fed ships' rations. Four or five ships, crowded
with passengers, had come and gone more than once at the
piers. These were ferrying passengers to the ships lying at
anchor in the harbor. Then they themselves retained their last
loads of passengers and, too, drawn away from the piers, out
in the harbor, rode at anchor. Many other passengers had
boarded the ships which had remained wharfed, such as the
*Tina* and *Tais*. The various ships were now crowded with the
men, women and children of Ar's Station. I doubted that any
one of them now held less than a hundred passengers.

It must be remembered, too, that these were river galleys
and, on the whole, smaller than the galleys of Thassa. Too,
the river galley, for those whom it might interest, is normally
shorter masted than a Thassa galley, seldom has more than
one mast, and seldom carries the varieties of sails, changed
on the yard according to wind conditions, that are carried by
a Thassa galley. River galleys, also, as would be expected,
seldom carry more than twenty oars to a side, and are almost
always single-banked.

Fifteen ships, mostly of Port Cos, were now at the piers,
which, now, except for armed men, were mostly empty. I
heard a battle horn sound, from the stern castle of the *Tais*. It
was, I gathered, the recall. In orderly fashion, unchallenged,
the numerous soldiers, guardsmen, armed oarsmen and such
who had lined the inner side of the piers, facing the inner
harbor, withdrew to the fifteen waiting ships. Many clam-
bered over the sides. Others made use of various planks and
gangplanks.

On some of the ships now there was scarcely room for the
oarsmen to ply their levers. Water lapped high on the hulls;
the rams were now at least a yard under the water; even the
lower tips of their shearing blades were submerged. Mariners
of some ships freed the mooring lines of others, and then
their own, and then boarded, some of them using the lines
themselves to regain the decks. Several of the ships then
departed from the piers, pushing off with the three traditional
poles. Among these was the ship called the *Tina*.

I looked out into the harbor.

I saw some of the ships there drawing up their anchors, generally two, one at the bow, one at the stern, and putting about, those that had faced the piers. The huge, painted eyes of these ships were then turning north, toward the mighty Vosk. The eyes of the other ships out in the harbor, those which had had the task of ferrying out passengers, already faced north. Such eyes are common on Gorean ships. How else, some mariners inquire, could she see her way? To the Gorean mariner, as to many who have followed the ways of the sea, learning her, fearing her, loving her, the ship is more than an engineered structure of iron and wood. It is more than tackle and blocks, beams and planks, canvas and calking. There is an indefinability and preciousness about her, a mystique which informs her, an exceeding of what is seen, a nature and wondrous mystery, like that of a companion and lover, a creature and friend. Though I have seldom heard them speak explicitly of this, particularly when landsmen are present, many Gorean mariners seem to believe that the ship is in some way alive. This is supposed to occur when the eyes have been painted. It is then, some say, that she comes alive, when she can see. I suppose this may be regarded as superstition; on the other hand, it may also be regarded as love.

The ships in the outer harbor which had been facing north now, too, drew up their anchors.

I looked back toward the landing and the citadel in the distance, across the inner harbor. I could see the remains of walkway from where I was. The citadel was burning.

I looked back to the harbor.

The first of the ships was now moving toward the river. Others were following her, in line.

Once again I looked back toward the citadel.

Smoke drifted out to the piers, too, from the city itself. Those fires, I supposed, might burn for two or three days yet.

I looked at the walkway. It had been a good fight, the fight that had been fought there. I did not think that those of either Cos or Ar's Station had cause to regret what had been done there. Glory is its own victory.

The last ships at the piers, one by one, began to depart their wharfage. I could see the water fall from the lifted oar blades into the harbor. Only the *Tais,* then, remained at the wharf.

"Captain?" said a voice. It was that of the young crossbowman.

His friend was with him.

They cast off the mooring lines and then followed me aboard. After our boarding the plank was drawn back, over the rail. Three mariners, managing the long poles, thrust the *Tais* from the pier.

"Out oars!" I heard the oar master call.

# 21
# THE RIVER

"Let the first of the two females be fetched," said Aemilianus.

It was now the middle of the morning. following yesterday's late-afternoon action at the piers.

The *Tais* moved with the current west on the Vosk. She led the main body of the flotilla westward. Ahead of us, in oblique formation, barely discernible, were four smaller galleys. These formed, as it were, an advance guard. Similarly, behind the main body of the flotilla, bringing up the rear, back a pasang or so, flying no colors, their markings concealed, were two galleys. One of these was the ship to whose captain I had spoken earlier, the *Tina*.

"Yes, Commander," said a man.

Aemilianus sat on the deck, rather before the steps leading up to the helm deck and, above that, to the height of the stern castle, leaning against a backrest of canvas and rope. Calliodorus of Port Cos, his friend, stood near him. Beside him, too, stood his aide, Surilius. Marsias, too, and the fellows whom I had encountered in the cell earlier, and who had fought with us on the walkway, were there, too. The grizzled fellow, too, had asked to be present. These were wounded. Marsias and one other fellow were lying on pallets. The others of the wounded sat on the deck. The young man, Marcus, was there, too. It was he who had made it through to Port Cos and returned with the ships which had made possible the evacuation from the piers. Now, in spite of his youth, he

stood high in these councils, those of the survivors of Ar's
Station. Many others were there, too, several of whom had
fought with me on the wall and elsewhere. Among them were
the two young fellows who had served me so well on the
wall, as my messengers, and had served well later, too, on
the landing. Those who stood with us here, I gathered, stood
high among the survivors of Ar's Station.

I looked about myself.

It was remarkable to see the difference in the fellows from
Ar's Station, now that they had had some food and a decent
night's sleep, though only stretched out on the crowded deck
of a galley. It had been perhaps the first night's sleep many of
them had had in weeks, not disrupted by watches or alarms.

The "first of the two females" had not yet been fetched.
They were arranging a special chaining for her. This would
be the one in the improvised hood. I had had her hood pushed
up yesterday evening and early this morning, though at neither time in such a way as to uncover her eyes, and, after
having had her warned to silence, had had her gag removed,
and had had her fed and watered. Though she would know
that she was on a galley and moving with the current on the
Vosk, thus west, she had no real idea as to where she was or
what was to be done with her. She was being kept with other
women, also ordered to silence, who, with one exception,
were slaves. The voices she had heard about her, for the most
part, naturally enough, given the crew of the *Tais*, would
have had Cosian accents, or accents akin to them.

Yesterday afternoon, shortly after we had cleared the harbor at Ar's Station, I had drawn the mask of Marsias from my
features, and had shaken my head, glad to feel the air of the
Vosk about me, so fresh and clear.

"I thought it was you," had said Aemilianus, weakly. "It
had to be you. Your escape and that of the heinous traitress,
Lady Claudia, became generally known after the recall of the
troops from the citadel, in the retreat to the landing. We were
informed of it by the good Marsias, and his fellow guardsmen.
Too, there was no sword like yours in Ar's Station."

"You might perhaps have joined with those of Cos," had
said a fellow, "in the fighting. Why did you not do so?"

"The wall needed defending," I had said. "One thing led
to another."

"Had you not held the wall as long as you did," had said Aemilianus. "And had you not further delayed Cos at the gate, and on the walkway, the day would have been finished long before the arrival of Calliodorus."

Several men had assented to this.

"It was nothing," I had said.

Back by the port side of the stairs leading to the helm deck, a few feet from where Aemilianus sat, knelt Shirley, his beautiful blond slave. No longer was she so pale and drawn as before. Now she was considerably freshened by rest and food. Her blond hair which had been closely cropped, if not shaved, early in the seige of Ar's Station was now growing out. And, already, with the rest and food, her beauty gave hints of returning to a voluptuousness that brings high prices on a slave block, and can drive a master half mad with passion. Too, looking at her, I realized that Aemilianus, too, must be feeling much better, and much stronger. She was in chains. Though the girl loves the master with all her heart and would never dream of fleeing from him, absurd though such a dream might be on Gor, given the branding, the collaring, the closeness of the society, and such, she knows that she is upon occasion to be put in chains. In this act is symbolized his desire of her, that she is worth chaining and keeping. And in this act is symbolized his power over her. Despite their love, she is still his, and a slave.

Even the gentlest and kindest of masters has absolute power over the slave. She is no less owned by him that she would be by the cruelest brute on Gor. Elated and reassured then is the woman that she is chained, in this finding continuing evidence of her master's desire for her, his passion for her, his prizing of her, his determination to keep her for himself. And for her part, she rejoices that she is helpless to escape him, that she truly belongs to him, that she is truly his, legally and otherwise, and that she must, as she intensely desires to do, continue to live for service and love. It is not merely pleasant to own a slave, to dress her as you please, if you wish to permit her clothing, to have her at your bidding, to do with her as you please; it is exalting. The man who has not owned a slave has no conception of the maximums of sexuality, nor has the woman who has not been owned.

"How is my old friend Callimachus, commander of the

forces of the Vosk League?'' asked Aemilianus of Calliodorus.
The body sovereign in the Vosk League, incidentally, at least
as I understand it, is its High Council, which is composed of
representatives from the member towns. This Callimachus, I
gathered, then, whoever he was, would be the appointee of
that council.

"Hard at work at his desk, attending to numerous adminis-
trative duties,'' said Calliodorus.

"Doubtless he will also be certain to be publicly visible in
Victoria,'' smiled Aemilianus.

"As would you in his situation,'' smiled Calliodorus.

"Doubtless he will be astonished to learn of yesterday's
action at Ar's Station.''

"Doubtless,'' agreed Calliodorus. "We may rest assured,
of course, that he will conduct a careful investigation.''

Aemilianus laughed.

The results of this investigation, I gathered, might prove to
be inconclusive.

We heard the sound of chain and saw the "first of the two
females to be fetched forth.''

It was she in the improvised hood.

She was led forth, before us, in her small steps, by a hand
on her left arm. Then she was sat on the deck, before
Aemilianus.

She sat there, hooded. I do not think she was sure, actually, where she was, except that she had presumably been
conducted further aft, or if anyone were about.

She sat there for a moment, listening. We were silent.

No longer wore she the leather collar, with its leash. No
longer were her hands thonged behind her.

But she was in sirik.

The metal collar was fastened on her throat. From it a long
chain, dangled downward. To this chain, near her waist, was
attached another chain, terminating at each end with a wrist
ring, into which rings her wrists had been placed and locked.
At the end of the chain dangling from the collar, to which the
wrist-ring chain was attached, was an ankle-ring chain, terminating at each end with an ankle ring, into which her ankles
had been placed and locked. The neck chain was rather long
and if she were to stand some of it would have lain upon the
deck. The device permits of numerous adjustments. As it was

now adjusted, her wrists had some twelve inches of play, her ankles some fourteen inches of play. The smallness of her steps had been a function of the current adjustment of her ankle chaining.

She sat on the deck. She felt the ankle rings and the chain between them, and the neck chain, and then, with each hand, she tried to slip the wrist ring from the opposite wrist. She could not, of course, begin to do so. She was exploring the device. Then she put her hands on the neck chain and moved up it, with her fingers, and pulled it against its staple on the collar. Then she felt the staple, jerked the chain again against it, and convinced herself that it was well secured there. Then she felt, wonderingly, the collar itself. It was well on her, and locked. She seemed puzzled, and frightened. The device had been only put on her a few moments ago. This was the first time, I gathered, that she had worn slave chains.

She probably had no idea how beautiful she looked in them.

Although she could now reach her hood and gag, given the length of the neck chain, which permitted her to lift her chained wrists to her head, she did not, of course, do so. She would not dare to so much as touch them, let alone remove them. She was not unfamiliar with Gorean disciplines.

"Kneel," said Aemilianus, gently.

Swiftly she knelt.

She began to tremble. The chains made small sounds.

I gathered that she did not know before whom she knelt. Also, interestingly, absurdly, it seemed that she was not altogether sure of her condition and status, obvious though it must be to anyone who looked upon her.

Aemilianus made a small sign to Calliodorus.

"You may put your head to the deck," said Calliodorus.

The girl did so, putting her palms on the deck.

"You may raise it," he said.

She raised her head. She was then kneeling as before, amongst us.

"Free her mouth," said Calliodorus.

I crouched beside the girl and undid the hood and pushed it up, and fastened it then as a half hood on her. In this way the effectiveness of the hood as a blindfold had not been compromised, for even an instant. I then untied the gag strips from the back of her neck, and pulled away the gag. I then, carefully, delicately, removed the mass of sopped wadding from her mouth. I put it on the deck beside her, heavy and sodden, with the rest of the gag In this way these things were at hand, and her mouth might then, at our convenience, if we wished, be restored swiftly to its former condition of helpless closure.

"You are not branded," observed Calliodorus.

"No! No!" she cried eagerly.

"Do you wish to live?" he inquired.

"Yes!" she said, fervently.

"Are you, or have you ever been, a woman of Ar's Station?" he asked.

"Yes!" she said.

"How came it then," he asked, "that you were in bonds on the piers, leashed and thonged, hooded and gagged?"

"An escaping prisoner did such things to me," she said. "Hooded, I was not recognized. Gagged, I could not make my plight known."

"Do you know what happened yesterday on the piers?" he asked.

"I have only a very imperfect understanding of what occurred," she said. "Twice on the piers I fainted, and was unconscious. I was awakened by the kicks of free women and conducted helplessly aboard this vessel."

"What do you think occurred on the piers?" he asked.

"Ships came to the piers," she said, "and I think that many on the piers, including myself, were embarked aboard them."

"Cosian ships?" he asked.

"I do not know," she said, miserably. "There were Cosian ships about."

"But surely you have learned much since you were brought on board," he said.

"I was kept with women," she said, "who were ordered to silence."

"What do you think was the fate of the women who brought you on board?" he asked.

"I do not know," she said.

"Do you think they were with you last night, similarly ordered to silence?"

"I do not know," she said.

"What have you heard on the ship?" he asked.

"Little," she said. "I have heard men conducting the business of the ship."

"Have you perhaps formed some conjectures as to the origins of these men?"

"Yes," she said.

"On what basis?" he asked.

"On their speech," she said.

"Their speech?" he asked.

"Their accents," she said.

"Does my speech have an accent?" asked Calliodorus, interested.

"Yes," she said.

Ah," he said. He, like most people, was not accustomed to thinking of his own speech as having an accent.

"And what is my accent?" he asked.

"I make it out to be Cosian," she whispered.

"And what of the accents of the men?" he asked,

"The same," she said.

"In whose power are you then?" he asked.

"In the power of Cosians!" she said, suddenly, now sure of it.

"You may speak," he said.

"Spare me!" she suddenly begged. "Spare me, noble Cosians!" She clasped her hands together piteously, holding them forth toward Calliodorus and Aemilianus. "Spare me!" she wept. "Take pity on a female!"

The men were silent, observant.

Their silence must have been disconcerting to the girl. She indicated her beauty, as she could, with her chained hands. "I think that I am not unattractive," she said, piteously, desperately. "See? See? And it is my hope that my face, too, should you be pleased to look upon it, may be found not unattractive!"

"Do you seek to interest your captors?" he asked.

"Yes!" she said.

"As a female?" he asked.

"Yes!" she said.

"Say it," said he.

"I seek to interest my captors," she said, "*as a female!*"

"What would you have of us?" he inquired.

"My life!" she wept.

"On what condition?" he asked.

"Any of your election," she said.

"Absolute bondage?" he asked.

"Of course!" she said unhesitantly.

"Even to Cosians?" he asked.

"Certainly!" she said.

"Why should Cosians accept you as a slave?" he asked.

"I—I do not understand," she faltered.

"Do you think it would be in their interest to accept you as a slave?" he asked.

"I do not understand," she said.

"Do you think you would prove to be of any value to them as a slave?"

"I would strive desperately to be of value," she said.

"Perhaps you should be bloodied and thrown overboard to river sharks."

"No!" she wept.

"Do you think that just any woman can make a satisfactory slave?"

"I do not know," she said, "but I beg the opportunity to try!"

"You would serve Cosians then?" he asked.

"Yes!" she wept.

"Belly," he said.

She slipped to her belly on the deck, her hands up, beneath her shoulders. She lifted herself a little from the deck, lifting her head, still half concealed in hood, to Calliodorus and Aemilianus. Her lips were lovely, and trembling.

"Go to your back," said Calliodorus.

She lay on her back.

Suddenly she lifted one knee, and pointed her toes. She had realized then, suddenly, that something was being done to her analogous, in its small way, to putting a girl through slave paces. She tried her best to be appealing.

"To your belly, again," said Calliodorus.

He had hardly spoken before she was on her belly, as before. Quick was she, she would show him, to obey.

"Kneel," he said.

She returned to her kneeling position.

"Of what are you worthy, female?" he inquired.

"Only to be a slave," she said.

"Speak," he said.

"I beg the inestimable honor and privilege of being made an absolute slave," she said.

"To Cosians?" he asked.

"To any man," she said.

It irritated me that she had spoken as she had to them for it was as if she were not already a slave, and an unconditional, categorical and absolute slave. She had not even addressed the men as "Master." Clearly she suspected, or hoped, and nothing had as yet occurred to gainsay this suspicion or hope, that they did not know she was already a slave, that she had only yesterday spoken self-irreversible words of self-enslavement on the upper battlements. She did not know, of course, that I was also on board.

"Unhood her," said Calliodorus.

I stepped back, so that the slave could not see me.

Then the slave was blinking and crying, and rubbing her eyes with the back of her fists.

Then, having managed to adjust somewhat to the light, and managing to achieve some grasp of her surroundings, and seeing in the midst of what men she knelt, she looked about herself wildly, in consternation.

"Is this the behavior typical of the women of Ar's Station?" smiled Calliodorus, glancing at Aemilianus.

"Say more simply it is the behavior typical of women," smiled Aemilianus.

"Commander," begged the girl.

"You are aboard the *Tais*, a warship of Port Cos," said Aemilianus. "You have had the honor of conversing with her captain, my former comrade in arms, and friend, Calliodorus."

"Port Cos!" she said.

"Yes," he said.

"That accounts for the accents," she said.

"Precisely," he said.

"It is true," said a man, "her face is not unattractive."

She blushed.

"I understand nothing of what is going on," she said to Aemilianus.

"Ten ships of Port Cos, and fifteen others," said Aemilianus, "entered the harbor of Ar's Station yesterday afternoon, shortly before what would presumably have been the last attack of Cos on the piers. These twenty-five ships neutralized what forces of Cos could be brought to bear at that point and succeeded in evacuating the piers."

"Then we are among friends," she said.

"Most of us," said Aemilianus.

"Why am I in chains?" she asked.

"Slave chains," said Aemilianus.

"Why am I in slave chains?" she asked.

"Do you not know?" he asked.

She was silent, wondering feverishly, doubtless, how much he knew.

"My commander can see," she then said, lightly, "that the only collar I wear is a portion of my chaining, and that I am not branded."

I stood rather behind her, my arms folded. My face must have appeared somewhat severe. Certainly I was angry. Though she had not explicitly claimed to be free, it seemed clear that she was hoping to be taken as such.

"Perhaps," she said, "my chains may now be removed, and I may be given suitable raiment, that of a free woman, that I may take a place among my free sisters." She had certainly worded that carefully, I thought. She had not said "my place," which might suggest she had a right to it, but "a place," which was compatible with it merely being a place she took, with or without title, so to speak.

"You are on trial," he said.

She looked at him, startled, aghast.

"Or," said he, "if you are a slave, you are being given a small hearing."

"I do not understand," she said.

"Perhaps you do," he said.

"On what charges?" she asked.

"The charges, if you are a free woman," he said, "are several, such as the intent to deceive with respect to caste, the jeopardizing of fellow citizenesses by disgarding traditional concealments and modesties, to your own advantage in the event of the taking of the city, for example, going barefoot and baring your calves, and such, and a lack of patriotism, as evidenced by having refused to cut your hair, to supply needed war material to your compatriots."

"But you can see, Commander," she said, suddenly lifting her hands to her head, "that my hair has been cut, and shortly, too!" She rubbed her hand over the brush of hair on her head.

"It is our understanding that your hair was shorn only yesterday, and against your will, in a cell in the citadel, by an escaping prisoner."

"Surely you do not believe that, Commander," she said.

"Lady Claudia, the traitress, and an undisputed free woman," he said, "is in our power. Shall she be brought forward to testify as to the circumstances in which, and the time at which, your hair was shorn?"

"No, Commander," said the girl.

"You do not dispute what I have said then?" he asked.

"No, Commander," she said, defeated.

"It is also believed that you carried much gold with you, in your purse, presumably, again, to improve your chances of persuading victorious Cosians to spare you, resources incidentally much beyond the reach of most women of Ar's Station, thus, again, supplying you with an advantage over them. Is this disputed?"

"No, Commander," she said. She knew, of course, that Lady Claudia could testify as to the presence of the gold in her purse. Indeed, interestingly, although this was not known to the girl, that very gold had been used after the fall of the gate to assist in the escape of Aemilianus and his colleagues to the piers. I had scattered it behind mercenaries, to clear a passage.

Aemilianus regarded her, evenly.

"You have not charged me," she said, "with not wearing robes of concealment."

"In Ar's Station," he said, "as in Ar, robes of concealment, precisely, are not legally obligatory for free women, no more than the veil. Such things are more a matter of custom. On the other hand, as you know, there are statutes prescribing certain standards of decorum for free women. For example, they may not appear naked in the streets, as may slaves. Indeed, a free woman who appears in public in violation of these standards of decorum, for example, with her arms or legs too much bared, may be made a slave."

"There was no crime then," she said, "in my appearing in public as I did, even though, say, I wore but a single layer and my calves, ankles and feet were bared."

"Whether the degree of your exposure was sufficient to violate the codes of decorum is a subtle point," said Aemilianus, "but I will not press it."

"Surely many low-caste girls go about with only as much, or even less," she said.

"But you are of the Merchants," said Aemilianus, smiling.

"A low caste!" she said.

I smiled. The Merchants often maintain that they are a high caste, and should, accordingly, be included in the councils of high caste. Now, however, it seemed she was eager to accept that, and stress that, the Merchants was not a high caste. The traditional high castes of Gor are the Initiates, Scribes, Builders, Physicians and Warriors.

"I do not press the point," said Aemilianus.

"And if I dressed in such a manner that my caste would not be clear," she said, "it is no more than many women do upon occasion. Surely some women even reserve the caste robes and colors for such things as formal occasions, and some even for ceremonial functions."

"True," said Aemilianus.

"I do not think then I should be held accountable under the charge of attempting to deceive with respect to caste," she said. "For example, I engaged in no business under false pretenses, and I never claimed explicitly to be of a caste other than my own." It seemed to me that she did have a point here. The legal problems connected with intent to deceive with respect to caste, of course, problems of the sort which presumably constitute the rationale of the law, usually come up in cases of fraud or impersonation, for example, with someone pretending to be of the Physicians. "And, too," she continued, "if conquering Cosians should have seen fit to take me for a simple, low-caste maid, I see no reason why the laws of Ar's Station should now be exercised against me. What would be the point of that, to protect Cosians from a mistake which they never had the opportunity to make?"

"You hoped by your mode of dress, and such," said

Aemilianus, "to conceal that you were of a caste on which vengeances might be visited, and thus to improve your chances of survival."

She tossed her head, and the chain dangling from her collar moved in its staple. "I am not a man," she said. "Indeed, I can barely lift, let alone wield, the weapons of men. I have nothing of their strength. I have nothing of their power. I am other than they. I am a woman. I am something quite different from a man. I think that I am entitled, then, to attempt to secure my survival as best I can, and in my own way."

"In the way of a female?" asked Aemilianus.

"Yes!" she said.

"In doing what you did," he said, "in going barefoot, in baring your calves, in not having your hair shortened, in carrying gold and such, you arrogated to yourself considerable advantages over other women in Ar's Station."

"It is every woman for herself," she said. "It is not my fault if other women were not as clever as I. It is not my fault if they did not judiciously bare their bodies, and design themselves clothing such as might appeal to a conquering invader. Too, it is not my fault if they lacked the gold wherewith to sweeten a petition to foes for the collar. Am I to be blamed, too, for being more beautiful than many women of Ar's Station, for I am certain that I am, and for thus having some additional unfair advantage over them?"

"Why did you not donate your hair to the defense of the city?" asked Aemilianus.

"I did not want to," she said.

"Why not?"

"It was pretty," she said, angrily.

"And?" he asked.

"I thought I would be more attractive with it," she said, angrily. "I thought if I were captured by Cosians, I would be more likely to be spared, if it was not cut."

"While the women of Ar's Station had theirs cut?"

"If they wished," she said.

"And thus might be less likely to be spared?" he asked.

"That is their business, not mine," she said.

"What of the desperate need of cordage for catapults?" he asked.

"Let the hair of slaves be shorn," she said.

"And what if there was not enough?" he asked.

"Then get hair from the women who are willing to give it," she said.

"What if there was not enough?" he asked.

"My hair would make no difference," she said.

"What if all the free women took that position?" he asked.

"They did not," she said.

"For one in chains you speak rather arrogantly," he observed.

"Surely they will be removed in a moment," she said.

"What did you do to contribute to the defense of the city?" he asked.

"I accepted a duty," she said.

"But it is true, is it not," he asked, "that you did this only late in the siege?"

"Yes," she said.

"And only after it had been made clear that women who did not participate in the efforts of defense were to be lowered over the wall at noon, naked, to Cosians."

"Yes," she said, angrily.

"What duty did you choose?" he asked.

"I served as a warder in the citadel," she said.

"Why did you choose that duty?" he asked.

"I thought it would be easy," she said.

"And in such a place," he said, "perhaps it would have seemed less inappropriate to wear garments such as you did, and go barefoot, and such?"

"Perhaps," she said.

"You did not choose to work on the wall?" he asked.

"No," she said.

"Why not?" he asked.

"I am not strong," she said.

"Straighten your back," he said.

She did so.

"There seems nothing wrong with your body," he said.

One or two of the men smiled.

"Slight as it is," he said, "it seems such that it could be appropriately subjected to lengthy servile labors."

She looked at him, frightened.

"Or perhaps more appropriately yet," he said, "to numerous, various labors of a more delightful sort, labors particularly suitable for females."

"Commander!" she protested.

He said nothing. I wondered if he were not, in his mercy, giving her an opportunity to request permission to speak. I was curious to see if she would ask such permission.

"Have I heard the sum of these charges?" she asked.

"Your behavior of this morning might be included," he said, "in which, before your compatriots, you in effect begged the collar of Cosians."

"I had no idea, Commander, that you or the others were here," she said.

"We gathered that," he said.

There was laughter.

"I beg your indulgence," she said. "I am only a female."

Aemilianus did not speak.

"I do not think my behavior so untoward, unpredictable or surprising for my sex," she said.

The face of Aemilianus remained expressionless.

"I do not think that other women, those of Ar's Station, or of other cities, under similar circumstances, would have behaved differently," she said.

"Do you think they would have behaved so, so readily?" he asked.

"I do not know," she said. "Perhaps the stupider women would not have. It is every woman for herself!"

"I understand," said Aemilianus.

"If that, then," she said, "is the sum of the charges against me, I request that they be dismissed. Surely my defense, even if you do not approve of me, is sound. Surely everything that I have done, including the matter of wanting to keep my hair, lies within the prerogatives of a free female. Similarly, it is surely within her rights to pursue her own best interests, selfishly or not, as she understands them. Similarly, it is not her fault if other women are not as favored as she with intelligence and wealth, and perhaps beauty. If there is any objection to my conduct, surely it must be merely that I was not, in your opinion, sufficiently patriotic, and surely it is no crime to be insufficiently patriotic. Therefore, remove my chains." At this point she lifted her chained wrists to Aemilianus.

"The matter," said Aemilianus, "is considerably more complex than you seem to understand. There are more subtleties here than you seem to realize. For one thing, your conviction that it is not a crime to be insufficiently patriotic may not be shared by everyone. In particular, it may not be shared by those who risked their lives in the defense of the city, those who, say, fought upon the wall, or at the gate, or on the landing or walkway. Secondly, there is the consideration, subtle at times, to be sure, of *conduct indicating suitability for the collar*."

She shuddered.

The principle he had alluded to pertains to conduct in a free woman which is taken as sufficient to warrant her reduction to slavery. The most common application of this principle occurs in areas such as fraud and theft. Other applications may occur, for example, in cases of indigency and vagrancy. Prostitution, rare on Gor because of female slaves, is another case. The women are taken, enslaved, cleaned up and controlled. Indulgence in sensuous dance is another case. Sensuous dance is almost always performed by slaves on Gor. A free woman who performs such dancing publicly is almost begging for the collar. In some cities the sentence of bondage is mandatory for such a woman.

"Conduct indicating suitability for the collar," of course, can be interpreted in various ways, and more broadly and narrowly. It is almost always understood, of course, fortunately for women, and as I suppose the phrase itself makes clear, in the special legal sense of the phrase, as having to do with *overt behavior* rather than psychological predispositions and such. Many Goreans believe that all women are natural slaves, and thus, in a sense, are all eminently suitable for the collar. But even taken in the appropriate, legal behavioral sense the phrase is, as may well be imagined, subject to diverse interpretations.

For example, in the present case, a judge would be expected to decide whether or not the behaviors of the sort performed, constituted behavior for which the collar might be suitably imposed. Also important, of course, at least in the eyes of some, might be her failures in the defense effort, her refusal to be shorn, contributing her hair for use as catapult cordage, in spite of the desperate need for such materials, and the fact that it was only after the imposition of a severe penalty for noncompliance that she accepted even a small duty in the siege.

It was on the basis of considerations such as these, and perhaps cumulatively, taking into consideration their conjoint weight, that a determination might be made as to whether or not it was fitting that she be made a slave. Her begging for a Cosian collar but moments ago, and her open admission of the fittingness and rightness of her being collared, interestingly, would probably not be considered at all. In most cities such things are taken for granted, the natural rightfulness of slavery for females, and such, and are accordingly seldom regarded as germane with respect to the legal imposition of a sentence of bondage.

"You do not think then that these charges should be dismissed out of hand?" she asked, faltering.

"I would certainly not think so," said Aemilianus.

"I see," she said, frightened. She was kneeling up, off her heels.

We heard a Vosk gull screaming overhead.

From where I stood I could see the linked ankle rings on her fair ankles, and part of the long chain running from the ankle-ring chain up, before her body, to the staple on her collar. The wrist-ring chain, in front, was attached to the same long chain. I could also see the metal collar on her neck. It was in plain view, of course, as I had cut her hair.

"What then is your decision upon the charges, Commander?" she asked.

" 'Charges'?" he asked.

"Yes," she said.

"*Charges*," he said, "are appropriate to free women."

"Commander?" she asked.

"They might be involved, for example," he said, "in a trial."

"Of course, Commander," she said.

"Whereas in your case," he said, "such considerations, being pertinent to free women, may be simply beside the point."

"But surely I have been on trial!" she said.

"Perhaps, rather," he said, "as I suggested earlier, we are not engaged here in a trial but in something quite different."

"I do not understand," she said.

"Perhaps this is more in the nature of a little hearing, a quite informal little hearing, or inquiry."

"Commander?" she faltered.

"And perhaps what we are really concerned with here are not charges, which are pertinent only to free persons, but causes for punishment, which are pertinent to slaves."

She looked at him in terror.

"To be sure," he said, "anything, with or without reason, may be done to a slave."

"Commander—" she said.

"I do not think we need now concern ourselves with matters such as intentional misrepresentations of caste, violations of decorum, arrogation of advantages, jeopardization of fellow citizens, and insufficiency of patriotism. We must rather consider matters which, I believe, are more pertinent in your case, and, I fear, unfortunately for you, far more serious."

"What matters?" she asked, terrified.

"Chief among them," he said, "would seem to be misrepresentation of status."

"I—I do not understand," she whispered.

"Impersonation of a free woman," he said.

She did not dare to speak.

"And, of course," he said, "there are several associated considerations, such as arrogant speech, speaking without permission, and failure to use the proper forms of address."

She shuddered.

"You may speak," he said.

She lifted her hands toward her collar. "You can see that the only collar I wear," she said, "is a portion of my chaining. You can see that I am not branded!"

"Are you, or are you not, a free woman?" asked Aemilianus. "Speak clearly."

She squirmed, kneeling on the deck. She trembled in the chains. She looked from one face to another, before her, and at the sides. Wildly she must have been considering whether or not there might be any there who had heard her speak the self-irreversible words of self-enslavement on the upper battlements. Then, kneeling up, again, off her heels, she straightened her back, and, I fear, was preparing to respond boldly, and negatively, to the question of Aemilianus.

She lifted her head, she drew in her breath.

"Consider your answer carefully," I said to her, from behind her.

Hearing my voice she suddenly uttered a shriek of misery, flung her hands up in the wrist rings, until the chaining impeded their further movements, and jerked helplessly in the chains. Then she lowered her hands and wavered. I feared she might faint. Then she bent over at the waist and put her head down, and turned half about, on her knees. Then, lifting her head a little, she looked up at me.

I looked down at the slave, my arms folded.

Then she again, quickly, put her head down.

She then turned again, on her knees, to face Aemilianus. "I am a slave !" she cried, prostrating herself before him, her chained wrists under her thighs. "Forgive me, Master! Have mercy on me, Master!"

She had seen me on the ship, standing there, a free man, among peers. She had had some concept, doubtless, of what I had done on the wall, if nowhere else. I did not think she was under any delusion as to who would be believed in any conflict of testimonies. Too, of course, Lady Claudia, still a free person, who could render free testimony, not even extracted under torture, for example, had been present. Too, the young crossbowman, though she would not know his identity, as she had been hooded, had been there later, when she had, by the code of whimpers, acknowledged herself a slave, and before him, and me, had performed an enticing, placatory slave behavior. She was surely under no delusion, now, as to whether Aemilianus and the others knew the truth. They had merely been playing with a slave.

"It is a serious matter," said Aemilianus to her, "when a she-tarsk claims not to be a she-tarsk."

"I did not claim explicitly to be a free woman, Master!" she wept.

There was laughter from those about. Even Aemilianus smiled. Her entire behavior had been calculated to deceive those about as to her status.

"Please forgive a slave, Master!" she wept. She lifted herself a little, timidly.

There was laughter.

I had not wanted her to assert, explicitly, in response to the question of Aemilianus, concerning her status, that she was a free woman. Although she did not realize it at the time, she was already then in deep enough difficulties. In making clear to her the futility of such a lie, sure to be devastating in its consequences, and, indeed, the futility of attempting to prolong her entire absurd charade, I had saved her subjection to hideous tortures, and perhaps her life. It is a very serious "cause for punishment" on the part of a slave to conceal or deny her status. Normally, of course, there is very little danger of this sort of thing occurring, as she is usually collared and branded, and, usually, is clad in a distinctive manner.

"Kneel," said Aemilianus.

The girl struggled up, in her chains, and then knelt before him. She crossed her chained hands over her breasts, covering herself. This was interesting, this sudden, poignant touch of frightened modesty, now that she was aware of her slave vulnerability.

Aemilianus' eyes were upon her. She lowered her hands. He continued to regard her. She then knelt back on her heels. Still his gaze did not leave her. She then, blushing, opened her knees.

"How did you become a slave?" he asked. He knew, of course.

"I confessed my natural slavery," she said, "and then spoke words of self-enslavement."

"At which point," said Aemilianus, "you ceased to be a person, and became a property."

"Yes, Master," she whispered.

"An animal."

"Yes, Master," she said.

"Do you think it is acceptable for properties, for animals, to pretend to the status of persons?"

"No, Master!" she said.

"But yet you did so."

"Forgive me, Master!" she begged.

"I have a mind to turn you over to free women," he said.

"Please, no, Master!" she wept, terrified.

"What do you think should be your disposition?" he asked.

She looked up, startled. It seemed she thought wildly, excitedly, for a moment. But then she put down her head, humbly, fearfully. "Whatever master pleases," she said.

"It is a suitable answer," said Aemilianus. I drew a deep breath. That, I feared, had been a close one.

"You are in slave chains," observed Aemilianus.

"It is fitting for me, Master," she said. "I am a slave."

"What is your name?" he asked.

"I have no name," she said. "I have not yet been named."

"You were eager to serve Cosians," he said.

"Or any man, Master," she whispered.

"You were not pleasing," he said.

"Forgive me, Master!" she said.

"Put her to one side," said Aemilianus, "and bring forth the other female."

Two men took the former Lady Publia, now an unnamed female slave, by the arms and pulled her to one side, where they put her on her belly on the deck, her chained wrists under her.

In another moment another figure, also in sirik, was produced. The sturdy collar of the sirik, from which the central vertical chain depended, could not be seen on her in front, or at the sides, because of her veil. One could see it, of course, at the back of her neck, below the white, scarflike turban. Too, of course, one could see, in front, the dependent chain, the wrist rings and ankle rings, and such. I saw the figure's eyes, frightened, meet mine as she was drawn forth, with small, hurried steps. She was put on her knees before Aemilianus. She looked to one side and saw the former Lady Publia, naked, in sirik, terrified, lying on her belly, on the deck.

"Consider," said Aemilianus, "the exciting costume in which the prisoner appears before us, the baring of so much of the arms, the baring of the calves, the ankles, the feet, the cling of it, indicating it conceals no undergarments but only female, how closely it resembles in many ways that of some simple, humble, impoverished, low-caste maid, and yet how cleverly it is contrived to display its occupant, and in a fashion calculated to stimulate the capture appetites of vigorous men, men accustomed to look upon females as slaves and loot, as prizes and pleasures."

There was assent to this. I am sure that more than one man there wished to tear those taunting rags from the beauty they bedecked.

The former Lady Publia, lying at the side, groaned. A fellow kicked her. She was then silent.

"Are these ingenious rags yours?" asked Aemilianus of the figure kneeling before him.

"No," she said.

"They belonged once, did they not, to a woman called Lady Publia, of Ar's Station?"

"Yes," she said.

"Why are you wearing them?" asked Aemilianus.

"I wore them that I not be recognized," she said.

"You would fear then," he asked, "to be recognized?"

"Yes," she said.

"You had wished to be taken, perhaps, for the former Lady Publia, of Ar's Station?"

"Yes," she said.

"Let us see who this woman is," said Aemilianus, "who has disguised herself as the former Lady Publia, and who for some reason, it seems, fears to be recognized." He made a small sign. A man then, carefully, not hurrying, removed the veil and turban.

The free woman knelt very straight. She held her head up, her neck in the closely fitting, now-visible collar, not trying to hide anything.

"Is she recognized?" asked Aemilianus.

"She is," said more than one man, grimly.

"I think I understand, now," said Aemilianus, "why you feared to be recognized."

Lady Claudia was silent.

"You are the traitress, Lady Claudia," he said.

"Yes," she said.

"You attempted to escape," he said.

"Yes," she said.

"But you have not escaped, have you?" he asked.

"No," she said. "I have not escaped." In a way, I thought that this was ironic. On the piers, had Cosians swarmed over them, doing slaughter, and, where it pleased them, making slaves, her beauty, which was considerable, bared and submitted, might have found favor with conquerors. She might even have been thrown chained to an officer, thenceforth to be his and serve him with perfection, at least until, say, he might tire of her, and, say, give or sell her to another. She might even have served in her way as a souvenir to one fellow or another of the action at Ar's Station. More mercy might she then have found in the wielder of a bloody sword on the piers than in the abstractions of the justice of her own city. The man with the sword is at least swayable; he is at least human and real.

"You have been found guilty of treason against your city, and are under sentence of impalement," said Aemilianus. "Do you gainsay either of these assertions?"

"No," she said.

Aemilianus turned to Marsias, who lay nearby, wounded, reclining on one elbow, on a pallet. "Marsias," said he, "have you the strength to carry out the sentence?"

The man nodded.

"Do you, Lady Claudia," asked Aemilianus, "regret your treason?"

"Keenly," she said.

"For you were apprehended," he said.

"Yes," she said. "But it goes much beyond such simplicities."

"Speak," he said.

"I have learned," she said, "in the cell, and in the arms of a man, what I am, truly. I forsook the softness and the reality of my being for ambition and cruelty. I had not understood earlier what it was to be a woman, or the joys, and meaning, of service and love. I sought power when I, rightfully, should have been subject to it, reveling in helplessness, submission and love. I did great wrong in seeking, one such as I, to interfere in the destiny of states, which is not my province. I have brought pain to myself and others. I am pleased only that my acts, as far as I know, had no consequences seriously deleterious to my city or her citizens."

"You accept the justice of your impalement?" he asked.

"Yes," she said, "as I am a free woman. But I think it would be more appropriate if I were fed to sleen."

"Such things are for slaves," he said.

"Yes, Commander," she said.

"Look over there," he said, indicating the former Lady Publia, chained and prone. "That is a slave," he said.

"Yes," said Lady Claudia.

"Are you like her?" he asked, scornfully.

"Yes," she said.

The former Lady Publia, so helpless, looked at her, gratefully, with tears in her eyes.

"No, you are not," said Aemilianus, "for you are free."

"But I envy her," said Lady Claudia. "She is at least free to be what she is, and wholly, but I am not."

The slave, frightened, moved a little in her chains. The links made a tiny sound on the deck, near her ankles. Looking about, I saw that more than one man would have been interested in having her.

"Has a suitable spear been prepared?" asked Aemilianus.

"I have seen to it," said Marsias.

"Let her garments be removed," said Aemilianus.

It took but a moment to pull the rags back, and down, from her body. It would take another moment or so to remove them completely, for them to be cut or torn from her, as they were now held on her by the chaining of the sirik, that of her wrists. Men's eyes glistened. I heard soft whistles, the intakings of breath, small, almost inadvertent gasps, and other tributes, somewhat more vulgar, things such as small clicks and the smackings of lips, to her beauty, noises which would generally be expected to greet the revelation of the beauty of a slave, rather than a free woman. She blushed, and yet was proud, I am sure, of her beauty. She did have superb slave curves. I did not doubt but what she would bring a good price in a slave market. Her entire body gloriously made clear a luscious hormonal richness and an exquisite femininity. She was a beautiful woman. The rags then had been cut from her and thrown to the side. She knelt then before us, beautifully. Many men, including myself, struck our left shoulders in applause.

There was little doubt that Aemilianus himself was impressed with her.

I think that any man might have been impressed with her, whether he found her as a free prisoner on the deck of the *Tais* or in some slave market, chained on a bench, awaiting a buyer.

"You could have been a bred slave," he said.

"In a sense I am a bred slave," she said, "for I am a woman."

"The spear is ready," said a man.

"Let her chains be removed," said Aemilianus, "and her hands tied behind her. Use a belly thong."

With the belly thong, presumably her hands would be tied closely, tightly, at the small of her back. This is an excellent, general tie. It is seldom, however, if ever, used in impalements. Apparently Aemilianus had called for the tie, in this context, as an act of mercy. He did not want her to be able to get her fingers on the spear which, in their futility and helplessness, might delay, or deepen or prolong the agony of impalement.

"May I speak?" I inquired.

One fellow, with a thong, and the key to the Lady Claudia's locks had already stepped forward. When I spoke, he halted, and stepped back. I assumed he would remove the Lady Claudia's wrist rings first, then affix the belly thong on her, fastening her hands behind her back, tightly, and then, and then only, remove the ankle rings and the collar, the remainder of the sirik. Such, at any rate, would have been a common Gorean manner of proceeding.

"Of course," said Aemilianus.

"In the cell, yesterday morning," I said, it seemed a long time ago now, "I gathered that my fate was not to be inextricably linked to that of Lady Claudia, that you had perhaps not convinced yourself, and quite properly, of my guilt in the matter of espionage."

"True," said Aemilianus. "I was not sure of you, what you were, or why you did what you did. There are still many things I do not understand, for example, about the military actions, and inactions, of the past months."

"Much would become clear," I said, "if you were willing to entertain the possibility of treason in Ar, treason in high places, treason of profound character and enormous scope."

"Only days ago," said Aemilianus, "that would have seemed unthinkable."

"But it is not so unthinkable now?" I asked.

"No," said Aemilianus.

"Clearly Ar's Station was abandoned, and presumably therewith the Vosk, and its basin, surrendered to Cos."

"My general sympathies," said Calliodorus, "as will be understood, are with Cos in these matters. Certainly I have no love for Ar. But if Cos thinks to hold sway upon the river I think, then, she has not reckoned with Port Cos, nor with the river towns themselves. We on the river will welcome neither the septered emissaries of Lurius of Jad nor Marlenus of Ar. Too, in the Vosk League, to which Port Cos is party, we have the nucleus of a vehicle for our alliance, a vehicle for common action if not common governance."

"Ar looks not with favor upon the Vosk League," said Aemilianus. "She sees in it the possibility of another Salerian Confederation."

"She did not permit Ar's Station to join the league," said Calliodorus.

"It was thought by many in Ar, seemingly Marlenus among them," said Aemilianus, "that entry into the league would appear to accept the principle that Ar was but one power among others on the river, and not the sole mistress of the waterway, as she would be. Cos may have acted more judiciously in the matter, thinking that Port Cos might dominate the league, and that she, in turn, might exercise her own control over it, through the might of Port Cos."

"If such were her intent, and I do not doubt it," said Calliodorus, "she misjudged the interests, the pride and temper of Port Cos. Though we have close ties, historical, cultural and political, with Cos, we are, unlike Ar's Station, a sovereign polity in our own right. We are in all ways institutionally and legally autonomous."

"Yes?" said Aemilianus, returning his attention to me.

"It had not pleased me," I said, "that this woman," and here I indicated the Lady Claudia by placing my foot against her, and thrusting her forward, so that she fell to all fours in her chains on the deck, "was to be impaled."

"It was the justice of Ar's Station," said Aemilianus.

"Look upon her," I said. "Does not impalement in this case seem a waste of slut?"

Lady Claudia, a free woman, gasped, so spoken of. Yet, too, she shuddered with pleasure in her chains, realizing that she had been found worthy by a man to have so familiar, vulgar and exciting an expression, and doubtlessly appropriately, applied to her.

"The question," said Aemilianus, "is not so much the suitability of the female for 'helpless-slut' status as one of justice."

"I determined then in the cell," I said, "to take action, not merely, of course, for her sake, but for mine as well, as I could not know for certain what you would eventually decide in my case, nor could I count on being released from a burning citadel by Cosians. After all, they might not take more interest in their enemies' criminals, and such, than in their enemies themselves. Also, Lady Claudia was to be well fed that morning, and so this put sustenance in my way, of which I took advantage. Indeed, I perhaps ate better than any in Ar's Station that morning."

"Your action on behalf of Lady Claudia," he said, "was very nearly successful. Had it not been for the timely arrival of our friend Calliodorus, and certain mysterious others, she might now be in the chains of Cosians rather than in those of Ar's Station. But, as it turned out, Calliodorus, and others, did arrive, and she did not escape. We are prepared to overlook your attempt to abet her escape, serious though this is, in view of your action on the wall, and elsewhere."

"My position on the matter, however," I said, "has not changed."

Lady Claudia rose to her knees, and turned, to face me, wildly. The former Lady Publia, the nameless, chained slave lying on her belly, on the deck, turned her head to look at me. Aemilianus' slave, Shirley, too, regarded me, her eyes wide, frightened. Men stepped back a little, uneasily. More than one loosened the blade in his sheath.

"Do you approve of treason?" asked Aemilianus.

"Not generally," I said.

"Perhaps you approve of it, however," he asked, "in this specific case, in the case of the Lady Claudia?"

"Not at all," I said.

"Surely a polity, even if it be one of pirates, if it is to survive, if it is to protect itself, must establish some forms of justice and law within its own precincts?"

"One would suppose so," I said.

"Even if it is of the rack and spear."

"I would suppose so," I said.

"By what title then would you presume to interfere, by that of the sword?"

"Please, noble sir," wept the Lady Claudia. "Risk nothing for me, a traitress! You have too much imperiled yourself already on my behalf, so unworthy an object!"

"Were you given permission to speak?" I asked her.

She was silent, startled. She was, after all, a free woman.

"I have no intention of imperiling myself on your behalf," I informed her.

She did not speak, confused.

"She looks well in slave chains, does she not?" I asked Aemilianus.

"Yes," he said. She was a dream in such chains, and their meaning. It lacked only that she should wear them truly, as a slave.

"The men of Ar's Station," I said, "I would suppose, have no particular interest, personally, in impaling this female."

Several of the men laughed.

"On the high spear of public, legal impalement, of course," I added.

There was more laughter.

The Lady Claudia shuddered, understanding what it might be to be at the mercy of men.

I turned to Aemilianus. "What do those of Ar's Station value most highly," I asked, "their justice—or their honor?"

Several of the men cried out, angrily. Lest some not understand their fury, let it be said, simply, that they were Goreans. Several hands grasped the hilts of swords.

"Their honor," said Aemilianus, quietly.

"I am not of Ar's Station," I said, "and I have little love for her. Indeed, I do not see why I should, as I was not well treated within her walls. But yet I have served her, and perhaps well. Is that not so?"

"It is so," said Aemilianus. "Indeed, had you not held the wall as long as you did, and the gate, and had you not aided in the evacuation of the landing, and had you not, with others, held the walkway until it could be destroyed behind you, I think there would be few of us here now who would be alive today."

"Then perhaps you will not think the less of me if I ask a boon," I said.

"You will not assure us it was nothing?" smiled Aemilianus.

"Was it nothing?" I asked.

"No," he smiled. "It was not nothing."

"I ask a boon then," I said.

"I am surprised that you would do so," he said.

"Think of me then as a mercenary," I said, "and I am speaking of my pay."

"We did not contract for your services," he said.

"I know," I said. "This is a matter of honor."

"Speak," he said.

"I ask the commutation of the sentence of impalement in the case of the Lady Claudia of Ar's Station."

"You do not ask for her freedom?" he asked.

"Or course not," I said. "She is guilty."

"You have no objection then," he said, "in view of her guilt, if a terrible and grievous penalty is inflicted upon her?"

"Of course not," I said.

"Even a fate 'worse than death'?" he smiled.

"Who speaks of it so?" I asked.

"Do not some free women speak of it so?" he asked.

"And are not those the very women who first bare their breasts to conquerors and beg the privilege of licking their feet?"

"Perhaps, upon occasion," said Aemilianus.

"If it were truly a fate worse than death," I said, "or even so unfortunate a lot, it seems it would be very hard to understand their happiness, their emotional fulfillments, their ecstasies, their willingness to die for their masters."

"Perhaps then," he said, "for all its demands and duties, it is not truly a fate worse than death."

"Perhaps not," I said, "else, after a time, they would not love it so."

"Perhaps those who would foolishly call it so do so only in their attempts to dissuade themselves from their desperate fascination with it, and longing for it."

"Perhaps," I said.

"At any rate," he smiled, "let them not make pronouncements on such matters until they have had some experience of that of which they speak, until they have had for a time, so to speak, the collar on their own necks.''

"Yet," I said, "slavery is a most serious matter."

"It is," he granted.

Gorean slavery is categorical and absolute. The slave is a property, an animal. She is incapable of doing anything to alter, change or affect her status. She is owned by the master, and owes him all. She can be bought and sold. She must serve with perfection.

Aemilianus looked at the Lady Claudia, "Do you understand the nature of our discourse, of that of which we speak?"

"Yes," she said.

"Good," he said.

She looked at him.

"Claudia, Lady of Ar's Station, free woman," he said, sternly.

She, kneeling before him, regarded him.

"Put your head to the deck," he said.

Men gasped, to see a free woman perform this act. More than one, I am sure, wanted to seize her.

"Lift your head," said Aemilianus.

She did so.

"You have been found guilty of treason," he said, "and sentenced to impalement. By the power that was vested in me I did this. By the same power, I now rescind the sentence of impalement."

"Commander!" she cried, tears in her eyes.

"Do you expect to escape punishment?" he asked.

She put down her head, shuddering.

"Do you know the sort of chains you wear?" he asked.

"Slave chains," she said.

"They look well on you," he said.

She did not speak.

Then, suddenly, in a moment, as of panic, seemingly unable to help herself, she tried the chains, those on her wrists, trying to slip them from her wrists, then jerking them, but they held her well.

"You understand clearly, do you not," he asked, "what I now propose to do?"

"Yes," she said, frightened.

"It is my intention," he said, "to sentence you to slavery. Do you understand this, and what it means?"

"I think so," she said, "—as far as any free woman can."

"Do you have anything to say before I pass such sentence upon you?"

"No," she said.

"I sentence you to slavery," he said, uttering the sentence. She trembled, sentenced.

"It only remains now," said Aemilianus, "for the sentence to be carried out. If you wish I, in the office of magistrate, shall carry it out. On the other hand, if you wish, you may yourself carry out the sentence."

"I?" she said.

"Yes," he said.

"You would have me proclaim myself slave?" she asked.

"Or I shall do it," he said. "In the end, it does not matter."

"In my heart," she said, "I am, and have been for years, a slave. It is fitting then, I suppose, that it should be I who say the words."

Aemilianus regarded her.

"I am a slave," she said.

Men cried out with pleasure and smote their left shoulders in Gorean applause, gazing on the new slave, looking about herself, frightened, kneeling chained before Aemilianus.

"Bring the other slave here, too," said Aemilianus, gesturing to the former Lady Publia.

In a moment the two slaves, naked, and in their siriks, were before him. Men adjusted the positions of the slaves, rudely, so that they knelt well, back on their heels, their backs straight, their knees spread.

"Calliodorus, my friend," said Aemilianus, "behold two slaves."

"I behold them," said Calliodorus.

"Do you find them pleasing?" asked Aemilianus.

"Yes," said Calliodorus. "Both were obviously born for the collar."

"This one," said Aemilianus, indicating the former Lady Publia, "at least for the time, we will call Publia."

"Who are you?" asked Calliodorus of the former Lady Publia.

"Publia!" she said.

"And this one," continued Aemilianus, indicating the former Lady Claudia, "at least for the time, we will call Claudia."

"Your name?" asked Calliodorus of the former Lady Claudia.

" 'Claudia'!" she said, quickly.

"It is my request, if it is not too much trouble," said Aemilianus to Calliodorus, "that both of these slaves be taken to Port Cos, and there properly branded and collared."

I smiled. It did not seem likely that in the future there would be any doubts about Publia's status, nor, indeed, that of Claudia either. I thought they would both look quite lovely in the garments of slaves, if they were permitted clothing.

"And then," said Aemilianus, "if you would, as one of these females was prepared to surrender herself to Cosians, and the other served Cosians, in betraying her city, see that they come into the keeping of Cosians."

"That will be easy to arrange," said Calliodorus. "There are many Cosians, envoys and such, in Port Cos."

The girls exchanged glances. Their fates were being decided by men, but I did not think unjustly.

"Do you have on board facilities for slaves?" inquired Aemilianus.

"Below decks," said Calliodorus, "we have some slave cages."

"Excellent," said Aemilianus. Then he addressed the slaves. "You may perform obeisance before masters," he said.

Both the girls then bent forward and, putting the palms of their hands on the deck, lowered their heads to the boards.

Aemilianus then nodded to Calliodorus. It was a small gesture. It indicated that he, at least at that time, had no further interest in the two women.

"Take them below decks," said Calliodorus to one of his men. "Cage them."

The fellow, standing behind and rather between the two girls took them each by an arm, Claudia by her right arm, and Publia by her left, and pulled them to their feet. Then, turning them and thrusting them forward, without relinquishing his hold on their arms, he conducted them ahead of him, toward a hatch.

"The cages," apologized Calliodorus, "are individual cages, and rather tiny. They are, in effect, punishment cages."

"No matter," said Aemilianus.

"But, of course," said Calliodorus, "it is probably best for them to begin to learn quickly that they are slaves."

"Certainly," said Aemilianus.

"Doubtless in the morning they will be willing and eager to leave the cages, under any conditions," said Calliodorus.

"Excellent," smiled Aemilianus.

"I would recommend, however," said Calliodorus, "that the one called Publia be taken from the cage for a time this evening, to be given a good hiding at the mast."

"Of course," said Aemilianus.

It was only fitting, after all, that she be punished, and well. She had attempted to take advantage of the fact that she had not yet been branded and collared. She had attempted to pass herself off as a free woman. In many cities, such a thing is a capital offense. Here, however, in accord with a fortune much greater than she would be likely to realize for a few days, she, a naive young slave, and guilty of what, in effect, was a first offense, was only to be whipped. Still, even so, I did not think she would be likely to forget her little bout this evening with the leather. For one thing, few slave girls forget their first whipping. Too, if nothing else it would impress upon her that she was a slave and that masters would think nothing of punishing her if she was not pleasing. That is a good thing for a girl to learn. I supposed, too, that it might have an effect in discouraging her, should the opportunity arise, as I did not think it would, from seeking to implement another deceit with respect to her status in the immediate future. Later, of course, as she began to understand what it was to be a slave girl, as she began to grasp something of the nature of her condition, and its categoricality, she would hastily, and fearfully, on her own, reject such thoughts. She would not dare to countenance them. She might find herself trembling in terror if even the smallest and most casual of such thoughts chanced to enter her mind.

I saw the fellow who had conducted the slaves to the hold emerge through the hatch and close it, after him. I supposed the slaves were in their cages. Calliodorus, too, seemed to note the reappearance of the fellow.

"The former Lady Claudia and I were cellmates," I said to Calliodorus. "I determined at that time that she, though then free, would make an excellent slave."

"Good," he said. Slaves, of course, are not only trained in a broad spectrum of sexual arts, such as how to kiss and caress, and such, but much attention is given, too, to their own responsiveness and pleasure. There is nothing surprising about this. Their reponsiveness and pleasure puts them far more under the master's power. Too, as might be imagined, it is very pleasant for a man to see the marvelous changes and effects which he can induce in a woman, for example, to have her thrashing helplessly at his touch, crying out her submission, begging for more. The slave, because of her training, her emotional freedom, thousands of times greater than that of a free woman, the discipline she is under, and such, can attain orgasm much more quickly than a free woman, sometimes, particularly if she has been deprived for a time, almost immediately. A response which might take a free woman a third to a half of an Ahn to attain a slave, and not an unusual slave, might attain in three or four Ehn. Beyond this the slave is often forced to endure lengthy, multiple orgasms, sometimes being carried by the will of the master for Ahn, whether she wills it or not, from one peak to another.

"She served Cosians, and declared for them," I said to Calliodorus. "Do you think that might put her in good stead with Cosians, should she come into their keeping, as that is what seems to be in store for her, at least in the near future?"

"In what way?" asked Calliodorus.

"That they might then see fit to reward her with her freedom," I said.

"No," said Calliodorus. "She is now a slave. That changes everything. Even if she had once been a Cosian girl, even of Telnus, of good family and high caste, she would still, now, be a slave, and only a slave. Too, Cosians, I assure you, are not overly fond of traitresses. One who is willing to betray her own Home Stone would presumably not hesitate to betray someone else's. Indeed, I would not have been surprised, had she surrendered herself at Ar's Station, claiming immunity, or such, that she would have quickly found herself, if, indeed, she were not slain, in the lowest of slaveries, as would seem fitting for her.''

"I see," I said. It was, of course, as I had supposed it would be.

"Her slavery, thus," he said, "will presumably be either simple, and uncompromised, or excessively cruel, and uncompromised.''

I nodded.

"But inasmuch as the crimes of the free woman are seldom held against the slave, for the slave has her own concerns, and fears, such as whether or not she is sufficiently pleasing, and so on, I would expect it to be simple, and uncompromised.''

"I think you are probably right," I said. Many theorists regard reduction to slavery as wiping the slate clean, so to speak. The woman is then thought, in effect, to be beginning life anew, but now as a mere property, a mere animal. To be sure, her past status and deeds do remain a part of her history, even if she is now only an animal. Thus, at least for a time, a master might relish the consideration that his abject slave was once perhaps a haughty free woman, or such. But, in time, it is likely that their relationship, mercifully, as such things fade into the past and tend to be forgotten, will become a simpler one, that merely of master and slave.

"In my uses of the former Lady Claudia, in the cell," I said, "I sometimes gave her the use name of 'Chloe'.''

"A Cosian name," observed Calliodorus.

"She had declared for Cos," I reminded him.

"Did the use name help her to dissociate herself from the proprieties which she might have thought appropriate to a Lady Claudia?'' he asked.

"I think it helped," I said. Certainly a woman's sexual relationship to a man is often improved when she begins to think of herself as having a quite different relationship to him than the one in which she has been accustomed to think of herself. The change of name can help in this matter. No woman, of course, takes her former name into slavery. In her reduction to bondage she loses that name. Even if the same name, in one sense, should be put on her as a slave, it is not the same name in the crucial sense; it is not now a legal name to which one has title in one's own right. It is a slave name.

In this sense, the name 'Claudia' as the name of a free woman is a quite different name from the name 'Claudia' as the name of a slave. The slave name, for example, can be changed at a master's whim. This loss of the old name, incidentally, and the susceptibility to being named, and the new name, if the master decides to give her a name, and such, although they are simple, legal consequences of the nature of reduction to bondage, are also, I think, psychologically useful in helping her understand that she is now a slave, and that she is now radically and absolutely different from what she was. Too, I think that such things, a new name, for example, showing her that she is now in a new reality, and so on, can help her make the transition more smoothly into bondage.

" 'Chloe' is an excellent name," he said. "I have known several slaves with that name."

"Do you think," asked Aemilianus of Calliodorus, "that 'Claudia' is too fine a name for a slave?"

"I think it is an excellent name for a slave," he smiled.

"You would," smiled Aemilianus. I supposed that Aemilianus might think that Cosian names might be better for slaves, whereas Calliodorus might tend to approve more of names more typical of the south, say, those of Venna or Ar. I myself thought there was much to be said for both, and, indeed, for many other sorts of names, as well. Many Goreans, incidentally, as is well known, regard Earth-girl names as slave names. Aemilianus's slave, for example, who was Gorean, was named "Shirley."

"I think there is little difficulty in the matter, in any event," said Calliodorus, "whether it is a fine name or not, as she now wears it as a slave name."

"I think you are right," said Aemilianus. "What do you think?" he asked me.

"I agree," I said. "It is now a mere slave name." Too, of course, it might easily be changed. In the odysseys of her bondage, her name would doubtless be changed many times.

"I wonder what will become of her," I said.

"She is curvaceous," said Calliodorus. "Perhaps she will be sold to a paga tavern."

That was a possibility. I hoped that eventually, however, she might come into the keeping of a single master, to whom she would be a love slave. I thought that there was something in the slave now called "Claudia" a precious, vulnerable, yearning love slave.

"Aemilianus, my friend," said Calliodorus.

"Yes?" said he.

"It will take us some days to reach Port Cos," said Calliodorus. "Would you mind if, tomorrow morning, the two slaves, Claudia and Publia, were made available to the crew?"

"Of course not," said Aemilianus.

"We will chain them by their necks to a ring in the deck, aft," said Calliodorus. "That way, if they are too initially dismayed, they will not be able to throw themselves overboard."

"By nightfall," said Aemilianus, "I do not think they would want to throw themselves overboard."

"I do not think so," agreed Calliodorus. "Too, aft, they will be out of the sight of free women."

"Use them as you please," said Aemilianus.

"My lads left Port Cos in a hurry," said Calliodorus, "and we did not know if there would be fighting, or not. Thus we did not include among our supplies any women for slave use."

"No explanations are necessary," said Aemilianus. "Too, if their masters do not object, you may avail yourself of any of the other slaves, there are a few, I believe, whom you embarked at Ar's Station, including, of course, my Shirley."

Shirley shrank back, a little. To be sure, even though she was the preferred slave of Aemilianus, her use could be handed about as easily as that of the lowest collar sluts on board, Claudia and Publia.

"I thank you for your generosity," said Calliodorus, "and I am sure that the other fellows of Ar's Station would be every bit as generous, but I think that after what you have been through, we would prefer, in all gentleness and courtesy, to let such slaves, including your Shirley, recollect in detail the pleasing of their own masters, perhaps amidships."

Shirley cried out with joy, looking upon Aemilianus.

"As you will," he smiled.

"And I think," said Calliodorus, "that the more extensive services then to be rendered by Claudia and Publia will be useful in helping them to comprehend more quickly and clearly the nature of their new condition."

"Undoubtedly," smiled Aemilianus.

"I wonder if I might ask an additional favor of you," said Calliodorus.

"Name it," said Aemilianus.

"When we enter Port Cos," he said, "I would like to do so in such a way as to make clear from afar that there is cause for rejoicing, that our business has been successfully conducted and that festivities are in order."

"Do as you wish," said Aemilianus.

"I will, then," he said, "with your permission, deck the ship with flags, and bunting and banners, and put prominently the flag of Ar's Station on the port stem line, and fly that of Port Cos on the starboard stem line."

"How is it," asked Aemilianus, "that you have a flag of Ar's Station on a ship of Port Cos?"

"One can never tell when such things might be useful," smiled Calliodorus. "And do you noble fellows of Ar's Station not carry flags of Port Cos, and perhaps of other towns, as well, in your vessels, perhaps in the chests in your stern castles?" That was a likely place to stow such paraphernalia. There it would both be out of the way, and yet handy.

"Perhaps," smiled Aemilianus.

"Dear friend," smiled Calliodorus.

"Dear friend," said Aemilianus.

Calliodorus bent down and clasped the upraised hand of Aemilianus. I had gathered that, long ago, these men had seen action together, probably on the river.

Calliodorus stood up.

There was, incidentally, one flag of Ar's Station on board which had been brought from Ar's Station itself, but that flag, large, rent, faded and tattered, was not the one, or ones, under discussion. That was the flag which had flown at the upper battlements. It had been there, staunch and defiant, throughout the siege. It had been brought to the *Tais* by the young man to whom I had entrusted it, the friend of the young crossbowman. He had given it to Aemilianus, who had, in turn, given it into the keeping of Surilius, his aide. I had little doubt that that flag was very precious to those of

Ar's Station. They would be very careful as to what lines on which it might be affixed.

"But, dear friend," said Aemilianus, "is there not one touch else that might be in order, to indicate a successful voyage?"

"I was thinking of asking about it," smiled Calliodorus.

"Hang them in chains, at the prow!" said Aemilianus.

"Good," grinned Calliodorus.

The slave girl, as Claudia and Publia would come to learn, has thousands of uses. And one of them, surely, is that of a display object. It is common for masters to be very proud of their girls and to desire to show them off. Indeed, one of the reasons for slave garb, aside from such things as its identificatory role, its stimulatory nature, both to the master and slave, its instructive role, and such, is its capacity to display the girl beautifully. Just as a man of Earth might be proud of his pictures, or his dogs or horses, so, too, a Gorean can be proud of his slave, or slaves. Some men like to travel with a naked slave afoot beside them, chained by the neck to their stirrup. Some rich men enjoy having lovely slaves, sometimes strings of them, follow them, chained by the neck, the leads of the chains fastened to slave bars at the back of their palanquins. In this case, Calliodorus was apparently interested in displaying two beauties, a pair of exquisite slaves, at his prow. Certainly they, suspended naked in their chains, would enhance his entry into the harbor at Port Cos.

"I must be about my duties, my friend," then said Calliodorus to Aemilianus. "Rest."

Most of the men about had, by now, drifted away.

Calliodorus stopped for a moment, as though he wanted to say something more to Amelianus, but he then seemed to think the better of it. He then climbed the steps behind Aemilianus, to the helm deck. I looked after him.

"He wanted to issue warnings," said Aemilianus, smiling.

"Warnings?" I asked.

"Yes," said Aemilianus. "He is a good fellow."

I gathered that it would be inopportune to inquire further into this matter, at least at the moment. But surely there could be little, or nothing, to fear now, at least for free persons.

"Commander," said I.

"Yes, Warrior," he responded.

"I thank you for your mercy in the case of the former Lady Claudia."

"Was it mercy?" he asked.

"I think so," I said.

"Well," he said, "her treacheries, however heinous and grievous, considered in the light of grander and more insidious designs, seemed paltry."

"And doubtless were," I said. "Is that why you spared her?"

"I spared her primarily," he said, "because you wished it."

"I am grateful," I said. "Too, I think she will make an excellent slave."

"I am sure of it," he said.

"Even Calliodorus thought she was born for the collar," I said.

"She and Publia," said Aemilianus.

"Yes," I said.

"I think he was right about both," he said.

"I think so, too," I said.

"My friend," he said.

"Yes," I said, startled.

"You said to her," he reminded me, "that you had no intention of imperiling your life for her."

"Yes," I said.

"Yet I think, had I not spared her," said he, "that you would have drawn your sword on her behalf."

"I said what I did," I said, "because I knew it would not be necessary to imperil my life for her."

"How could you know that?" he asked.

"Because Aemilianus, and those like him," I said, "are honorable men."

"You were counting on that?" he asked.

"Yes," I said.

"And had we not, in your opinion, behaved honorably?" he asked.

"Then I would have drawn my sword," I said.

"I thought so," he said.

"I am sorry," I said.

"Even were I other than I am," he smiled, "I do not think I would have wanted you to draw your sword against us."

I did not respond.

"Particularly over a woman," he said. He held out his hand to Shirley, and she came quickly to kneel beside him and took his hand, and lifted it to her lips, kissing it, softly.

"Of course," I said.

"And in particular," said Aemilianus, "one who was soon to become a mere slave."

"Of course," I said.

Shirley, holding and pressing her lips to the hand of Aemilianus, looked up at me.

I smiled. Swords are often drawn on Gor over women, and particularly over lovely slaves. Women are prizes, perfections and treasures. It is no wonder that men fight over them with ferocity.

Wars have been fought to recover a stolen slave.

I then, quietly, withdrew from the presence of Aemilianus, permitting Shirley to attend him.

I went forward. In doing so I passed some slaves and masters, amidships. How beautiful were the slaves in their collars and brief tunics. I then proceeded farther forward, taking my way beside free women, and some children, and climbed to the tiny bow deck, forward of the stem castle, immediately behind the prow. I stood there, and looked down the river. I could see the advance ships some quarter of a pasang, or so, ahead. I wondered what the warnings of Calliodorus, if Aemilianus had read him aright, might have been about.

# 22
# PUBLIA; SLAVE

Publia lay before me, on her stomach, over a pile of rope, aft on the *Tais*. Her head was down. Her neck was chained to a ring in the deck.

"You?" she said.

"Yes," I said.

"Please be kind to a woman who is now only a slave," she said.

I laughed, softly.

She shuddered.

She was pretty, lying on her belly, over the ropes, her head down.

But yet, I thought, as she is a slave, surely she should be permitted to beg for kindness.

"Do not hurt me," she begged.

"That is muchly up to you," I said.

"To me?" she asked.

"Yes," I said. "I do not have any intention, at least at present, of hurting you. On the other hand, if you prove to be in the least disagreeable, do not fear. I will not hesitate to inflict discipline, and severe discipline, upon you."

"I understand," she said.

"You were once Lady Publia, of Ar's Station," I said.

"Yes," she said, frightened.

"Who are you now?" I asked.

"Publia," she said, "a slave."

"Lift yourself, Publia, slave," I said.

She cried out, softly, perhaps not anticipating the sternness of my grip upon her.

"Master," she said.

She clutched ropes in the coils on which she lay. "Ohhh," she said, suddenly. Then she began to gasp, and make helpless noises.

The moons were full. The slave was pretty. It was late. We were two days yet from Port Cos.

I then crouched beside her, and turned her, and lifted her. I held her knees up, close to her belly. Her body was a small, curvaceous delight. I then put her on her back, on the coils of rope. I bent over her and then, with one hand, behind the back of her neck, gripping it, lifted her head, bringing her face beneath mine, forcing it there. I then kissed her, and let her lie back on the ropes. Her eyes were wide, and soft, and frightened.

"You were a pretty warder," I said.

"I am a slave," she whispered, "only a slave."

"Perhaps you desire to be pleasing?" I asked.

"Yes," she said, fervently. "I desire to be pleasing!" She then reached out for me and put her hands behind the back of my neck. She then lifted her lips timidly to mine, fearing, it seemed, that her overture might be refused, that they might be rejected. "I do desire to be pleasing, Master," she whispered. I permitted her to kiss me.

Later we lay together, side by side.

It was near morning now. I had waited until the crew had finished with her, until late, before I had approached her. In this way I could have more time with her. I supposed that in an Ahn or so a fellow would come by, to release her from the chain, to return her to the hold. They were no longer kept in the tiny cages. They were free in the hold, though the hatch was locked. Claudia had been put at the ring earlier and returned to the hold earlier. Publia had been put at the ring later, and would be returned to the hold later. For a time during the evening, both had been at the ring. Tomorrow night, as it was on alternate nights, Claudia would be put at the ring later, and Publia earlier.

"On the day after tomorrow," I said, "we reach Port Cos."

"I know," she whispered.

"The ship will be decorated," I said. "You and Claudia will be displayed at the prow."

"I have heard that," she whispered. "How will we be dressed for that honor?"

"You will be naked," I said.

"And in chains?" she asked.

"Yes," I said, "or perhaps ropes. You surely know how women are displayed at prows."

"How will it be done?" she asked.

"You will probably be hung there," I said, "one on each side of the prow."

"Doubtless it is a great honor," she said.

"Yes," I said.

"But," she said, "I gather, given the apparent desire to protect the slaves of Ar's Station, it is only to be expected that it be Claudia and I, and we alone, who are to be accorded that honor."

"Yes," I said. "But do not fear. I am sure that both of you, even if there were a cargo of superb captures aboard, would still be excellent candidates for the honor."

"I am not accustomed to thinking of myself as an ornament," she said.

"It is one of the purposes to which a slave girl may be put," I said.

"But now I find myself intrigued by the idea of serving so," she whispered.

"Oh?" I said.

"Yes," she whispered, "of being found so beautiful that men would display me so. Oh, I fear it, but, too, I find it exciting, and meaningful and thrilling. I am coming to understand now how marvelous it is to be beautiful and attractive to men. I feel so much myself, and so real, and female! Will not other women, I wonder, resent and hate me that it was I who was put at the prow and not they?"

"Perhaps," I said.

"Sometimes, when I was a free woman," she said, "I wondered, secretly, of course, what it might be like, to be so displayed."

"You will soon know," I said.

"Am I beautiful?" she asked.

"Yes," I said, "and you will discover that in bondage you will become even more beautiful. Indeed, you will find you have little choice in the matter. There are many reasons for it, physical and psychological."

"I want to be beautiful," she said, "and I am proud to be beautiful!"

"Beware of free women," I said.

"Surely masters will protect me from serious harm," she said.

"They will usually endeavor to do so," I admitted.

"I will be proud, being put at the prow!" she said.

"Beware of becoming too proud," I said.

"Master?" she asked.

"Do you wish to be whipped again?" I asked.

"No!" she said. She had been whipped on our second night out, from Ar's Station.

"The whip is an excellent device for taking pride from a woman," I said.

"I do not doubt it," she said.

"Or, generally," I said, "for bringing about reforms in her character."

"Yes," she laughed, "and for bringing us to you in any way you please to have us."

I then kissed her, and left her.

# 23
# CLAUDIA, SLAVE

The slave lay before me, on her stomach, over a pile of rope, aft on the *Tais*. Her head was down. Her neck was chained to a ring on the deck.

"Is it you?" she asked.

"Yes," I said.

"I am afraid of you," she said. As a slave she had a right to this fear, indeed, a right to the fear of any man.

"Do you wish to beg for mercy?" I asked.

"Would my pleas be meaningful?" she asked. "I am a slave. Will masters not do with me as they please, regardless of my pleas?"

"They will do with you as they please," I said, "but if they harken to your pleas, then it may be that what will please them will be to do with you as you plead."

"Then by all means," she said, "I plead for mercy!"

"But will it be shown to you?" I asked.

"I do not know, Master," she whispered.

"That, you see," I said, "is what the masters will decide."

"Yes, Master," she said.

"You were once Lady Claudia, of Ar's Station," I said.

"Yes, Master," she said.

"Who are you now?" I asked.

"Claudia," she said, "a slave."

She was pretty, lying on her belly, on the ropes, her head down.

"Lift yourself, Claudia, slave," I said.

"Oh!" she said.

She was then held helplessly. She could not so much as move without giving me great pleasure.

"What is wrong?" I asked.

"I am afraid I will yield to you," she whispered.

"And what is wrong with that?" I asked.

"But as a shameless slave!" she wept.

"Do so," I said.

Then, sobbing, then gasping with elation, with relief, she yielded. I could hardly hold her for a moment, even with her small body, so grateful, so wild, so eager she was in her sudden, joyous spasmodic helplessness.

Then she was on her belly, sobbing, pressing down into the ropes, as though she would hide herself in them. Her head was down, turned to the side, the side of it pressed against the ropes. She sobbed wildly, helplessly, poignantly, not able to understand her own behavior, shamed.

I crouched beside her.

"So that is how a slave is used!" she gasped.

"Sometimes," I said.

"Surely no free woman would be used in such a manner!" she said.

"Presumably not often, at any rate," I granted her. I did know that free women might be, and occasionally were, used in that way, for example, to insult them, or prepare them for the collar. To be sure, the man who used them in that fashion might as well be, I supposed, for most practical purposes, their master.

"Do you presume, incidentally," I asked, "to arrogate to yourself the rights or modesties, or the least of the prerogatives of the free woman?"

"No, Master!" she said.

"Do you presume, further," I asked, "to inquire into even the least of the sexual habits or activities of free women, whatever they might be?"

"No, Master!" she said. Her response amused me. Naturally both free women and slaves, as both are women, are very much interested in one another's sexual activities. It is very natural. To be sure, unless the slave is a bred slave, most of this interest is on the part of the free women, for the slaves have usually, at one time or another, been free women, and have a very good idea of how narrow, dull, limited and mediocre is the sex life of the free woman. Indeed, the matter is paradoxical, for the free women have a tendency both to inquire eagerly into the behaviors expected of slaves, and enjoined upon them, and, at the same time, commonly profess horror and scandal at what they hear.

"Such things are no longer of concern to you, are they?"

"No, Master!" she said.

"And you are a little liar, aren't you?" I asked.

"Forgive me, Master!" she said.

"In any event," I said, "you need not concern yourself any longer with the sexual activities, the proprieties, and such, of the free woman. Your attention is now to be more properly focused on your own business and concerns, for example, such things as the many intricate, exciting, complex and delicious sexual modalities and behaviors of the female slave."

"Yes, Master," she said.

The moons were full. The slave was pretty. It was late. We were one day out from Port Cos.

I then turned her, and lifted her, as I had Publia, holding her knees up, close to her belly. Her body, like Publia's, was a small, curvaceous delight. I then put her on her back, as I had Publia, on the coils of rope.

She turned her face away from me, that our eyes not meet.

"Look at me," I said.

She turned her eyes toward mine, reluctantly, but helplessly, commanded to do so. They were filled with tears. Her lip trembled.

"Surely," I said, "you have been richly used before now. This is not your first night at the ring."

"But I know you," she said.

"And do you think any man can be known as well as a slave knows her master," I asked, "or that any woman can be known as well as a slave is known by her master?"

"I do not know," she said.

"No," I said. "The relationship of master and slave is the relation of total, helpless intimacy."

"Yes, Master," she whispered, frightened.

"To be sure," I said, "the knowing of a master by his

slave, and of a slave by her master, cannot occur immediately. It is a natural relationship, and thus like any other natural relationship, for example, between a sleen and its master, it will take time."

"Of course," she said.

"Do you have any questions?" I asked.

"How can a man who truly knows a woman treat her as a slave?" she asked.

"It is easy," I said.

She regarded me, frightened.

"His knowledge even facilitates the matter," I said.

"Yes," she said, thoughtfully. "It would."

"There is even a special pleasure in doing so," I said, "in mastering, and commanding, she who is most intimately known."

"I understand," she said.

"Similarly," I said, "the nature of women, what they truly are, most deeply within themselves, apart from, and beneath, the gross, accumulated encrustations of artificialities and conventions, which must be peeled away, to reveal the true woman, naked and loving, is important."

"I love men," she confessed, seemingly scarcely daring to whisper it.

"Are you ashamed of that?" I asked.

"Should I not be?" she asked.

"No," I said. "You are no longer a free woman. You no longer need conceal your feelings. You may now openly and freely admit your interest in men and your love for them."

"The intimacies of which you spoke, the knowledges, the closeness," she said, breathlessly, holding to me. "Such things are at the discretion of the master, are they not?"

"Largely," I said.

"And not all masters grant them, do they?" she asked.

"Of course not," I said. I could not deny to her that some masters are heartless, that some are inflexible and cruel. And the coins of such men, of course, have as much buying power as those of anyone else. In fact, sometimes I have suspected that slavers enjoy throwing a girl who is still proud, or who has given them some difficulties, into such clutches. Sometimes after only a week in the power of such brutes a girl is almost willing to give her life to achieve a kind word, or a moment of intimacy. She is then ready to be a slave fully. The slave may be given more or less leash, as seems fitting, but she must always understand that it can be shortened at a moment's notice, and that the whip is always ready.

"How proud I was as a free woman!" she said, shuddering.

"You are no longer a free woman," I said.

"And even a moment ago," she said, "I, a slave, dared to question your usage of me!"

"That is more serious," I said.

"How proud I was!" she exclaimed. "Punish me!"

"No," I said.

"I was not pleasing!" she said.

"Do not concern yourself with the matter," I said. To be sure, had I taken offense, I would have seen to it that she was much concerned with the matter.

"In the cell, the day you escaped," she said, smiling, "do you remember how you lay over me, covering my body with your own."

"Yes," I said.

"I thought you were trying to protect me, like a gentleman," she laughed.

"I was protecting you," I said.

"But you used me!" she laughed.

"Yes," I said.

"From behind!" she said.

"That was natural," I said, "as we were lying, as I was protecting you."

"I was so surprised," she said.

"You were only a naive free woman then," I said.

"But I was a free woman!" she said.

"True," I said.

"Yet you used me so, in spite of the fact that I was a free woman!"

"Of course," I said.

"How could you dare to do so?" she asked.

"It was easy," I said.

"Undoubtedly," she said.

"Also you were convenient, in that position," I said.

"I see," she said.

I lay back, looking up at the stars. The sail was furled. We were using the current to proceed downstream.

"I think you used me to relieve your tensions," she said.

"Oh?" I said.

"Yes," she said, chidingly, cuddling up to me. "I have heard men talking about such things. Some use their slave girls, before battle, to relieve their tensions. I think you used me merely to relax yourself before the door to the cell was opened."

" 'Merely'?" I asked.

"Yes!" she pouted.

"Do not underestimate yourself," I said.

"Master!" she laughed, kissing me.

"On your stomach," I said.

She obeyed immediately, unquestioningly. "I love being a slave," she said, "and serving!"

We heard a fellow stirring about, on the deck.

"It is my keeper," she said, clinging to me. "He will put me below, in the hold!"

"Yes," I said.

"Can you not keep me a little longer in your arms?" she asked, anxiously.

"A moment longer," I said.

"Oh!" she said, softly.

Then I stood up, drawing my tunic about me.

She then half sat, half knelt, the chain depending from her collar, her head down.

I buckled the sword belt about me.

She looked up at me, reproachfully.

"Do you object?" I asked.

"No, Master," she said, quickly, kneeling. But her hands were on the chain depending from her collar. She drew on it a little. It was on her.

"How is she?" asked the fellow, coming up to us.

Immediately, before her keeper, she put her head down to the deck.

"Excellent," I said.

"Master," she said, timidly, not daring to raise her head, "my I speak?"

"Yes," he said.

"Publia, slave, has told Claudia, slave, that we are to be put at the prow. May Claudia inquire of master if it be true?"

"It is true," he said.

She raised her head a little, timidly. "May Claudia inquire how it is to be done?"

"We use a harness of chains and leather," he said. "The female is absolutely helpless, but is beautifully displayed."

"Does it hurt?" she asked.

"No," he said.

"I do not know how to be displayed at the prow," she said.

"Do you not think the chains and leather will take care of that matter?" he asked.

"But I mean with respect to my own appearance," she said.

"You will be naked, of course," he said.

"Yes, Master," she said, in misery, teased.

The fellow laughed. "There are many different ways," he said. "Free captures are often encouraged to volubly bemoan their fate, to appear tragically sorrowful, to beg mercy and lenience, to cover their bodies with tears, and so on, as they are carried helplessly into bondage. This is amusing to the crowds at the piers. They are then marched through the streets, to the house of one slaver or another."

"Much depends," she said, "on who has contracted for captures in advance?"

"Usually," he said.

"Seasoned slaves, on the other hand," he said, "usually appear pleased, even elated and joyful, and, if they do not appear so readily, they usually soon do so, once again encouraged. Sometimes the woman is required to appear proud, even contemptuous, for there are then fellows who will, so to speak, lie in wait for her at her sale, and bid high for her, hoping to bring her within the scope of their power, to get her, who was proud and contemptuous, into their collar. She will not remain proud and contemptuous for long. Other women are encouraged to appear terrified, or fearful. Fear in a woman is stimulating to a male and also to the female, making her more desperate to please, more eager to feel, more zealous to yield satisfactorily. These, and various other attitudes, may be required of women at the prow."

"And if they are not properly exhibited, or exhibited to the satisfaction of masters," she said, "then the women receive encouragement?"

"Yes," he said.

"And may I inquire the nature of this encouragement?" she asked.

"The women at the prow," he said, "are suspended within reach of a slave whip."

"I see," she said. The chain trembled, moving in the staple welded to the collar.

Usually, as far as I knew, the placing of women at the prow was not attended by such considerations. For example, when I had put women at my own prow, from time to time, I had usually let them behave or appear in any fashion they pleased. It was enough for me, and, I suppose, for them, that they were at the prow, displayed and helpless. Still, it was an intriguing idea, instructing them in the behavior they were to exhibit at the prow. In such a manner one might, rather as if decorating the ship in a certain way, say, with bunting and garlands, exercise more control over the impression one created in entering the harbor.

Too, of course, one might by such a device ready the crowds for bidding on a certain female, raise up her price, and so on. Certainly it was no secret that slavers, particularly in the more expensive houses, occasionally planned the sale of women in great detail, carefully regulating the order, arrangement, style, pacing and presentation of the goods, sometimes, in effect, even choreographing or staging the sale. But even without special attentions the behavior of women at prows varied considerably, from such things as free women hysterically writhing and screaming in their bonds to saucy slave girls exchanging quips with the crowd. Sometimes, indeed, a girl would single out a desirable male in the crowd and signal to him in no uncertain manner that she begs to wear his collar, and that she wants only the opportunity to become for him a dream of love and pleasure.

"And may Claudia inquire as to what behaviors may be required of herself and Publia?" she asked.

"I do not know what the captain will decide," he said. "I suppose that perhaps, as you are slaves, but new slaves, it might be required that you adopt an attitude of apprehensive ambiguity, of informed trepidation, of fearful uncertainty, as you have some concept of what it is to be a slave, and are being carried into a new bondage."

"Yes, Master," she said.

I supposed that even the most seasoned of slave girls must have some apprehension every time she finds herself in a new bondage. After all, what does she know of her new master? Very little, except that she is completely his, and that he has total power over her.

"On your stomach, head down, over the ropes," said the fellow to Claudia. She turned about, instantly, an obedient slave. He then braceleted her hands behind her back. He then thrust the heavy key he carried into the lock at the back of her hinged collar, and dropped it to the side, near the ring, with the coil of chain, on the deck. He then looked at her, braceleted and helpless. I left them alone and went to the rail, on the starboard side, amidships. In a few Ihn he brought her to the hatch, holding her by the arm. She looked at me, and then lowered her eyes. He knelt her there and unfastened the lock on the hatch. He opened the hatch, unbraceleted her, and indicated that she should descend into the hold. She did so, carefully, holding to the sides of the ladderlike stairs. She looked at me once more. Then she descended and he swung the heavy wooden grating back in place and padlocked it shut.

After he had left I went and looked down through the grating, into the hold. By means of the moonlight I could see a reticulated pattern of light and shadows there, which fell across two girls, one, Publia, sleeping, the other, Claudia, still standing, near the bottom of the ladderlike stairs, who looked up at me. Seeing my eyes on her, those of a free man, she knelt. I then turned away, and went toward the prow. There, standing on the tiny bow deck, I looked downriver. Tomorrow, in the afternoon, we were due to arrive at Port Cos.

# 24
# PORT COS

"There," said Calliodorus, standing on the bow deck, "is the *pharos* of Port Cos."

Aemilianus, standing now, but supported by Surilius, was there with us. Others, too, were about, such as the young warrior, Marcus, who had come days before to Port Cos, to obtain succor for the besieged of Ar's Station, and the young crossbowman and his friend, so young, and yet men by battle.

We looked at the tall, cylindrical structure which lay on a promontory, at the southwesternmost point of the harbor. It was perhaps one hundred and fifty feet high. It tapered upward, and was perhaps some twenty feet in diameter at the top. It was yellow and red, in horizontal sections, the colors of the Builders and Warriors, the Builders the caste that had supervised its construction and the Warriors the caste that maintained its facilities. It was as much a keep as a landmark. At night, in virtue of fires and mirrors, it served as a beacon. This morning a dispatch ship had been ushered through the advance ships, bringing news of some sort to Calliodorus. He had shared this with Aemilianus, it seemed. On the other hand, whatever might have been the contents of the sealed leather cylinder delivered into his hands with signs and countersigns I did not know. The dispatch ship had then hurried back, ahead of the flotilla, to Port Cos.

Two narrow beams, with attachment points for tackle, lay

at the sides of the bow deck. There were mounts in which they could be inserted.

"I had never thought to come in this way to Port Cos," said Aemilianus.

"Nor had I ever thought to go to Ar's Station in the capacity I did," said Calliodorus.

Some men began to attach tackle, chains and harness, to the two beams.

I glanced at the face of the young man, Marcus, who had brought the ships of Port Cos, and, apparently, those of certain other towns, as well, to the aid of Ar's Station. His face seemed resolute, and grim. In his way, he was a hero, and yet, for all he had done, he, and those with him, of Ar's Station, were coming to this town, once their greatest rival on the Vosk, as refugees, with little more than the clothing on their backs. There was little left now of Ar's Station, I speculated. There were some men, and some women and children, and a flag, that and little else. To be sure, the Home Stone, somewhere, supposedly, survived. At least I hoped it did. That, to Goreans, would be extremely important. It had apparently been sent southward toward Ar. I suspected that if its departure from the city had been much delayed, perhaps even for a few days, it would not have been sent toward Ar. I did not think that those of Ar's Station now bore those of Ar much love.

"Out oars!" called the oar master, from his place before the helmsmen, aft.

I heard the great, counterweighted levers thrust through the thole ports. The oarsmen of Port Cos were in their best today, their tunics bright, their leather polished, their brimless, jaunty caps atilt on their heads. They were in high spirits. They were nearing home. They would cut quite a figure with the lasses of Port Cos, I was sure. Doubtless there would be crowds on the docks to welcome them.

Among these, too, I was sure there would be many girls in brief tunics and collars, waving and joyous, and not just girls released for the occasion from the taverns and brothels either, but from the shops, and the laundries and kitchens, and homes, from all over the city. Such makes a sailor's return even more joyous. Indeed, some of the girls would undoubt-edly belong to one or another of the oarsmen. They would thus be eagerly, joyously welcoming, almost beside themselves, not only returning heroes but their masters.

The slave girl within the city, incidentally, commonly receives a great deal of freedom. She normally can do much what she wants, and go much where she wishes. Her mobility and freedom in such respects is often much greater than that accorded to free women. This freedom and mobility does not matter greatly, of course, for she is branded and collared. To be sure, she is seldom allowed outside the walls of a city unless she is in the company of a free person. Similarly, if an appropriate free person is available, she must request permission to leave the house. At this time, she will probably also have the Ahn of her return specified for her. Similarly, if an appropriate free person is available, she must report in to that person, when she returns. It is better for her, incidentally, to report in before or at the time that has been specified for her. It is sometimes amusing to see these girls hurrying to get home in time. Many houses are strict about such matters. Being late can be a matter for discipline.

"That is the *pharos*," a mother told her child, holding him up to look.

The refugees, save for some of the men, were glad enough, I think, to see the *pharos*, to know that the harbor of Port Cos was near. This harbor meant haven and refuge for them. The nightmare of the siege was over.

There was pleasure in the eyes of the free women. I had seen that even the briefly tunicked slave girls on deck, kneeling together amidships, properties of various masters on board, were eager, happy and excited. Among them, with no special sign of her status, as being the preferred slave of Aemilianus himself, was Shirley, only one slave among others.

The two beams, by fellows of Port Cos, were put in the mounts, the chains and harness pulled back inside, within the rail. They jutted out, on either side of the sloping, concave bow.

I saw those small ships which had been in our advance now slowing their progress. In a bit, they would be abeam, and later astern. Our ship, that of Calliodorus, the *Tais*, it seemed, would be the first ship into the harbor.

I met the eyes of the young crossbowman and his friend. We smiled at one another, then looked apart. His name was

Fabius. The name of his friend was Quintus. They were eager, it seemed, to see Port Cos. How marvelous, how remarkable, how astonishing is the resilience of youth! To look at them, and see their anticipation and eagerness, one would not have thought that they had endured trials that would have harrowed many a brave fellow, that they had stood on the wall, that they had served on the landing and near the piers. I had given each of them a handful of coins that they might buy themselves a girl in Port Cos, coins from those taken from the looter, met in the corridor of the citadel, leading out to the landing.

The advance ships were now astern.

"Stroke!" called the oar master.

The oars entered the water in unison, drew and rose, shining, dripping, from the river.

I looked again at the tall, cylindrical *pharos*. At night, its beacon aflame, the light multiplied and reflected in the mirrors, it could presumably be seen for pasangs up and down the river.

We were now, I conjectured, some three or four pasangs from the harbor.

"Stroke!" called the oar master.

Calliodorus was near me. So, too, was Aemilianus, supported by Surilius.

The ship was bedecked with flags and streamers. Conspicuous at the port stem line snapped a flag of Ar's Station. On the starboard stem line flew that of Port Cos. Aemilianus could not have asked for more honor. He was being conducted into Port Cos not as a piteous refugee but as a welcome and respected ally.

I went back over various things in my mind, the Crooked Tarn, the camp of the Cosians, the trenches, the approach to the wall, my captivity, my escape, the fighting at Ar's Station, the escape from the piers. How complex and desperate had become the world. I felt so small, like a particle adrift on a vast sea, beneath a vast sky, a particle taken here and there, at the mercy of the tides, the currents, the winds, not understanding. But there were compasses and landmarks, as palpable to me as the stars by which I might navigate on Thassa, as solid and undoubted as the great brick structure of the *pharos* of Port Cos itself. There were the codes, and honor, and steel.

Two slaves were brought forward, to stand on the bow deck. I looked at one, whose name was Claudia. Then she lowered her eyes, timidly. I watched metal bonds placed on their wrists and ankles, these bonds attached to the chains running to the jutting beams. I watched their bodies fitted into the chain-and-leather harnesses, these harnesses also attached to the chains. The harnesses were then buckled shut and secured with small padlocks put through rings. They were then put prone on the bow deck, one on each side, their manacled wrists extended before them, over their head. The head of Claudia was turned to the left, her head between her arms; the head of Publia was turned to the right, her head between her arms.

I heard a drummer testing his instrument. I heard, too, some pipes.

Treason, of horrid and grand dimension, was abroad on Gor. I was confident, too, from long ago, it seemed now, from captured papers, taken in Brundisium, that I knew at least one of the participants in these treacheries, one who was perhaps an arch conspirator, one who was perhaps even the prime architect of these devious asnd insidious designs. And I, like a fool, who had had her once in my grasp, in Port Kar, had had her freed, even when she had mocked and scorned me, thinking me crippled, and had had her returned in honor and safety to Ar! I considered her. How insolent she had been. How high she had flown. I wondered what should be her fate.

We were now nearing the harbor.

I considered the face of the young warrior, Marcus, near me. How set it seemed, how grim.

"My place, now," said Calliodorus, "is on the stern castle." With a bow he withdrew.

A curule chair was brought for Aemilianus and set on the bow deck. Some of his high officers were gathered about him.

Various thoughts passed through my mind. I recalled lovely Phoebe, of Telnus, so slim, with her very dark hair, her very white skin. How lonely and unhappy she had been as a free woman! How right she looked, clad in the garments of a

slave! Yet I had not enslaved her. but had kept her, to her
frustration, merely as a full servant. On the morning I had
gone to the trenches I had first taken her, clad only in a slave
strip, to the wagon of my friend, Ephialtes, the sutler, met at
the Crooked Tarn. There I had had her put on the coffle of
women he was holding for me, those whom I had redeemed
at the Crooked Tarn. I recalled the well-curved, auburn-
haired Temione, of Cos, who had worked inside, in the paga
room. Then there were the women I had met outside, chained
beneath the eaves of the left wing, Amina, the Vennan,
Elene, from Tyros, and Klio, Rimice and Liomache, these
latter three, like Temione, from Cos. The somewhat venal
master of the Crooked Tarn had had the heads of all these
shaved, to sell their hair for catapult cordage. I also recalled
the slave, Liadne, whom I had used beneath her master's
wagon, in the storm. It had amused me to have her put, once
purchased for me by Ephialtes, over the free women on the
chain, as first girl.

I had given Ephialtes my permission, of course, to do
much with the women as he wished, for example, renting
them, trading them, selling them, reducing them to bondage,
and so on, as the conditions of the market might seem to
make most judicious. I did not know, of course, if I would
ever see him again. I had myself sold Elene and Klio in the
trenches, in making my way toward the foot of the wall, at
Ar's Station.

I had also, I recalled, met a fellow in the trenches who had
been defrauded by a Liomache. I did not know if it were the
same Liomache as the one on my chain, of course. I rather
hoped for her sake that it was not. After the fall of Ar's
Station the Cosian troops, and their allies, mercenary and
otherwise, would have much more freedom. Too, there might
not be so many women available for the men, given the large
numbers shipped west toward Brundisium, and other destinations, some destined doubtless even for the markets of Cos
and Tyros themselves. Poor Liomache, held there on her
chain, helpless, would be exposed to the scrutiny of anyone
who passed by, and under the conditions, it was almost
certain that several would pass by. If the fellow from the
trench caught sight of her I pitied her. Her captivity, that of a
free person would be almost certain to be promptly replaced

with bondage, and a master into whose clutches she might have most feared to fall.

I recalled, too, the bearded fellow from the Crooked Tarn who had so humiliated and scorned poor Temione, refusing even to be served by her. He did seem to be a rude chap. Too, I did not think he would have been too pleased with me, either, with how I had tricked him, and made away with his dispatches and his tarn. I had last seen him chained naked to a ring in the courtyard of the Crooked Tarn, unable, thanks to me, it seems, to pay his somewhat extravagant bills. I wondered if he had managed to secure redemption from some passing Cosian, perhaps a comrade in arms who might have recognized him. This seemed to me not unlikely. The Crooked Tarn was a likely stopping place for couriers, and such. It did not seem to me likely that I would meet that fellow again. That seemed to me just as well.

I saw some small boats, wreathed with garlands, coming out to meet the flotilla. They swarmed about. In them, men, and slave girls, clinging to the masts, kneeling in the stern sheets, waved. They would escort us into the harbor.

"Gentlemen," said Aemilianus, from his curule chair, "as we are nearing Port Cos, it behooves me to speak plainly to you. Not all that I say will be welcome to your ears. Yet much of it you will have suspected."

"Speak, Commander," said a man.

I did not withdraw from the bow deck, as no one seemed to pay me much attention. Had they not wanted me there, or thought that I should not hear, surely I would have been advised of this. Too, I gathered that what was to be said, if secret now, would soon be common knowledge. Too, there were two or three fellows of Port Cos there, those who had set up the outjutting display beams, and would presumably handle the forward lines in wharfing. Too, of course, prone on the deck, in their shackles, their shackles and chain-and-leather harnesses attached to the beam chains, were the two slaves. No matters of prolonged moment would be likely to be discussed in the presence of such. Normally slave girls, with a snap of the fingers or a wave of the hand, are dismissed from an area when sensitive information is to be discussed. They then scurry away, until summoned back. Also, interestingly, they will usually take pains on their own behalf to avoid such areas. Total ignorance, they know, as they are mere slaves, is often in their best interest. If they hear too much they know that it is only too easy to dispose of them.

"What I tell you now," said Aemilianus, "is already common knowledge in Port Cos."

"But these things were brought by the dispatch boat this morning?" said a man.

"Yes," said he, "and with the routines of the couriers of Port Cos, that we might learn them before we disembarked. But there is little here that I have not suspected, and that our friend, Calliodorus, recently, has not intimated to me, privately."

I recalled that Calliodorus, even on the first morning out from Ar's Station, after we had attended to the females, those who were now both slaves, and lay near us in their chains, had seemed ready, then not ready, to speak to Aemilianus of certain weighty matters, that he might have been considering conveying to him warnings, or perhaps confiding suspicions or misgivings. He had hesitated then, I suspected, because he was not yet sure of such matters, or, perhaps, because he had thought it wise to hold them in abeyance until his friend was stronger.

"Stand," said the keeper of the two slaves, one of the fellows of Port Cos, on the bow deck, to the two slaves. They stood up. He checked the chain and leather of their harnesses. He lifted their shackled wrists over their head, lifting with them part of the chain to which they were attached. Then he let them stand there, with their shackled wrists lowered, before them. He did adjust their posture, rudely, with a slap or two. Then they stood there, softly, beautifully erect, on the bow deck.

"Hail Port Cos!" cried a fellow in a small boat, off the bow to starboard. Behind him there stood a long-legged, half-naked slave girl in a bit of a rag. "Hail Port Cos!" she cried, happily, waving. "Hail Port Cos!" She was rather nice. The collar looked well on her neck. I thought that she, too, might have been worthy to put at a prow. Seeing her, both Publia and Claudia stood even a little straighter, though apparently paying her no attention.

One of the fellows on the bow deck waved to them. "Hail Port Cos!" he responded.

"We are coming to Port Cos," said Aemilianus. "That will seem to confirm the story circulating in Ar, which, I take it, is the official version of what occurred at Ar's Station."

"Speak, Commander," urged the young warrior, Marcus.

"It will be of interest to you to learn that Ar's Station was surrendered to Cos more than two months ago," he said, drily, "before the relief forces could reach it. Lacking siege equipment that is why they did not proceed directly to Ar's Station but went into winter quarters."

"Ar's Station was never surrendered!" said a man.

"I do not understand," said another. "She fell but seven days ago this afternoon."

"Thousands must know the falsity of such allegations!" cried another man.

"Not officially, not in Ar," said Aemilianus. "They know, on the whole, except for rumors, only what they are permitted to know. I suspect it would even be unwise to speak certain truths in Ar herself."

"I do not understand," repeated the fellow who had spoken before.

"The situation is reputed to stand thus," said Aemilianus. "Supposedly, over two months ago, I, and my high officers, and the caste officials, and councils of the city, treasonously, and without a fight, surrendered Ar's Station to a delegation of Cosians. In return for this perfidy we received much gold and were granted safe passage to Port Cos, within whose walls we are to receive domicile and security."

"Our arrival here will make it seem so!" cried a man.

"I fear so," said another.

"Would you rather return to the ashes of Ar's Station?" asked Aemilianus, bitterly.

"Surely those of Port Cos do not believe such lies!" cried a man.

"Of course not," said Aemilianus. "The truth is generally known here. It is in Ar, and the south, that it will not be known."

"Where have you learned of such matters?" asked a man.

"Specifically, from the dispatches," said Aemilianus. "Cos, it seems, has many spies. Too, it seems she possesses swift, covert channels of communication. I do not doubt but what her work on the continent has been long in preparation. Naturally Cosians are in close contact with those of Port Cos, whose support to them is important on the river. I would not suppose that there is complete openness between them, but there seems to be no problem about sharing information of this sort.''

"Captain Calliodorus takes these reports seriously?" asked a man.

"Yes," said Aemilianus. "Indeed, he had even anticipated, as I had, given the abandoning of Ar's Station by Ar, that matters might be construed in some such perspective."

"It seems the spies of Cos are efficient," said a fellow.

"It is said," said Aemilianus, "as Calliodorus has told me, that even a whisper in Ar is heard in Telnus by nightfall."

We were now nearing the harbor.

There were clouds of small sails about us now, as many small boats had come out to meet us.

"Oh!" said Publia, as one of the fellows of Port Cos lifted her up lightly in his arms and threw her over the rail of the port side of the bow deck. There was a sound of chain, pulling against the beam ring, the links suddenly growing taut, and Publia, suspended from the beam, in her chain-and-leather harness, hung at the port side, out, about a yard from the rail, her feet now slightly below the level of the bow deck, over the water. There was a shout of pleasure from several of the small boats. Although her weight was substantially borne by the harness her small wrists were pulled high over her head, and held in place there, close to the chain, by her wrist shackles. Her ankles, too, were closely shackled. I considered her small hands. How piteous they appeared, so held in place, so helpless in their inflexible metal bonds. The steel, too, clasped her fair ankles closely.

"There is more," said Aemilianus, bitterly, "We of Ar's Station, and those who abetted us, not surprisingly, given the falsified and distorted accounts of our actions, are held in official dishonor and contempt."

There were several cries of rage. Hands clasped the hilts of swords.

"The proclamations have been posted," he said.

One of the fellows of Port Cos then went to Claudia. She

looked at me, wildly. Then she was lifted up, lightly, in the chain-and-leather harness. The fellow held her for a moment, his left hand behind her knees, his right hand behind her back. Her eyes were on mine, frightened. Then they widened, suddenly, and she gasped, and was thrown over the rail. Then, a moment later, her hands pulled high over her head, suspended in her harness, she hung off the starboard rail of the bow deck, as Publia did off the port rail. There was a cry of pleasure, and admiration, from several of the men about in the small boats. I saw her hands twist in the shackles, high above her head. Her body, suspended in the harness, swung a bit, and then turned from side to side, over the water. I glanced from her to Publia, and then back to her. I agreed with the shouts of pleasure and commendation from the small boats. Both slaves were excellent. Calliodorus was sure to be congratulated on his display.

"Is that the extent of the dispatches, Commander?" asked a man.

"It is perhaps as much as you should know now," said Aemilianus, grimly.

"Commander!" protested the man.

"The occasion is festive," said Aemilianus. "Perhaps it is well that you learn the rest later."

"Please, Commander," said a man.

"The Home Stone has reached Ar," he said.

"Good," said a man, overjoyed.

"Better it had never done so," said Aemilianus.

"Commander!" said a fellow.

"It is under guard near the Central Cylinder, on the Avenue of the Central Cylinder," he said. "There it is exposed that the citizens of Ar, and any who please, may file past it and spit upon it."

"Vengeance!" cried the young warrior, Marcus.

"And we, of course, and all those who abetted us, have been pronounced renegades."

"Vengeance!" wept the young warrior, Marcus. His sword was out of its sheath.

"Vengeance!" cried a man.

"Vengeance!" cried others.

There were cries of rage. Swords were drawn,

"Sheath your swords, beloved friends," said Aemilianus.

"Let us now, upon this holiday, to be declared the day of the Topaz, put aside all thoughts of fury and blood. Rather hasten to brush your garments and put smiles upon your faces. Consider your mien. Upon your countenances, I beg you, this day, let there be only the appearance of joy. Let this day rightfully redound to the glory of Port Cos, our brethren of the river, and let us rejoice with them, and with ourselves, for our deliverance. Our gratitude has been richly deserved. Let us not be sparing in its expression. Surely you realize that the fidelity of Port Cos to the pledge of the Topaz may cost her greatly in the future."

"Those of Port Cos have proved better friends to us than those of Ar," said a man bitterly.

"Perhaps the river is its own place," said a man.

"Perhaps," said another.

I could hear music now, coming from the piers of Port Cos. As the bow swung about to enter the harbor I could see the piers were jammed with crowds in their holiday finery. It seemed all the caste colors of Gor might be there.

I heard the sudden crack of a long, plaited, single-bladed slave whip on the bow deck. The whip was in the hand of the fellow from Port Cos who, on the journey downriver, had acted as the keeper of the two slaves. Slaves are always, directly or indirectly, in the keeping of one free person or another. He had not struck anyone with the whip. He had only, so to speak, readied the tool. Publia had cried out, startled, and in misery. She knew what it was to feel the whip. Claudia had cried out, startled, but, too, in fear. She knew she was subject to it.

"Publia," said the keeper.

"Yes, Master!" she cried.

"Claudia," said he.

"Yes, Master!" she cried.

He then, gently, lightly, with a small movement of the wrist, little more than a toss, snaked the whip out to the port side. Its single blade harmlessly but meaningfully more than encircled Publia. She shuddered. He then repeated this action to starboard.

"When I speak, you will attend to me," he said.

"Yes, Master!" said Publia.

"Yes, Master!" said Claudia.

"Beloved friends," said Aemilianus, "prepare yourselves to be received by our friends of Port Cos."

Swords were sheathed.

Most of those about Aemilianus then withdrew from the bow deck. Surilius remained, and the young warrior, Marcus, and some others. I, too, remained.

"Surely Ar herself will cry out for vengeance," I said, "for the loss of Ar's Station, her pride upon the Vosk,"

"Such seems to be the spirit in the northern camp of Ar," said Aemilianus.

"This you have, too, from the dispatches?" I asked,

"Yes," he said,

"The forces of Ar in the north," I said, "should move south with rapidity, before the spring, to engage the main power of Cos. Were it not for the action of Dietrich of Tarnburg at Torcadino, she would already be at the gates of Ar."

"But they will not do so, will they?" asked Aemilianus.

"They must do so," I said.

"They are apparently intent upon destroying the Cosian expeditionary force in the north," said Aemilianus.

"That would seem easy enough to do," said Marcus, bitterly. "Although the Cosians outnumbered us ten to one, their numbers would be no match for what, I gather, is nearly the full might of Ar,"

"Even so, they might not have as easy a time of it as they think," said Aemilianus. "They think that force has been in winter quarters, like themselves, though at Ar's Station. They do not realize it is battle hardened, that it has been in action for months."

"But if you were the Cosian commander in the north," I said to Aemilianus, "you would surely, if possible, avoid engaging the main body of Ar."

"True," said Aemilianus.

"He will not be able to do so," said Marcus. "Ar's northern forces are interposed between Ar's Station and Brundisium. They could also cut off a retreat to Torcadino."

"It would seem so," said Aemilianus.

"It would be difficult for them to cross the river, to the north," said Marcus, "and, even so, they could be followed. Too, they are unlikely to withdraw to the terrain of the

Salerian Confederation, for it will not wish to risk war with Ar. If they try to intrude by force into those territories they could well find themselves between the Salerians and Ar. The fate of the Cosians in the north is a foregone conclusion.''

"Few conclusions in war, my eager young friend," said Aemilianus, "are foregone.''

"With all due respect, Commander," said Marcus, "Ar's position in the north is ideal for destroying the expeditionary force.''

"But they would have to encounter it first," said Aemilianus.

"It is an army," said Marcus, "not ten men traveling at night.''

"Cos controls the skies," said Aemilianus.

"Even so," protested Marcus.

"It would not surprise me," said Aemilianus, quietly, "if the expeditionary force slipped past the men of Ar.''

"Between the winter camp and the southern bank of the Vosk," I said.

"Precisely," said Aemilianus, grimly.

"That is absurd," said Marcus. "They would be pinned against the river. It would be a slaughter.''

"But only if they were caught," said Aemilianus.

"No sane commander would elect such a route," said Marcus.

"Unless he knew something which you do not," said Aemilianus.

"The whole idea is absurd," said Marcus.

"Is it any the less absurd," asked Aemilianus, "that Ar should have been digging latrines in winter camp while the walls of Ar's Station were crumbling?''

"But Ar might still be apprised of these movements in time to interpose herself between the expeditionary force and its base at Brundisium," said Marcus, slowly. "Thus, to what end west?''

"What lies west on the Vosk," asked Aemilianus.

"On the southern bank, Ven," said Marcus. Turmus, which is the last major town west on the Vosk, is on the northern bank.

"And what beyond Ven?" asked Aemilianus.

"The delta," said Marcus.

"Precisely," said Aemilianus.

"I do not think I understand these things," said Marcus, slowly.

"I hope that I do not either," said Aemilianus. "But I am afraid, terribly afraid."

"In the fall," I said, "I spoke with Dietrich of Tarnburg, in Torcadino. He had similar apprehensions."

"I understand nothing of this," said Marcus.

"You are young in the ways of war," said Aemilianus. "Not everything in war is nodding plumes and the sun flashing from silvered shields."

"If Ar is in danger," he said, "she must be warned."

"By renegades?" asked Aemilianus.

"Renegades?" he asked.

"Surely," said Aemilianus. "I, you, the others, all of us, we have all been pronounced renegades."

"Should Ar not be warned?" he asked.

"And what do you think we, we who were abandoned by Ar, we whom she holds in dishonor and contempt, we whose Home Stone she spits upon, we whom she has pronounced renegades owe to her—now?"

"We owe her nothing," said Marcus, bitterly. "But I would still see her warned."

"And so, too, would I," said Aemilianus, smiling. "So, too, would I."

"But of what is she to be warned?" he asked.

"And to whom would you speak?" I asked.

"We do not know for certain what is going to happen," said Aemilianus. "At the moment we have little but our suspicions, our fears."

"Ar will destroy the Cosians in the north, and then destroy them in the south," said Marcus.

"Quite possibly," said Aemilianus.

"Then there is nothing to do," he said, slowly.

"Not now," said Aemilianus.

We were now within the harbor at Port Cos. The piers were some three hundred yards away, jammed with people. Music came from them. Pennons waved. The *pharos* on its promontory was behind us now, to port, something like a pasang away. The flotilla, entering the harbor, with its flags and streamers, would be a splendid sight. Already, too, from the piers, it would be able to be seen that two slaves hung from the outjutting display beams on either side of the concave bow of the *Tais*.

"Do not concern yourself now about such matters," said Aemilianus to the young warrior. "Rejoice now. We have come safe to Port Cos."

The slave whip snapped again, loudly, sharply, unmistakable in its definition and authority. The two girls cried out again, startled. Publia jerked in her harness as though she might have been struck, but it had not touched her. Claudia, too, winced, but, too, it had not touched her.

"Publia, Claudia!" said their keeper.

"Yes, Master!" said Publia.

"Yes, Master!" said Claudia.

"You, Publia," he said, "prepared well to surrender yourself to Cosians."

"Yes, Master," she wept.

"You, Claudia," he said, "were a traitress to your city."

"Yes, Master," she wept.

"And you are now both slaves," he said.

"Yes, Master!" they said.

"And so," he said, "you will enter Port Cos as the slaves, and sluts, you are."

"Master?" asked Publia.

"The movements of your hips, and your squirmings and glances," he said, "will leave no doubt as to the fittingness of your bondage."

"Master!" wept Publia, in protest.

"Please, no, Master!" called Claudia.

"Your movements for the most part," said the keeper, "will be slow and sensuous, but terribly meaningful, sexually. These may be mixed upon occasion with sudden, perhaps surprising, movements, almost spasmodic, or spasmodic, in nature. I trust that you understand these things. If there is difficulty in the matter it may perhaps be clarified by the whip."

Publia threw back her head and wept, in the harness.

"You. Publia, first," he said. He then required of her a variety of forward and backward movements of the lower belly, and then lateral movements of the hips. These things ranged, in their varieties, from almost imperceptible extensions and shadings, to sharp, forward thrusts, such as bumps and buckings, and from scarcely detectible lateral movements, to tantalizing or abrupt movements, to rhythmical swayings. He had Claudia, too, do these things. "Now," said he, "consider transitions among such movements." My hands clenched on the rail. The slaves were beautiful. "Now," said he, "slow, rotatory movements of the hips, slow, agonizingly slow, grinding movements!" I thought that many on the piers might have to hurry their own girls home, if they could make it that far. I was almost in pain.

"Well done, girls," said the keeper. "And do not forget the beauty of your breasts, and your squirmings, your glances and smiles."

Publia cried out in misery.

We were now something like a hundred yards from the piers. Two of the fellows on the bow deck already had the forward lines in hand.

"It has been decided, slaves," said the keeper to them, "that you will be sold at auction. In order, however, that you come into the keeping of Cosians, attendance at the auction, save by sales personnel, will be limited to Cosians. After a Cosian buys you, of course, he can do with you what he wants. We are now nearing the pier. I will point out various Cosians in the crowd, for there will be several. They are recognizable by their habiliments. You will then direct your glances and your movements particularly to them. Be pretty. Arouse interest in yourselves, We want them sweating blood when they bid for you!"

Aemilianus was already raising his hand to the crowds. There was much cheering.

"Look!" cried a fellow on the dock, pointing to the slaves.

"Yes!" said a man. "Yes!" cried another.

"Sensuous sluts!" laughed a man.

Claudia cried out with misery, but did not cease to move.

As so many were waving to us, I, too, with many of the others, at the starboard rail, waved back.

All seemed a riot of music and color.

"There," said the keeper, gesturing with his whip, as we drew alongside the pier. "There is a fellow of Cos! Present yourselves to him! You are female slaves! Do it! And there is another!"

"I am not such a girl!" suddenly cried Claudia.

Then she threw back her head and shrieked, as the lash, like lightning and fire, struck about her body.

She dangled and jerked in the harness, sobbing, though she had been struck but once.

"I am such a girl!" cried Publia, fervently, seeing the keeper turn toward her. "I am such a girl!"

"If she is recalcitrant, or not pleasing," cried slave girls on the pier, "strike her! Strike her! Punish her! Punish her! Punish her severely!"

Slave girls, kept under strict discipline themselves, they wanted it imposed on others with the same authority, exactness and perfection that it was imposed upon them. They were deeply concerned that Claudia not be permitted to get away with anything, no more than they. Was she, too, not a slave girl? Thus, interestingly, it is often slave girls themselves who are most zealous to see that masters are strict with their slaves.

The keeper turned back toward Claudia.

"I, too, am such a girl!" she cried out, wildly, swinging in the harness. Clearly she did not wish another blow from the disciplinary instrument. Yet, too, I think that the matter was far deeper than that, and this became clear but an instant later. The chain-and-leather harness, incidentally, is muchly open. This is what one would expect, considering its display purposes. On the other hand, a consequence of this openness, also, of course, is that it affords little, or no, protection, from the slave whip. Claudia swung in the harness to face me. Our eyes met. "Yes!" she cried. "Yes! I am such a girl!"

"You are," I assured her.

"Yes!" she wept. "Yes!"

I saw then that her small rebellion had been no more than a foolish sop to her pride, one perhaps she thought in order, I wondered if she had uttered her silly noise only because I was there, who had known her when she was a mere free woman. I hoped not. But in any case, whether because of her own pride, in itself, or her concern that I who had known her as a free woman was about, or because of the strangers in the crowd, or the other slave girls, or whatever, how woefully out of place was that absurd utterance in her new reality! But then I saw in her eyes, she half laughing, half crying, that whatever had been her motivation, whether some or all of the things I had wondered about, or even others, that she had only wanted the reassurance of the whip, the reassurance of the inflexibility of the will of men, that she must now obey, and was truly a slave. Moving as she did, and being what she was, a slave, was the deepest and most wonderful thing in her being, and she reveled in it, and loved it! She had wanted only the clear understanding that she must now surrender to it, that she was now truly a slave. She was elated in the harness.

"There!" said the keeper, pointing out a fellow with the coiled whip.

She swung about. "Am I pretty, Master?" she cried. "Will you bid upon me?"

"Bid upon me!" cried Publia to him. "I need a collar and a man!"

"There is another," said the keeper.

"Perhaps it will be you who will own me?" called Claudia to him.

The forward lines were cast to fellows on the pier. In a moment they were made fast to mooring cleats.

There was much cheering, and waving, and calling out, between the pier and the railing. Drums and pipes on board the *Tais* sounded. A plank was being run out to the pier. The following ships in the flotilla, scarcely less resplendent than the *Tais* herself would, in moments, in turn, take their own berths.

"What manner of slaves are those?" called a fellow on the pier, apparently, by his garb, a Cosian, to the keeper on the bow deck. "Are they common slaves?"

"They are as common as you will have them!" shouted back the keeper.

"They are not branded, are they?" asked the fellow. "They are not collared!"

"Such details will be soon attended to," laughed the keeper. I did not doubt it. Goreans are efficient about such matters. For an instant Publia, startled, and Claudia, frightened, stopped writhing in the harnesses. It was, after all, their own branding and collaring of which the men were speaking!

"Move," growled the keeper.

Then again they moved, frightened, obedient slave girls.

There was laughter from the pier.

"Wriggle!" called out a slave girl to them.

"Squirm! Squirm, Kajirae!" called out another.

"Do you not know how to squirm?" laughed another girl.

"How is it that these two are at the prow?" called another fellow.

"They squirm well," said a man.

"Writhe—writhe—more slowly," said the keeper to them.

"Aiii!" cried a man.

"How is it that these two are at the prow?" called the fellow again.

"Stop," said the keeper to the two slaves. Motionless were they then, their arms high, their bodies beautifully elongated, stretched out, suspended from the outjutting beams in the shackles and harness.

"Beautiful!" cried a man.

The keeper then, with his coiled whip, in two expansive gestures, one to port, one to starboard, indicated, and called attention to, the lineaments of the figures of the two lovely slaves. "Can you not guess?" he asked the fellow who had asked the question.

"Yes!" said the fellow.

"Are they not worthy to be at the prow?" asked the keeper.

"They are!" called out more than one man. And they were worthy not only because of the beauty of their figures, so well displayed, but because of their facial beauty as well.

I saw a slave girl in her skimpy tunic, scarcely a rag on her, nuzzling a fellow, rubbing her face and head against his left shoulder. She was trying to distract him from the suspended slaves. She was urging a consideration of her own not inconsiderable charms upon his attention.

"But perhaps, too, there is another reason!" hinted the keeper.

"Oh?" asked his questioner.

"This one we call 'Publia,' " said the keeper, "and this one 'Claudia.' " As he said these names, he reached out, and, in turn, Publia first, flicked each of them with the whip. At this touch, even as light and playful as it was, each of them recoiled in dread. Both had now felt the whip at one time or another, indeed, Claudia only a moment ago. There was more laughter. "They were both free women of Ar's Station," continued the keeper. "Publia dressed in such a way that her caste, that of the Merchants, would be concealed."

A Cosian merchant in the crowd cried out in anger.

"And that none would know she was wealthy!" said the keeper.

"She is not wealthy now!" cried a man.

"Let her now serve the wealthy!" called out a well-dressed fellow.

"Or serve a master of low caste," called out a fellow in the garb of the metal workers, "with the same or greater perfections than would be required of her in a high house!" I smiled. A great deal, indeed, is expected in low-caste domiciles of slaves who were formerly of high caste. To be sure, they no longer have caste then, of any sort. Even the lowest of castes is then undreamt-of heights above them, for in such houses they are only animals.

"She was determined to survive the fall of Ar's Station, whatever might prove to be the fate of her sisters in the city," said the keeper.

There were cries of anger.

"Thus, by such means as provocative dress and habiliments, baring even her calves, hoping then to be taken for a lowly, beautiful, meaningless maid, by even refusing to cut her hair on behalf of the city's needs, an act by means of which she hoped to appear more attractive to strong men, more attractive than might her sheared sisters, and a lack which, incidentally, as you can see, has been made up upon her, and by carrying gold with her, not shared with her sisters, with which she hoped to bribe captors to spare her for a nose ring and cord, she gave great attention to the readying of herself for a Cosian master."

There was much laughter.

"And thus," said the keeper, lifting the whip, "we think it is only appropriate that her planning not have gone for naught. It is to a Cosian, some Cosian, that she will be sold!"

Men, hearing this, slapped their thighs with pleasure. Slave girls, too, laughed.

"I am a Cosian!" called out a fellow. He, to be sure, did not wear the habiliments of Cos.

"Perhaps, then," said the keeper, "yours will be the collar she will wear!"

"Perhaps," he laughed.

"And this one," said the keeper, indicating Claudia, "betrayed her compatriots, declared for Cos and took Cosian gold for treason!"

"But she is a slave now?" called a man.

"Yes," said the keeper.

"Traitress!" cried a fellow, angrily, one in the habiliments of Cos.

Claudia looked wildly at the keeper. He nodded. He would permit her to speak.

"I regret what I did!" cried Claudia. "And I am only a slave now! Please have mercy on a slave!"

"She, too," said the keeper, "is to be sold to a Cosian."

"Traitress!" cried a Cosian. "Traitress!" cried another.

"Perhaps I will buy you!" cried another. "The whips in my house lash hard!"

"I will try to be pleasing, Master!" she wept.

It was very hard to hear now. The drums and pipes aboard the *Tais* were sounding. There was other music, too, here and there, from the piers, greeting other ships. There was much shouting, and calling, and raillery, between the piers and ships.

Aemilianus, pausing now and then to wave to the crowd, and partly supported by Surilius, and most of those with him were conducted back from the bow deck. Calliodorus, I suspected, had now left the stern castle and was awaiting his friend, Aemilianus, amidships. Aemilianus, who had commanded at Ar's Station, it seemed, would be the first to disembark. I, and some others, including the young warrior, Marcus, remained where we were. In a few moments, then, to drums and pipes, and cheers, I saw Aemilianus, unsupported, but obviously weak, make his own way down the gangplank. Behind him were Calliodorus and Surilius. Aemilianus and Calliodorus, and other officers, were embraced by several fellows wearing medallions of office at the foot of the gangplank.

Following this official party, so to speak, the refugees of Ar's Station disembarked, a few clutching tiny bundles containing meager belongings, and some of their other belongings following timidly, on their own bare feet. Much of the crowd, in a few Ehn, then, had followed the procession of

officials and officers, and refugees, and properties, from the
wharf. Oars were inboard, stowed. Oarsmen and sailors now,
save for a watch, weapons and sea bags over their shoulders,
entering upon their leaves, and other fellows, their service
now discharged, passed down the gangplank. Reunions were
common and often demonstrative, those with relatives and
friends, those of companions, those of masters with eager,
scantily clad, loving slaves. Much the same sort of thing was
occurring elsewhere, at other piers.

"It was a good voyage," said the keeper, reaching out
with a staff and hook to draw Publia, by the chain from
which her harness was suspended, close to the rail.

"Yes," I said.

When Publia had been drawn closer to the rail two other
fellows reached out and pulled her to the bow deck where
they knelt her, in the shackles, in the harness, still attached to
the chain. In a moment he, and the others, similarly, had
retrieved Claudia and she, too, knelt on the bow deck.

"I gather," said the keeper, "that you have had some
relationship, or something to do, with these two slaves."

"Yes," I said.

"Slaves," said the keeper.

"Yes, Master," said Publia.

"Yes, Master," said Claudia.

"You may bid him farewell," said the keeper, "in a
manner suitable for slaves."

"I wish you well, Master," said Publia, humbly, kneeling
before me in her shackles and harness, putting down her
head, kissing my feet.

"I wish you well, slave," I said.

Claudia then, too, as had Publia, was kneeling before me.
She, too, put down her head. "I, too, wish you well, Master," she said. She then softly, delicately, kissed my feet.

"I wish you well, slave," I said.

The young warrior, Marcus, was not looking toward the
piers, or the town, ascending from the harbor. His attentions
seemed to be outward, and back, toward the entrance of the
harbor.

I looked back to the pier. Here and there, lingering, some
four or five of them, were slave girls,

The keeper was now crouching by Publia, He freed her

wrist shackles from the chain and then her wrists from the shackles. He then pulled her small wrists behind her back and locked them there, in slave bracelets. He then, similarly, removed her ankle shackles from the chain and then freed her ankles from the shackles themselves. He then removed her harness. He similarly handled Claudia.

"You do not seem eager to see Port Cos," I said to the young warrior.

"Where," asked he, "do you think the northern forces of Ar are?"

"South of the river," I said, "back, to the east, somewhere."

"The expeditionary force of Cos will never be able to slip between them and the river," he said.

"Perhaps not," I said.

"It would be impossible," he said.

"Perhaps," I said.

I turned about. A fellow had brought two slave hoods and a neck chain, it appeared to be about five feet in length, terminating at each end with a collar. I watched while Publia was turned about and set, kneeling, before the kneeling Claudia. Claudia's neck was the first locked in the collar. Publia appeared apprehensive, but did not dare turn about. The second collar was locked on her neck. The two slaves were now linked together. The chain was, indeed, some five feet in length. Claudia's eyes, frightened, met mine. Then she was hooded, and the hood straps, beneath her chin, drawn snug, and buckled shut, behind the back of her neck. In a moment Publia, too, similarly, had been hooded. Publia was then drawn to her feet by an arm and conducted back, through the passage between the starboard rail and the stem castle, back amidships, to the gangplank, Claudia, responding to the cues of the chain, helpless in the hood, with tiny steps, hurrying behind.

I looked toward the *pharos*, on the promontory. Its light at night could be seen, it was said, pasangs east and west on the river.

"What are you thinking of?" I asked the young warrior, Marcus.

"Of vengeance," he said, bitterly, "and loyalty."

"An odd juxtaposition of thoughts," I commented.

I then turned about and watched Publia and Claudia,

hooded, naked, on their common chain, their wrists braceleted behind them, being herded along the pier, among boxes and bales, Beyond the pier, abutting on harborside wharfage, there were numerous buildings, mostly shops, such as those of sailmakers, oarmakers and sawyers, and warehouses, and, here and there, between these buildings, narrow streets, stretching up toward the city. I expected that they would be herded up one of these streets to the house of some slaver or other. They would have very little idea, at this time, of what Port Cos was like. Their hoods would be removed, presumably, only in the slaver's house. They would be very helpless, and muchly disoriented. Later, perhaps never having been given access to a window, or never having been outside unhooded, they would find themselves auctioned. From that time on, what was permitted to them would be determined by their master.

"I am angry," said the young man, perhaps more to himself than to me.

"Why is that?" I asked.

"There are many things I do not understand," he said.

"There are many things which none of us understand," I said.

"I am bitter," he said.

"Because war is not all nodding plumes and the sun flashing from silvered shields?" I asked, recalling the words of Aemilianus.

"Perhaps," he said.

I looked to the pier. There were still some slave girls there. I now saw three. Two were bare-breasted.

"Put dark thoughts from you," I said. "You have come safe to Port Cos. Rejoice. See the city. Come, if you like, and sup with me. Let us see what Port Cos has to offer in the way of enslaved females. She is noted, like Victoria, and certain other towns, for excellent wares in that respect."

"I thank you," said he. "But go on without me."

"You are a hero, and a warrior," I said. "Surely you do not mind squeezing luscious female flesh, branded and collared, in your arms."

"Outrage at treachery and blood, and confusion, and hatred, are now in my thoughts," he said, "not the belled, perfumed bodies of female slaves."

"Yes," said I, "such are pleasant, crawling and licking about your feet and legs, looking up at you, begging to please. Make use of them, Use them for recreation. They are your due."

"No," said he.

"It is hard to suppose that you would not be pleased to see them dancing before you, in the beads and chains of slaves."

"It is on less pleasant things that my thoughts now dwell," he said.

"For some," I said, "you might give your purse, and even draw your sword, to take them from the auction block."

"I do not have such feelings now," he said.

"Some," I said, "the curvy little sluts, in their collars, can make you scream with pleasure."

He was silent, looking to the east.

"It is hard to lose ideals," I said. "But sometimes one can purchase them back, by deeds, in a new form." I recalled the delta of the Vosk. I recalled Torvaldsland.

He was silent.

"I wish you well," I said.

"I wish you well," he said.

I then went back, amidships, and gathered up a sea bag and a few articles, a shaving knife, and such, which I had purchased on the ship from one or another of the good fellows of Port Cos. Then, my blade over my shoulder, I lifted my hand to the deck officer and took leave of the *Tais*.

I had scarcely set foot on the pier when the three girls came quickly forward, and knelt down.

"Come to the Dina!" said the first. "All our girls are dinas!" She turned her left thigh to me and drew up her tunic, showing me the dina brand. The dina is a small, roselike flower. It is popularly called the "slave flower." The dina brand, or slave-flower brand, is a common one on Gor.

"Come to the Veminium!" said the second. The veminium is a delicate, five-petaled blue flower common in both the northern and southern hemispheres of Gor. "We are not so expensive!" The use of the veminium, as a name for the tavern, given the widely spread range of the flower was perhaps supposed to suggest affordable beauty. The second and the third girls were the ones who were bare-breasted.

"My master's tavern is the Larma!" said the third.

I smiled. The larma is luscious. It has a rather hard shell but the shell is brittle and easily broken. Within, the fleshy endocarp, the fruit, is delicious, and very juicy. Sometimes, when a woman is referred to as a "larma," it is suggested that her hard or frigid exterior conceals a rather different sort of interior, one likely to be quite delicious. Once the shell has been broken through or removed, irrevocably, there is, you see, exposed, soft, vulnerable, juicy and helpless, the interior, in the fruit, the fleshy endocarp, in the woman, the slave.

"Are all the paga taverns in Port Cos named for flowers or fruits?" I asked.

"No!" laughed the first.

"Surely there is a connection," I said, "through ownership, or tradition?"

"Many towns have a tavern of dinas, Master," said the first.

"That is true," I granted her.

" 'Veminium' is a pretty name," said the second.

"True," I said. "Incidentally, what is the point of the name? Is it to suggest that the girls there, like the veminia, are cheap and pretty?"

The second girl, she from the Veminium, gasped, suddenly, laughing, putting her hand before her mouth. "I do not know!" she said, looking at the others, scandalized, laughing. "I never thought of it! Perhaps, Master!"

"And are all the girls there cheap and pretty?" I asked.

"I think we are pretty," she laughed. "I do not know if we are so cheap."

I smiled. I had wondered if perhaps the name had not been chosen more to lure fellows inward, than to supply an objective assessment of the commercial competitiveness of the contained services and merchandise.

"There are many paga taverns in Port Cos, Master," said the first. "Not all are named for flowers or fruits. There is the Cage, the Jewels of Telnus, Artemidorus' Cargo, the Secret Basement, the Hold, the Scarlet Whip, the Tavern of the Collar of the Two Chains, and many others."

"I am pleased to hear it," I said. "I take it that you are all friends."

"Yes, Master," said the first.

"The Veminium and the Larma are owned by brothers," said the first.

"They are near one another," said the second,

I was pleased to hear these things. The girls were friends, which suggested they might be from similar style and level institutions. Certainly girls from high taverns and from low taverns seldom consort with one another. And two of the places were owned by brothers and were near one another. These were connections, at least of some sort.

"And what of the girls at the Larma?" I asked. "Are they expensive?"

"We, like those at the Dina and Veminium, are affordable," she said. "Our uses go much for the standard prices."

"Were the girls at the Larma all once larmas?" I asked.

"I suppose some, Master," laughed the third girl.

"Were you a larma?" I asked her.

"No, Master," she laughed. "I have known that I was a slave since puberty, and I never pretended to be otherwise, perhaps because I feared someone might see through me and beat me."

"Of what caste were you?" I asked.

"Of the Peasants," she said. "We had too many daughters, too few sons. Two of my older sisters had already been sold into slavery before I was fifteen. One autumn my father's fields again failed, We were starving. I begged him to sell me. He then beat me, and bound me, and sold me."

"You are happy as a slave?" I asked.

"Yes, Master," she said. "It is what I am, and want to be. I hope only that someday I may have a private master, a love master, to whom I may be his devoted and obedient love slave."

"You long," I asked, "for a master who is strong, and love?"

"Yes, Master," she said.

She was a pretty young thing. She had very dark hair and very light skin, and, for a girl who had once been of the Peasants, was surprisingly slim. She reminded me a little of Phoebe, from Telnus, whom I had left on the coffle with the remainder of the debtor sluts I had redeemed, and obtained, at the Crooked Tarn, Temione, Amina, Rimice and Liomache.

"Master!" she said.

I had put down the sea bag and, crouching before her, lifted back the beads about her body.

"Are you typical of the girls at the Larma?" I asked her.

"I think so, Master," she said.

"You are, of course, soliciting for your master's tavern," I said.

"Yes, Master," she said.

"But are you, yourself, rentable?" I asked,

"Of course, Master," she said.

"And what of you others?" I asked.

"Yes, Master," said the dina.

"Of course, Master," said the girl from the Veminium.

"Ho, Warrior," I said, getting up, addressing the young fellow, Marcus, who had only now descended the gangplank and was going to make his way up the pier, toward the warehouses, the shops, the town.

He turned to regard us, and I beckoned that he should join us.

"Line up," I said to the kneeling slaves. "Straighten your backs, get your knees wider."

Then they were indeed presented as an excellent display of slaves.

The young warrior looked upon them.

"What do you think of them?" I asked. I thought they would make a nice set.

"They are appealing," he said.

His interest encouraged me. He needed a woman, and the best of such are slaves.

"Who are you?" I asked the slaves.

"Roxanne, of the Dina, slave of Simonides, tavener of Port Cos," said the first.

"Korinne, of the Veminium, slave of Agathocles, tavener of Port Cos," said the second.

"Yakube, of the Larms, slave of Panicrates, tavener of Port Cos," said the third.

"That is a Tahari name," said Marcus, looking at her closely. Indeed, of the three women it was she, the young slave from the Larma, to whom he seemed most drawn, in whom he seemed most interested. She was, I gathered, as I presumed they did not know one another, a type of woman whom he found extremely and excitingly attractive, a sort toward whom he seemed powerfully, perhaps almost irresistibly drawn, I was pleased to see his interest in her, as I hoped that she, or she and another, or she and the others, might distract him from his moody reflections. Slaves are excellent at relaxing a man, and giving him happiness. But something in his tone of voice had been menacing, and chilling.

"Yes, Master," said the girl, hesitantly. She was clearly aware of the implicit menace in his tone. Slave girls are extremely sensitive to such things. I could see that she was frightened.

"But you are not of the Tahari, are you?" he asked.

"No, Master," she said. Her coloring, of course, did not suggest that of a woman native to the Tahari region. Many males of the Tahari, of course, are fond of fair-skinned slaves, and such, shipped south and east, bring excellent prices in their markets. Thereafter they learn to serve their dark masters well, within the recesses of the cool, white buildings of the oases and cities, and out on the desert, in the tents. In such places they learn the wearing of the garments of the Tahari, and, if the master pleases, the stride-measuring ankle chains of the area, worn even by many free women. It is expected, too, that they will quickly become adept in the manifold labors of the Tahari woman, and, in particular, in their cases, those of the Tahari slave woman. In the latter respect, swiftly are the many meanings of the submission mat taught to them, where their slavery in their master's house or tent begins, but is not likely to end. To it they may be from time to time returned.

"Why do you have a Tahari name?" he asked.

"It was given to me, Master," she said.

This sort of thing is not all that unusual. For example, last fall, after accepting her as a slave, I had named the former Lady Charlotte of Samnium "Feiqa," which is a Tahari name. The name, which I had soon determined, had done wonders for new understanding of herself, and for her sexuality. To be sure, much depends on the woman. Certain names on Gor tend to be used almost exclusively as slave names, such as Dina, Lita, Lana, Tafa, Tela, Tula, and so on. Perhaps because of the commonness and simplicity of such names, as well as their exciting beauty, many girls respond quite well to them.

Many masters, in acquiring a slave, will change her name that she may understand that she is now, in effect, beginning her life anew. Indeed, some masters, even with the same girl, and not simply as a matter of discipline or reward, may change her name, to startle her, to impress their will upon her, and, perhaps, to freshen their relationship, she understanding, in effect, that she must now begin anew.

"It is not to disguise another name?" he asked.

"No, Master," she said.

He regarded her.

I did not understand his seeming anger, his seeming suspicion.

"I have worn many names, Master," she said. "I am a slave. Men name me, as is fitting for me, as they please."

"Are you a bred slave?" he asked.

"Not in the legal sense of the term, Master," she said.

"Speak clearly," he said.

"Though I am a natural slave," she said, "there was a time when I was not a legal slave. I was once, in the eyes of the law, a free woman."

"What was your name, when you were free?" he asked.

She squirmed beneath his gaze, which was like edged steel. I was sure she wished that she might reach up and bring the strands of beads, which I had lifted and thrown back, about her collar, that they might dangle behind her, obscuring the less my vision of her loveliness, back again before her, as though such tiny, colorful objects might protect her to some extent from that imperious scrutiny. But she did not dare to lift her hands from her thighs where, in one of the common positions of the pleasure slave, they now reposed. I had little doubt but what their palms were sweating. She moved her knees a little further apart, presumably in an effort to make clear her desire to be pleasing. How lovely her throat looked in its closely fitting steel collar.

" 'Prokne'," she said.

His eyes blazed.

She trembled. She knew, of course, from his insignia, that he had come from Ar's Station.

His hands went to his belt, and she shrank back. I thought that perhaps he was considering removing it, to lash her.

"Are you from Cos?" he asked.

"No, Master!" she said. "The fields of my father were north of White Water!"

White Water is called such because of rapids in its vicinity. It is a town on the northern bank of the Vosk. It is a member of the Vosk League. It is the first major town west of Lara, which is located at the confluence of the Vosk and Olni. Lara is the westernmost city in the Salerian Confederation. White Water is east of Ar's Station. There are three major towns between Ar's Station and White Water. They are Forest Port, Iskander and Tancred's Landing, which three towns, like White Water, are members of the Vosk League.

Most of the major towns on the Vosk are on the northern bank. This is undoubtedly because of a one-time policy of Ar to maintain a margin of desolation to the north, one stretching to the river, across which it would be difficult for an invader to bring an army. The major route south was then, as it is now, the Viktel Aria, which by means of its camps and posts, Ar then controlled. Thus, supposedly, Ar could move north with ease, but it would be difficult for other forces to move south, unless challenging Ar for the Viktel Aria. The margin of desolation, however, has not been maintained for years. Its military significance declined with the development of large-scale tarn transport, capable of supplying troops in the field. Too, as Ar's population increased she began to move northward. Indeed, her interests in the Vosk Basin are well known. In the past few years, particularly under the governance of Marlenus of Ar, the policies of Ar have tended to be expansionistic. Accordingly, it seems clear that in time the strategists of Ar came to view the margin of desolation less as a rampart than a barrier.

"Such names," he said, "are not so common east on the river."

"Yes, Master," she said.

"You are a long way from White Water," he said.

"Yes, Master," she said.

I saw his hands tighten on the belt, near its buckle. This was not lost on the slave, either.

"You came from the vicinity of White Water?" he asked.

"Yes, Master," she said.

"With a name like 'Prokne'?"

"Yes, Master," she said.

"I wonder if you are lying," he said.

"No, Master," she said. "I am not lying! The slave, Yakube, does not lie to the free man! She would not dare to do so!"

"Perhaps you are indeed from far away," he said.

"Yes, Master," she said.

He looked at her.

"Men take me where they wish, they do with me as they please," she said.

Slave girls, of course, as goods, as exchangeable properties, and so on, are likely to see a great deal more of their world than the average free woman. Many free persons on Gor seldom travel more than a few pasangs fom their village or the walls of their city. An important exception to this is the pilgrimage to the Sardar, which every Gorean, male and female, is expected to undertake at least once in his life. The journey, of course, from many points on Gor to the Sardar is, at least in certain parts, dangerous. It is not unknown for a young woman who sets out in the pilgrim's white to arrive as a chained slave, who will be sold at one of the fairs. Her glimpse of the Sardar is likely to be obtained from the height of a sales platform.

"But perhaps you are from the west, and not the east," he said.

"Master?" she said.

"Might you be from Cos?" he asked, his eyes narrow, his hands on the belt, near the buckle.

"No, Master!" she said.

"It is well for you, that you are not," he said.

"Yes, Master," she whispered.

His voice had been low, but it had been terrible in its menace. He then removed his hands from his belt. Yakube shuddered. I was afraid for a moment that she might faint. The other girls, too, were frightened. There was no mistaking the menace, the fury, of the young warrior.

"I shall look for lodging for the night," he said to me. "I wish you well."

"I wish you well," I said. I no longer ventured to suggest that we sup together, or pleasure ourselves with slaves.

We watched him depart.

"May we be dismissed, Master?" asked Roxanne.

"All but Yakube," I said.

Gratefully Roxanne and Korinne leapt up and hurried away. Yakube looked up at me.

"I will not hurt you," I said.

She trembled, kneeling on the pier.

"Do you know him?" I asked.

"No!" she said. "No!"

I continued to look after him.

"Why does he hate me so?" she asked.

"I do not think he hates you," I said. "I think, rather, you trouble him. I think, indeed, and am sure of it, that you are the sort of woman he finds inordinately exciting, maddeningly attractive."

She shuddered.

"It is Cos he hates," I said.

"I am pleased that I am not of Cos!" she said.

"You may go," I said.

Quickly, gratefully, she drew her beads again about herself, before her, then leapt up and hurried after her friends. I saw that they had waited at the end of the pier. When she had joined them, they hurried away together. They took care not to take the same street as that followed by the young warrior.

There was a cold wind now. It came from the east.

I thought of Dietrich of Tarnburg, holding Torcadino, of Ar, of Cos, of the expeditionary force in the north, of the forces of Ar, and the delta.

I was afraid.

I then turned my attention once more to the street which the young warrior had entered. It was one of those narrow streets leading up between buildings, leading up, away from the wharves. It was now empty.

# STAR BOOKS BESTSELLERS

## GOR SERIES

| | | |
|---|---|---|
| TARNSMAN OF GOR | John Norman | £1.80* |
| OUTLAW OF GOR | John Norman | £1.80* |
| PRIEST-KINGS OF GOR | John Norman | £2.25* |
| NOMADS OF GOR | John Norman | £2.25* |
| ASSASSINS OF GOR | John Norman | £2.50* |
| RAIDERS OF GOR | John Norman | £2.25* |
| CAPTIVE OF GOR | John Norman | £2.35* |
| HUNTERS OF GOR | John Norman | £2.25* |
| MARAUDERS OF GOR | John Norman | £2.50* |
| TRIBESMEN OF GOR | John Norman | £2.35* |
| SLAVE GIRL OF GOR | John Norman | £2.50* |
| BEASTS OF GOR | John Norman | £2.60* |
| EXPLORERS OF GOR | John Norman | £2.50* |
| FIGHTING SLAVE OF GOR | John Norman | £2.50* |
| ROGUE OF GOR | John Norman | £2.25* |
| GUARDSMAN OF GOR | John Norman | £2.50* |
| SAVAGES OF GOR | John Norman | £2.25* |
| BLOOD BROTHERS OF GOR | John Norman | £2.50* |
| KAJIRA OF GOR | John Norman | £2.50* |
| PLAYERS OF GOR | John Norman | £2.50* |
| MERCENARIES OF GOR | John Norman | £2.50* |

*STAR Books are obtainable from many booksellers and newsagents. If you have any difficulty tick the titles you want and fill in the form below.*

Name _____

Address _____

_____

Send to: Star Books Cash Sales, P.O. Box 11, Falmouth, Cornwall, TR10 9EN.

Please send a cheque or postal order to the value of the cover price plus:
UK: 55p for the first book, 22p for the second book and 14p for each additional book ordered to the maximum charge of £1.75.

BFPO and EIRE: 55p for the first book, 22p for the second book, 14p per copy for the next 7 books, thereafter 8p per book.

OVERSEAS: £1.00 for the first book and 25p per copy for each additional book.

*While every effort is made to keep prices low, it is sometimes necessary to increase prices at short notice. Star Books reserve the right to show new retail prices on covers which may differ from those advertised in the text or elsewhere.*

*NOT FOR SALE IN CANADA